Also by Stefanie London

Bad Bachelors
Bad Bachelor
Bad Reputation

Bad Influence

STEFANIE LONDON

sourcebooks
casablanca

Sourcebooks and the colophon are registered trademarks of Sourcebooks, Inc.

Published by Sourcebooks Casablanca, an imprint of Sourcebooks, Inc.
P.O. Box 4410, Naperville, Illinois 60567-4410
(630) 961-3900
Fax: (630) 961-2168
sourcebooks.com

Printed and bound in Canada.
MBP 10 9 8 7 6 5 4 3 2 1

Prologue

Three years ago…

JOSEPH WOULD FORGIVE HER FOR CHANGING HER MIND; he *had* to. They were family. Sure, they might not be married yet, but she'd seen the ring. The elaborate hunk of a stone, a cushion-cut masterpiece surrounded by a spray of smaller diamonds, nestled in navy velvet, and tucked away in the depths of his sock drawer. It meant something. A future. A symbol of their bond.

Wasn't forgiveness what family was all about?

Or was it compromise?

Annie Maxwell leaned against the wall outside their bedroom, her heart in her mouth, as she surveyed the boxes stacked all over the apartment. Her neat handwriting in black Sharpie labeled them for the move: kitchen, bathroom, bedroom. She had a bad feeling about this conversation.

Maybe you're worrying for nothing.

He loved her, and she loved him. That was all that mattered…right?

Annie's hand fluttered over the fancy brass doorknob. They'd picked it together at an antique shop in an effort to give their apartment some character.

After half an hour of arguing over brass and wrought iron options, Joseph had given in and let Annie have her choice so long as he got to choose the curtains.

See, compromise.

This was different. They weren't talking about aesthetics or design choices. They were talking about the difference between family and careers. Her family, his career. Supporting one meant giving up the other. How were they supposed to find compromise in that?

She needed to put her mother first, because there was no way she could move halfway around the world for Joseph's new job when the diagnosis was the big C. And especially not when her mother, Connie, had called her in tears, begging her to stay.

Funny how one little cluster of cells could wreak so much havoc.

Last week, when her parents had announced Connie's diagnosis, her mother had seemed fine. They'd known about the cancer for a while but had been waiting for the right moment to tell the kids. Waiting until they had a plan and could reassure them that everything would be okay. The doctor claimed catching the tumor in her mother's right breast at this early stage boded well. He predicted recovery. Ninety-three percent survival rate. That sounded good…didn't it?

But then he'd thrown around words like *mastectomy* and *chemo* and *hormone therapy*.

And when the phone rang half an hour ago, her mother was a mess. Annie hadn't heard her cry like that in a long time.

Please don't go, Annie. I need you here. I can't do this without you.

How could she leave the woman who'd raised her—who'd *sacrificed* for her—when she needed her most?

Living overseas would mean being too far away to help with appointments or household chores or hugs. Joseph had promised she could fly back every month if she wanted. But her mother needed her here. Now.

Singapore would have to wait.

Never mind that they'd been planning this move for months. Never mind that Joseph had been offered his dream job on a silver platter. Never mind that their apartment was in boxes because the movers were due to arrive tomorrow. That they were due to *leave* tomorrow.

The bank had offered Joseph a golden opportunity—a signing bonus, money to cover relocation, a salary with more zeroes than she could comprehend. They'd put him in charge of a whole technology department and had him reporting to the chief information officer. At his age, it was nothing short of incredible. She'd never seen Joseph so excited.

If only her mother didn't have that lump.

Shaking her hands, Annie let out a long breath. Perhaps all this worrying would be for nothing. He would understand her decision…wouldn't he?

"Joe?" Annie forced down her nerves and walked into the bedroom. "Can we talk?"

He looked up, his eyes the blue of a frozen lake—cold. Impenetrable. A suitcase lay open in the middle of their bed, a stack of shirts folded neatly inside. His ties were rolled and nestled against the edge of the suitcase—silvers, grays, and navy with the occasional pop of red. Plus the vibrant sky-blue one she'd bought him because it matched the color of his eyes. It was his favorite.

Hers too. He was utterly delectable in that tie.

She waited for a smile, a response…something. But Joseph's face was unreadable, his mouth set in a taut line. Fear churned in her gut. He'd resigned almost a month ago. As had she. They'd spent the last week packing everything they owned, wrapping each item with care as they talked about their future. As they planned their dream life.

And now she was going to take a lit match to it all.

"We need to talk," she said, more assertive this time. Her fingers curled over the wooden bed frame for support. "About Singapore."

"There's nothing to say." He turned away and riffled through his closet, the slim gold hangers clinking in the quiet as he pulled out a short, black coat. "You've made up your mind, haven't you?"

Her heart pounded, rapid and uneven. Like a horse trying to gallop through thick mud. "What do you mean?"

He laid the coat on the bed and folded it in that fastidious way of his until the garment had been manipulated into a perfect square. "I overheard your conversation with your mother. You told her you had no intention of moving to Singapore."

"You make it sound like I'd planned to back out all along."

"The result is the same, isn't it?"

Heaviness settled in the pit of Annie's stomach. Her mother knew they were ready to move. Knew what it meant to their dreams of having great careers and seeing the world together. It was what they'd both been working toward since they'd gone from being friends to lovers that starry, late-summer night in her first year of college.

"She was crying, Joseph. I didn't know how to make it stop." Her fingers intertwined and she squeezed until the joints ached.

"It's not true then? We're still making this decision together?"

She detected the barest hint of hope in his voice, though his face revealed nothing. Like always. She'd vowed early on in their relationship never to play poker with Joseph after he'd cleaned her dry one night and left all the money beneath her pillow. He didn't need the money. Winning was his drug.

"It's not that I have no intention of moving, but now...I can't. I can't leave her." Lip trembling, Annie drew a deep breath. "But it's still *our* decision."

"That's a lie, because you've already made the decision and now you're here to *tell* me what we're doing instead of discussing it with me first." He flipped the lid of the suitcase. "I was always going to be left out of the loop, wasn't I?"

"You're not left out of the loop." She cringed. Because he was right—she *had* made the decision without him. A decision that affected them both, that *denied* them both.

"And here I was thinking there were only going to

be two people in this relationship. Turns out I'm the third wheel."

"No, you're not." She pressed her fingers to her temples and rubbed in slow circles, the throbbing escalating from a dull thump to a roaring pound. "I love you."

"Then why didn't you talk to me?" The pain on his face sliced through her chest. "We're supposed to be leaving tomorrow. I've already quit my job. What are you expecting me to do, walk back in there and say, 'Oops, sorry about that'?"

"They'd give it back to you." She sucked in a breath, knowing she was on thin ice. "They wanted you to stay, right? They offered you more money."

"Jake pulled me aside on my last day and told me he was glad I didn't accept the counteroffer. Because this job is…" He threw his hands in the air. "It was going to change everything for us. We were going to start a new life together, be independent. It would be *our* money, and we wouldn't have to rely on my father anymore. We could travel. See the whole world. You wouldn't have to work a job you hate. We could do anything."

Anything, except be close to her mother when she needed her most. "Things have changed."

"I get that, I really do. You know I care about your parents. I *want* your mom to get better." For a minute he was soft again, his eyes warm and caring. He didn't often allow himself to be like that. Vulnerable. But she'd seen that face before, through eyelids cracked open so slightly that he'd thought she was still sleeping. "And I offered to fly you back as much as you needed. I'll fly you back every goddamn weekend."

"It's not the same. If she calls me, I can't be by her side right away if I'm on the other side of the world."

"Then why didn't you tell *me* that? Why did you leave me for last like you always do?"

"I don't—"

"No? What about that time you got promoted, and I only found out when your sister texted me to organize a surprise dinner?" His voice was so quiet. Oh, so quiet. Because Joseph never yelled. He didn't need to.

"I told you I was sorry." She swallowed against the panic clawing up her throat, mingling with the anger that he'd held on to such a petty thing for so long.

"Yeah, you also promised me it wouldn't happen again."

"You're being selfish, Joe."

"*I'm* being selfish?" He looked at her and shook his head. "You're the one who changed your mind on both our behalves without even talking to me first. You always pick them."

His acid tone made her blood boil. "This isn't about taking sides."

"No? Because I want us to make decisions *together*, and that means *you* need to put me first for a change."

"This is ridiculous."

"No, it's not." He drew the zipper around the outside of the suitcase, sealing the lid shut with an eerie calm. "At some point, I needed to see the writing on the wall."

"You really want to choose your career over her?" Annie's voice wavered, shaken by the ugly emotions warring inside her. "Over me?"

"I can't waste this opportunity, because a chance like this won't come around again. It's everything *we* wanted. We talked about the life we were going to create. Remember?"

Hot tears pricked at the backs of her eyes, causing her to blink rapidly. "I won't leave her."

"I never said you had to leave her. I wanted to find the middle ground. A compromise."

There was that word again.

"I can't compromise when it comes to my family," she said.

Emotion flickered across his face for an instant.

That was all she ever got with him…an instant. Emotion had no place in Joseph's life, because he'd packed years of it down until he'd become unable to demonstrate it at all. It wasn't his fault his parents demanded perfection. That they expected everyone and everything to meet their exacting standards.

He didn't know how to be loved.

She'd been ready to accept that…in the hope that one day he'd change. That maybe she could be the positive influence to help him deal with his issues.

And she *had* seen some improvement. Her family had started to teach him what it meant to be part of a team instead of always playing by himself. But this argument told her the changes weren't enough—he would *never* understand what it meant to sacrifice something for another person. Because the truth was, she *wanted* to go to Singapore with him. She wanted the life they'd planned together. The future they'd been working toward.

More than anything, she wanted him. Forever and always.

But she had to put her mother's needs first.

Pain tore through her chest, her breathing shallow. Could this really be it?

"We could make it work. Singapore is *not* that far away." He rested his hands on the suitcase and leaned forward, his Adam's apple bobbing as he swallowed. "I'll pay for as many plane tickets as you need."

Annie shook her head. "I'm not going anywhere until she's better. I can't."

"Can't or won't?"

An ugly mélange of emotion swirled within her: anger, sadness, frustration. She would not be bullied into leaving. "Both."

He pulled the suitcase off the bed and set it down beside him. "Then it looks like we have a few calls to make."

Chapter 1

"Dear Bad Bachelors, before your app came along,
I truly believed I was going to die alone."

—SincerelySingle

ANNIE MAXWELL HAD NEVER BEEN HELD AT PASTRY-point before. Thankfully, she'd never been held at gunpoint either, but there was something about the way her stepfather thrust the freshly piped cannoli in her direction that made her want to avoid any sudden movements. She stood in the middle of his café, still empty since it hadn't yet opened.

"I'm about to go for a run." She gestured to her hot-pink Nikes and leggings. "I don't need a pastry. Besides, I'm catching up with the girls."

Well, girl. Singular. Of her two best friends, only one was currently speaking to her. But *girls* slipped out like it always did, because they were supposed to be a group.

Not this tense, fractured mess.

Sal Russo's dark eyes narrowed as he appraised his stepdaughter with pursed lips. "You should eat breakfast."

"I hate to break it to you, but that isn't breakfast."

She gestured to the pastry. "It's a dessert. At the very best, you might be able to call it a snack. But it's most certainly *not* breakfast."

Still, Sal had to give the people of Bensonhurst what they wanted...and that included flaky, sugar-laden non-breakfast foods.

Sal huffed and placed the tray of cannoli down. A sprinkling of white icing sugar dusted the edge of his dark mustache, telling Annie that he'd already tucked into the goods that morning. No matter how she cajoled and pleaded, he couldn't—or rather *wouldn't*—curb his sweet tooth.

"Italians have eaten this way for generations."

"Exactly. Why do you think Nonno has trouble with his blood sugar now? Too many cannoli." She shook her head. Worrying about her grandfather's health was almost as pointless as worrying about her stepfather's. If she had her way, they'd live forever. "Not to mention all that damn salami he eats. And the prosciutto...and the creamy gnocchi."

"Now you want to take our pasta away from us?" Sal feigned mock outrage.

"God forbid."

"I'm just trying to say that you..." He shook his head. "You don't have to be perfect all the time. You put too much pressure on yourself."

He looked like he was about to say something else, but no words came out. At one point, he would have joked that he'd never be able to marry her off if she was so uptight—purposefully goading her into a lecture about a woman's right to choose marriage or whatever lifestyle she pleased—which was exactly what Sal believed too. He wanted his daughters to be strong and independent, despite his teasing. But no one joked about the m-word around her anymore. Hell, it was only ever uttered when absolutely necessary, and even then, it was accompanied by furtive glances and sympathetic eyes.

Poor Annie. What if she never finds anyone else? Lucky he has two other daughters who'll do the family proud and give him a couple of adorable nipoti.

Ugh. Her *zia* didn't know she'd overheard that conversation. And even though Annie didn't believe Sal cared much about whether or not she gave him grandchildren, the remark still stung. Even months later.

"I'm perfectly happy, and I enjoy running." She squared her shoulders. "You should try it sometime."

He laughed, the tension melting from his face as he pulled her in for a bear hug. She was sure to have smears of icing sugar all over her hoodie now.

"I'm too old for that shit."

Despite her worry, Annie chuckled. There wasn't much that couldn't be fixed by a bear hug from her stepfather. In fact, when he'd decided to quit his job and follow his dream of opening a café, the family had decided to name the place after his hulking frame. Café l'Orso, or the Bear Café when translated into English. In two years, Sal's place had become a hipster hot spot a mere five minutes down the road from the family home.

"Ma is so proud of you, you know that?" she said, looking around the café with a warm feeling in her chest.

"Just your mother?"

Annie chuckled. "Well, I am too. But we all know her opinion is the only one that matters."

Sal squeezed her tightly. "True. It's strange to think her cancer was the catalyst for something so great. It forced us to appreciate life more."

Her parents had changed a lot in the last three years. Sal had let go of his need to make decisions based on security, and her mother—who'd always been feisty and outspoken—had learned to chill out and roll with the punches more. But they were happier than ever. *Stronger* than ever as a couple.

Annie swallowed back the lump blocking her throat. "I should get going."

The view outside the café beckoned. Sunlight sparkled off the puddles from an earlier shower, giving the late-fall foliage an extra degree of golden warmth. Soon the café would be busy, and Annie wanted out before she guilted herself into helping with the swarm of locals looking for their weekend caffeine fix. After all, it was her first free day in almost a month and she had plans. This morning she would catch up with her friend, Darcy. Then she could crack open her bullet journal and tackle her to-do list.

"You know you don't have to check on me on your day off." Sal smiled and waved her away. "I suppose I should be grateful that I raised three conscientious, hardworking daughters. You're my favorite though."

Never once had Sal made Annie feel like she wasn't part of the family, even though she was the only daughter not related to him by blood.

"I bet you say that to all the girls. Mom included."

Annie laughed, knowing without a doubt that her father *did* in fact say it to each of them. "We're on to your tricks, you know."

"Yeah, yeah. Get out of here."

He turned and moved behind the counter, turning on the coffee machine and pouring beans into the grinder. A loud hiss of steam drowned out the clatter from the kitchen as Annie left the café and stepped out into the crisp fall morning.

Annie loved the early weekend mornings, when Brooklyn was still asleep. She loved the way the sky transitioned from indigo to lilac to gold and finally to blue. She loved the peace and quiet. It had taken her a long time to be at peace in the silence after Joseph left, since her mind would play their breakup on a loop. But now the quiet comforted her.

She headed toward the subway and caught the D Train to Columbus Circle. Though she lived in Manhattan, which meant a long schlep to Brooklyn to visit her family every weekend, she appreciated the ability to fit in a run before work instead of having to commute.

When the subway slid to a stop, Annie exited, almost walking straight into Darcy.

"Hey," she said with a wave. Darcy grumbled a half-hearted return greeting.

"I still don't understand why I needed to come all this way to go for a run." Darcy's dark hair was slicked back into a ponytail, and her chin was buried in an oversize Mets hoodie. Given it was almost as long as a dress, Annie assumed it belonged to Darcy's fiancé, Reed. "Exercise is stupid."

Annie rolled her eyes. "You asked for *my* help, remember? I thought you wanted to support Reed."

A week ago, Darcy had come to her with questions about running, explaining that Reed was taking part in a four-mile charity run through Central Park and that he'd bribed her into participating. Given that her next question had been whether she could run in Doc Martens, Annie had designed a training plan.

"And supporting him means getting up at the buttcrack of dawn to trek into the city?" Darcy yawned. "I'm usually in bed for at least four more hours on my day off."

"It's good to understand the terrain. If you're going to be running here on the day, then it makes sense to train here." They walked up the steps and out onto the street. "What did he say to convince you, anyway?"

Darcy's cheeks turned pink. "Nothing I feel comfortable repeating in public."

Central Park shone with autumnal color. Eager tourists were out in force, cameras dangling from their necks and selfie sticks in hand. The air was crisp, but the day was unseasonably warm for this time of year. In other words, it was a perfect day for a run.

"You stayed at your parents' place last night?" Darcy asked as they walked into the park.

"Yeah, Allegra was home from college for the weekend, and Sofia decided we should have a movie marathon." Her stepsisters were twenty-one and seventeen, respectively. "A chick-flick movie marathon. It was fun. We ate popcorn and ordered pizza. But they're seriously boy crazy. Sofia spent half the night getting us to help figure out which Halloween party she should attend based on which boy would be in attendance."

"Count me relieved that I *never* have to experience high school again."

"Me too." They stopped next to a bench to stretch out. Annie pulled her ankle up behind her butt to loosen her quads. "They're so…"

"Hormonal?"

"I was going to say naive."

"You mean they haven't been tarred by the cynicism that comes from being someone *formerly* in a relationship?" Darcy quipped. That was one of the things Annie loved about her best friend. She was never short of a smart-ass remark. She also had the best resting bitch face Annie had ever seen, an in-depth knowledge of classic literature, and a penchant for beautiful tattoos.

She was also one of the most forgiving people Annie had ever met.

"The early twenties were a simpler time, that's for damn sure." Annie sighed. "And don't you go acting all smug now that you're coupled up."

"I'm just saying, if *I* found someone, then there's hope for literally everyone." She laughed. "Which means you don't need to shrivel up and become an old prune."

Annie switched legs and swatted Darcy with her free hand. "Old prune? Screw you."

"If you don't use it, you lose it," Darcy said with a sage nod. "Isn't that what you said to me?"

"I believe that was Remi."

An uncomfortable silence settled over the duo. It had been two months since the big fight. And apart from seeing Remi's performance at the *Out of Bounds* opening night, there had been zero contact. Annie was the kind of person who chose her friends carefully and infrequently, so Remi's absence had left a big hole in her life. Not to mention a big hole in her heart.

She *would* fix things. Eventually. But Remi needed her space, and this time Annie was going to respect that.

"She'll come around," Darcy said, as if reading her friend's thoughts.

"I hope so." But hope might not be enough. She'd really hurt Remi and it haunted her every day.

"Hey." Darcy leaned over, pressing the back of her hand to Annie's forehead. "Are you okay? You look pale."

"I'm fine." Annie waved her hand. "I'm tired. I've been working a lot lately."

"Work's not everything, you know."

Darcy was right, of course. Work *wasn't* everything... for most people. But right now, the only thing keeping Annie going was her work. And not her job either. But the work that was her true purpose in life.

Bad Bachelors. The website and app she'd created to change the way women dated. By being able to rate and review men, the women of New York could avoid the players and the cheaters. They could go into a relationship with their eyes open. She believed in the good it could do, but it had certainly caused a lot of trouble as well.

Beyond the fight with Remi and the issues with Bad Bachelors, however, something else had her feeling queasy. Next week marked three years since the love of her life had packed his suitcase and walked out on her. Three long years since she'd swallowed her hurt and anger and regret and tried to find something to channel her energy into.

Each anniversary had gone much the same way. Quietly, but noticeably. She wallowed in her misery alone, usually while watching sad movies and crying her eyes out like a Bridget Jones wannabe.

This year, however, she was determined to avoid that unproductive behavior by keeping busy.

"All right," Annie said, bouncing up and down on the balls of her feet. "We're going to jog over to the pond, go around, and then come back. It'll be about one and a half miles, so then we can see how you're doing."

"What if I'm dying?"

"Then we can walk for a bit." Annie grinned. "Unless you're legitimately dying. Then I'll call an ambulance."

"Why did I agree to do this?" Darcy whined. "I'm going to get sweaty, aren't I?"

Annie chuckled. "Not sure how you ended up with a guy like Reed if you have an aversion to getting sweaty."

Before Darcy could retort, Annie jogged into the park at a slower pace than she would have if running alone. Darcy caught up quickly, and they weaved through the growing clusters of people. With each stride, she felt farther away from her problems.

Running was the most effective form of therapy Annie had found and, at this point in her life, she'd tried her fair share. It wasn't only the injection of vitamin D, the picturesque scenery blurring past, or the blood pounding in her veins that made her love running so much. It was the feeling of progress. Despite the success of both her job and Bad Bachelors, the last few years had felt like a giant step backward. Running gave her a sense of accomplishment that had been otherwise lacking in her personal life.

Shaking off the nagging thoughts, she jogged on, checking on Darcy every so often to make sure she was keeping up. A few times they slowed to a walk for a couple of steps so she could catch her breath but, to her credit, Darcy powered on. Sunlight streamed down, bright beams of light reflecting off the rain-soaked sections of the pavement. Manhattan's temperamental weather patterns meant a downpour could come at any moment. Sometimes it only lasted a few minutes, but it would be enough to cover the ground in mirrorlike puddles.

Since she'd forgotten her sunglasses, Annie tried to shield her eyes as she ran. But holding her arm in front of her face threw off her rhythm. Squinting, she rounded the corner of the pond toward the area where people tended to stop and take photos. It might not have been the best route to take, given how busy the park was getting, but they were stuck now. Dodging a woman with a stroller, Annie skirted a puddle and forged on. But her run came to a sudden halt when she slammed full force into something. Less than a second later, a curse in a deep baritone rang out, followed by a splash.

"Oh my God!" Annie dropped to her knees and peered over the edge of the rocks outlining the curve of the pond. "I'm so sorr—"

The apology died on her lips.

The man in the water wasn't an innocent stranger. She recognized those light-blue eyes, knew that they were the exact shade of a pale spring morning. She knew the full lips intimately. She knew the exact texture of his sandy-brown hair, though now it was saturated with water and looked closer to dark brown. She knew every inch of him, inside and out.

After all, she'd wanted to marry him.

Chapter 2

"I can only guess you're some ugly spinster, sitting behind your keyboard feeling powerful for creating this bullshit website. Eventually someone will unearth your identity."

—WaitingForRevenge

"ARE YOU GOING TO JUST STAND THERE?" JOSEPH PRESTON swam to the edge of the pond.

Annie contemplated turning around and jogging in the other direction. It was exactly what he deserved. But she never was one to leave a person in need... unlike him.

Clasping a hand around his outstretched arm, she heaved. His grip was slippery, and she struggled to get leverage against the slick rocks ringing the pond. Her small frame was no match for the weight of his much larger one. If she wasn't mistaken, he'd bulked up since he left.

"A thanks would be nice," she said as he got to his feet.

"You pushed me into a pond."

"I hardly pushed you." It was so like him to blame it all on her.

"If I'm not mistaken, you're dry and comfortable, and I'm the one covered in pond scum." He stood, water pooling around his feet. One expensive-looking loafer was on his left foot, its companion nowhere to be seen.

Still, he managed to look devastatingly handsome, even with the missing shoe, ruined suit, and foliage sticking to his hair. He had a beard now, which was unexpected. But it gave his face a darker edge. A *harder* edge and an air of unabashed and striking masculinity. His blue eyes blazed, and his white shirt clung to the muscles on his chest. Yeah, he'd filled out all right.

Her stomach somersaulted.

"Darcy, nice to see you," he said drily.

"Joe. It's been a while." Her eyes narrowed. "Though not long enough, in my humble opinion."

Joseph ignored the dig and plucked a leaf from his arm, letting it drop to the ground with a splat. "I don't suppose either of you know where I might be able to clean up and dry out my suit?"

"No idea." Annie folded her arms across her chest, suddenly feeling very naked in her skin-tight leggings.

He looked her up and down, as though drinking in her image inch by inch, committing her to memory. Or *re*committing her to memory. "None at all?"

A breath caught in her throat, her body threatening to combust with the angry swirl of emotions competing for dominance inside her. "Nope."

"Not even an apartment that I might be able to get access to?" His eyes bored into hers.

"Can't think of one…" She shook her head.

"We should go." Darcy tugged on her arm. "You don't owe him anything."

Joseph didn't react to Darcy's statement, even though she'd said it loud enough that everyone around them could hear. They'd drawn quite the crowd. Murmurs skittered among the onlookers, but Annie couldn't drag her eyes away from him. Joseph was here…in New York…in the flesh.

And what the hell was he doing in a suit on a Saturday?

"Annie." Her name was a growl on his lips. He stretched the two syllables out into an endless rumble, like thunder warning of a storm.

Three years. Three goddamn years, and seeing him was still like taking a shotgun to her heart. The worst thing was, not a single part of her wanted to walk away right now. He'd always had that kind of pull. A magnetic energy that encircled him like his own special atmosphere.

She turned to Darcy, pretending her heart wasn't lodged somewhere in her windpipe. "It's fine. You go on. I can deal with this."

"No." Darcy shook her head. While Annie was trying her hardest to internalize her emotions, Darcy's anger was raw and visible. "You don't need to help him."

"You can have a shower at my place," Annie said to Joseph with an efficient nod. She placed a hand on Darcy's arm. "It's fine. I'll catch up with you later."

Darcy looked like she was about to spit fire, but she sucked in a breath and nodded. With a dirty look hurled in Joseph's direction, she turned and headed back the way they'd come, with her hands balled into fists. Her reaction wasn't surprising. She'd been by Annie's side all through the breakup, all through her mother's treatment, and every day since. Joseph's name was a dirty word in their circle.

What was surprising, however, was that Annie wasn't turning on her heel and following Darcy. Maybe it was some sick curiosity that compelled her to offer him a warm shower. Or maybe it was that she wanted him to see that she'd moved on…even if that was an illusion.

They walked. The only sound breaking the tense silence between them was the squelch of Joseph's soggy clothes. He'd taken off his single shoe and it dangled limply from one hand. There were so many things she wanted to ask, like what the hell was he doing in their old spot?

She swallowed. "Their spot" was the section of the park surrounding the pond. She couldn't seem to go running without tracing the water's edge, torturing herself with memories of when he'd confessed his love for the first time.

She had so many questions. They all rushed for priority position, clambering over one another, but where the hell did she even start? There was so much to sift through, and she didn't trust herself not to cry or throw him overboard again if she dared open her mouth.

So she said nothing, and neither did he.

Joseph didn't need to be guided to her apartment off Sixth Avenue. She wondered if he would be shocked by how it looked now with all signs that he'd lived there scrubbed clean until the place was sanitized of his presence.

Would he even notice?

Joseph cleared his throat. "I wondered if you might move out one day."

"Why would I? I love this apartment." She kept her eyes firmly fixed on the path ahead, not daring to look at him. Her limbs moved heavily, gracelessly. She may as well have been wading through a swamp.

"I loved it too." There wasn't a hint of emotion in his voice. Good old Preston stoicism. Like father, like son.

"You loved a lot of things at one point."

He had the good sense to keep his mouth shut as they walked through the lobby of the apartment building. The security guard behind the counter raised an eyebrow at Joseph's appearance, but he didn't stop them. If he remembered Joseph, he didn't say, and Annie let out a sigh of relief. She couldn't handle questions right now...particularly ones she didn't have answers to.

Fifteen minutes later, Joseph sat on the soft, gray couch, freshly showered and wrapped in a towel. He nursed a cup of coffee between his palms, and as he blew on the steam, he watched Annie intently.

This was *not* how things should be going down. The smart thing would have been to kick him out as soon as he'd finished showering. Instead, she'd been making a coffee for herself and had automatically made one for him.

Muscle memory...what a bitch.

Perching herself on the arm of the sofa, she tapped a silent beat with her foot. Sunlight streamed in from the floor-to-ceiling windows, bathing them both in gold. The scene was so familiar that it unsettled her down to the marrow of her bones. How many weekend mornings had they sat in this exact space, drinking coffee and planning their future? How many times had they abandoned breakfast to make love on the couch, the floor…that one incredible time on the coffee table?

It had been the first thing she'd sold when he left.

The memory of sorting through the boxes, deciding what should follow Joseph to Singapore and what should stay behind with her, burned like a newly lit flame in her chest.

"Did you really have to push me into the pond?" He raked a hand through his hair, sending a few droplets scattering over his shoulders and chest.

The towel did little to hide his perfect physique. He'd always been on the lean side, but now his thighs pressed against the soft fabric of the towel and the ripple of muscle in his abdomen was more pronounced. His shoulders appeared bigger, as did the generous shape of his biceps and the curve of his calves.

Annie swallowed against the dryness in her mouth.

"Honestly? I've thought about it many times." She cradled her coffee, thankful for something to occupy her hands. "I guess some dreams *do* come true."

"What a special day." His voice was dry. Was he more upset that he'd ended up in her care or that she'd ruined a Zegna? Knowing Joseph, probably the latter.

"How many times do I have to say I'm sorry?"

Her gaze roamed around the room, looking at everything but him. The place had changed a lot, with sharp modern art replaced by softer, more feminine pieces. The stylish minimalist gray tones had been updated with muted pinks and blues.

"Once would be fine," he drawled.

Of all the scenarios she'd played in her head about what would happen when they met again, this was not one of them. Her slapping him across the face and telling him what a fool he was? Yep, that could happen. Her flaunting her new running-fit body in some impossibly skimpy outfit and him collecting his jaw from the ground? Absolutely.

Her knocking him on his ass and then him bullying his way into their old home? *Hell. No.*

"If either one of us has cause to provide an apology, I know who it is," she said. "I'll give you a clue. It's not me."

"Well, you've got some force. I'll give you that. When did you take up running?"

"When you left."

It was the one statement guaranteed to kill conversation. No point in beating around the bush. They'd been reunited by some cruel joke of the universe. It didn't change anything, despite his attempt at semipolite conversation. She hadn't even known he was back in the country. Why would she? It's not like he'd called, or texted, or emailed…in three years.

Joseph sipped his coffee and continued to study her. His inquisitive blue eyes analyzed the changes in her, the changes in their old home. *Her* home.

She didn't want to talk to him, didn't want to have him so close to her. Old urges were simmering below the surface, masked beneath resentment that snowballed by the minute. She had to break the silence before it broke her.

Tell him to leave. Get him out of here!

"How was Singapore?" she asked, mentally cursing herself.

"Busy." He set the cup down on the table in front of him. "Exhausting."

Lonely. She could hear it in his voice, a tiny change in tone that revealed more than his words. When they were together, she'd become adept at interpreting tone. Being with Joseph had required master-level skills in translating body language. She'd become an expert in pitch and subtext and the minutia of him.

Was he regretting his decision to leave? Had he missed her?

Her chest constricted. "Why did you come back?"

"New opportunities. HSBC had given me what I needed, and it was time for me to move on."

"And how *is* your career going?" Annie couldn't keep the edge out of her voice. "Are you on your way to world domination yet?"

He sat up straighter, his broad shoulders stretching to their full breadth. She forced herself not stare at the muscles flexing in his chest and arms as he shifted position. One wrong move, and that towel would be nothing more than window dressing.

"Did you say you had something I could change into?" He ignored her question.

And like that, conversation time was over. Some things never changed. "No, I didn't say that."

"You expect me to walk out of here naked?"

Annie smirked. "Why not? I'm sure the ladies of Manhattan wouldn't mind. It's over fifty degrees, so you shouldn't have too much shrinkage."

"That's never been a problem, and you know it." He narrowed his eyes at her. "And I'm not going to get booked for indecent exposure my first weekend back in the city."

"That sounds like your problem." She waited for him to squirm. He didn't. "How you walk out of here is up to you, but your options are pretty limited."

"And what exactly *are* my options?"

She smiled. "Your suit or a towel or a pair of my running tights."

Joseph's eyes dropped to the dark fabric hugging her hips and thighs, outlining her to perfection. Even if he could squeeze into them—which was *highly* unlikely— he'd maintain his modesty better with a face cloth. But damn, she looked good in them. Her legs were lean and toned. Shapely.

The rest of her was as stunning as he remembered— cocoa-colored eyes framed by thick lashes, fine nose, high cheekbones. She had a smile that could light up a room…not that he'd be likely to see it anytime soon.

"Surely there's something else I can wear," he said.

She shook her head. "Not that I can think of."

"You haven't got any baggy sweatpants?"

"I'm afraid not." She looked like she was having *far* too much fun with this scenario.

"You seriously have nothing else?"

He was tempted to ask her if an old boyfriend—or a current one—might have left any clothing he could borrow. But he wasn't sure he wanted to know the answer to that.

"What about a sock?" She cocked her head, a smirk tugging at her lips. "Or maybe a strategically tied scarf?"

Clearly she wasn't going to budge. Wasn't this the ultimate post-breakup fantasy? Catching your ex in a compromising position and mercilessly holding it over them?

Since his suit was currently soaked through, it looked like he'd be making the journey back to his new apartment in a towel. Part of negotiation was knowing when to stop, and she'd made it crystal clear that pushing would not get him what he wanted.

If she thought he was going to stay here and whine about it, she was sorely mistaken.

"Fine." He stood, tightening his grip on the knot at his waist.

Annie's eyes lingered there, something dark and forbidden flickering over her features. Joseph willed himself not to react. An untimely erection would only make his situation more precarious. But it was hard not to remember all the times they'd torn each other's clothes off right here. Annie was the kind of woman who'd been brimming with passion, and she'd often instigated sex with rough kisses that spiked his body temperature and made him insatiably hungry for her.

Chemistry was *never* their problem.

He squared his shoulders and walked across the room, studiously ignoring the internal voices taunting him with all the ways he'd screwed up. He hovered at her front door, her name on his lips.

There was so much he wanted to say to her, but talking about his feelings ranked low on his list of skills. And desires.

"What about your suit and shoes? Well, shoe. Singular." The amusement in Annie's voice needled at him. Yeah, she enjoyed having the upper hand, all right. "It'll all be ruined if you squish it into a bag now."

"I'll pick everything up later, after my appointment."

He opened her door and walked out into the hall. Nobody else appeared to be coming or going from their apartment and he made it down to the foyer without anyone seeing him. But that's where his luck ran out. The concierge lifted a brow as Joseph strode through the lobby, the towel clutched in one hand and his soggy wallet in the other.

"Can I help you with something?" the concierge asked. But Joseph walked silent and barefoot right out onto the street, automatically sticking his hand out to hail a cab.

The cool air chilled his skin. Hypothermia was the least of his concerns, however. Because even though New York had a reputation for being an intensely crazy city, a half-naked man standing on the corner of Sixth Avenue in Midtown would most certainly attract attention. And he was less worried about a cop stumbling across him than he was going viral on Snapchat.

That would *not* be the right way to start off his stint as the "youngest CIO of any American bank."

"Oh my *God!*" A group of teenage girls giggled as they walked past him, arms linked. One of them held her phone up, the rhinestone-encrusted case glittering in warning.

Mercifully, a cab pulled over right then, and Joseph ducked his head as he slid into the back seat. If the girl got a photo, at least it wouldn't show his face.

"Sutton Place," he said, following up with the exact address.

The driver, a woman, winked at him in the rearview mirror. "It's not every day I pick up a guy in a towel. Got a story to go with that outfit?"

"My ex-girlfriend pushed me into a pond."

A raspy chuckle filled the cab. "Good for her."

His new home wasn't too far from their old building. *Her* building. The sun shone brightly through the window, warming his exposed skin as he kept a hand gripping the towel tightly in front of his privates. The last thing he wanted was to accidentally flash the cabbie.

He was pissed. Surprisingly, it wasn't because he'd been forced to head home in locker-room attire. He was pissed because he'd lost control over his first meeting with Annie after his absence. He had planned to see her again, of course, but it would have been on his terms when he wasn't in such an…exposed state.

Literally *and* figuratively.

Now she knew he was here, and his scrambled mind hadn't allowed him to communicate properly. He'd come across like an arrogant SOB, forcing his way into her apartment because he couldn't bear to pry himself away. Curiosity had gotten the better of him, proof that within five seconds Annie could shatter his legendary control just as she always had. He'd wanted to see what their old place looked like now. Had she kept any of the things they'd bought together? Was there even a trace of him left? Had she replaced them with the belongings of another man?

The thought of another guy being with Annie in their old apartment made Joseph's blood boil. He was completely aware that being jealous if she'd moved on made him a first-class hypocrite, but that didn't stop the surge of ugly emotion rocketing through him at full speed. Not that anyone would ever see it. He'd make damn sure of that.

But the apartment looked like it was set up for one. No photos of any other men besides her stepfather or grandfather in the living room. No manly objects marred the feminine softness of the furniture or decor, which was Annie to a T. It shouldn't have relieved him…but it did.

When the cab pulled up at his building, he handed the wet bills over, paying more than double for the fare. He could only hope the swipe card to his new building would still work, since the front desk team didn't know him by face yet. It took him several attempts, but eventually the card let him in, and his key was tucked safely in the coin pouch of the wallet.

He strode through the lobby, his bare feet making sucking noises against the tiles. The security guard lifted his head and looked at Joseph quizzically.

He didn't break pace. "Don't even ask, buddy."

After avoiding the strange glances from a woman in the elevator, he marched down the hallway to his door and let himself in. Tossing his wallet onto the kitchen bench, he frowned when it landed with a wet slap. In all likelihood, he'd need to replace the wallet as well as his suit and shoes. What about his phone? *Crap.* That was also lost to the depths of the pond, since it'd been in his hand when he'd fallen. He'd have to look up his new boss's number. Not exactly the best way to make an impression on the guy, since they were supposed to be meeting at some upscale place for lunch in less than an hour.

He shouldn't even have been in Central Park. But it was on the way, and he'd gone early to have some fresh air and time to clear his head. The second he'd spotted the path leading to their spot…

Their spot. They'd been one of those sickeningly sweet couples with a spot and a song and a takeout place. Annie had made sure they documented all their special moments, assigning things of importance like cocktails and meals and venues to the memories as a way to anchor them in the present. To allow them to be replicated.

Fuck. This wasn't how he'd wanted to see her again.

Joseph dropped the towel to the floor and walked naked to his home office. The window was full-length but it faced the glittering line of the East River, so no one would witness him working in his birthday suit.

Right now, he had more immediate concerns than sorting through the shit between him and Annie. But his ruined clothing was still at her place, so at least he had a reason to go back unless she decided to dump everything in the trash.

He opened his laptop, found the email with the restaurant details, and called to let them know he'd be late. Then he selected a fresh suit along with a crisp, white shirt from his closet and a blue-and-red tie. Company colors. They *might* make up for the fact that he was late. Never mind that he was having a business meeting on a Saturday. That was his life now.

Personal time wasn't a luxury afforded to people in his line of work. And he was young—almost *too* young—for the job he had, which meant needing to prove himself at every turn. Not many major worldwide banks had a CIO who was thirty. So, people were watching him.

He was about to leave the apartment when the landline rang. "Hello?"

"Joseph." The commanding voice of his father boomed through the phone line.

"Dad, what a pleasure," he said drily. After this morning, he didn't want to deal with Morris Preston and couldn't even muster the energy to fake it.

"You could sound a little happier, Son." One of his father's signature dramatic pauses stretched on. Joseph knew to prepare himself for the sting. "Have you had a rough start to your repatriation?"

"Something like that," Joseph muttered. "And I'm running late for a meeting."

"Already tardy."

The admonishment made his cheeks burn. Only his father could reduce him to feeling like a naughty child in less than a minute of conversation. He resisted the urge to recite the lines of his résumé as proof he knew how to handle his career.

Instead, he took a silent breath and said, "It'll be fine."

"It's that careless attitude that caused you to have so many problems in Singapore."

"I didn't have many problems in Singapore." Just one. A *big* one.

"But you're not denying you had a careless attitude?"

"I—"

"It was a rhetorical question. If you're going to sleep your way around the expat scene, perhaps don't choose the daughter of a board member next time."

Joseph resisted the urge to hurl the phone against the wall. In "sleeping his way around the expat scene," he'd had *one* relationship in the three years he was there. *One* woman in his bed. And while hindsight had shown him it was a bad decision, he was hardly a playboy or a womanizer. But trust his father to bring up the topic of his fall from grace the second he arrived back home. Would he ever hear the end of it? Not likely.

"Did you have a reason for calling, or was it just to remind me why I enjoyed being away?" Joseph couldn't keep the barb out of his voice, cursing himself immediately as soon as the words left his lips.

There was no point antagonizing Morris. He was stubborn as a mule, and bitching him out would only make it worse.

"What a shame Singapore didn't improve your manners. I'd hoped the experience might have been a good influence on you. Seems I was wrong." Morris cleared his throat. "Anyway, the reason that I called is because I'd like to have lunch. I figured if I left it up to you, I'd be waiting some time."

"I'm surprised you didn't have your assistant call. I'm honored."

"I'll let that one slide. Meet me at Per Se next Sunday. I'll have Millie reserve a table."

Joseph hung up the phone and groaned. He'd only arrived in Manhattan two days ago, and already everything was turning pear-shaped—running into Annie unprepared, winding his father up… What next?

Sighing, Joseph headed for the front door. So much for the welcome wagon.

Chapter 3

"Dear Bad Bachelors...whoever you are, thank
you."

—UnBroken

ANNIE STARED AT HER FRONT DOOR. SHE HADN'T MOVED
from her perch since Joseph left wearing her towel.

Joseph.

Deadweight rooted her to the spot as the memories
swirled like a tornado in her head. He was back in
Manhattan, wandering around their old spot. It was
exactly what she'd prayed for right after he left. In the
throes of her anger and grief, she'd willed him to come
to his senses, to come home. To her.

But one lonely night in her would-be marriage bed
had turned into two, ten, a hundred.

Three years.

When her mother had been diagnosed, it'd felt
like the world had crumbled. Joseph leaving had been
the final swing of the wrecking ball. She'd needed to
become a new person. A *different* person. Over the next
few years, the pieces had been put back together, bit by
bit. She'd created a new life without him, tried to close

the Joseph-shaped hole by pouring her energy into her work and her family. Into Bad Bachelors.

And now he turned up out of the blue like it was nothing. Annie let out a shaky breath. The universe worked in mysterious ways, her mother had always said.

The universe was an asshole.

"This doesn't change anything," she said as she walked across the room to the small desk where her laptop sat, the screen dark. "This doesn't fix things."

Maybe not. But a heads-up would have been nice. It was asking too much, in reality, because what reason would he have had to contact her? Last she'd heard, he was living in Singapore, engaged to a woman from some prestigious family who looked like a supermodel. The kind of woman who would no doubt satisfy his parents. Their precious lineage wouldn't be sullied by someone unworthy.

Annie jabbed at the power button on her laptop and folded her arms across her chest while it booted up. As if the anniversary hadn't been hard enough, now she had to contend with the fact that Manhattan was no longer safe. Her runs through Central Park could be interrupted by him; her morning walk to work could be derailed by him. Every time she saw a guy in a suit with broad shoulders and endless legs, she'd wonder… Is it him?

The only way to combat this would be work. Bad Bachelors had saved her at a time when she'd needed to be busy. Needed to be distracted. Quickly, the emails—good and bad—had poured in. Slowly, she'd gotten better. Now she'd have to rely on it again. The Bad Bachelors inbox was jam-packed. On average, she received close to four hundred emails a day, ranging from praise and gratitude to threats of all kinds. What would today have in store?

She scanned the subject list, deleting the ones that were obviously angry people looking to vent. On a daily basis, she was told that Jesus hated her, that she was going to hell, that she should kill herself…and worse. Thankfully, the douche canoes writing those emails always made their subject lines super obvious, so she went on her merry deleting spree, stopping only to read the good ones. Because the only emails she cared about were the "you've changed my life" ones and the "I never thought I could date again" ones.

Dear Bad Bachelors…whoever you are, thank you.

When I came across your site, my life had been sex-free for five years. Not because I didn't want it, not because I didn't have the opportunities. After my husband passed away, I couldn't seem to function anymore. I didn't want to move on. A friend forwarded me your article about dating as a widow, along with the interview you posted. I decided that day I was going to try again.

My neighbor had asked me out a few times, but I'd always said no. I hadn't told anyone in Manhattan I was a widow, because I moved here to get away from the questions and the sympathy. But the day I read the article, I decided to look him up on your site. He only had one review, and it was very positive. So I went to his apartment and told him I'd changed my mind about going on a date with him.

We're taking it really slow, and I have a good
feeling about it.

—UnBroken

According to what people wrote, she'd helped assault
victims find the courage to go out with someone because
they could research their dates first. She'd helped heart-
broken women find the desire to put themselves back out
into the world. She'd also helped some women come
to terms with the fact that they were happier alone.
People wrote to her about all kinds of things: strug-
gles with sex and sexuality, with emotional intimacy,
with body confidence and knowing how to stand up
for themselves. Others shared hilarious stories of their
dating misadventures.

She didn't respond to them all, because that would
be a full-time job in itself. But the emails that spoke
to her, like the one from UnBroken, made her stop
and take a few minutes to reply. Annie could easily lose
a few hours in her inbox. And while the bad emails
came as steadily as the good, she never doubted what
she'd created. Bad Bachelors had caused a stir. Sure, it
wasn't something that would please everybody. Even
now, with Darcy and Reed engaged, he was still a little
wary of Annie. But he loved Darcy, and so did Annie,
so they made the effort to get along. It wasn't perfect...
but that was life. They weren't actors in a movie. Real
life was messy, and as much as that wasn't her forte, she
knew not to expect perfection.

Annie continued scrolling down the inbox until
something made her hand freeze. A single email with the

subject line You're not hiding anymore made her heart thump in her chest. Emails like this weren't unusual. Every other day she'd receive one saying that people were hunting her down or working to expose her. She even had a few saying they were watching her right that second. But she'd spent enough time online to know that such threats were about as real as the names people used when contacting her. Talk was cheap and easy. And anonymous.

Action wasn't.

Besides, Annie was nothing if not careful. As much as she hated it, she always used her full name, Leanne, when communicating with people. And, after the incident with Reed tracking her down, she'd abandoned her favorite coffee place, rotating her meeting place for interviews. Face-to-face was risky, of course, but it was still safer than handing out her phone number because that implied continued contact, which she didn't want. And she heavily vetted people she met and always chose a public meeting place where she could observe her contacts before she approached them.

But this email…something about it made her senses prickle.

She clicked. The blurry shot of security camera footage was small, too small to see clearly, but a figure was positioned at the bottom, entering the building. It *could* be her apartment building.

A cold fist closed around her throat.

Or it could be any one of the thousands of other buildings in this city.

Annie squinted, but no distinguishing details could be made out. It would be easy enough to google *security footage* and find a similar image with a woman in the frame. From the picture, it was hard to tell anything other than the woman had darkish hair. That was it.

Rolling her eyes, Annie decided not to waste any more time on it. Her identity was well protected, and she'd made every effort to cover her tracks. Because Reed McMahon hadn't been the only person looking for the "big bad" behind Bad Bachelors. Not by a long shot. She'd racked up plenty of enemies.

But Annie had made privacy priority number one when she'd set out to change the way women dated in Manhattan. First, she'd cited a fake company called Bad Bachelors Inc. on the website. Several articles referenced this company name, indicating the journalists hadn't done much digging. That was layer number one. Her second and more robust layer of protection came in the form of her *real* company, Maximum Holdings. This was the company under which she registered her developer licenses with the major app stores, and it was used anytime she had to list a company name in the course of her work.

The thing about Maximum Holdings was, however, that it was an anonymous LLC registered in Delaware. After doing some research, she'd discovered that privacy laws there allowed people to set up an LLC without disclosing the name of the owners or requiring the members or managers to be residents of the state. In other words, it was the perfect legal shroud.

The assholes who threatened her via email every day could spit and snarl all they liked, but Annie wasn't dumb. She *knew* her work was going to upset people. The truth often had that effect. People didn't like their bad behavior to be called out, especially by a woman online.

Annie deleted the email and decided not to give it a second thought. If she was the kind of person to let an email like that upset her, Bad Bachelors wouldn't have lasted more than a week.

Her cell phone rang, the cheerful electronic sound splitting through the silent apartment. "Hello?"

"I'm checking in to make sure you're home alone." Darcy's tone was laced with worry.

"Yes, I'm home alone."

"No bad decisions?"

"Do you think I'm so weak that I'd jump into bed with him the second I saw him again? It's not like he has some superpowered dick that makes my clothes fly off the second he's in my vicinity."

Darcy snorted. "That would have been awkward at the park."

"I let him use my shower, and then I sent him packing...in a towel."

"You *what*?"

A sly smile lifted Annie's lips. "There was nothing for him to change into."

The thought of high-and-mighty Joseph Preston standing in the middle of a busy Manhattan street, trying to hail a cab in only a towel, gave her a deep sense of perverse pleasure. For a guy who'd been dressed in designer clothing from the second he'd emerged from his mother's womb, it was quite the step down. Part of her had wanted to tell him that the towels were from Target, just to see if he'd break out in hives.

Darcy chuckled. "Oh boy, I would have paid good money to see that."

"I thought his eyes were going to pop out of his head. And I wasn't a total jerk. I offered him a pair of my running tights." She absently scrolled through her emails with her free hand. "Seriously, though. You don't have to worry about me. I'm fine."

"Did he say why he came back?"

"Apparently Singapore had given him what he needed."

But that wasn't the question Darcy was really asking, and they both knew it. It was the question Annie had forced herself *not* to ask while he'd sat there in front of her, half-naked, scowling, and hotter than ever.

Is he still getting married to someone else?

It had been a bad day when Annie had seen the tabloid shot of him and his striking fiancée wearing the precious antique ring she'd once thought was intended for her. There was no mistaking it—the large cushion-cut diamond surrounded by smaller diamonds in an art deco setting was easily identified. It had belonged to his grandmother.

She'd been so excited when she'd stumbled across it. They'd talked about marriage, of course. But not with any timelines attached to it.

Annie swallowed. "I didn't ask him to elaborate. Frankly, I don't care."

Liar.

She couldn't afford to care, because she'd already devoted too many hours of her life to him, and for what? So he could give the ring meant for her to someone else? *Ugh.* She might still be nursing a few bruises on her heart, but that didn't mean she was dumb enough to fantasize about getting Joseph back. That door was closed. Permanently.

An email subject line caught her attention—Bad Bachelors Interview Questions. She clicked on it as Darcy gave her a pep talk about how she'd "grown so much" and that she didn't need "some self-entitled asshole" in her life.

"Mmm-hmm." Annie murmured a generic agreement. Right now, she wanted to be alone to wallow, or at least to distract herself from thoughts of Joseph.

The email made her smile. A user of the app had reached out to her last week with a tale of how she'd found love with her accountant thanks to Bad Bachelors. Annie had asked if the woman would like to be interviewed for an upcoming blog series she was running on love in unlikely places, and the user had agreed, although she would only answer questions over email because she wasn't comfortable meeting in person. Perhaps it might be time to invest in a burner phone so she could do phone interviews.

"Anyway, I'm here for you," Darcy said. "If you feel like you're going to drunk dial him, then call me first, okay? I'll talk you off the ledge."

"Thanks. But you really don't have to worry about me," Annie replied, clicking on the Word document attached to the email so she could read the interviewee's responses. "Everything is perfectly fine."

Later that day, Joseph walked down Sixth Avenue, relishing the feeling of being home. The kaleidoscope of sensations—hovering just before the point of being overwhelming—was quintessentially New York. Horns blared and people shouted, and the scent of pretzels and car exhaust and expensive perfume danced around him. It was like living inside a manic rainbow. The blend of wealth and grit was a pleasing combination that Singapore had failed to give him. It hadn't taken him long to resent how much he'd missed the sound of smacking gum and people saying "fuck you" like they meant it with every fiber of their being.

God, he'd missed this place.

Everywhere in this city there was life. Vibrant extremes.

Right after the move, he'd been lured in by the expat lifestyle: the drinking, the partying, the people from all around the globe. It was a glittering, cosmopolitan world of style and abundance…or so he'd thought. But he'd soon learned that it was a transient existence. People came and went. Friendships of proximity didn't hold up with transfers. And those who stayed enjoyed all the things about Singapore that rubbed him the wrong way—the cleanliness, the rules. The obsession with hierarchy.

He'd missed the seasons, especially fall, feeling the crisp breeze chill the back of his neck. Not to mention being able to get his coffee the way he liked it and a bottle of his favorite wine.

Most of all, he'd missed Annie.

A shoulder jostled him as someone shoved past, snapping his attention to the present. He could see his old apartment building—no, *Annie's* apartment building—looming ahead. Should he stop in and pick up his suit, or should he give her another day to recover?

Who was he kidding? He'd turned up three years after walking out the day before he was going to propose. Another day here or there wasn't going to make any difference. He'd be fighting an uphill battle in trying to atone for his sins, no matter which day he stopped by.

Slinging his jacket over one arm and loosening his tie, he approached the entrance. He had no idea what on earth he was going to say to her. Despite all his careful planning about how he might have that first, awkward conversation, their encounter that morning had flipped everything on its head. His plans were now a pile of smoking rubble.

But his darkest days in Singapore had proven he belonged in Manhattan. And he'd thrown that away for what? A chance to fast-track his career and earn himself a big reputation? Another failed attempt to gain the respect of his father? Perhaps Morris was right. Joseph *was* a disappointment. A giant, colossal fuckup.

The glass door of Annie's apartment building reflected the sun, causing Joseph to squint. He punched the apartment number into the intercom panel and waited for her to pick up. The speaker rang and rang, but no voice greeted him. A second later, the doors opened and a security guard in a navy uniform peered at him curiously.

"Mr. Preston?"

"That's me."

"I, uh…saw you earlier this morning." He handed over a yellow sticky note. "Ms. Maxwell asked me to pass on a message."

The flowery writing punched Joseph straight in the gut. Annie had always written in this elaborate cursive that looked better suited to poetry than Post-its. It was totally at odds with the rest of her efficient, by-the-book personality. Yet every Christmas and birthday card had been filled with curling lines of it.

> *I dropped your stuff off at the dry cleaners. The old place. It's under your name and already paid for. No need for you to return the money.*

The message couldn't have been clearer: stay the hell away.

"Thanks very much," he said stiffly, plucking the note from the security guard's finger.

A small part of him—a dark and selfish part he'd rather ignore—warmed at the note. She could easily have dumped his wet clothing into the trash. But that wasn't Annie. Even with the person she probably hated most in the world, she took the time to do the right thing.

But that meant he'd need another excuse to talk to her.

And what are you going to say that'll make a lick of difference?

That was the more difficult question. *Shit.* He needed a drink. Perhaps downing a couple of beers in the fading daylight might help him get his head together. Then he could figure out what kind of magic it would take to get Annie to hear him out. The need to apologize had been weighing on him ever since he'd decided to come home, and the feeling had only grown stronger as the hours passed.

He was meant to be home, and it wasn't simply because of a lucrative job offer. He needed closure.

Grabbing the prepaid phone he'd bought to keep him going until a replacement work phone could be procured, he racked his memory for someone to call. Despite all the people in New York City, it could be a lonely place sometimes. And Joseph hadn't exactly maintained a lot of relationships after he'd left. But he still remembered the number for one of his oldest friends. The one person who didn't appear to completely detest him.

Ten minutes later, he was perched on a high stool, a cold pint in his hand. The bar was an old favorite, a common "on the way home" watering hole that he and Annie had frequented when they'd worked only a block from each other. He swiped his thumb through the condensation on the glass and let out a hollow laugh.

How fucking stupid he'd been back then. He'd had the world at his feet, and he hadn't appreciated it one bit.

"Joe?"

A familiar voice caught his attention.

Andrew, an old friend and former colleague, clapped a hand on his back and reached for the beer waiting for him. "How long has it been?"

Joseph tamped down the feeling of relief. These days, he really needed a friend, even if he didn't necessarily deserve one.

"Too long," Joseph replied, raising his beer to Andrew's. "Feels like a goddamn decade."

"I heard you were coming back."

"Word travels fast." The negotiations for this job had been kept quiet. Joseph hadn't even flown in for the interviews, since it'd all been done over Skype. Even after the paperwork had been signed, they hadn't announced it right away.

Because his appointment caused waves. In tech companies and start-ups, it wasn't uncommon to have a younger person at the helm. Hell, it was probably the norm. But banking was one of the world's last corporate dinosaurs. Anyone under forty-five "couldn't possibly" have the experience to take on such a challenge, as he'd already been told. Joseph had heard the discontent and all the comments about his father giving him a leg up, and questions about his experience were being lobbed at him left, right, and center. Technically, he didn't start until Monday, so who knew how much worse it would get.

"C I fucking O. You make me sick," Andrew said. "How old are you, like twelve?"

"Thirteen." Joseph winked. "And a half."

"And they're giving you the keys to the kingdom." Andrew shook his head. "I'm impressed."

"Talent knows no age, my friend."

Andrew snorted. "I thought you said you were going to kick the corporate stuff after a few years. Focus on starting up your white-hat business."

That had certainly been the plan. With cybercrime on the rise, the need for ethical hacking was growing at a rapid rate. Data breaches were fast becoming a major concern for large corporations, and there was money to be made. But of course, being an entrepreneur wasn't quite prestigious enough for the son of Morris Preston.

As far as his father was concerned, internet security was a passing fad that would leave Joseph penniless like a dot-com crash victim.

"Goals change," he said with a shrug.

"It's good to see you." Andrew grinned and took a swig of his beer. "I knew you couldn't stay away."

"Manhattan tends to have that effect on people."

"The job brought you home?"

"I was ready to come home. If it wasn't this job, it would have been another. Singapore was great, but I had cabin fever." He shot his friend a rueful smile. "It's very…insular in the expat community."

He nodded. "Does Annie know you're back?"

"You don't waste any time with hard-hitting questions, do you?" Joseph shook his head.

"Sorry, man. That's what consulting has done to me. Time is money, no beating around the bush."

"I bumped into her this morning." Joseph's lip twitched at his choice of words. "Completely by coincidence."

"And?"

"It was awkward. She was shocked." Joseph took a long gulp of his beer, relishing the cool liquid sliding down his dry throat. "I didn't want it to go down like that."

"But fate got in the way." Andrew nodded sagely.

"Probably more karma than fate. Payback for being a stupid son of a bitch," he muttered.

"Can't argue with that."

Andrew was one of several people who had sent him a "What the hell is going on?" message when it had come out that Joseph was leaving and Annie was staying behind. He and Andrew had kept up loose contact—an email here and there—over the last few years. But Andrew had made it clear from the get-go that he thought Joseph was being an idiot.

"Did you tell *anyone* you were coming home?" Andrew narrowed his eyes.

"I emailed my parents last week." Joseph shrugged. "But I suspect Dad already knew. Industry gossip… You know what it's like."

"That's dysfunctional."

Dysfunction was the only thing his family excelled at as a group. And he'd emailed to save himself a lecture from his mother, not because he thought they'd want to meet him at the other end.

"What happened to the girl you were going to marry?" Joseph's hand tightened around his beer. "It's over."

He could still hear the sound of Annika screaming at him, at the burst of a vase against the wall like a glittering, violent firework. Her shaking the picture of Annie that she'd found hidden in his passport wallet.

I can't compete with her. I can't make you forget about her.

Joseph needed a plan. A plan for how to deal with his parents. A plan for how to speak to Annie so he could let go and move on. A plan for how to get his life back on track. Because now it felt like he was standing at the edge of a sinkhole, and it was only a matter of time before his mistakes pulled him under.

Chapter 4

"You made one too many mistakes. Look out, I'm coming for you."

—MrNiceGuy

"I MEAN, HE'S CUTE AND ALL, BUT WE'RE ABOUT TO GO off to college next year. I don't know if I'm ready to be tied down like that." Sofia paused to take a sip of her coffee—some crème brûlée–flavored confection that was more whipped cream than it was coffee. "You know, commitment is scary."

Annie had to bite her tongue. The only commitment her seventeen-year-old sister had encountered so far in her life was to choose between two types of Lululemon leggings for her birthday present. But Annie had learned that pointing such things out would only result in her sister talking to her less, which was not at all what she wanted.

"Might be good to keep your options open," Annie said, bringing her latte to her lips and finding the cup empty. She tossed it into a trash can as they approached her apartment building. "And you've got better things to worry about besides boys."

"You sound like Mom." Sofia rolled her eyes. "Although I guess that shouldn't be too surprising, since you *are* blood-related."

"Hate to break it to you, Sof. *All* moms and big sisters sound like that."

"And I thought big sisters were supposed to tell you to take risks and live your life." Sofia wrinkled her nose. "Not say boys are a waste of time."

"I said you had better things to worry about, not that they're a waste of time."

Annie swiped her access card and let Sofia go ahead of her. She watched as her sister's long, dark ponytail swished above a pair of jeans so tight they could have been spray-painted on. A thin ribbon of skin was bared at her back, where a cropped sweater failed to meet the waistband of her jeans. It was chilly today, too cold for that kind of outfit.

You really do *sound like your mother.*

"Is that why you never have a boyfriend anymore?" Sofia asked with a raised brow. "Because you have better things to worry about?"

It was partly that. Between her day job working as a business analyst for a software development firm, managing Bad Bachelors, and visiting her family, there wasn't much time left over at the end of the week. Annie chose to spend it reading, running, or hanging out with Darcy.

But that was only an excuse she told herself to keep the truth at bay. Fact was, the thought of dating again terrified Annie. There had been a brief time when she'd tried to put herself out into the dating scene after Joseph. But it had been an epic disaster.

No chemistry, bad conversation, long, awkward pauses that made her want to pull her hair out. Oh, and the dick pics. *Ew*. Then there was the guy who'd point-blank told her in the middle of dinner that he had a ten-inch cock, and after him, she wouldn't be able to enjoy sex with other men.

Ugh, hard pass. No pun intended.

"Dating is not a priority for me right now," she said. As they walked through the lobby, the concierge flagged them down.

"Ms. Maxwell." The young guy nodded. "A parcel came in for you today. Would you like to grab it now?"

Annie nodded, and the man disappeared into the storeroom to retrieve it. "I mean, if the right guy comes along, I won't say no, but I'm not actively looking."

You mean if the right guy runs smack into you in the middle of Central Park...

"But the right guy won't find you if you do nothing but be a"—Sofia narrowed her eyes—"hermit."

"I'm *not* a hermit."

"You're kind of a hermit."

Annie smoothed a hand over her hair and prayed for strength. "It's called being an adult, Sof. You'll learn about that one day."

"Responsibilities, bills, jobs. Blah, blah, blah." Sofia made a talking motion with her hand. "*Boring!*"

"Here, make yourself useful and hold this." Annie handed over the bag containing their takeout dinner as the concierge returned with a large cardboard envelope.

"You might want to contact whoever sent you this," he said. "They had the building number, but not the apartment number. Usually we mark these 'return to sender,' but I recognized your name so I put it aside."

"Thank you." She scribbled her signature onto the electronic signing pad. "I appreciate that."

"What did you order?" Sofia asked, peering at the label as they walked to the elevators.

"No idea." Annie turned the item over in her hands. There were no distinguishing markings, no information on the label to jog her memory. Just her name and address, along with a sticker that said *Do not bend*. "Let that be a lesson to you—don't drink and Prime."

Sofia giggled. "Drunk online shopping… Now *that* sounds fun."

"And you can do it in four years' time." The elevator's mirrored doors opened with a soft *swish*.

"Seriously, what do you think I should do? Matt wants to go out, but I don't want him to, like, get the wrong idea or anything." Sofia fiddled with the clasp on her bag. "He said he's always getting stuck in the friend zone."

"The friend zone is bullshit, Sof." The elevator pinged, and they walked into the hallway. "You're not under any obligation to date a boy. Ever. And there's nothing wrong with being friends, so if he can't deal with it, that sounds a whole lot like *his* problem. Not yours. You're not punishing him by saying no."

Sofia laughed. "Thanks for the advice, Mama Bear."

Annie dug her keys out of her purse and let Sofia into her apartment. Through the big windows, the sky was turning dark and the city lights shimmered. Annie tossed her keys into a bowl by the door and set the envelope on the kitchen counter.

"I guess I don't really like him like that," Sofia said as she started to unpack their dinner. "And he's a little intense, you know? I felt bad after Emily dumped him and then Frieda rejected him. So when he asked me, I said I'd think about it. But then he started hounding me for an answer."

It was probably a good thing that Annie lived in Manhattan. Because if she was close to Sofia's school in Bensonhurst, she might be liable to turn up and teach the little shit a lesson. But that was the thing about Sofia; she had her father's giant heart. The thought of upsetting anyone always made her worry. It was less of an issue with Allegra, who was only too happy to tell people to fuck off if it was required. But Sofia was Sal's daughter through and through. Soft, sensitive souls who were ripe for people taking advantage of their good natures.

"A pity date doesn't help anyone," Annie replied. "And if he's hounding you now, what will he be like if you say yes?"

Sofia nodded. "Good point."

"What do you do if he gives you a hard time?" She stared her sister down.

"Tell him no and walk away." She sighed, as if being made to recite her times tables. "And if he touches me when I said no, I knee him in the nuts and get to someplace safe so I can call you or Dad."

"That's right."

Sofia opened the containers one by one. They always got dinner from the Chinese restaurant down the street when Sofia stayed over before a Manhattan-based school excursion. There was vegetable soup with tofu for Annie, wonton soup for Sofia, jumbo shrimp with broccoli, sweet and sour chicken, and steamed rice for them both.

Annie was busy shrugging out of her coat and kicking off her heels, shedding the workday like a snake shedding skin. Her bare feet hit the floorboards, and she almost groaned at the feeling of freedom. Nothing like releasing one's toes from patent-leather hell to make a woman feel happy to be home. That was, until her phone beeped with a text from an unknown number.

It's Joseph. Can we talk?

She swallowed, her heart pounding suddenly as if the message had triggered her fight-or-flight response. She ran her thumb over a smudge at the corner of the phone's screen. It had been five days since their "encounter" in Central Park. Five days of wondering whether he'd try to contact her again. Of not knowing whether she'd be more upset if he did or didn't. She hadn't changed her number in the last three years; maybe that was a mistake.

Respond or ignore?

"Who's messaging you?" Sofia asked as she collected bowls from the kitchen. "Is it Darcy? Tell her to come have dinner with us."

"It's no one," Annie lied. "Boring work stuff."

She dropped the phone into her bag and closed the zipper as if needing to seal the nervous energy inside.

This wasn't something she wanted to deal with right now. Especially since she hadn't decided whether to tell her family that Joseph was back in town…and that he'd been in her apartment. Her eyes strayed to the couch where he'd sat, hair dripping wet and his cut body barely concealed in her towel. *Oh boy.* It was not an image that would quickly fade.

Joseph's name had become a forbidden word in their house after the breakup. She reached for the envelope, desperate for something to distract her. Annie pulled the tab open. Inside was a single sheet of paper. She frowned. Not a piece of paper, actually. She pulled it out. It was a photograph. Of her.

It appeared to have been taken with the webcam in her laptop.

Annie blinked, hoping it was some crazy trick her mind was playing on her. Or perhaps it was a sick joke? A doctored photo? But the angle of the camera was right, and it captured the funky plant she kept in the corner, with the unique geometric design on the pot. In the photo, Annie had her hair wrapped up in a towel, like she did most days when she washed her hair and answered emails while it dried.

"Are you coming to eat?" Sofia asked from the table. She was occupied by her phone and so hadn't noticed Annie staring at the contents of the envelope.

She quickly stashed the photo in a drawer and sat down with her sister. But her legs wobbled like Jell-O, and she caught sight of her reflection in the decorative mirror across the room. Her face was ashen. Petrified.

Someone knew she was behind Bad Bachelors.

Later that night, Annie lay awake in bed, staring up at the ceiling. Normally, she closed her blinds tightly, trying to preserve as much darkness as one could living in a city that sparkled the way Manhattan did. But tonight she had them open, leaving her room in a state of half-darkness that allowed her to see the outlines of everything in her room. With each creak of the building or shuffling sound from the apartment next door, her fists curled tighter into her duvet. Never once had she felt unsafe in her home. Never once had she been the kind of person who worried about bumps in the night.

But that security had been well and truly obliterated.

She'd smuggled the photo into her room after Sofia had gone to sleep, because she didn't want her sister to worry. But there *was* cause for worry. Someone had hacked into her laptop and watched her via her webcam. A sick sensation cemented in her stomach.

Someone. Had. Been. Watching. Her.

She pushed up in her bed, pressing a hand to her chest in the hope that it might steady her fluttering heart. It didn't. The feeling of violation was so strong, it was like her home had been broken into. Her skin crawled, like a thousand beetles were prickling her. All her senses were on high alert, her nerves frayed, her heartbeat uneven and quick.

Annie swung her legs over the edge of the bed and braced her forearms against her thighs, breathing deeply in the semidarkness. The view from her bedroom was partially blocked by another building, and Annie watched the lights flicking on and off in the windows facing her. Shadowy figures moved behind blinds, but some were more careless, leaving their windows uncovered and their rooms bared for her to see, falsely secure in the belief that no one was paying attention.

Her phone sat on the nightstand, calling to her with a siren song.

If someone had hacked into her computer, she needed to figure out how to get them out. But hackers were far beyond her level of technical skill. She was fine with building websites and installing security code and running her antivirus software. But beyond that... Hacking was a specialized skill, and she had no idea how to find out which "door" they'd used to get in. Nor how to stop them from watching her now.

Taking her laptop to a computer repair place would mean letting more people know who she was. That *she* was the person behind Bad Bachelors. How could she trust some computer-repair guy with that information? What if he'd been reviewed on the site? What if he sold her information to the tabloids...or worse, what if he sold her information on the internet somewhere? To people who could really hurt her? How could she protect herself then?

Annie had ended up in the one position that could make her truly vulnerable: needing help from the very last person she wanted to ask.

Why is the most-talked-about website and app in Manhattan not making any money?

By Andrea Steinberg (*Mint Money Online* technology reporter)

Unless you've been living under a rock, you've probably heard about the website and app that allow New York women to rate their dates. While it's not surprising to see another dating-related tool taking off, what *is* different about Bad Bachelors is something that has a lot of people scratching their heads.

Monetization...or lack thereof.

Many online dating tools feature a freemium model, with certain features open to all and upgraded features available for a fee. Most have advertising built into their platforms.

But Bad Bachelors features no obvious revenue streams. That can only lead us to speculate about the person behind it and why they would choose not to cash in on this venture. But despite multiple attempts to unearth the identity of the Bad Bachelor's creator, little information has been forthcoming.

This isn't entirely surprising, since the concept has certainly sparked a lot of debate. Have people forgotten the origins of Facebook? It's not the first time we've used the internet to rate and compare people. Still, many have spoken out against Bad Bachelors due to its potential for lasting reputational damage.

That hasn't stopped whispers that investors are starting to circle. There's money to be made, and if the creator isn't going to capitalize on the concept while it's in its prime, perhaps others will.

At any rate, whoever is behind Bad Bachelors appears to be keeping quiet, and their motives remain unknown.

Joseph looked up from his laptop and pulled his reading glasses off so he could grind his fists into his bleary eyes. It was close to midnight and he really should call it quits, but he hadn't even changed out of his suit yet. Day four in his new role had been the longest yet, finally ending after a meeting with the CEO stretched well past 10:00 p.m. Joseph had come home, grabbed an apple from his fridge, and promptly collapsed onto the couch to start reading the media pack that his executive assistant prepared for him each day.

It wasn't enough to be in the office for fourteen hours straight; he had to keep on top of the latest industry information as well. Not that he was sure why he was reading about a bachelor-review site, but perhaps his assistant thought it might come up in conversation. After all, Joseph *had* asked for some local knowledge articles. Three years was a long time to be away from any city, but it was light-years for Manhattan.

He glanced at his phone again. The damn thing had been mercilessly silent all night. He'd fired off a text to Annie between meetings sometime around seven in the evening and had received nothing but stone-wall silence.

Did you really expect any different?

He hadn't. It was a miracle she still had her old number. And he only knew that because he'd drilled Andrew for information, receiving a noncommittal "I don't know if she changed her number" when he'd asked. Which meant, of course, she hadn't. But Andrew was trying hard not to pick sides.

Just as Joseph was about to look away, the screen lit up.

ANNIE: Why do you want to talk?

He stared at the message. Why *did* he want to talk? It wasn't like he had anything planned. Talking about one's feelings was a very *un*-Preston thing to do. His mother had always classed deep and meaningful conversation as something to be avoided at all costs. Like pleather. And cheap champagne.

JOSEPH: I wanted to thank you for not throwing my suit out of your window.
ANNIE: No need to thank me.

And what on earth was she doing up at this hour, texting him? The Annie he knew was always asleep by ten thirty. She *loved* sleep. Loved being in bed even if she wasn't sleeping. He used to get up at the crack of dawn to go running on the weekends, and when he'd returned, he often found her still in bed but with a cup of coffee and a book, looking happy as a puppy with a lap to curl up on.

He swallowed against the tightness in his throat. How many times had he torn the book out of her hands and pressed his lips to her neck while she swatted him playfully and claimed he was gross and sweaty? That was, until he'd started kissing down her body, and those playful swats had turned to a viselike grip on his hair.

Fuck, he missed those Sunday mornings.

JOSEPH: I wanted to see how you're doing.
ANNIE: I'm peachy.

His lip quirked. One time he'd asked her what *peachy* actually meant, because it didn't really make any sense to him. Why were peaches chosen to represent human emotion? Why not apples or cherries? True to form, Annie had then used the word as often as possible in order to tease him for getting so annoyed about it in the first place. Just one of the games they'd played.

He swallowed. There was so much he wanted to say, so much he needed to untangle. He'd decided when he boarded the plane to JFK that he would find a way to apologize to Annie for what he'd done. He wasn't about to take sole blame for the dissolution of their relationship, but back then he hadn't even been willing to accept a portion of it. Which made him an asshole first and an idiot second. She deserved an apology. But that couldn't happen over the phone.

ANNIE: Actually, I need your help with something.

Joseph blinked to make sure his mind wasn't playing tricks on him. But there in the blue-bubble text message was a request for help.

JOSEPH: What do you need?
ANNIE: Come to my place tomorrow when you finish work. Doesn't matter if it's late.

His mind whirred. It must be something serious

to prompt an invitation. Beyond serious. A hard knot settled in his gut.

JOSEPH: I'll be there.

Chapter 5

"Dear Bad Bachelors, one day you're going to realize that you've hurt people in an irreparable way. Is that the legacy you want to leave behind?"

—Unhappy

THE FOLLOWING DAY, JOSEPH FINISHED WORK AS EARLY as he could. His head was a wasteland, with nothing but thoughts of Annie and her request occupying his attention. It'd made him feel slow. Sluggish. Like the power that his body usually required to function was dedicated to the endlessly spinning wheel of worry.

He watched the city crawl by outside the cab's window as they drove from the Financial District to Midtown. It was almost eight thirty in the evening, and the streets were still clogged, meaning the journey was marked by the blare of horns and grumblings from the cab driver who shook his head repeatedly.

Despite having spent most of the day thinking about what Annie could possibly want, Joseph hadn't come up with an answer. When they'd lived together, she hadn't needed much help with anything. The woman was an IKEA master, a whiz in the kitchen, and unafraid of spiders or cockroaches. She'd painted the place on her own while he'd been away for business, and rearranged the furniture periodically. She was meticulous. Independent, confident. It was the very thing he'd loved about her—that she wasn't with him because she needed him, but rather simply because she *wanted* him.

For a boy who'd grown up with shoulders weighed down by obligation and expectation, to be wanted instead of needed was a very refreshing thing.

When the cabbie pulled up in front of the building, Joseph paid and stepped out onto the sidewalk. The air was bitterly cold and blustery, causing the bottom of his coat to flap open and the skin on his neck to ripple with goose bumps. He walked over to the front of her building and jabbed the apartment code into the intercom.

"Hello?" Her voice was distorted by the speakers.

"It's me."

The only response was the slight click the door made when the lock was released. Joseph waited an extra heartbeat to see if she would say anything else, but she didn't. The air inside the foyer of the building was stuffy, and he shrugged out of his coat as he walked to the elevator. He didn't recognize any of the people coming or going. Three years was plenty of time for people to move in and out, for faces to change. He wondered if the elderly Italian woman with the three corgis still lived on their floor.

Annie's floor.

He would have to correct himself a few more times before it stuck. Being back here had made him regress into old habits, like thinking this was *his* place. Like feeling as though he'd come home. It needed to stop.

By the time he made it upstairs, he was still no closer to figuring out what possible catalyst might have brought him here. Nor what the hell he was going to say to her. The only saving grace was that at least this time he was dry and had both shoes.

And hopefully he wouldn't be going home in a towel.

Joseph knocked on Annie's door, and a few seconds later, it swung open.

"Hey." Her eyes almost met his, but not quite. "Come in."

She looked dressed for battle. Black pencil skirt, black silk blouse, and black pearls in her ears. He recognized the outfit—it was one she wore whenever she had to face down a problem at work. Or if she had to negotiate. Black made her feel fearless.

But what could she possibly have to negotiate with him?

"Long day at the office?" he asked.

She held her hand out, gesturing with a subtle wriggle of her fingers. "Isn't it always?"

She hung his coat on the stand near the door, and the sight of it—the long line of black cashmere next to her much smaller gray coat with oversize gold buttons—wrenched in his chest. Just like old times…

"So, uh, the reason I asked you here…" She wrung her hands in front of her. "I need some help with my computer."

He raised a brow. Annie was pretty tech-savvy, so it mustn't be an average computer problem. "What sort of help?"

"I think it's malware-related."

Now that he looked at her more closely, something was definitely amiss. She'd lost weight since he left— he'd noticed that last time. Her curvy figure had been honed into a leaner, fitter machine. But today…today was something else. There were dark hollows under her eyes that the bare flick of mascara did little to compensate for. And her skin tone seemed off. Sickly white.

Malware clearly wasn't the only issue.

He wanted to ask if everything was okay, but he bit his tongue. Asking her something like that would only make her shut down. Being here to help would have to be enough for the moment.

It's enough. Period. You're not back in Manhattan to re-create the past.

"I can take a look," he said. "But malware isn't my specialty these days, so I'm not up on the latest technology in that area. You might have to take it to a specialist."

"I'd prefer not to," she said, folding her arms over her chest.

He went to the desk in the corner of the room. It had a view of the city, and her laptop sat on a stand in the middle. The rest of the desk was as neat as a pin. No surprises there. "What makes you think you have malware?"

He dropped down into the seat, rolling it back slightly so he could fit his legs under the desk without bumping his knees. When Annie didn't respond, he turned to glance up at her.

"I need to know what I'm looking for," he said.

"Just a feeling." Her face revealed nothing.

"I'm assuming you ran an antivirus scan?"

She nodded. "Nothing came up."

"But you still have a feeling that something is off?" He watched her poker face closely. "I'll have more chance of finding something if I know what to look for."

Worry flickered over her face, but she didn't say anything else. The strange behavior did nothing to quell Joseph's intuition that something was deeply wrong. The second he'd gotten her text, his concerns had mounted. He'd tried to brush the intuition off as leftovers of their relationship—like muscle memory or phantom feelings—but his gut was hardly ever wrong.

He turned back to the computer, unsure where to start, when something caught his eye. A piece of black tape covered the webcam at the top of her screen. It made his blood run cold.

Back when he was still working in information security, he'd told her to cover up the camera and she'd laughed, teasing him about conspiracy theories and paranoia. That night at dinner, she'd fashioned him a miniature hat out of tinfoil.

He scratched at the corner of the tape with his nail, ready to peel it off.

"Don't!" she said suddenly. "Don't take it off."

"What the hell is going on?" He looked at her, the fear in her expression blowing a hole through his chest. But he went with frustration instead, because that seemed more manageable. "You *need* to level with me."

She bit down on her lip and pulled open the drawer by his thigh. Inside was a photo printed on thick white paper that showed Annie looking ahead, close to the camera. Her expression was neutral, a small line between her brows that he knew to be her mark of concentration.

"It's from the camera," she said. "I didn't take it."

He shook his head. "You think someone hacked into your computer and used your webcam to take a photo of you?"

She nodded.

"Fucking hell. And they emailed it to you?"

"Sent it," she corrected. "In the mail."

"So they have your address?" He tried to calm his mind enough so he wouldn't blow this one chance to do something good for her. But all his primal, protective instincts were fired up, screaming at him to make sure nobody could hurt her ever again.

You fucking hypocrite.

"Yes, they have my address," she said tersely. "Well, the building address anyway. Whoever sent it didn't use my apartment number. So the only reason I received it was because the concierge recognized my name."

"Still, they know you live here. In this building."

"I understand the gravity of this situation." She leveled him with a look. "Can you help me?"

"I'll see what I can find." He swallowed down the questions that were piling up in the back of his throat, choking him. Right now, he needed to do what she'd asked. *Then* he'd find out what was going on.

"Have you eaten?" she asked softly. "You used to forget to have dinner when you worked long hours. And don't tell me you had an apple, because that doesn't count."

Through all the crazy, swirling emotions in his head, a smile ghosted over his lips. "No, I haven't eaten."

"I've got some leftover soup. I'll heat it up for you."

Her heels clicked over the floorboards as she left him alone, the taped-over webcam staring back at him like the unblinking eye of a monster. Why would anyone be spying on Annie? Not just spying. Intimidating. Threatening. Because the only reason someone would take a photo like that and send it in the mail was if they wanted something.

Annie stood in the kitchen, her feet aching from being in heels since early that morning, trembling hands gripping the edge of the countertop. She'd drifted through the day in a zombielike state, equally nervous about the people watching her as she was about having to ask Joseph for help. Not because she thought he might refuse—she knew he wouldn't—but because relying on him was far too familiar.

She sucked in a breath and fished the leftover sweet potato soup from the fridge, forcing herself to focus on the task at hand rather than letting her mind spin like a Ferris wheel out of control. From the kitchen, she could easily see him sitting at the computer, too big for the quaint little desk she'd jammed into the corner. He leaned forward, silent in concentration, the back of his suit creating a sexy, broad line from strong shoulders to a trim waist. He'd worn a navy pinstripe today. No doubt an upgrade from the one she remembered, since he had them tailored annually.

Damn, it looked good.

Okay, so Joseph Preston was as hot as ever. Big deal.

Annie knew better than to be lured in by good looks and a suit that fit so well it was a perfectionist's wet dream. She *especially* knew not be lured in by his calm capability and willingness to come to her aid.

Snapping her eyes back to the glass container in front of her, she set about spooning the soup into a pot on the stove. While it was heating, she pulled a bowl down from the cupboard in front of her, wincing at her shoes. They were a recent purchase and not yet broken in, but they made her legs look good, and right now she needed all the confidence she could get. Because there was a very real chance that everything was about to crumble around her.

She stirred Joseph's soup aimlessly, watching him as he worked. Every so often, he would reach behind his neck and knead the muscles there, the way he always did when deep in thought. It was hard not to remember how his hands felt—strong, firm, and forever in control. Annie lowered her eyes, her pulse thumping. He'd always had an insatiable appetite and enjoyed keeping her in a state of near-exhausted satisfaction. Lovemaking had never been their issue—it was their makeup routine, their Sunday morning routine, their halfway-through-a-movie-that-wasn't-quite-grabbing-their-attention routine.

You're really thinking about sex right now? What the hell is wrong with you?

It seemed a better option than worrying about what he might find on her computer.

Are you worried about who's spying on you or about him finding out about Bad Bachelors?

It should be the former. But there was a healthy dose of the latter too, if she was being honest with herself.

"Why do you care what he thinks? It's not like he's on the damn site," she muttered as she tested the temperature of the soup.

Joseph looked over his shoulder suddenly, as though he'd heard her. Which would be impossible since he was across the room. But the invisible thread that had once made them so in tune with each other—a bond they'd nurtured on and off for a huge chunk of her life—was still there. It unnerved the hell out of her. How was it possible that a three-year absence and total emotional devastation hadn't quite destroyed it?

"That smells amazing," he said, pushing up from the desk chair. He shrugged out of his suit jacket and undid the red tie at his neck, his strong fingers moving over the gleaming silk with a sureness that settled like a stone in the pit of her stomach.

"It's nothing fancy." She ladled the soup into a bowl and carried it to the coffee table. They used to have a small dining table in the apartment, but that extra space was now taken up by her desk. Which meant dinners were usually eaten on the couch. "What did you find?"

He folded himself into one corner of the couch, his long legs extending past the coffee table where he rested his crossed ankles. The hem of his suit pants pulled up to reveal blue-and-red-striped socks. Company colors, she would guess. That was Joseph's MO. Even the smallest details had significance.

"Would you sit down?" he said. "I'm not going to bite."

Annie's stomach twisted at the words, but she forced herself not to show any reaction. The couch was small, made for two people, so there was no way to get distance from him. She squished herself into the opposite corner, trying to make herself as small as possible in a desperate attempt to avoid any accidental brushing of limbs.

"There's a system-monitoring program accessing your webcam," he said, reaching for his dinner. "I've removed it from your computer, but I would say that whoever installed it would know by now that you've figured out someone was watching."

"Because I covered the camera up?"

"Yeah."

She bobbed her head. "I'm guessing they're the same people who sent me the picture. Surely they would be expecting a reaction."

"I would say so."

She frowned. "Why wouldn't my antivirus software pick the program up?"

"Antivirus usually picks up spyware, but not always. Since the monitoring program isn't doing anything malicious to the computer, they were able to make it act like a regular background process." He spooned some of the soup into his mouth. "But that wasn't all."

Annie shut her eyes for a moment. "There's more?"

"They weren't only monitoring your webcam." He looked over at her. It was shocking how those light, icy eyes still made her heart flutter. "They were looking through your computer. Probably got your IP address, and that's how they narrowed your street address down to this building."

"Right." She slowly bobbed her head.

"Do you have any idea why someone might be doing this?" His brows creased, and he set his half-empty bowl on the coffee table. It was harder to look at him now, because the concern poured out of him like a pheromone, and it wasn't his job to be concerned about her.

"I have some idea." She swallowed past the tightness in her throat.

Silence stretched between them, and eventually the sound of traffic and life outside trickled in.

"Care to share?" he asked.

His intense gaze made her feel hot and cold at the same time. Joseph had always liked to feast with his eyes, so she'd often stripped for him slowly and steadily, letting his insatiable desire churn like a storm until he couldn't take the anticipation anymore.

"No," she replied. "Just tell me what I need to do."

"Take it to a repair place and have a professional do a proper sweep."

"You *are* a professional."

He cocked his head. "I'm a CIO, Annie. My head's been in strategy and spreadsheets the last three years. That kind of technology moves fast, and I haven't been keeping up to date."

He'd moved on. And his dream to open a white-hat hacking business must have fallen by the wayside along with their relationship. It was comforting not to be the only casualty of his ruthless ambition.

"And if I can't take it to a repair place?"

"Wipe it." He leveled her with a stare. "Many of these programs are built to regenerate and reinstall themselves. You can kill it off, and then it grows back like a weed. The safest thing to do would be to back up your files and do a factory reset."

"Is that something you can do?"

Joseph leaned back against the couch, one arm coming to rest along the back. The pose was relaxed, as though he was totally at ease in this situation. In her space. His crisp white shirt was now unbuttoned at the base of his neck, and his waist was highlighted by a slim, tan belt. It matched his shoes to perfection. Annie had always been a sucker for a well-dressed guy. It'd attracted her back then—he'd been the only well-dressed guy in the whole frat house when everyone else had been wearing cheesy fedora hats and other assorted fashion atrocities of the mid-2000s. Not that it had stopped her from teasing him about his slacks and shirt, just for the excuse to talk to him.

"I can wipe it for you, but it'll take a while. A few hours at least."

"Why did you agree to help me?" she asked suddenly. The question was like a grenade lobbed into the air by accident. "Actually, don't answer that. I don't care."

"I know things ended...badly."

She rolled her eyes. "You're a regular freaking Sherlock, aren't you?"

"But that doesn't erase what we shared," he finished. "If you ask for my help, I will always provide it."

She didn't want to hear that. She didn't want the god-awful position of being stuck between a rock and a hard place, forced to lean on him out of sheer necessity and preservation. It made her sick to her stomach.

"But it's not a 'no questions asked' kind of deal?" She picked at the hem of her skirt, fixated with a small dangling thread. She dragged her nail over it, worrying the imperfection until the thread started to pull.

Annie jumped when a warm hand closed over hers. The touch was simultaneously too wrong and too right. Comforting and jarring in equal measure. She yanked her hand back.

"This is serious, Annie. You're smart, and you know how to protect yourself online. I taught you everything I could. Which means that for someone to have gotten this kind of software onto your computer, there's been some social engineering." He dropped both hands into his lap. "This kind of stuff doesn't happen by accident."

"Social engineering?"

"Psychological manipulation. Hackers use confidence tricks and other methods to convince people to do what they want—usually divulging confidential information or granting some kind of system access. Or it could have been a phishing exercise. They convince you to click on a seemingly innocent link or open an attachment that installs the spyware."

"And you think I got tricked?" She stood suddenly, unsure what to do with her hands so she reached for his half-eaten soup and took it to the kitchen to wash up.

"I don't want to frighten you, but I also don't want you to think that me wiping your computer is going to solve whatever problem led you to this point."

Tears welled in her eyes. Every part of her body ached for the comfort only he could provide. Joseph was the one man who'd always calmed her anxious personality.

She was that high-strung kid, the type A high achiever who always fussed over every little detail. But around him, she'd turned into this carefree, confident woman. A flower blossoming under the perfect amount of sunshine.

"I can stay and do the wipe now if your backups are up to date," he said.

"It's late," she said, glancing at the clock hanging on the wall. "If you start now, you won't finish 'til the middle of the night."

"I'd rather know you weren't in this place alone." His tone was stiff.

"I can't have you sleep over."

God, she wouldn't be able to handle it. Knowing he was in the other room while she was feeling at her most exposed. Every part of her was soft now. Raw and vulnerable and all those other words that made her skin scrawl.

"I don't think I could sleep a wink anyway," he replied. "I'll be gone before you get up."

Annie considered her options. Truth be told, she was frightened of being alone at the moment. And she'd already planned to spend the weekend at her parents' place, just to get out of the apartment. If Joseph was here tonight, then she could put off dealing with the situation for a few more days. That might give her enough time to figure out how to deal with this threat. How to protect herself and Bad Bachelors.

"Okay," she said with a sharp nod. "Thank you."

Chapter 6

"Bad Bachelors helped me to realize something: nobody is perfect. In fact, most of us are fundamentally flawed."

—JustAGirl

ANNIE LAY AWAKE IN HER BED, STARING UP AT THE ceiling and unable to sleep for the second night in a row. The apartment was silent. Whatever Joseph was doing in the other room, he managed to operate with the stealth of a ninja.

Had he found Bad Bachelors yet? Would he judge her? Assume that she was so broken by him that she'd started it in some misplaced general revenge against men?

Didn't you?

He'd been the spark, certainly. Or rather, the photo of him with his brand-new fiancée. Then Darcy had been cheated on. Remi had arrived from Australia by that point too, fleeing the carnage of a relationship that'd ended her career, at least temporarily. All three of them were strong, independent women who were good at their jobs, generous with their spirits. Women that any man would be lucky to date.

Yet they were all ruined in their own ways by relationship failures. Darcy had turned in on herself, her introvert tendencies guiding her away from dating. Remi had turned to casual dating and no-strings sex, happy to have the physical connection but not the emotional. And Annie had taken action in secret, building Bad Bachelors in the hope that other women might be able to avoid the pain she and her friends were currently experiencing. She wanted to *help* women. Give them a tool with which to protect themselves.

It was never supposed to go viral.

Annie turned onto her side, unable to get comfortable. Knowing Joseph was in the next room, separated by only a wall, had her on edge. And not because she didn't want him to be there. Because she was trying her hardest not to get out of bed and go to him.

She turned again, burying her face in her pillow. But it didn't help. Sure, she felt safe knowing he was there. Physically, anyway. But every other emotion battled for supremacy inside her. Want, need, and desire drew swords against fear, anger, and doubt. Huffing, she swung her legs over the edge of the bed. The floorboards were cool beneath her bare feet. Soothing, even.

She wandered to the huge window and opened the blinds so she could look out at the city. Resting her cheek against the glass, she tried to concentrate on the feeling of coolness instead of the vicious churn of thoughts in her head.

Why did he have to ruin what they had?

He wasn't the only one who ruined things.

She'd been trying to be everything to everyone—a

loving partner and supporter of his career ambitions, as well as a doting and devoted daughter to her parents. But those two things had been at odds. They'd drawn her in opposite directions, pulling so hard that she'd been ready to break apart.

Annie padded over to her door and pressed her ear to it. Silence. Maybe he'd left already? But she hadn't heard the front door latch, and it was right next to her room. Ignoring the screeching *Do not proceed* in her head, she pushed the door open. As quietly as gravity would allow, she tiptoed out into the entryway, which opened directly into the living room.

In the far corner of the room, Joseph sat at her computer desk. All the overhead lights were off, and an eerie bluish glow created a fuzzy halo, silhouetting his broad shoulders. It must have been after 2:00 a.m. Possibly later.

But it wasn't the time or the darkness that made the breath stick in the back of Annie's throat. It was the image on the laptop screen in front of Joseph. A photo was the source of the bluish light, her once *favorite* photo. They'd gone to the Greek islands for a vacation, and a friend had captured them frolicking in the ocean. Joseph had Annie on his shoulders, with her almost toppling off from laughter and his face radiating a pure, uninhibited joyfulness that he rarely showed the outside world. It was the week before she'd found out that her mother had breast cancer.

Before everything crumbled.

Annie stepped back. She wasn't ready to face Joseph like this, and she should have stayed in her room until he left. But she backed up too quickly and bumped into the side table, the corner of it jabbing into her lower back so that she had to stifle a yelp. In the silent apartment, the sound might as well have been a gunshot.

Joseph quickly closed the laptop and whirled around. "What are you doing up?"

"I couldn't sleep." She could barely force the words out. Suddenly, everything tumbled down on her like an avalanche. Joseph's return, the creepy photo, the spyware on her computer, the weight of so many angry emails and threats. The dissolution of her friendship with Remi. Tears filled her eyes to the brim, but she blinked furiously, chasing them away with gritted teeth and balled fists, praying he couldn't see her weakness.

He strode toward her. They were enveloped by shadows, with only the twinkle of city lights keeping the room from being pitch-black. Annie curled her hands around the edge of the table behind her, needing something to keep her upright. Each step he took was like a knife twisting in her gut, because at her base level she still craved him like he'd never been away. Her body hadn't gotten the memo that Joseph Preston was not on the menu, because her hands tingled and that sweet spot between her legs pulsed like she was about to get some.

You're not *about to get some.*

"Were you able to fix it?" she asked. Her voice was barely above a whisper, because anything louder would feel like too much and she wanted to dwell in this limbo between dreaming and the real world.

"It's good as new. All your files are back on there, and there's a backup on the USB hard drive." He was close, but not too close. Not as close as her body wanted. "You shouldn't be staying here alone."

"I'm crashing at Mom and Dad's over the weekend."

His pale eyes were ethereal in the shadows. "Do they know what's going on?"

She shook her head. "They would freak."

"Rightly so," he said. "I want you to call me if you see anything at all suspicious. If you hear a bump in the night, if you get something weird in your mailbox, just…call me."

"No questions asked?"

"I'm always going to ask questions."

She let out a sharp laugh. Of course he would. Joseph never held back on poking and prodding, even if she asked him to back off. That was always the bone of contention between them, because it was the one area where he was happy to dish it out but reluctant to take it in return.

"You haven't changed," she whispered.

"Haven't I?" He took a step closer. "I certainly feel changed. But I'm not about to stay quiet when I think your safety is at stake."

"I'm not your concern. This issue isn't your concern." That was a steaming pile of bullshit, and she knew it. She'd brought him here; she'd *involved* him.

"Will you promise to call me if something seems off?" His tone was hard now, jagged. "I don't care if I'm the last resort after you've called everyone else you know. I'm telling you, if you need me, I will be here."

"This time." She couldn't stop the bitter little words from popping out, her nerves frayed and brittle. "I shouldn't have—"

"Yeah, you should have."

They stood in the dark, the air so thick between them that Annie wondered if he might need to swim the last few steps toward her. Beneath the oversize flannel shirt she'd worn to bed, her body was wound tighter than a spring.

"I don't want to get into this now." She bunched the ends of her nightshirt in her hands, trying so hard to remember why she hated him.

He left you when you needed him most. He has no regard for your family or your feelings. He was going to marry someone else with the ring meant for you.

But those thoughts had cycled in her head so many times that they'd lost color and meaning. Instead of growing like a bonfire, they'd become dull and soft.

"Annie." He came closer, the sound of her name like a plea and a prayer. "I don't... *Fuck.*"

Yeah, *fuck* was the right word, all right. What the hell were they doing, whispering in the dark and talking about how he wanted her to lean on him? The famil-iarity of it gripped her with relentless hands, forcing her to believe for a heartbeat that maybe she'd wound the clock back. Or that maybe she'd imagined the last three years, and they were still together. Still in love.

Joseph reached out and brushed a strand of hair from her forehead, neatly tucking it behind her ear. The action—so simple and so tender—unlatched something deep down. She stepped forward, closing the last foot between them and placing her hands on his chest. God, he felt good. Hard and honed, covered in a cotton shirt so soft it made her sigh.

He drove his hands into her hair, his fingers curving around her nape. A shudder rippled through her, and before she had time to think about the consequences, his lips were on hers. The kiss was almost feral—with too much teeth and too much pulling and too much pent-up anger. From both sides.

Annie stepped back, her hips hitting the table behind her, but she didn't care. She yanked him toward her by his shirt, and he growled in that brief moment their mouths were separated.

Then he was on her again, sliding his tongue into her mouth and cradling her head so she had no option but to submit. His beard scratched her skin in a way that was new and exciting. One hand was at her waist, smoothing up her body, over her rib cage, until it connected with the swell of her breast. Annie groaned into him. *Yes!* And then Joseph's other hand delved behind her, nudging aside the decorative bowl and carefully arranged stack of antique books. Something fell over the edge with a loud *thump*.

He hoisted her up, placing her butt on the surface and nudging her knees apart so he could stand between her legs. *More.* This was how she remembered him—furiously passionate, unstoppable in his seduction. Not smooth and definitely not charming. He was almost rough. Primal and visceral and operating on pure instinct.

He tore at her shirt, clumsily popping the buttons open until he palmed her bare breast. Everywhere, she ached. Her nipples beaded intensely, the feeling bordering on pain, and sweet relief came when he rolled one between his thumb and forefinger, bringing her straight to the edge of mind-numbing pleasure with a speed that was both terrifying and soul-soothingly satisfying. He *knew* her. Knew her body, knew her pleasure points, knew exactly how to ride the line of hardness and softness that drove her wild.

She fisted her hands in his hair, pulling his head down so that his lips scorched a trail down the side of her neck until he hit her collarbone. Joseph would burn her alive if she let him, and right in that moment, she wanted nothing more than to be turned to ash. The scent of faded aftershave on his skin, the lingering taste of the spearmint gum he favored dancing on her tongue, brought memories rushing back. All the times they'd made love—from that very first time, awkward and tender under the stars, to the last time while she'd blanked out her adult worries—swirled into one memory blob.

"No," she whispered. His lips closed around her nipple and he sucked, causing her to arch into him with a sound that was barely human. It felt better than anything on earth. "No, stop."

Joseph jerked his head up, eyes wide like he'd snapped out of a trance. He released her and stepped back as though she'd burned him, reality slapping her in the face so hard it brought fresh tears to her eyes.

"You need to leave." She shimmied down from the table and tugged her shirt closed, her shaking fingers fumbling with the buttons as she attempted to cover herself. "Thank you for your help, but please go. Right now."

He looked at her for a long moment, his brow furrowed and his jaw set. But then he turned and walked to the front door, collecting his coat before exiting her apartment and letting the door close behind him with a soft click.

Annie slid down to the floor, her heart thundering in her chest. What the hell had she done?

Sunday afternoon at Per Se was a who's who of Manhattan society. The exclusive restaurant was peppered with everyone from property and media moguls to important political players, old-money heirs, CEOs, and other corporate bigwigs. The old fogies on the bank's board—the same ones who'd unsuccessfully objected to his employment—would also dine here.

These people epitomized everything his father stood for: privilege, high-society expectations, and the "old way" of doing things. Morris Preston was well aware of his son's feelings. No doubt that was why he'd chosen the restaurant. Anything to pull Joseph into line.

He scanned the crowded room for his father. After dreading this lunch all week, the event hanging over him like a black cloud, he wanted it over with. The damn thing had eclipsed the small wins he'd made at work as well as the encounter with Annie. Not that it could be counted as a win, necessarily. They'd kissed and she'd told him to leave. Hardly a raging success. But he'd be lying if he said he hadn't thought about it on a loop ever since.

A waving hand caught his attention, the pigeon-egg-sized bauble on the woman's finger glinting in the light.

"Mother, I didn't know you were coming." He bent down to kiss her, not daring to actually put cheek to cheek lest he mess up her carefully styled hair.

"Why wouldn't I? I'm so happy to have you back home." She smiled warmly, her light-blue eyes crinkling.

"Dad." He stuck out his hand.

Morris accepted the gesture and nearly crushed Joseph's bones in a vigorous handshake. "Son."

His father had always told him that a firm handshake asserted dominance, and he never let an opportunity go by to remind his only son of the family hierarchy. Even at what was supposed to be a "pleasant" lunch.

"I still can't believe you're home," his mother said, reaching for her champagne flute and almost blinding him with another flash of her ring. "It feels like yesterday you were leaving."

"Time flies when you're having fun," he said drily.

She sipped. "And you didn't even tell us you were coming home until it had all been organized. We could have helped you find a place."

"I didn't want to trouble you with something as trivial as that. The bank has people who sort out housing for executives."

"A home is not a trivial thing, Joseph," his mother admonished, clucking her tongue. "Home is where the heart is... Isn't that what they say?"

That might be true if one had a heart.

Joseph glanced at his father and waited for a response. But Morris simply lifted his whiskey to his mouth and drank, long and slow. Clearly, matters of the heart were not in his conversational repertoire.

Shocker.

"How's the job going?" Morris leaned back in his chair and watched Joseph with a cool gaze. "McMartin tells me you've had an interesting start."

One of his father's minions had obviously been gathering intel for him. Fucking brilliant.

"Well. The CEO's new organizational structure has been implemented and people seem to be settling in. Only time will tell if the changes actually fix the problems they've been having. But so far, so good." He signaled to a waiter and ordered himself a beer. He had a feeling he was going to need it. "We can press on with the digital strategy now that the people changes are complete."

"People changes," Morris scoffed, waving his hand. "They spend far too much time and energy on that stuff. Why they don't outsource the whole delivery segment is beyond me."

Joseph bit his tongue. His father had earned the title of the Executioner for the many jobs he'd cut in his long career.

"Please tell me I won't have to listen to you two talk shop for the next hour," his mother said, sighing and shaking her head. "I get enough of that at home."

To anyone listening in, it might have been missed that his mother was a powerful businesswoman in her own right. A CEO of one the world's largest cosmetics companies, she was a highly respected industry player. But her approach to family time was that work had no place intruding on it. At least, she'd gotten that way in the last decade or so. It had been a different story through his childhood years.

"Still taking conference calls at the dinner table?" Joseph asked with a raised brow. That kind of question was like pouring gasoline on an open flame, but after finding out that his dad was keeping tabs on him, Joseph felt he deserved a return shot.

"No." His mother gave her son a self-satisfied smile. "I've instructed Marcie not to feed him if he's on the phone."

"How is Marcie?"

"She's a cook. Why do you care how she is?" Morris shook his head. "I pay her. Well, I might add."

An awkward silence descended on the table, and Joseph pretended to look over the lunch menu. The older he got, the harder it was to bite his tongue, but he always tried to find a way if his mother was around. Conflict between the two men in her life was the thing she hated most, and he'd seen her reduced to tears enough times in his life already. For some reason, she genuinely loved her husband, despite the fact that Morris Preston seemed physically incapable of giving a shit about anyone but himself.

His mother cut the silence with a tinkling laugh, as if enthralled by her husband's humor. It wouldn't do to be seen in public looking like they weren't the Most Perfect Family Ever.

"I heard that Emily Halstead is back from her stint in Seattle," she said, changing the topic. "Why don't you give her a call? I always thought you two would be lovely together."

"I'm not interested in dating." Joseph nodded at the waiter who'd arrived with his beer and grabbed the cold glass gratefully. "I'm concentrating on work."

"Like father, like son," his mother said with a proud tone.

Joseph quashed the visceral repulsion by clearing his throat.

"He's not concentrating on work," Morris scoffed. "If he was, he wouldn't have come back here."

"Oh, really? Do tell me how I'm living my life the wrong way. I so enjoy hearing it."

"I told you that you needed ten years' experience overseas. This position might seem like the biggest jump now, but you're shortsighted and inexperienced. You should have done at least five years in Asia, then a stint in Europe. I could have connected you with any of the majors—Deutsche Bank, Lloyds, RBS, Barclays—"

"I wanted to come home."

His father snorted. "Why, because you think you're going to get that girl back?"

Rage ricocheted around Joseph's head. His father had always called Annie "that girl," as if she was something for him to turn his nose up at. That girl. The maid's daughter. Whatshername. Leanne, if he had to address her by name. Never Annie.

Joseph sucked in a breath. He'd lost count of the number of times his father had told him that Annie wasn't suitable because she and her mother had once cleaned their house.

Why would you want to marry a girl like that? She's probably after your money.

"Is that true?" his mother asked, her fine blond eyebrows creasing above her nose.

"I came back for my career," Joseph said.

You'd think being the bank's youngest CIO in its hundred-plus-year history would be a good enough reason to come home. Apparently not. No, he was "shortsighted and inexperienced."

"Except that you quit before this job came up." Morris eyeballed his son with a cold expression. "Didn't you?"

How in the hell would he know that?

Joseph leveled his father with a stare. "No," he lied.

"That's not what I heard."

"Now you're spying on me?" Joseph shook his head, taking a long gulp of his drink. "Don't you have anything better to do with your time?"

"I spent a fortune on your education. I will not have you throwing it all away for some girl who, frankly, is beneath you." Morris looked him up and down, the corners of his lips downturned.

Joseph's hands ached from how tightly he'd balled them into fists. Heat flared into his face as he fought for control. Oh, how he'd love to stand up and thrust his fist straight into his father's nose!

"Is it going to work if I threaten to cut you off again?" Morris said.

"Boys," his mother admonished. "This is *not* suitable public conversation. What have I said about airing dirty laundry in public? Somebody might overhear."

The look of horror on her face made Joseph want to shake his head. She lived for her company, for her high-profile career, and the thought of the Ladies Who Lunch gossiping about her was "positively terrifying."

Joseph could think of something more terrifying: living life in debt to Morris Preston. That was *exactly* how he'd been made to feel his whole life, as if the privileges and education his parents had given him were a loan to be repaid in blood.

"You know we only want what's best for you." His mother placed her hand over his, her fingertips cold from where she'd been handling her chilled champagne glass.

Joseph shrank away. "Then don't interfere with my life."

"You didn't seem to mind me interfering when I got you that job in Singapore." Morris shrugged.

"Only because you told me I'd no longer be your son if I turned it down." He drained the rest of his beer. "I was too stupid to see that the threat of no money and no family was nothing compared to losing someone who actually cared about me."

His mother gasped. "How can you say that? Of *course* we care about you."

Joseph turned to his father and waited from him to echo the sentiment. It would have been quicker to wait for a blade of grass to sprout out of the ground.

"Morris, darling, tell Joseph how much we care about him."

Morris looked at his watch as if he had somewhere he'd rather be. "A man shouldn't need to be coddled like that."

"Yeah, I think that about justifies my decision." Joseph stood and patted his mother on the shoulder.

"Thanks for the beer. Sorry I won't be staying for lunch."

"Joseph, don't be rash. Your father doesn't mean any harm."

A part of him—the part that still desperately craved his father's love—wanted to give Morris another chance to prove him wrong. To prove that he wasn't a heartless man hell-bent on mentally beating his son into obedience.

But that part was on life support.

"Let him go, Melinda." Morris waved his hand as if shooing an insect. "The boy won't listen. He never did before, and he won't start now."

Joseph threaded his way through the restaurant, forcing himself to walk with slow, even steps. His father wouldn't ruffle him anymore. He'd tried for too long to please the old man, and he'd paid dearly for it.

Never again would he make that mistake.

Chapter 7

"Dear Bad Bachelors, if it weren't for you, I might never have found true love right under my nose."

—EternallyGrateful

ANNIE SMOOTHED HER FLAT IRON OVER HER HAIR, forcing out any kinks until it hung in a shiny shoulder-length sheet around her. Then she applied a touch of makeup—a subtle pink to her cheeks so she didn't look completely dead, and a healthy dab of concealer to hide her dark circles from a night of tossing and turning. She needed a disguise right now, and looking put together on the outside would hopefully hide that she was a wreck on the inside.

After Joseph had left her apartment in the dead of night, she'd gone back to bed and stared into the darkness until daybreak. Then she'd packed her things and gone straight to her parents' place. It was Sunday afternoon now, and for once, being around her family *hadn't* made her feel better. After a day of hanging out with her sister and her mother, not feeling any more relaxed, she'd slipped into tortured sleep intermittently last night. The hours had been punctuated by nightmares of a masked intruder clamping a hand over her mouth. Those dreams gave way to ones where she hadn't turned her ex away—where he'd stayed and carried her to bed. She'd woken up in a cold sweat, her mind reeling from the ping-ponging visuals.

The voice on the radio told her it was almost two, and that meant she had about three minutes to get dressed before lunch would be served. The scent of her mother's cooking wafted under the door, teasing Annie's senses with the aroma of fresh basil, tomato, and pecorino. Wriggling her hips, she tugged a pair of jeans over her legs and tried to button them up while looking for her shoes.

Her foot connected with the corner of her bed. "Ow!"

"Annie?" Sofia's voice came from the other side of the door. "You okay?"

"I'm fine." She bent down to inspect her big toe. No blood. "Just being clumsy."

"Maybe we should Annie-proof the house," Sofia said, laughing. "We'll get those corner protectors they use for babies."

Annie shook her head as she fished a cream sweater out of her overnight bag. "Very funny."

"You ready?" Sofia asked. "Mom's calling us, and Darcy is here."

"Uh, yeah. Just a sec."

"Annie, come *on!*" Sofia pounded on the door. "You're supposed to help set the table."

It figured Sofia would be there waiting for her, despite all the times growing up in this house that Annie had set the table while her sisters conveniently needed to use the bathroom whenever it was time to do chores.

"Crack that whip, Sofia." Another voice sounded as someone came up the stairs. Darcy. "Do I have to drag you out?"

"Way to have some loyalty." Annie yanked the door open and put on her best smile. "Who invited you anyway?"

A few minutes later, the table was set and people took their seats. As Annie placed the last dish on the table, the family's Irish wolfhound, Lupo, sat patiently by her legs. The top of his head came to midthigh, his large paws stepping all over her ballet flats. To anyone else, he might have looked like a fearsome guard dog, but to Russo/Maxwell family members, he was merely a canine version of their grandfather: a grumpy but lovable old soul with a hearty appetite for cold meat and leftovers.

Annie was half-Italian—on her mother's side—and she fit right in with the noisy Calabrese on Sal's side of the family, enjoying the way the house always felt so warm and so full of love when they were all together.

"Hey, Lupo." Darcy scratched the dog's head as she walked past.

The group sat at a long table in the dining room. Nonno Pietro, Sal's father, was perched at the head of the table, as usual. His T-shirt had already been spattered with pasta sauce, and he chatted in Italian with Zia Carla.

Food spread out across the table in a rainbow of variety: ragù pasta, assorted meats, radicchio smothered in olive oil and vinegar. At some point, they'd given up on the traditional courses of an Italian lunch, and now all the food ended up on the table together, save for the dolci, which were either in the fridge or on the kitchen counter.

Annie dropped into a chair between Darcy and Carla's daughter, Viv.

"Tell me someone brought some green stuff," Viv said with a shake of her head. "If I keep eating here every weekend, I'm going to end up with clogged arteries and an ass the size of Brooklyn."

"Of course." Annie passed the glass bowl containing the salad.

"I love it." Darcy speared an olive and a piece of soppressata with a toothpick. "Food from the old country."

"And if by 'the old country' you mean Trader Joe's, then sure." Viv piled a generous amount of salad onto her plate.

"Potato, po-*tah*-to," Darcy said cheerfully.

Ever since they'd become friends in their school days, Darcy had been coming to the family lunches. If too many months passed without Darcy showing her face, Annie's mother, Connie, would fuss and worry. Darcy was as much a part of the family as Annie herself.

Annie took the salad bowl from Viv and added a generous mound next to her helping of Zia Carla's famous roasted swordfish. "Speaking of which, how's your training going for the run?"

"You're running now, Darcy?" Viv raised a brow. "That's great."

Darcy chuckled. "I don't know if I'd call it 'running,' to be honest. Plodding, maybe. Shuffling, at best."

"Reed roped her into a charity run," Annie explained. "Four miles."

Viv nodded. "That's a good place to start."

"Maybe for you two," Darcy said. "But for someone whose only current form of exercise is holding a copy of *The Lord of the Rings* upright, four miles is torture."

"Load up on the salad then." Viv pushed it toward Darcy. "Kale is good for helping with joint inflammation."

"Thanks, Doc." Knives and forks clattered, and conversation slowed as everyone dug in. "But that stuff tastes like ass."

"How do you know what ass tastes like?" Annie quipped, and Sofia shrieked.

"Ew!"

Darcy shrugged. "It's an educated guess. I'm ninety-nine-point-nine percent sure kale is gross."

Viv frowned. Being the family doctor, she was always quick to dole out advice. "Greens are important. They're good for your immune system, for your skin and hair."

"And cheese is important for my happiness." Darcy grinned and sprinkled her pasta generously with grated Parmesan.

"Life's short," Sofia chimed in.

Annie *loathed* that saying. It implied an impending deadline that she did *not* want to think about. Ever since her mother's battle with the big C, mortality was on her list of things to ignore at all costs.

"Life doesn't have to be short," she snapped. "I wish everybody would stop saying that."

Across the table, Connie frowned. Her mother and father thought she'd become "obsessed" with health and wellness since the diagnosis. And maybe she had. But what she put into her body was something she could control. Along with her daily runs, it was a coping mechanism.

"I'll be eighty this year." Nonno Pietro's booming voice made Annie turn toward the head of the table. "And I eat plenty of cheese. God will take you when he sees fit. We have no control over it."

She swallowed down the sick feeling. The outburst was *so* not like her; she didn't get riled up in front of people like that. It was Joseph and that stupid, searing kiss. Or her security troubles.

Or both.

"Hey." Darcy put a hand on her shoulder. "What's going on?"

"It's all that kale," Sofia said with a giggle. "It's turning her brain into a salad."

Connie stifled a smirk and went back to swirling her pasta. As the conversation resumed, Annie pushed her food around her plate. She felt the intense burn of Darcy's eyes on her.

"He came over," she said under her breath so no one else would hear.

"What? Are you serious?" Darcy hissed.

Annie silenced her with a look. Discussing her excommunicated ex-almost-fiancé at the dinner table wouldn't go down well. Her mother would be livid, and Sal would be devastated. Annie didn't know which was worse. Her father had taken Joseph under his wing, like the son he'd never had. And her mother had always had a soft spot for the polite little boy who was the son of her clients. She'd been thrilled when they'd started dating. Joseph had become part of their tight-knit group, almost like he was real family.

Needless to say, they did not take Joseph's departure well.

"I was having trouble with my computer. He helped. It's no big deal."

That was as plainly as she could put it without lying. Annie wasn't ready to tell Darcy or anyone else about her creepy internet stalker until that situation was further under control. She wasn't about to confess to the kiss either.

"You called him?" Darcy shook her head. "I don't believe it."

Annie caught her younger sister peering on curiously, so she motioned for Darcy to keep quiet. "We'll talk later."

They managed to get through the rest of the meal without Darcy prodding her for more information. But when she volunteered them for clean-up duty after lunch, Annie knew she'd have to spill the beans.

"You're not thinking about seeing him again, are you?" Darcy shoved the sleeve of her sweater up, exposing her elaborate tattoos. "Please tell me you're not in self-destruct mode."

"I'm not," Annie said, unsure which of the two things she was actually addressing.

She *should* be repulsed by the thought of having him back in her life. Spitting in anger that he'd waltzed back into Manhattan and was hanging around "their place" without warning her. But the fact was, Friday night had shifted something between them. He'd come to her rescue when she'd needed him.

This time. Let's not forget that his presence and attention are conditional.

Darcy pulled on a pair of pink rubber gloves and wrenched Annie's mother's old, squeaky taps. "Look me in the eye and tell me you're not thinking about seeing him again."

The answer should have been an immediate *absolutely not*, but the words didn't spring to Annie's lips. "Maybe it'll give me some closure."

"It's been three years. What other information could change the way you feel?" Darcy had a point.

"I don't know."

"The answer is none. Nothing will change what happened." She squirted detergent into the basin and Annie watched the luminescent bubbles multiply under the hot water. "Think about the reasons why he might want to talk to you. One, he wants to apologize. In which case, fuck him. Two, he wants you back. In which case, fuck him."

Annie smirked. "I'm seeing a theme here."

"Stay the hell away. Trust me, your sanity will thank you."

Of course, she knew Darcy was right. When Joseph had walked out, she'd fallen to pieces. Her friends had helped put her back together. They'd crashed at her place that first night—Darcy and Remi sleeping on the cramped pullout sofa bed—to make sure she got up the next morning and ate a proper breakfast. They'd stood by her while she called her boss and asked for a few days off to deal with it. They'd plied her with wine and pizza and cheesy movies.

They'd gone to the hospital with her after her mother's mastectomy, held her hand, and promised her that everything would be okay. Things *he* should have done.

God, she missed Remi. Her life wasn't the same without the bubbly Aussie who loved to crack jokes and put a smile on everyone's face. She was a good friend, and her absence was like a fracture in Annie's life.

Swallowing down her guilt and regret, she focused on the task at hand. She had no idea how to make it up to Remi, and thinking about that right now was only going to make her feel worse.

"What are you two gossiping about?" Her mother appeared in the doorway, a knowing smile on her lips. Only she wouldn't be smiling if she actually knew that their "boy talk" was about *he who should not be named*.

Darcy shot Annie a look. "Your daughter is harassing me about my charity run."

Connie snorted. "That sounds like her."

"Ma! You're supposed to be on my side."

Her mother walked over and wrapped her arms around her, her head barely coming up to Annie's chin. She smelled like lemon and sweet basil and perfume. Like always. It struck Annie, even now, that her mother's shape was so permanently changed. She'd decided not to have reconstructive surgery after the double mastectomy—one to address the cancer and one as a preventive measure—having always hated her huge bust. But they'd never actually talked about it. And Annie hadn't wanted to pressure her mother when she knew it was still a painful topic.

Her mother and Sal had always been determined to "protect" their kids from anything painful in life, including their health problems. At the time, they'd hid Connie's diagnosis until it was decided she needed to have surgery. Had Annie known about her mother's situation earlier, she might never have agreed to go to Singapore. Perhaps with that on the table from the get-go, things might have turned out differently between Annie and Joseph.

But it hadn't, and knowing her parents were inclined to harbor such big secrets had made Annie jittery. And untrusting.

Wow, and the hypocrite of the year award goes to…?

"You know I love you, *topolina*. But you are a giant pain in the ass sometimes." Connie's loud laugh ricocheted off the worn linoleum and weathered walls.

"Charming," Annie replied, extracting herself from her mother's embrace and heading behind the breakfast bar to gather more dishes. "Let me know when we want to do dessert, and I'll get some coffee going."

"Soon. The girls have gone for a walk and the boys are in the garage." She attempted to muscle her way into the kitchen to help, but both women waved her away.

Connie rested against the breakfast bar. Her once-chocolate-brown hair was now peppered with gray. The lines had deepened around her eyes, which still had a mischievous twinkle, and she wore her signature bright-pink lipstick.

To Annie, she would always be the most beautiful woman on the face of the earth. And the bravest.

"So," Connie said. Annie's ears pricked up at her tone.

It was the *I've heard something interesting* tone. "When were you going to tell me Joseph is back in town?"

Darcy made a choking sound and Annie froze, her back to her mother as she dried one of the white ceramic platters. "Huh?"

"I ran into Zia Mariella at Costco, who said she'd had lunch with Anna-Maria from down the street, and *she* had spoken with Petra—Petra who's married to Tony—whose grandson works for one of the banks, and he read an article saying Joseph is now the chief something-or-other."

Annie blinked as her brain took the necessary time to catch up with her mother's story. "Wait, *which* Petra?"

Connie ignored her question and narrowed her eyes. "Did you know?"

Darcy looked like she was about to back out of the kitchen, so Annie grabbed her wrist, shooting her a *Don't you dare leave me* look. *Crap.* What was she supposed to do now? She never lied to her parents. Ever.

"Uhhh…"

"You *did* know." Connie's lips flattened into a line so thin that almost all of the pink lipstick disappeared. "How could you not tell me?"

"I didn't think you'd want to know, to be honest." Annie tucked her hair behind her ear. *Shit*. This was not a time for her tells. When it came to dealing with her mother's warpath, the mantra needed to be: Show no weakness!

"Well, I do." Connie planted her hands on her hips. "So now I can tell him to leave again. He's not welcome in this city."

Her mother would definitely freak the hell out if she knew he'd been in Annie's apartment.

"Thanks, Mayor Mama. I'll be sure to revoke his Connie visa." She rolled her eyes.

"He hasn't contacted you, has he?" Her mother was practically vibrating with anger.

That's how it was in her family. You wrong one person, you wrong everyone.

How the hell was she going to get around this?

All of a sudden, water sprayed up from the sink, catching Annie right in the face. She shrieked and recoiled, bringing her hands up to cover her face.

"Sorry!" Darcy quickly wrenched the taps, shutting the water off. "This thing has a mind of its own."

"I'll get some towels." Connie disappeared into the hallway.

Annie shook her hands, sending water droplets all over the countertop. Her hair stuck to her face, and when she rubbed her eyes, her hand came away coated in black mascara smudges.

"You could have distracted her without shooting me in the face," Annie grumbled.

"I'll assume you don't know how to correctly pronounce 'thank you.'" Darcy tore off a piece of paper towel. "That's called quick thinking."

She sounded as smug as hell. Evil thing. "I'd call it taking advantage of the situation."

"At least now you've got time to think up some excuse for why he contacted you...unless you're planning on lying?"

Annie dabbed at her face. Well, if her parents saw fit

to "protect" her from things, then maybe it was time to start doing the same.

"I'm going to say I knew he was back, but that we haven't seen each other," she said, already feeling guilty about lying. But her parents didn't need the added stress of worrying about their daughter's feelings, and since her contact with Joseph was limited and soon to be terminated, it wasn't *that* big a deal. "Don't you dare say a word."

Joseph had done a lot of difficult things in his life. He'd also done a lot of stupid things.

Hanging out in the lobby of Annie's building, waiting for her to get back from her parents' place, could fall into either of those buckets. But he had little to lose and a lot to gain, a position that was totally foreign to him. Right now, the only thing he cared about was Annie's safety.

Thankfully, the guy working at the concierge desk tonight had been around for years and he'd recognized Joseph right away. It was the only reason he'd been allowed to chill out on one of the chairs dotting the reception area, instead of waiting out on the street in the blustery evening.

Since he'd returned home sometime around three thirty on Saturday morning, thoughts of Annie had plagued him. Sure, after their breakup he'd tossed and turned many a night away, but nothing like this. He'd woken with bruise-like smudges under his eyes and not a single answer about what to do next. But he couldn't stay away. Not when his gut told him that the person watching her wasn't going to be content with sending creepy photos.

The last three years weighed on Joseph like a slab of granite.

He'd come home with a single purpose: to do things right this time. That meant leaving Singapore in the past, instead of doing what his father wanted. Because this was home.

It always would be.

Annie walked through the front entrance of the building, talking to a man with dark hair and a thick army-green jacket. She wore a pair of skinny jeans that hugged her thighs and hips to perfection, along with a pair of black ankle boots and a gray coat. She always looked elegant, even in the simplest of outfits. *Especially* in the simplest of outfits. He'd grown up with his parents' "more is more" approach to style—shining baubles, Hermès silk, and bespoke tailoring. But Annie had a subtle flair that allowed her to walk into H&M with fifty bucks and walk out looking like she'd spent a million.

She didn't notice Joseph. Her companion gesticulated with his hands as he made a joke, his face open and friendly. Annie's genuine smile was like a knife to Joseph's gut. It had been eons since a woman had smiled at him like that, longer still since he'd seen Annie's beautiful face light up with humor.

Joseph fought back the urge to launch himself at the guy and tear him away from Annie. His hands twitched by his sides, restless. Useless.

Do you really think she's been alone while you were off

getting engaged? Get real. Men would have been lining up once you were out of the picture.

Annie smiled at her companion and waved as he headed off to the elevators. The second he was gone, her smile dropped into a tired, worn-out expression. Okay, so not a boyfriend then. A sigh of relief rushed out of his mouth, and Joseph uncurled his fists. What a wreck. He couldn't even watch her talk to another man without his body switching to full-blown caveman mode.

He'd turned into his father.

If there was one thing he wanted to avoid in his life, it was turning out like dear old Dad. His lips twisted at the thought. Then, as if drawn by magnetic intuition, she suddenly turned her eyes on him.

"What the hell are you doing here?"

"I called." He stood, his whole body alight with the desire to lean in and embrace her. Instead, he held himself stiff as a monument. "I wanted to check that everything was okay with your computer and…"

He couldn't even bring himself to say it. But the thought of her returning alone to her apartment had given him this ice-cold, creeped-out feeling he couldn't shake. He didn't have to stay with her, but he wanted to at least walk her up so they could make sure no one had broken in over the weekend.

Yeah, he sounded like a tinfoil hat–wearing paranoid asshole. So what?

"I didn't answer your call for a reason," she said. "I'm fine. I appreciate the tech support on such short notice, but you don't need to do anything else."

"Yes, I do."

"How do you know I don't have someone waiting for me? I might have an amazing boyfriend whose only goal in life is to make me feel good." She folded her arms across her chest.

"Do you?" He squared his shoulders as if preparing for a fight.

She swallowed. "Yes."

"You're lying."

No malice tainted his words. The simple statement only served to demonstrate that he knew her far better than any other person on the face of the earth. Better than her sisters or her cousins. Better than her mother and her stepdad. Better, at times, than she knew herself.

He'd held that important place once, and something told him he hadn't slipped entirely.

"So what if I am?" She shrugged. "It's none of your business."

In any other argument he'd be hunting for that spot, the chink in the armor. He was used to exploiting those vulnerabilities to get what he wanted. That skill had served him incredibly well in his career. It was also the thing that had earned him the label of selfish in his personal relationships.

And he wasn't about to repeat that mistake.

"You're right, it's not my business." He nodded. "Let me walk you upstairs and make sure your apartment is secure. I won't set foot inside your place," he promised. "I'll wait at the door while you check inside, and when you give me the all clear, I'll go."

Her expression softened slightly. "Stubborn as ever, I see."

"Please." It wasn't a word he used often.

She looked at him for a long moment, rolling her bottom lip between her teeth as if weighing her options. "Okay, fine."

They headed to the elevators, awkward silence clogging the air around them. Even the other people waiting there—a young couple with a child of about five—gave them a wide berth. Was the tension that obvious? Likely. He felt it rolling off Annie in waves as they rode the carriage up to her floor.

"So…" She hitched her overnight bag higher up on her shoulder as they exited the elevator. "Are you living in Manhattan?"

"Yeah, on Sutton Place."

"You mean to tell me that when you barged into my apartment last weekend, you had your own place to go to?" She frowned at him as she dug her key out of her bag.

He glanced at her with a wry smile. "Yeah."

"You're unbelievable." She shook her head. "You told me you didn't have anywhere to go."

"I didn't say that exactly."

"You *implied* it."

"Yes, I implied it." He shoved his hands into his pockets. "I hadn't expected to run into you so soon, and I wanted to see how you were."

"So instead of asking me, you decided it would be better to convince me to let you into my home?"

"You pushed me into the pond."

"You *fell* into the pond."

He snorted. "Yes, totally of my own accord. That little accident had nothing to do with you."

She stared straight ahead as they walked.

"Would you have answered me if I'd asked?"

"Probably not," she admitted. "But that doesn't give you the right to lie by omission so I'll take pity on you."

"You took pity on me? It seemed like you enjoyed me sitting there in only a towel."

"I preferred the idea of you walking home in it." A smirk passed over her lips, and she shoved her key into her lock.

"I'll wait here," he said, leaning against the wall.

"And what, I scream bloody murder if I find someone inside?" She turned to him, her dark eyes brimming with something intense. Something primal.

"If I don't hear from you in a minute, I'll barge in."

"This is stupid." She huffed. "Don't wait outside like a dog. We'll check it together, and then you can go."

That was her way of saying thank you, even though she clearly hated to need his assistance. Whatever. She could be as prickly as she liked; it didn't matter. The only way he'd have a hope in hell of sleeping tonight was if he knew she was alone in this apartment with a working lock between her and the outside world.

Chapter 8

"You're done for now, you stupid bitch. Watch your
back."

—TheEveryMan

WHY COULDN'T SHE EVER STAND HER GROUND WITH
Joseph Preston? He'd managed to barge into her apartment the morning of the pond incident with the same
driving persistence he'd used on her throughout their
entire relationship.

*Are we going to ignore that your stomach was in knots the
entire subway ride just thinking about walking into this place
by yourself?*

Yes, she was *absolutely* going to ignore that. *Avoid,*
the little voice in her head urged. *Avoid, avoid, avoid!*

But avoiding the issue of her creepy hacker wouldn't
work now. Joseph was right. Simply doing a reset on her
computer wasn't going to cut it. She didn't even know
how the hacker had gotten access in the first place.

"How long were you waiting?" she asked as they
walked slowly through her apartment. She flipped every
single light switch on as she went.

"Not long. Half an hour."

Wow. He'd gotten cranky if she was more than five minutes late when they used to be together. Maybe he *had* changed.

They walked into her bedroom, and she reached for the light but miscalculated and accidentally clipped the edge of her chest of drawers. A string of curse words flew out of her mouth as she finally found the switch.

Joseph had gotten her all riled up. Her palms were slick with sweat, and her heart thudded an erratic beat against her rib cage. Dark hair fell into her eyes, and she blew it out of the way in an agitated huff.

"Everything okay?" he asked. His presence behind her was as comforting as it was unsettling. No matter how hard she tried to concentrate, it was like her body reacted by flipping every freaking "on" switch in her nervous system.

"I'm fine. Everything's fine."

His lip twitched, but he stopped short of smiling. "You always did swear like a sailor."

"It's my one vice."

They stood awkwardly in her room as she looked around. It wasn't the biggest space, just enough for a queen-size bed and one bedside table. A small chest of drawers was pushed against one wall. Memories flickered before her eyes—her fists curling into his chest, tugging him to the bed. The weight of him pressing her down, hot kisses on her neck.

She cleared her throat. "Mom asked me why I didn't tell her you were back," she said. That was one conversation guaranteed to kill any latent sexual desire dead in the water.

"Who spilled the beans?"

"She ran into Zia Mariella at Costco, who said she'd had lunch with Anna-Maria from down the street and *she* had spoken with Petra—Petra who's married to Tony—whose grandson works for one of the banks, and he read an article saying that you were now the 'chief something-or-other,' as she put it."

"Chief something-or-other. It's what I've always aspired to be," he quipped, his eyes scanning her face. "I bet she cursed my name until you lied and told her you hadn't talked to me."

She hated how astute he was, how his eyes seemed to break her down piece by piece until they found what they were looking for. A weak spot.

"Pretty much."

"How's the family?" he asked. His expression was difficult to read. "How's…Connie's health?"

"She's doing well. Sofia is looking into colleges, and Allegra is loving living away from home."

"And your dad?" This time there was a catch in his voice.

"Paving his way to a heart attack with cannoli and sfogliatelle." She let out a dry laugh. "You'd think after everything that's happened, his health would be number one."

"You're his number one. You and Connie and the girls." Joseph sounded almost wistful.

"Not much good he can do us if he's dead."

The words came out sharper than she'd intended, her voice brimming with emotion. Damn it, couldn't she keep her cool for five minutes around Joseph?

If she'd wanted to come off as unaffected and distant, she'd blown that to smithereens. She'd always promised herself that if she ever bumped into him, she'd make it known that her life was better without him. *Ha!* She could chalk that up to a big, fat fail.

"Don't be so hard on him. He does nothing but support you and your sisters."

"You always take his side." For a moment, the anger melted away, and she remembered why she'd wanted to marry him.

He'd slotted into her family seemingly overnight, immediately becoming best buds with Sal and learning enough Italian to put a smile on Nonno's face. He'd attended every family event by her side, learned all their traditions and cultural quirks.

He'd worked so hard to be accepted even though he didn't need to. They would have loved him no matter what.

"Well, you *used* to take his side," she corrected herself.

"Shit, Annie." Joseph paused, swallowing. "I know I fucked things up between us. I know I've been an absolute bastard."

She turned away, her throat constricting. "I'm glad you've finally caught up with the rest of us."

His sandalwood and cologne scent invaded her nostrils, dredging up the past. She'd been trying to ignore it ever since they'd gotten into the elevator together. It was the expensive soap she'd bought him so he'd have something nice in the shower when he stayed over. Back then, she was still studying, working as a barista and stocking shelves at a supermarket to save so she wouldn't have an enormous student debt hanging over her head. That soap had cost more than a whole day's work.

But it smelled like he still used the same one now.

In her periphery, his jaw clenched. "I wish I could do it over."

Tears filled her eyes like hot, angry needles. There was no way she would let him see her cry—not again. Not *ever* again.

He sighed. "I should have let you know I was coming home."

"No." She whirled around to face him, heat racing through her veins. "You shouldn't have left in the first place. Then you wouldn't have had to tell me you were coming home because you'd already *be* home."

His mouth hung open, those perfectly shaped lips parted in surprise. Those lips had been her world once, his every kiss filling her with desire, hope, and purpose.

She balled her fists, pressing her nails into the heels of her hands. "You left me when I needed you more than I ever had. She…she could have died."

The wave of emotion hit her out of nowhere, pain and anger filling her nose and throat and ears. Drowning her. Suffocating her.

"I'm sorry, I—"

The sound of her phone ringing cut him off. Saved by the bell. "Hello?"

Silence. Then breathing.

"Hello?" A tremor raced the length of her spine. Was it possible for such a soft sound, barely perceptible to her ears, to feel threatening? "Who's there?"

"Leanne Maxwell." The voice was disguised with a robotic tone.

She sucked in a breath and yanked the phone away from her ear, stabbing at the speaker button with her finger. Joseph's eyes snapped to hers.

"I'm coming to get you," the robotic voice continued. "Leanne Maxwell in apartment fifteen-twenty... See you soon."

Joseph grabbed the phone from her hands, but the call had disconnected. "Fuck."

Annie's hands shook as she sank, mute, onto her bed. He had *her apartment number*!

"You've probably been doxed." Joseph's voice was hard-edged.

Doxed. Her mind spun. The term sounded familiar, but in her panicked state, she couldn't grasp what it meant. "What?"

"It's when someone publishes your personal information online." His expression told her all she needed to know. If someone had done that, then an unwanted phone call was about to be the least of her worries.

"But you fixed my computer." Her chest heaved as she sucked in air. "You wiped everything, right?"

"They must have already had what they needed."

"Then why the photo?" Her pitch climbed higher, panic flooding her system like a toxin. "Why do that?"

"Maybe they were toying with you?" He shoved a hand through his hair. "We're getting out of here. Now. You're coming back to my place."

Oh, hell no. Not a chance.

But what else could she do? Go back to her parents

and have to fess up about what she'd done? About Bad Bachelors and the hacking and…everything? To Darcy's place, where she lived with her fiancé who'd been a target of Annie's site? To Remi's place? Remi wasn't speaking to her because of Bad Bachelors.

Where else could she turn?

"Don't even try to argue with me." The raw edge to his tone was like a knife's blade running along her nerves. "If you think I'm letting you stay here on your own, you're mistaken. Come on."

She grabbed his arm, halting him. Muscles flexed through the fine wool of his sweater, but he didn't brush her hand away. Unnerved, she let go.

"I don't want go to your apartment." The fear that tinted her words made her cringe. "I'll stay at a hotel instead."

"What if someone's watching you now? What if they follow you?" He shook his head. "No. A hotel isn't secure enough. We're going to my place."

Was he overreacting? What was the worst someone would do?

You're really asking that? After the vicious, violent emails you've received?

But what people said online wasn't the same as how they acted in person, right? They wouldn't *actually* go through with it…would they?

Watch your back.

How many times had she read that in an email? Her app and website hadn't only pissed off the men of Manhattan, or even the entire state. What she'd done had pissed off men everywhere. Women too. As much as she truly believed she was helping some people, it was hard to deny she'd hurt others.

But that was life, wasn't it? Existing in the gray area between good and bad, hoping that you were inching closer to the former. Pleasing the entire world just wasn't possible.

"Grab a bag," Joseph said. "Throw in some clothes and your laptop. Then we're getting the hell out of here."

———————

It didn't take long to get to Joseph's place. In fact, the cab ride was so short that Annie knew she wouldn't be able to get out of her head how close he was. Maybe that was simply her brain fixating on something safer than her current situation. Although calling proximity to her ex *safe* was kind of laughable. A month ago, this would have been the worst thing in the world.

Now, he was the only guy she could trust.

As the elevator in his apartment building whisked them up to the penthouse floor—because *of course* he had a penthouse suite—the silence made her antsy. She leaned against the back of the elevator, an overnight bag hanging heavy on her shoulder, trying to remember what she'd thrown inside. Probably a mismatched outfit that she wouldn't even be able to leave the house in. Had she remembered clean socks? Clean underwear? Who the hell knew?

They exited at the top floor. Plush carpet muffled their footsteps, and not a peep came from the only other apartment on this level. The hallway was like a tomb.

For some reason, Annie didn't want to know what was behind Joseph's front door. Because this would be the final nail in the coffin of knowing that he was home for good. Of knowing that she couldn't shove him back into a dark corner of her mind, smothering her memories with a mental blanket, hoping to snuff them out like a candle. He had a home. Here.

He was back.

Joseph shoved his key into the lock, and the door open soundlessly. He motioned for her to walk in ahead of him, and she held her breath, her bag bumping against her hip with each step. The apartment was sprawling, so large that if she'd seen a picture of it, she would have claimed that it couldn't possibly be located in Manhattan. Looked like his new CIO gig was paying well.

White couches faced a window framing the river below. There was a sleek chrome-and-glass coffee table with nothing on it. The kitchen occupied a generous corner of space, and was also white and silver and glass. So sleek. Harshly modern. And totally lacking in personality.

The apartment was like a showroom for a high-end interior designer. This wasn't a home that was lived in or loved, nor was it a place that reflected the occupant. It was a mask.

"You get to christen the spare room," he said. "Haven't had a use for it yet, other than stashing some boxes that I haven't unpacked."

"No guests?" she asked.

He shook his head.

Annie wanted to clarify whether that meant no guests who'd stayed in the spare room, or no guests who'd visited at all. But even thinking that question caused a riot of unpleasant images to flash in her mind—of sweaty bodies and greedy hands and desperate lips that weren't hers. What right did she have to feel jealous? None. Absolutely none. Still, common sense wasn't enough to stop the swishing in her stomach, that ugly, vicious, painful churning that was all too familiar.

"Why don't you unpack, and I'll organize something for dinner. If you want to freshen up, there's a second bathroom next to your room."

Her room. She decided not to comment on that.

"I'll grab you some towels." He looked at her long and hard, like he was trying to figure something out. She knew that look.

She tucked her hair behind her ears. "This is an untenable situation."

An expression tugged at the edge of Joseph's lips. A smile? A smirk? She couldn't tell. "Untenable?"

"What I mean to say is… I can't stay here. Not for long."

He nodded. "I know. We'll find a solution. But right now, the only thing I give a shit about is keeping you safe. You have no idea what these people are capable of."

"And you do? This could all be a hoax."

"Do you really want to take that risk? This kind of stuff doesn't happen without a catalyst. Something has triggered these assholes."

Annie wanted to know why he cared. He didn't have any responsibility for her. Period. This was her issue, her problem. Her punishment. Not his.

She debated whether to tell him about Bad Bachelors

and that she knew exactly *why* this was happening to her. But she kept her mouth shut. It was the only way she could see to get through this mess.

Joseph kept himself busy while Annie took a shower. The last thing he needed was to think about what her luscious body looked like with water streaming all over it. Shower sex had been one of their favorites. She'd often snuck into the bathroom while he was getting ready for work, stripped down to nothing, and climbed in behind him, her hands slipping over his soap-covered skin to work him into a frenzy.

He couldn't even count the number of times she'd made him late for work. They'd never been able to get enough of each other.

"Focus," he said to himself. "Figure out what to do about the situation *now*."

He drummed his fingers on the kitchen counter. This whole thing with the stalker had his stomach in knots. Intuition prickled, raising the hairs on the back of his neck. Before he'd followed in his father's footsteps on the path to CIO, his bread and butter had been internet security: white-hat hacking, social engineering, penetration testing, and studying the bad guys. He knew the internet had an evil underbelly. By now, that was common knowledge, but he'd seen it in action. Analyzed it. Tried to learn how it behaved.

And he knew that despite the perception that what happened online wasn't part of the real world, the internet wasn't the safest place for women. He'd worked on many a case where the victim was female, where old threats were made new and more effective with technology. But there was *always* a motivation for an attack, always something that sparked the flame. A catalyst. And even though he had no right to demand it, he wanted to know what trouble Annie was in.

"Why are you getting involved in this?"

The question could have come from his mind. It was a legitimate one. Joseph looked up to see Annie standing in the doorway. "If memory serves me correctly, *you* came to *me*."

She had her hair wrapped in a towel. Faded blue jeans and a pink sweater covered her body. "I'm grateful that you helped, but all I asked was for you to fix my computer. You didn't have to take me in like some stray." As she walked forward, her bare feet made soft slapping noises against the hardwood floor. "I'll be fine."

"Then why did you tell me you'd go to a hotel?" He watched her stifle her reaction, the quick flash of vulnerability telling him everything he needed to know. "Is it because you have nowhere else to go?"

"Of *course* I have somewhere else to go," she said. The irritation in her voice was only further evidence. Annie never got mad when she knew she was in the right. "But I'd rather not worry people."

"So you *do* think there's cause for worry?"

She licked her lips. The action was quick, and the flash of pink did little to stop Joseph from thinking about what they might have been doing if this was them three years ago. He wanted to catch her tongue between his lips, press her against the kitchen counter like everything was good and right and safe in the world. Like they hadn't fucked their relationship into the ground.

"If this was happening to Sofia or Allegra, what would you tell them to do?"

She nailed him with a stare. "I would tell them to get help. I would tell them to get out of their place and go somewhere safe."

At least she could acknowledge that. "It'll be easier for me to help you if you tell me what's going on."

She didn't trust him. And why would she? Right now though, the fact she was here with him and not with any of the other people in her life said a lot.

"How do you think you're going to help me? Are you planning to sit outside my door and guard me all night? Are you going to monitor my emails? Because what else am I supposed to do?"

He flipped his coffee machine on, desperate for something to occupy his hands so he didn't have to stand there locked in this argument. It was like the chicken and the egg: she wouldn't tell him anything until she knew how he could help, and he couldn't help until she told him what had happened. For all he knew, if she went back to her apartment alone, there was a very real chance something bad could happen.

"Do you want to know why I left Singapore?" The coffee machine whirred to life. He pulled the cupboard open above his head and grabbed two mugs. "The real reason."

"I thought you said you got what you needed," she replied.

"That's part of it." He stuck a mug under the spout and pushed the button for a double shot. "I thought working in Singapore would change things. I thought it would make my career, and then my life would be exactly what I wanted it to be."

"Aren't you the banking industry's youngest CIO? Isn't *that* what you wanted?"

He turned and offered her the mug, and she hesitated a moment before accepting it. But then she wrapped her hands around the smooth white china and leaned against the breakfast bar. A tendril of damp, dark hair escaped the confines of the towel and hung softly against her cheek. "I wanted the whole package. The prestigious job, the loving wife, a life that would make my parents respect me."

Emotion simmered in the depths of her dark eyes, something like the love child of fury and regret turning her sweet face hard-edged and brittle. "You *could* have had that, with me. With my family. Here."

So he was still fully to blame in her mind? He felt the past rear up inside him, like some smoking demon that he'd tried—and failed—to bury. To shackle in the depths of his mind so that it wouldn't come out without his permission.

"I wanted it with *our* family. Ours." He jammed another mug under the coffee machine and jabbed the start button with his finger. "I've been an afterthought in my family for my whole life, so why the hell would I want to be an afterthought in yours?"

"I don't want to get into this." She shook her head. "I didn't come here to rehash all of the conversations I hated having the first time around."

"Maybe if we'd *had* those conversations properly the first time around, we wouldn't be needing a do-over." Dark liquid spilled into his cup, and steam curled upward. Being around Annie dredged everything up, all the good memories and the bad. The things that haunted him. Everything.

"Did you think it was easy living with you? Did you think it was easy trying to keep everyone happy? I *wanted* to go with you, but I couldn't. I couldn't leave my mom." She stared into her cup, her eyes dry despite the wavering emotion in her voice. "And I stand by my decision."

"You stand by the fact that you made such a momentous decision without me? A decision we were supposed to make together? You didn't think to discuss it with me *before* you decided to change things?" Now his thoughts spilled out, like a champagne bottle that had been shaken and uncorked. Everything they'd bottled up and tried to forget was fizzing up and over. "How was I supposed to feel like we were a team when you shut me out like that?"

That was the part that had hurt him the most. Being shut out. Because it was like all those times he'd tried to go to his father for advice or help or to share some excitement, and he'd watch that big, heavy door swing shut in his face. As he'd gotten older, he'd stopped trying to build that relationship. There was only so much rejection a person could take before it became easier not to try.

"What was I supposed to do? Say, 'Hey, Mom, I know you have cancer and all, but I really need to leave you behind and go overseas with my boyfriend because his career is more important than your life'?" She set the cup down and curled her hands over the edge of the breakfast bar, her knuckles turning white. "I don't know how that situation would have gone down in your family, because frankly, I'd have a better chance understanding aliens than I would understanding them. But in *my* family, we look after one another. We don't leave when things get tough."

"No, and I imagine you don't stop communicating when things get tough either." That was exactly his point. There had been a set of rules for her family, rules for how to love, and nurture, and support. Binding contracts that they all held in the highest regard, because they knew the love they had for one another was more important than anything else in the world. And, ultimately, her love for her family had been more important than what she felt for him.

All he'd wanted was for her to prioritize him the way he prioritized her. In his life, Annie was the be-all and end-all. She was his *everything*. The reason he woke in the morning, and the reason he worked his ass off all day. And it had killed him to know that he would never be that important to her.

"For the record," he said, clearing his throat, "it was never about the fact that you wanted to stay behind with her. It was about the fact that you didn't even give me a chance to be part of that decision. I would have done *anything* to make it work."

"Then why did you leave?" Now her eyes shimmered. Tears brought out the tiny, almost imperceptible flecks of green that he knew were there only because he'd stared into her eyes for so many years. Since they were kids playing in his parents' house, since they were lovesick college students. "Do you have any idea what I went through?"

When a tear dropped onto her cheek, she swiped at it angrily with the back of her hand. Annie had always hated crying in front of people.

"You were it," she continued. "You were the only man I ever wanted, and then I had to watch you put *my* ring on someone else's finger."

Her ring? He swallowed. The ring he'd given his ex-fiancée was a family heirloom, a treasured item from his grandmother that should never have been used for such a farce as his engagement to Annika Van Beek. In his desperation to move on from the past, he'd done something monumentally stupid. Annie had never seen that ring…had she?

"I found the ring, in case you hadn't worked that out already." She looked at him dead-on. That was his Annie, never one to shy away from the tough things in life. "In your sock drawer."

He could practically hear the question bouncing around in her head. *When were you going to ask me…?*

What she didn't know was he'd had it all planned out. A fancy hotel room in Singapore, booked for the night they were due to land and start their new life together. He'd arranged for the best suite in the place, with all those clichéd things like flower petals on the bed and a bottle of champagne chilled and waiting. A bouquet of flowers to be delivered shortly after their arrival. It would have been the most special moment of his life. Only, he'd boarded the plane alone. Arrived in his new country alone.

Her eyes bored into him. "Are you going to make me ask?"

"Why does it matter? It's in the past."

She bobbed her head slowly. "You're right. There's no point rehashing this."

The buzzer rang and they both jumped, the harsh sound cutting through the tension like a knife. It was the delivery guy. Joseph had almost forgotten he'd ordered them dinner. He paid for their food and set it out on the table, boxes of stir-fries and noodles and saucy dishes in almost every flavor. He didn't want to assume her tastes had stayed the same, so he'd ordered a little of everything.

While he was setting up dinner, Annie went into the bathroom and returned without the towel on her head. Damp, dark hair hung around her face, curling and kinking every which way. It was something that had always made him smile, the way her hair was so unruly. A bird's nest, she called it. Not that anyone outside her house would ever see her like that. She kept a tight handle on her appearance at all times. But he was one of the lucky few that got to see her unfiltered and unedited, the real her.

The fact that some of their old comfortable habits lingered made him feel tight in the chest.

"So what happens now?" she asked, taking a seat at his dining table and reaching for a bowl. "I stay here tonight, and I skip work tomorrow. Not exactly a long-term solution."

"The main thing we need to establish is whether you've been doxed. I've still got accounts on some of the old forums I used to go to, white-hat forums, so I can ask around. See what I can dig up." He reached for a pair of chopsticks and pulled them apart with a sharp snap. "If your address and phone number have been published, then your place will be unsafe for a while."

"And if that information hasn't been published?"

"Then hopefully we're only dealing with one sick fucker instead of multiple." He grabbed a piece of chicken with his chopsticks. "If we're only chasing one person, we've got a better chance of figuring out who he is."

"You're assuming it's a he?" She raised her brow.

"In most of the instances I've seen, the person doing the stalking was a man." He shrugged. "But that's speculation until I find out more."

She toyed with her food, digging her chopsticks into the small pile of noodles in her bowl, picking rather than eating. "Don't you have anything better to do with your time than look after me?"

"I have plenty of better things to do." He tried to muster a smile, hoping to take the seriousness of the conversation down a notch. "I've got a white paper on big data and intelligence metrics that I'd much rather be reading."

The twitch of her lips told him she'd picked up on his note of sarcasm. "Don't tell me your big important job only involves reading a bunch of white papers?"

"The higher you go, the more you read and the less you do. It's all spreadsheets and board packs and emails these days."

They ate in silence for a few moments. Annie looked

deep in thought, her brows furrowed as she hunted out a piece of tofu with her chopsticks. He wanted to tell her that she could trust him, that he would do what he could to help her. But without knowing what she was hiding from, he was hunting for a needle in a haystack. And to make matters worse, his brain was now clogged with all other kinds of questions. Angry questions and defensive questions that would do nothing but open Pandora's box. So much water was under the bridge that he was worried it might drown them.

She looked up at him, her expression unreadable. "Have you heard of Bad Bachelors?"

He blinked. "Yeah, actually I have."

"I created it."

Holy. Shit.

She didn't say anything further. She didn't need to. But that one piece of information put everything else into context. It was like going from a single puzzle piece to zooming out until you could see the entire picture. This was a hell of a catalyst.

"I don't want to talk about it. But you wanted a reason, so that's it." Her eyes challenged him. "You're staring at the most wanted woman in New York City."

Chapter 9

"Dear Bad Bachelors, thank you for standing up for the broken hearts."

—Ms.Manhattan

JOSEPH DROPPED DOWN INTO THE LEATHER CHAIR IN HIS office, both hands coming up to rub vigorously over his face. He was running on three hours of sleep and twice as many cups of coffee, which made for frayed nerves, a wavering attention span, and a short temper.

After dinner last night, Annie had retired to his spare room and hadn't come out again. They hadn't spoken further about her confession, but armed with this new information, Joseph had started digging. When Annie had called herself the most wanted woman in New York City, she wasn't joking. Bad Bachelors was the topic on everyone's lips—or was that fingertips? It came up in news articles, gossip columns, blogs, forums, and on every social media platform there was. With equal strength, she had supporters and those who wanted to see her fall.

There were entire websites dedicated to finding out who was behind Bad Bachelors. Though it seemed little had been dug up, what he'd seen written on some of those message boards had made his skin crawl. It was like she'd roused the demons of the internet, the slithering, gutter-dwelling bottom-feeders of the internet. Angry posters on 4chan…and worse. They wanted blood.

However, knowing the root cause of her troubles gave him more opportunity to figure out *who* was after her. Annie had given him access to her emails and anything else he might need, and it hadn't taken long to pinpoint how the hacker had gained access to her computer. It looked as though many others had tried. Annie had absorbed at least some of the lessons he'd taught her back in his internet security days. She'd been careful. Meticulously so.

But one piece of brilliant social engineering had tripped her up. On the day the malware was installed on her computer, she'd received an email with what looked to be a Word attachment containing answers to interview questions. To the untrained eye, it would look completely innocent. But the Word document was not what it appeared to be. The file had installed the spyware that allowed someone to take the picture with her webcam.

The brilliance of it was that Annie had asked *them* if they would like to be interviewed, based on a short, emotional email praising her site. They must have hoped she'd take the bait…and she had. Social engineering at its finest, because she wouldn't have thought twice about opening that attachment.

Who knew what information they'd taken? But they'd been watching, that was for damn sure.

"Knock, knock." Joseph's assistant, Dave, poked his head into Joseph's office. "Just wanted to check you haven't passed out on your desk."

Joseph laughed and looked at the stack of empty cups in front of him. "Given the amount of caffeine I've had today, I'm not likely to sleep for a week."

"That's a benefit in your job."

Joseph had been in his new role for a little over a week, and in that time he'd decided he liked Dave. The guy was organized, efficient, and most importantly, was well connected to the other assistants in the company. If there was one thing Joseph's career had taught him, it was that information was king. Especially the kind of information that wasn't available through any official channels.

In banking, those who couldn't navigate the political waters would be quickly chewed up and spat out by the corporate sharks. It wasn't a game Joseph enjoyed playing, but it *was* necessary. And having someone like Dave on his side was key.

"Can I ask you something?" Joseph waved Dave into the office. "I'm assuming you've heard of Bad Bachelors, that date-rating website and app? You put an article in my media pack about it."

Dave raised a brow. "That's right. I know a bit about it, but I'm a married man. Not exactly the target audience."

Joseph had seen the picture on Dave's desk, the one that showed him and his wife grinning with the Eiffel Tower in the background. "I'm more curious if you've heard people talking about it."

"Sure." Dave shrugged. "I think everybody is talking

about it, aren't they? I can't look at Twitter without seeing someone complaining about a review."

"What exactly have you heard?"

Dave looked at him strangely, his blue eyes narrowed. Then he looked over his shoulder before closing the office door behind him and leaning his lanky frame against it. "Do we have a situation that we need to manage?"

"No, no. Nothing like that. I've been out of the country for the last three years." How could he frame his questions without revealing any key information? The last thing he wanted was for anyone to know that his ex-girlfriend was the woman behind Bad Bachelors. That would *not* do good things for his career. "I read the article. I thought it was interesting."

Dave folded his arms across the front of his sharp navy suit. "It *is* interesting. One of the hottest websites and apps in the country, and there's speculation it's not making any money. What's the point, if not to cash in? They'd need a helluva motive, considering the earning potential. I heard there've been offers on it for over five million."

"What's your take on it?"

"You want my theory?" Dave tapped a long, slim finger against his clean-shaven chin. "Woman scorned, I think. Someone who had one too many failed relationships. There was speculation it was an ex-girlfriend of that PR guy Bad Bachelors was ragging on a few months back. Reed Something-or-other. They went after him hard. But it could be anyone."

Would anyone suspect Annie? She certainly fit the bill. A woman scorned? Well, if their argument last night was anything to go on, she definitely put herself in that category.

"I had a friend who got caught up in the reviews. He broke up with his ex recently, and it wasn't pretty. They're having a custody battle, and she decided to use the site against him by posting a bad review." Dave twisted his wedding band around his finger, brows knitted. "But then I've got another friend who swears by it. Her husband died five years ago, and she was terrified about dating again. Someone convinced her to download the app and she decided to give it a go. I'm not sure she would have tried without some kind of safety net like that. So I don't really know what to think."

"Kind of in a gray area, isn't it?" Joseph pushed out of his chair and turned to the giant window behind him. It was a dream office—a corner space with big windows and lots of light. A proper Wall Street bigwig view. Too bad he spent most of his time hunched over his laptop and couldn't truly enjoy it. "I guess if people only used it for its intended purpose that wouldn't be so bad."

"Who's to say what the intended purpose is, though? Maybe this is exactly what the creator was going for."

Dave's words struck Joseph in the chest like a blow from a hammer. Is that *why* Annie had created this app? To give people a way to hurt their exes? Maybe she felt helpless and wanted to lash out at him, but didn't have an avenue for it. That didn't sound like her though. She'd always been the kind of woman who saw the best in people.

Maybe you changed that about her. Maybe when you left, it turned her into the kind of person who wants to hurt others.

"I'm not usually a fan of giving unsolicited advice,"

Dave said, "but if I were you, I'd do my best to stay off Bad Bachelors. There are a lot of eyes on you, and personally I'm psyched to work with the youngest CIO in our company's history, but there are board members who will be looking to prove you're not up to the task. You're a threat to their security. To their pensions and their piles of money. They don't want young people taking their jobs."

Joseph turned sharply. "What have you heard?"

"Nothing outrageous. Comments about your age, mostly. A few people saying you only got the job because of your father, which is bullshit. But I've been around the block here. I know how it works. Hiring you was a risk because it sends a message that maybe their jobs aren't as secure as they once thought." Dave bobbed his head. "So they'll be watching, waiting for you to trip up."

"I *won't* trip up."

Dave looked as though he was about to say something else, but then he smiled and opened the door. He let it click shut softly behind him, leaving Joseph with a handful of confused thoughts and no more clarity than he'd had five minutes ago.

Getting involved in Annie's mess could really screw things up here. At this level, there was no such thing as a second chance. They were paying him the big bucks, and that meant he either delivered or they'd get rid of him. He would do everything in his power to protect Annie, but he would have to keep it quiet.

Nobody could know about his connection to the person behind Bad Bachelors.

Being stuck in Joseph's apartment all day had made Annie feel like a caged animal. By the time 6:00 p.m. rolled around, she was going stir-crazy.

The anonymous caller had flashed up on her screen several times today. Each time the number appeared, accompanied by the shrill ringtone she'd assigned it so she would know not to answer, her blood pressure soared higher and higher. Until eventually she'd shut the damn device off.

She'd made every effort to distract herself with work, partly to ease her guilt over taking a day off when she wasn't really sick and partly because if she didn't do something to keep her mind active, she'd go mad with worry. But eventually she'd drifted into the Bad Bachelors inbox, which was clogged with its usual sea of abuse and praise. More threats, more people thanking her profusely. Everything in between.

She was trying her hardest not to speculate on what Joseph might think about the whole thing. She'd heard him tapping away at the computer last night while she lay in his spare bed, staring at the ceiling, wondering if she'd ever sleep properly again. Was he judging her? Was he feeling guilty about their argument? Did he agree with the people who called her evil and heartless and a bad influence on society? A feminazi?

Eventually, Annie abandoned her laptop and found herself digging through Joseph's refrigerator. She figured cooking might be a better way to keep her hands and her mind occupied, rather than looking through her inbox and wondering what the hell she was going to do.

"Old Mother Hubbard ain't got nothing on this fridge," she muttered to herself.

What was the point of having a giant, gleaming silver behemoth in your kitchen if you were going to leave it empty?

Half an hour later, she'd managed to locate his spare key, make her way to the little bodega next to his building, and return with ingredients for some gourmet sandwiches. It wasn't much, but at least it would get them through the night. She was juggling her shopping bags while trying to get his key into the lock when she heard the ping of the elevators behind her. Placing the bags on the floor, she turned.

"About time…" she said, her voice dying when she saw who was striding through the hallway.

After Joseph had left her, there was only one face she'd wanted to see *less* than his. Only one person she hated more.

"Well, this isn't what I was expecting to find." Morris Preston looked at her the way he always had—like she were an offensive piece of gum on the bottom of his shoe.

"For all you know, I'm here to do the cleaning," she retorted, issuing her best withering glare. "It's all my family is good for, isn't it?"

"Always so defensive, Leanne."

"It's Annie. Or is your memory starting to go?" She jammed the key into the lock. "I haven't been Leanne for a long time."

But of course, in Morris's eyes, she would only ever be the little wisp of a girl who was the daughter of their housekeeper. The hired help. He'd scolded her once—for running around his house when her mother had brought her to work after their sitter canceled, and she'd been bored out of her brain. Who could blame a five-year-old girl for getting fidgety in a house where she wasn't allowed to touch anything? Morris expected everyone around him to adhere to his rules. At all times. Without exception.

That's why he'd hated her from the start. Not only did she not come from "good breeding," but she had a mind of her own. And he didn't like that.

"Joseph isn't here." She pushed the door open and held it with a foot while she bent to pick up her bags. Unsurprisingly, Morris didn't offer any assistance. "I don't know when he'll be back."

"I'll wait."

Morris hadn't changed a bit. Well, maybe his silver hair had thinned a little. But he was still a large, imposing man with shoulders enhanced by a double-breasted suit, and the ice-cold gaze of someone who knew that power was theirs at all times. He still had that big, booming voice that was rumored to reduce a man to a quivering mess in an instant. He'd tried that on her once. It was the one time he'd actually voiced what she knew he'd been thinking all along: that Annie was some gold digger from the wrong side of the tracks, a common mutt who would never be accepted in their family.

"Then you can wait downstairs." She stood in the doorway, not caring that she didn't have a right to say who could and couldn't enter Joseph's apartment. The last thing she wanted in the midst of all this drama was to be stuck with the man who'd never done anything but make her doubt herself.

Morris took a step forward, his hands clasped in front of him. A heavy gold watch glinted from one wrist, matching the band on his ring finger. "From what I understand, you already have one of his apartments. Are you planning on stealing this one too?"

In less than thirty seconds, he'd found something to throw in her face. "If you're here to see Joseph, I've already told you he's not here. If you're here to harass me, then consider it a job well done. Now, if you'll excuse me, I'm going inside."

The sound of someone clearing their throat made her head snap to the side. Joseph stood there, arms folded across the front of his slick black suit. Fire in his eyes. She hadn't even heard the elevator open.

"Are you two done with this pissing match yet?"

God, she remembered that tone. For a fleeting second, guilt streaked through her. Joseph had always been stuck in the middle—the buffer between his difficult-to-please parents and the girlfriend who could never live up to their expectations. He'd tried so hard. Probably harder than most would have. And it still wasn't enough. By setting up that job for him in Singapore, Morris had eventually gotten his claws in and widened the wedge between them.

"I was in the neighborhood." As always, Morris was cool as a cucumber. "I wasn't aware you had company."

"It's *my* apartment. Sometimes I have company. You can always call ahead if you're uncertain."

Well, *that* was new. There was frost in Joseph's voice,

a glacial edge that she hadn't heard before, at least not when he was talking to his father.

Morris raised a brow. "And which one of you should I call?"

"I don't live here." She was still in the doorway, her foot keeping the door open and the grocery bags feeling heavier by the second. She was tempted to dump the lot on the floor and get the hell out of there, because the one good thing about *not* being in a relationship with Joseph anymore was that she didn't have to take any shit from his family. "And you're not welcome to have my phone number."

"You haven't changed a bit." The insult couldn't have been clearer.

"I could say the same for you."

"Enough!" Joseph slapped his hand against the wall, and the sound echoed through the hallway. "Is it too much to ask that we behave like adults? I've had a long fucking day and, frankly, I don't have the patience for this. Dad, I'm busy. Next time, call ahead and I'll let you know if I'm free."

Joseph stalked toward the door and Annie took a step back, unsure if he was going to kick her out too. She'd be taking the stairs; that was damn sure. Because there was no way in hell she'd let herself be stuck in an elevator with Morris Preston.

"Get inside," Joseph said, his tone heavy. "Unless you want to hang out with my dad some more."

"Hard pass."

He pressed his shoulder to the door and took the grocery bags from her, motioning for her to go ahead.

Morris gaped while Joseph let the door swing shut in his face. That's when Annie realized her pulse was racing, despite the fact that she'd done her best to seem cold and unaffected on the surface. Unfortunately, making other people feel inferior was Morris's superpower. Even now that she owed him nothing and needed nothing from him, he still managed to reduce her to unpleasant visceral reactions.

Only this time, instead of defusing the situation, Joseph had taken her side. At least that's how it seemed.

"I thought I told you not to leave the house." He raked a hand through his hair, strong fingers driving through thick strands that stubbornly flopped back into place the second he dropped his arm.

"And you expect a girl to starve?" She walked to the kitchen and dumped the bags on the counter. Then she started to unpack the cold meats, fresh bread rolls, and the little slab of cheese that had cost a fortune, but that she knew he would like. "Your fridge is a ghost town."

"I wasn't expecting to have two mouths to feed."

"It doesn't look like you were expecting to have one mouth to feed either." She shot him a pointed look. "Are you getting on that new air diet that everyone is talking about?"

His harsh expression softened a touch, a smirk tugging at his lips. "It would certainly suit my lifestyle. Pretty easy to do meal prep."

She opened the bag containing the rolls and grabbed a cutting board sitting neatly against the kitchen backsplash. A funny feeling had settled in her stomach, something like butterflies but not as pretty. He'd chosen her this time, over his father. It was something she'd asked him to do so many times before, especially when Morris had seemed determined to break her. And yet Joseph had always played piggy in the middle, never choosing a side or taking a stand.

At least not in public.

"Your dad is a delight, as usual." She yanked a bread knife from the wooden block and noticed it still had a sticker on the handle. The guy hadn't even cut a piece of bread since he moved in?

"And you were giving him what he wanted. As usual." Joseph shrugged out of his suit jacket and yanked at the tie around his neck, his movements sharp and jerky. She tried not to stare at the way his fitted white shirt stretched across his chest as he moved. But her mouth was watering, and it had nothing to do with the food in front of her. "Almost like I never left."

She wanted to snap at him. It felt too soon for that joke, even though it wasn't. Instead, she ran the serrated blade over the crispy roll until she hit the soft, fluffy center. Crumbs skittered over the cutting board.

"What did he say?" Joseph's voice drifted down the hall as he walked into his bedroom. There was a rustling of fabric, and Annie forced herself not to think about what he would look like getting changed. "Or don't I want to know?"

"You know what it's like with him. It's more *how* he says things than what he actually says."

"That sounds about right."

She made their sandwiches, layering prosciutto with

sun-dried tomatoes and crumbly pieces of cheese. "I thought you might kick me out."

"Why would I do that when I was worried about you leaving the house?"

She kept her eyes on the cutting board as his footsteps grew louder behind her, causing a tremor to run the length of her spine. Her body anticipated his touch— waited for a hand to curve over her hip, to slide up her waist and under her top. Her flesh tingled with want, with need, with memories of him.

"You didn't have to speak to him." He was close behind her now, not touching, although the air between them bristled with electricity. "You don't owe him anything."

"No, I don't. But he's not very good at taking no for an answer." She reached up to the cupboard above and pulled down two plates, well aware that her sweater would rise up enough to reveal a band of skin above her jeans. The feeling of being watched intensified, sliding over her skin and winding through her blood. "One of the many traits you inherited from him."

"Don't compare me to him."

She wanted to turn and look at him. But she couldn't. Because seeing him care about her well-being, care about the past, and choosing her over his father cracked the layer of ice around her heart. And that was danger- ous. She needed that ice, that protection.

"I am *nothing* like him."

"You chose your job over the person you supposedly loved." The words were bitter on her tongue. She was lashing out to take the focus off what truly frightened her—that she needed him. That she *didn't* have anywhere else to go. "I thought you'd turned into him."

"You can at least look me in the eye when you insult me like that."

Annie sucked in a breath and counted to three before she slowly turned. It was like peering over the edge of a volcano, shimmering and bright. The heat so intense, she was worried her eyelashes might singe right off. The old Joseph would never have engaged in such an argument. His specialty was storming off, slamming doors. Avoidance.

But now he looked armed and ready for battle, ready to stand his ground.

And for some ungodly reason, it put Annie's entire body on red alert. Right then, it was like being in an alternate reality. One where he'd never left, where she'd never let her fear push him away. Where they had both been more mature and better equipped to deal with the curveballs that life had thrown them. Where they were exactly where they were supposed to be—together.

"Care to say that again?" His jaw ticked. The hard expression on his face was completely misleading, because she knew that underneath that layer of anger and resentment was something far more primal. His spring-morning eyes were darkened, blackened.

He was as excited as she was.

"I thought you had turned into him," she repeated, tipping her face up and nailing him with her gaze. If there was one thing that Annie never did, it was back down. "Like father, like son."

Chapter 10

"Why are you doing this? Don't you know good men
are being hurt by your website? Do you even care?"

—ConcernedMom

THERE WAS NO WAY IN HELL JOSEPH SHOULD HAVE BEEN
turned on. If there had been a single cell left functioning
in his brain, he would have been able to turn and walk
away. But judging by the thunderstorm of emotions—
the toxic and enticing mix of anger, resentment, and
lust—that caused his body to propel forward, the only
thing in his head right now was a pile of Jell-O. Her
eyes widened as he stalked forward, hands balled into
fists and teeth grinding together so hard he thought they
might crack.

"Like father, like son, huh?" he growled. "Why are
you here? If you have so many people to call on and I'm
such an asshole, why the hell are you here?"

Her hands came up to his chest, and it was only then
that he realized how close he'd gotten. He was in her
space, in her orbit. For a second he thought she'd push
him away, but instead she curled her fists into his shirt
and yanked him closer. His hips wedged her against the

kitchen counter, and as though driven by instinct, his hands smoothed over her waist. Through the thin fabric of her sweater, he felt that delicious dip, the perfect spot that allowed his thumbs to sweep up over her rib cage and to barely brush the rounded underside of her breasts.

"I guess I'm a glutton for punishment." Her chest heaved as she sucked in a shaky breath, but there wasn't an ounce of fear in her expression. Nor could he find any emotion that might allow him to grasp sensibility and step away: no hesitation, no reservations, not even a flash of remorse. "You've always had that effect on me."

"What effect?"

"The ability to make me forget all the things I *should* be doing." Her eyes were dark pools, sucking him in. "To lead me blindly into bad decisions."

Bad decisions. That's what it would be if he let need overcome him now. They would wake up in the morning and regret everything. His hands flexed at her waist, knowing he should let go but unable to force himself to do it. His body was trying to make up for the mistakes of his heart, of his head. To make up for the stupid actions he'd taken in the name of trying to please his family.

"You're not so innocent yourself. If I remember correctly, you were the one who dragged me into the bushes at that awful wedding."

Her lips curved into a sinful smile. "You said you were dying of boredom. I needed to administer mouth-to-mouth resuscitation."

All the blood in his body surged south, and he pressed against her, his cock aching. "If your lips had only been on my mouth, I wouldn't have had much to worry about."

"You weren't complaining at the time." Her face tilted up, lips parted, eyes pleading, and nose shoved ever so slightly in the air. "I got the impression you quite enjoyed it, not being such a good boy for once."

"If you think I only 'quite enjoyed it,' then you're sorely mistaken." He lowered his head, sucking in the scent of her—mixed with his soap and shampoo—and spoke directly into her ear. "I would say I enjoyed it very fucking much."

Bad influence. Wasn't that what his parents had said about her? The girl who came from nothing, whose family loved so openly and fiercely they were like an alien species, and who made him feel like perhaps someone *could* love him. The first day he'd run into her at college—after not seeing her for years—she'd taken one look at his starched shirt, Gucci loafers, and neatly styled hair and told him that wasn't how he was supposed to dress for a frat party. So she'd grabbed a beer, shaken it up, and sprayed his top, all the while smiling like the devil himself had painted her expression. In that moment, he'd fallen head over heels.

It was the first event of many where she'd stolen him away for kisses and more.

"I still think about it," he added.

"You still think about it? Or you still think about me?"

Of course he still thought about her, but confirming that would do more damage than staying silent. Because he couldn't let her know he'd booked his one-way ticket from Singapore back to Manhattan with a head full of memories. With a head full of her. He couldn't tell her that the woman he'd proposed to had accused him of still loving her. At the time, he'd convinced himself it was nothing but Annika's paranoia, but right now, with everything feeling so damn right, he wondered if she'd been onto something.

"Pleading the fifth, huh?" Annie cocked her head. "Why am I not surprised?"

That was more like it. Defensiveness was easier. Arguing was easier. He stepped back and shoved his hands into his pockets, needing some kind of physical barrier to keep him from reaching out again. "There's no point in having this conversation."

"You're right." She looked up at him. "What are you going to tell your dad?"

"Nothing. It's none of his business."

"But he'll think we're back together." She shook her head and turned to the counter, picking up the plates and carrying them to the table as though their conversation hadn't been interrupted by a brief moment of fantasy-induced insanity. "Isn't he going to give you a hard time?"

"Let him think whatever he wants. I really don't care."

For once, that was the truth.

She toyed with a strand of her hair, rubbing the ends back and forth between her thumb and forefinger for a moment before tucking it behind her ear. Nervous habit. Good thing she wasn't playing poker right now. "I should probably go home tonight."

"Tomorrow. I'm waiting to hear back from a few old

contacts that I reached out to about your situation." He held up a hand before she could say anything. "Don't worry, I didn't give them your name. I only wanted to see if they'd heard anything about Bad Bachelors."

They took their seats at the table, but there was a stiffness between them. An awkwardness thickening the air. "Did you find anything in my inbox?"

"Not really. There's no more malware on the computer. And the emails didn't give me anything." He shook his head. "Nothing useful, anyway."

He didn't tell her that he'd been horrified by some of what he'd read. It wasn't as though he hadn't anticipated abusive emails, but there had been a few where it had taken everything in his power not to hunt the assholes down.

"Anything you agreed with?" she asked. He wasn't fool enough to take the casual question at face value.

"I'm trying to figure out who's threatening you. I'm not here to judge."

A soft little noise escaped her lips, something between a laugh and a huff. "I'm not sure why I care."

Neither of them had touched their food. All this to-and-fro-ing had left him without an appetite. Well, that wasn't entirely true. He was ravenous…but not for food. Sparring with her had always gotten him hot and bothered.

Don't even think about it. There are so many ways you can mess up this situation right now, and sex is at the top of that list.

"I'm going to see if anyone's gotten back to me." He grabbed his plate and headed toward his study. "I'll let you know what I find."

Annie tossed out her half-eaten sandwich and paced around Joseph's kitchen for a good ten minutes, trying to figure out what to do next. She'd turned her cell back on and found her voicemail filled with short breathing-only messages from the number that'd been calling her since yesterday.

This time, she blocked the caller. It's what she should have done yesterday, but a small part of her had hoped they might reveal some important information. However, now she feared she was simply giving this asshole what he wanted. And frankly, there was only so much she could take. Tomorrow, she'd be getting a new phone number.

In the meantime, Annie wasn't ready to go home. When she'd asked about what Joseph had found, his expression had told her enough. Not only was he legitimately *not* judging her…he was worried. And Joseph had never been the kind of guy to worry needlessly, despite her tinfoil-hat jokes. Which meant she had to sit tight for another evening.

She rubbed her hands over her face. When her phone trilled from the back pocket of her jeans, vibrating against her butt, she almost shot twenty feet in the air.

"Shit." She fumbled with the phone, sighing in relief when Darcy's name flashed on the screen. "Hello?"

"Hey." Darcy was chewing on something. The sound of a bubble popping made Annie jerk the phone away from her ear. "Reed ditched me for the night because he's got some event at the college. Want to hang out?"

"Uh…" She glanced across the apartment to where Joseph's office door sat ajar. "I can't, sorry."

"I was going to get Remi to come along. Figured we could have a good old-fashioned girls' night out." She paused. "You know, like we used to."

Out of nowhere, Annie's lip quivered. A girls' night. God, it felt like a lifetime since they'd had one of those! Before Annie had put the final nail in the coffin of her friendship with Remi, before Joseph had come back, before she was in hiding from someone who wanted to hurt her.

"I wish I could…"

"Don't tell me you're *still* at work," Darcy said. "It's almost nine. I'll pry you away from your keyboard with a crowbar if I have to."

"I'm not at work."

"Oh. Where are you? I tried buzzing your apartment first."

Shit. "I have a life, Darcy. I do other things besides working and staying at home," she snapped. Then she cringed. Wow, she was in full bitch mode tonight. "Sorry, I didn't mean to snap. I'm cranky today."

"It's cool. Everything okay?" The concern in her friend's voice made Annie feel even worse. With everything she'd done in her life, she was quite convinced she did not deserve a friend as good as Darcy.

"I had a run-in with Joseph's dad." It would be so much easier if she could control how she felt about Morris, but he was her kryptonite. The one person guaranteed to make her feel an inch tall with only a glance.

It royally pissed her off. How was she not above that?

It'd been three years since she'd broken up with Joseph. The old man meant nothing to her. So why did it still sting that he thought of her as a lowlife?

"Whoa. What did that douche canoe have to say for himself?" She could practically see Darcy curling her lip. "I hope you punched him in the nutsack."

Annie snorted. "I wish."

"Consider it a favor to society so he doesn't bring any more assholes into the world."

It was really freaking hard to put Joseph in that category right now. Because he was a total gentleman.

"Anyway, it was brief. Thankfully." Annie headed past the study and into the guest room. "He made a crack about how Joseph gave me the apartment."

"Don't remind me he did that. I want to hate him, remember?"

When he'd left, he'd handed the keys over to her, essentially giving her the apartment for nothing. There'd been no discussion about selling it and settling up. No suggestion that she buy him out. He knew she'd never be able to afford it. And that was that. The man had basically given her a million-dollar property without a word.

She'd been foaming at the mouth for a fight. But he hadn't given her the chance. If there was a gentlemanly way to extricate oneself from a breakup, Joseph had done exactly that. There were no angry texts or drunk dials or arguments about stupid stuff.

He'd been there one day, and gone the next. Almost like she'd imagined the whole relationship.

"Have you seen him since he came over?" Darcy asked.

"No," Annie lied, crossing her fingers the way she'd done as a little girl. She hated lying, especially to Darcy, but answering truthfully would open a can of worms that she had no hope of controlling.

You'll make it up to her once you have more information. It's a temporary lie.

A weak justification, at best.

"Good. You've moved on, and you're better off without him." There was a clanging sound in the background, like Darcy was puttering around in her kitchen. "You're *not* the same person he left behind."

"No, I'm not," Annie echoed.

The breakup had changed her. She was less idealistic, more practical and analytical. She'd become an expert in assessing risks and protecting herself. Which was precisely why she'd spent the last three years not dating and not having sex and trying to act like that didn't bother her.

What her friends and family didn't know was that she'd tried to date in the early days. Tinder, Bumble, OkCupid, and something ridiculous called Coffee Meets Bagel. She'd even gone on a blind date.

But all it had done was reinforce the idea behind Bad Bachelors. The dating jungle required a guide— because men seemed to think that picking up the check meant she should open her legs. Not that there was anything wrong with women having sex on the first date—absolutely *not*—but it shouldn't be expected. It was *her* choice. And some of her dates had turned nasty when she refused to go back to their place for a "drink." Others had simply shrugged and told her she was only one of a half-dozen dates they had lined up that week. That someone else would put out.

That she was nothing special.

One or two of the guys had been genuinely sweet. But by then she'd had her walls so well-fortified that nobody was getting in. Three years without sex. She'd even googled to see if it was possible for her to lose interest for good. If maybe prolonged abstinence would damage her libido beyond repair.

But her suspicions had been well and truly dashed tonight. Turned out she wanted sex…but only with one person.

"You there?" Darcy asked. "I should go. I'm still going to call Remi, so if you change your mind, I'll text you the bar details just in case."

"Thanks," she whispered.

Annie ended the call and tossed the phone onto the bed. What a mess. Now on top of everything else, she was lying to her best friend. For a person who craved rules and boundaries and control, Annie felt like she was in a downward spiral. Everything had gotten so far out of hand that she didn't know what to do anymore.

She sucked in a long breath and attempted to quell the panic rushing up the back of her throat. "You are a grown-ass woman, and you can handle this," she said to herself. "You'll come clean with Darcy, and she will understand. You'll make it up to Remi, and everything will go back to normal. This internet stalker thing will get resolved if you let Joseph do what he does best."

She let her breath out slowly. Everything would be fine. She had to keep telling herself that. The universe worked in mysterious ways, as her mother used to say, and she had weathered worse storms. Annie was a changed woman. Stronger, smarter, more equipped to deal with life's curves and bumps.

Smart enough to know that baiting your ex is a bad idea?

Was she baiting him, though? The moment he'd stalked toward her in the kitchen and her hands had found purchase in his shirt, she'd been baiting *herself.* Because as much as it would be a hell of a lot easier to hang on to the anger and hurt and shame, she had to be truthful. Annie was no less attracted to him now than she had been when they'd first met.

Not even a little bit.

Acknowledging that was no easy task, because it meant she couldn't brush off the thrill when his gaze raked over her skin. She couldn't blame it on "muscle memory" or phantom feelings or some weird little quirk in her brain. She still wanted him. Even now. Even after everything.

Letting out a long breath, she tipped her face up to the ceiling. Like a sign from the heavens, she heard the sound of running water coming from the bathroom next to his bedroom. The picture was already bright and vivid in her mind, colors and shapes enhanced by the strongest of her memories. Foggy glass. Water sliding over his smooth skin, running in rivulets down the length of his spine and over the athletic curve of his ass.

Joseph had always had a great ass. Even in their college days when he was much lankier.

Dammit. Why did she still have to feel this way about him? Why couldn't she be like a normal person and feel revulsion at the sight of her ex? Why couldn't she focus on the bad instead of the good?

Maybe because you know he's a good person, despite what happened. Maybe because you're also to blame for the breakup.

He'd come to her rescue the second she'd asked—without hesitation and without judgment. He'd given her a safe place to hide out, had stayed up late working on something that didn't benefit him in the slightest. And then she'd thrown it all in his face by saying he was like his father, which was possibly the biggest piece of bullshit to ever come out of her mouth.

Because Joseph *wasn't* like Morris. At all.

She rubbed her hands over her face. Couldn't she pretend to hate him? Or at least pretend she hadn't thought about jumping his bones?

The running water continued to taunt her. It was like her body had suddenly realized that it missed sex, and now her libido was playing catch-up for the last three years. Her senses hummed with awareness.

She rose from the bed and walked into the hall. The bathroom door was slightly ajar, and steam billowed out through the small space. He *always* forgot to turn on the exhaust fan. Shaking her head, she reached inside with the intention of flipping the fan's switch, but her arm bumped the door open a little further.

The mirror was quickly being consumed by fog, but a clear patch reflected slick, bare skin.

Against her better judgment, she pushed the door open a little wider. The steam and hot air settled on her skin, and when she raised her hand to touch her cheek, it was warm. The bathroom was huge, with another door on the opposite side that led straight into his bedroom. The shower was floor-to-ceiling glass, and it offered a hazy view of him from head to toe. He had one forearm braced against the tiles, head bowed to the rushing water. It was like a modern art exhibition, his perfect body sculpted straight from fantasy with every muscle toned and taut, every line clean and smooth.

This is the part where you turn around and leave. Go back to your room, do whatever you can to bleach this from your brain.

Her brain was so good at dispensing advice but not all that great at following it. It seemed that whatever part was responsible for motor function was on Team Get Some. She closed her eyes for a second, willing sensibility to kick in and drag her horny ass back out of there.

But a soft sound shattered whatever scraps of willpower she'd mustered up. Behind the cloudy glass, Joseph's arm worked up and down. Holy shit, was he really…

He was.

The muscles in his arms and his back flexed as he worked himself over. Every so often, his ass would clench as he thrust into his fist. The foggy glass hid all the details, but her mind could easily color in the rest—the soft trail of hair from his belly button down to his cock, the hard, strong length of him.

The jolt of arousal hit her so hard it might as well have been administered by jumper cables. Her body was a live wire, crackling and seriously, desperately hot.

Watching him was like being in his head; his feelings were hers. His pleasure was hers.

Was he thinking about her?

Her hands came to the hem of her sweater, like someone else had the remote control to her brain. She dragged the fabric up over her stomach, over her breasts, and over her head.

"Annie, what the fuck? What the hell are you doing in here?"

She popped the button on her jeans. Now he faced her, the steamy glass attempting—and failing—to hide his mouthwatering body.

"I'm sick of dancing around it." She drew the zipper down on her jeans and shoved the fabric over her hips, taking her underwear along with it. "It's obvious you and I have some unfinished business. I'd rather deal with it now and get it out of the way."

"Unfinished business?" He shook his head. "You think sex is the problem we never dealt with?"

She unhooked her bra and let it slide down her body. His indignant act was all well and good, but he wasn't exactly averting his eyes. And his erection bobbed in front of him. "We've been circling each other like animals. It's clear there's tension."

"We were just winding each other up. Isn't that our thing?" He still hadn't covered himself. That was something she'd always admired about him, how confident he was in his own skin. He used to be perfectly happy walking around the apartment totally naked, that glorious ass always on display.

"Winding you up enough that I walked in on you

taking care of business." She stepped away from her pile of clothes and headed toward the shower.

His fiery gaze roamed over her. "And you want to give me a hand?"

Did she ever. "Think of this as scratching an itch. There won't be any cuddling or false promises or bullshit. It's just sex. Nothing more."

"Well, how could I possibly refuse when you put it in such enticing terms?" he said drily. "You think I'm looking for a fuck buddy?"

His tone was saying one thing, but the flare of darkness in his eyes said something else entirely. He wanted her. This was the one area where she was an expert in him. His every tell was logged deep in her brain—the way his nostrils flared ever so slightly, the tensing and release of his hands, and the way his full lips would part a fraction. She would bet the last cent in her bank account that he wanted her. Now.

"We're both mature adults." She wrapped her hand around the edge of the sliding glass door, pushing it open further, enough to accommodate the width of her shoulders and hips. "We don't have to deny ourselves."

Yeah, you're definitely not denying yourself anything. Tomorrow you'll have all the regret and shame that you can possibly handle.

But stopping now wasn't going to happen. That horse had already bolted, and the realization that she still wanted him put fire in her veins. She would not be sated until she had him.

"There's that bad influence again." He wrapped a

hand around her wrist. "There's no going back from this. You know that, right?"

"There is no going forward from it either." She stepped into the shower, allowing him to pull her close. "It is what it is. Nothing yesterday. Nothing tomorrow. Just now."

Chapter 11

"The perfect man is too good to be true. He doesn't exist. You're selling a lie."

—Jaded

IT WAS LIKE WATCHING A MOVIE WHERE YOU DIDN'T know what was reality and what was in the character's head. He'd had this dream before—Annie naked in front of him, arms outstretched. That coy little smile on her lips, the one that had always told him she was in the mood. He'd been so attuned to her then, so in sync with her. And now, she was tempting him. Promising him everything and nothing.

Her hair was pulled back, so he reached behind her head and found the thin elastic, tugging until it came loose. Then he drove his fingers through the silky strands.

"Don't think this means I forgive you," she said. Her voice was husky and warm, and he let himself be mesmerized by the movement of her lips.

"Wouldn't dream of it," he drawled, tipping her head back. The action exposed the length of her neck, now glistening with moisture from steam and water droplets. "I know you better than that."

"Yes, you do," she whispered.

This is a very bad idea. Repeat: this is a very fucking bad idea.

He turned them both and backed Annie against the tiles, thanking the heavens this place had a double shower. He'd assumed at the time it was a waste of space, since he'd be showering alone. But now...now.

"You're still so beautiful." He lowered his head to hers. "Still so goddamn difficult and demanding and beautiful."

Her head rolled back against the tiles, and she chuckled. "You told me once you didn't like yes people. Guess that's why you were attracted to me."

"Among other things." He slid a hand up her rib cage to cup her breast, capturing her nipple between his thumb and the pad of his forefinger. She arched into him, gasping.

"So goddamn sexy," he growled, rubbing his other thumb over her lip.

Eyes glinting, she sucked his thumb into her mouth, swirling her tongue around and around. He grunted and shoved his hips against hers, pinning her to the wall. The hard length of his cock rubbed against her smooth, taut belly as he pushed his thumb further between her lips.

"God, that dirty little mouth."

Her lashes were dewy, her eyes smoky. She was fully aware of how easily she could tug his strings. Damn her. He made it easy, too. Didn't hold anything back. Not during sex, anyway.

Her full lips formed a tight O around his thumb, and then she sank her teeth into him just enough to make pain snap through the barrier of pleasure. That was Annie in a nutshell...all sweetness, until she decided to bite.

"Bad girl." He slipped both hands down her back to grab her ass as he pressed his mouth to hers.

Her lips were hungry and willing, and she tasted so achingly familiar. So perfectly, frighteningly, wonderfully familiar. The rightness of it made him want to fall to his knees. But there was no way he could let on that this was anything more than sex. That it was anything more than primal need and pent-up lust and the consequences of too much work and not enough play.

"Are you going to tell me if you were fantasizing about me before?" She peppered his face with kisses, her fingers tangling in his hair as she stood on her tiptoes. Warm water sluiced over them.

"Before?"

"I saw you, Joseph." She shot him a look.

Shit. Maybe it had been a risky thing to do, knowing she was so close, but he'd figured it might help ease some of his tension. Because walking around his apartment with a hard-on while he tried not to eye-fuck his ex-girlfriend wasn't going to lead anywhere good. So he'd stepped into the shower and found himself already hard enough to drill through concrete.

She always did that to him. *Every. Damn. Time.*

"Saw me what?" Maybe he could get her to back down. Just this once.

"I saw you stroking yourself." She reached down between them, wrapping her hands around him. He grunted as she squeezed, twisting her hand around the sensitive, throbbing head. "I saw you tugging on your cock like your life depended on it."

His one-handed attempt paled in comparison to this. Masturbation was all well and good, but anyone who said it held a candle to the two-player version was full of shit.

"And?" He pressed his forehead to hers.

"You were thinking about me." Her gaze wavered.

"You asking or telling?"

She swallowed. "Telling."

Her hand worked him up and down, and since he'd been well on his way before he'd found her stripping in his bathroom, he was precariously close to the edge. Joseph wrapped his fingers around her wrists and brought them above her head, holding her hands against the tiles. She looked like a meal. A decadent dessert waiting for him to take a bite.

"Tell me, since you seem to know so much, what *was* I thinking exactly?" He held her in place with one hand and lowered his head to her breasts, dragging his tongue over one distended pink nipple.

The muscles in her wrists flexed under his hard grip as she arched against his mouth. "You were thinking about this." The last word was like a snake's hiss, a warning slithering through his veins. "You were thinking about all the times I used to get on my knees in the shower for you."

Hell. Yes.

"All the times I'd sink down and open my mouth for your big cock. You used to love—" Her words broke off into a sharp gasp when he scraped his teeth over her nipple. "You used to love grabbing my hair and holding my head while you fucked my mouth."

The memories splintered—fragments and fractures of every time they'd made love spinning and shimmering until he couldn't tell one from the other. Until he couldn't tell the past from the present, or fantasy from reality. Everything had melted together.

"You want me to do it now, baby?" She pressed her hips forward and rubbed herself against him. "Give you what you want?"

God, yes. But holding on would be seriously difficult.

"If you do that, this little game is going to be over quickly." He ground the words out between clenched teeth. There wasn't a single person on the face of the earth that managed to turn him on like her. "And I don't like to rush. Keep your hands above your head, sweetheart. It's my turn to play."

He slipped a hand between her legs and found her hot and wet. Ready. But this was as much to give him time to calm down as it was to wrench some of his power back. To put them on even footing. Because he knew that if he let her take control, he'd give her anything. Everything.

Only this time they weren't playing for keeps, and he needed to remember that.

"Widen those legs." His lips were at her ear, each word causing them to brush against the delicate shell. She'd forgotten to take her pearl studs out, and they gleamed. "Let me feel all of you."

He pressed his fingers into her wetness, sliding one deep into her while he rubbed the heel of his palm against her most sensitive spot. Her dark eyes were ablaze, a mix of lust and rebellion swirling like fire batons. Nothing was ever easy with this woman. Even sex had a hint of combativeness.

And damn if he didn't love the fight.

"You haven't lost your touch." Her head lolled back, and her eyes clamped shut. "Still know how to find all the good spots."

What was she trying to say? That he'd had a lot of "practice" since her? If only she knew…

"You're not exactly rusty yourself."

Her eyes snapped open and she glared at him, the hard expression holding its power for only a second before she swirled her hips against his hand and lost herself in a rhythm of her own making. "I want you. Please."

"Tell me." He worked her over mercilessly, chasing the spot that made her flutter. "What do you need?"

"You. Inside me." Her jaw was tight. "Now."

The thought of burying himself between her smooth legs was like a lit match to a pool of gasoline. "We should…" He shook his head. "I don't know if I have any condoms."

He was pretty sure he didn't. Because sex had been the last thing on his mind when he'd moved in. In fact, he would have been happy never to think about it again— until that night at Annie's place, where she'd walked into the room wearing her nightshirt. Until she'd stomped all over his plans to quietly slip back into life here. Alone.

"I'm safe." That's when her mask slipped, and he caught a rare glimpse of her vulnerability. No hard outer shell, no piercing glare. Just his Annie. "I, uh… I keep up with my tests."

He didn't want to feel jealous, thinking about her going to the doctor for some other guy. But fucking hell, it made him want to smash down walls and tear through the city like a monster.

"I'm still on the pill," she added.

"I'm safe too." Aside from being meticulously careful, he'd needed to be doubly sure after everything imploding in Singapore. Which made his jealous feelings hypocrisy of the highest order. "Are you sure you want this?"

"Yes." She chuckled, and the throaty sound dragged over his nerves like a razor blade. "Sex with you is the one thing I've never had doubts about."

"Do you remember the first time?" He slipped his hands under her thighs and lifted her up. Her legs wrapped around his waist, and he held her fast with one arm, his other hand braced against the tiles. "Do you remember how good it was?"

"With sticks and rocks poking into my ass?" She sucked on the side of his neck as he rubbed against her, drawing out the moment they'd been working toward. "How could I forget? You laid the sleeping bag down so carefully, brought that adorable picnic so we could eat outside. I'd never seen stars like that before."

He'd taken her to his family's cottage in upstate New York. But rather than staying inside, they'd gone to sleep under the night sky, the moon reflecting off the lake's gently rippling surface. They'd only been dating a few weeks, but he already knew he loved her.

"Then you thought you heard a coyote." He laughed against her neck.

Annie had always been a city girl, through and

through. The wide outdoors fascinated her. It was strange and foreign, with so many shadows she wanted to explore. It was exactly how he'd felt falling for her. Love wasn't something he knew much about.

It's still not something you know much about.

"Joe," she whispered. She hadn't called him that since they'd bumped into each other in the park. It had always been Joseph. Formal. Stiff. Unfamiliar. "If you don't stop rubbing against me, I'm going to go crazy. Don't make me beg."

"Never." He pushed forward, dragging the head of his cock through her wetness until he found the right spot.

When he slid inside her, the tight heat of her sex made his head swim. God, she felt good. While they were both acting on instinct, it all came rushing back. The drag of her nails on his shoulders, her teeth at his neck—she loved to bite. Not hard, and not to do any damage. But sharp, little nips that left him with tiny red marks the morning after. She liked to mark him. Claim him.

And he wanted to do the same.

"That feels…" Her breath was hot on his ear. Little puffs of fire that swept through him. "So incredible."

He brought his hands down to her ass, digging his fingers into her smooth, firm flesh. Her body was different—changed. But the way she loved him was like no time had passed. For a moment, he wished it hadn't. He wished that his time in Singapore was a nightmare he'd finally woken from.

I've missed you.

He drove up into her, primal instinct fueling his movements. Her thighs started to flutter at his waist, her muscles tensing and relaxing in quick succession, indicating that an orgasm was close.

"Oh God…" she gasped. "It feels so strong, so—"

"Don't fight it." His mouth covered hers, his tongue driving between her lips as he thrust up into her. Her face was wet from the spray of the shower, the water droplets sliding along her cheeks and catching on her lips.

"Joe," she mewled into his neck as the first wave of her orgasm hit hard, making her arms tighten around him like a vise. "I've missed you."

The words were so hoarse. Had he imagined them? Was he hearing what his subconscious wanted? Pretending his words had come from her? The rushing water and slap of skin on skin had nearly drowned her out. Or had they? Perhaps his mind was filling in the blanks. Taking the words from his head and putting them into her mouth.

There wasn't much more he could do to hold on. Annie's body was heaven in his arms; the way she clung to him was a balm for his soul. And the way she rocked her hips, a wicked glint in her dark eyes, left no opportunity to draw things out. With one last thrust, he seated himself deep inside her and came hard, cradling her head with his hands and pressing their foreheads together.

Yeah, this was an epic mistake.

Annie held on to Joseph's arms as she lowered herself down. Her legs were Jell-O infused, making the rest of her body shaky and uncertain.

You told him you missed him. What the hell were you thinking?

At least she'd managed to keep her celibacy a secret. That would have been worse. That she was so pathetic in her pining for him that she hadn't been able to move on.

Sucking in a big breath, she looked up. "Well, that was…"

"Fun? Reckless?" He was so disheveled and handsome that it was physically painful to look at him. "Ill-advised?"

"All of the above." She sucked on her lower lip.

The water was still warm—one of the perks of living in an expensive condo building. She shifted under the spray to clean herself up and then wrenched the taps shut. Joseph kept a hand on her shoulder as he reached outside the shower to grab a towel, like he thought she might bolt.

She would have if it wasn't for the stupid Jell-O legs.

"Do you regret coming in here?" He wrapped a towel around her shoulders and rubbed his hands up and down her arms.

"No." It was the only honest way she could answer him. Because her body hadn't felt this satisfied in a long time. Her limbs ached, and the spots where his facial hair had rubbed against her skin felt sensitized in a way that was exciting and new. But that was the key thing to remember: it was physical. Nothing more.

Any feelings attempting to push their way into the equation could be written off as nostalgia. They'd had good times. A lot of them, in fact. But that didn't change anything.

They stood in the shower, his magnificent body spattered with water droplets and looking so perfectly cut, she suddenly felt a little intimidated. She tugged the towel tighter around herself. Joseph's hair was darkened by the water, and against the slate-and-stone backdrop of the bathroom, his eyes appeared even more vibrant.

"So…" She averted her gaze. "This is a little awkward."

Usually after sex, they would curl up on the couch or in bed. They'd talk and laugh and often end up going for round two. And since she had no other experiences to draw on, she wasn't sure what to do. Neither one of them was making the first move.

"I can make some coffee," he offered. "Is that… Fuck, I don't know what I'm doing."

"Yeah, me neither. This is kind of unchartered territory."

The tension eased a little in her chest. For some reason, the fact that he also seemed a little awkward made her feel better. If he'd turned into a playboy with smooth moves, she would have wondered how he'd honed those skills. And with whom.

You know he's been with one other woman since you. At least.

Annika Van Beek. Daughter of wealthy Dutch expats living in Singapore. Tall, blond, slim but curvaceous like a Victoria's Secret model. An It Girl who frequently graced society pages. She'd even been photographed for the *Sartorialist* in leather trousers and vintage YSL. And the one interview Annie had read about her made it seem like she was a genuinely lovely person.

The woman was literally everything Annie was not.

"Why don't you get changed? I'll get us something to drink." Joseph's lips pulled into a smirk. "Something stronger than coffee."

"Stronger is good." Annie swallowed and went to turn away.

But before she could leave the fantastical bubble they'd created in his shower, Joseph lowered his lips to hers. The kiss was searing and exploratory; he coaxed her mouth open and tipped her head back. It was possessive. Passionate. The kind of kiss that could truly destroy her.

When he released her, she groped for the shower door to steady herself. This was insanity. Tomorrow she would wake up, and the world would be colored by this mistake.

You've done it now. Having a drink isn't going to make a difference.

Annie clutched the towel as she padded to the guest bedroom to change into something warm. Outside, rain pelted the windows, blurring the city skyline and making streaky patterns on the glass.

"Just a drink." She shook her head and wriggled back into her jeans and a fresh sweater. She was out of clothes now, having not packed enough for more than two nights. Tomorrow, she would need to face her apartment. "One drink. Keep your hands to yourself."

Easier said than done. Even after shower sex hot enough to melt the floorboards beneath her feet, she didn't feel sated. There was a lot of catching up to do, and her body's needs would not be hushed with this one offering. No matter how good.

She followed the sound of clinking crystal and found Joseph in the main room. He stood at the sideboard, sweatpants hanging low on his hips, broad shoulders hugged by a white cotton T-shirt. It wasn't anything special, but on him… Well, the guy could make a potato sack look like a million bucks.

She watched the muscles in his back flex as he moved, grabbing two heavy tumblers from the cupboard. There were three crystal decanters sitting on a silver tray, but only one had anything in it. She recognized the items from when they'd lived together. Two of them were old—family heirlooms that'd belonged to his grandfather. The other had been a gift from her. A ship's decanter that she'd found for a steal at an antique market.

For some reason, it surprised her that he still had it. Maybe because she'd scrubbed all presence of him from her possessions, tossing out gifts and cards and mementos as she'd found them. Every so often she'd come across something tucked away at the back of a drawer or in the pocket of a bag that hadn't been used for some time. And every single time, that item would be donated, sold, or tossed in the trash.

Yet he'd kept that special item. Perhaps he'd forgotten who had gifted it?

"Don't hover, come and get a drink." He hadn't even turned around, yet he knew she was there, quiet as a mouse.

He poured two glasses of whiskey and went to fetch her an ice cube.

"You remembered?"

"That you like to butcher your drinks?" A cheeky smile crossed his lips.

It was an old joke. Something he'd teased her about. On their second date at a fancy bar, she'd wanted to do something nice for him. Knowing he liked whiskey, she'd forked out more than she could afford for a glass of Blue Label…with Coke. At the time, he'd politely drunk it and hadn't said a word, but later on, he taught her to appreciate his favorite drink. Although she preferred it with ice, and he would always go for a splash of water.

"Yeah, I remembered." He handed her glass over and held his up. The soft chime of their clinking crystal rang through the room.

Annie took a sip, relishing the warmth in the back of her throat contrasting with the cool knock of the ice cube against her lips. "So, do we need to set some ground rules for this thing?"

She walked over to the couch and sank deep into the corner. Then she pulled one of the throw pillows into her lap for added protection.

"This thing?" Joseph followed her and sank down into the opposite corner. He pulled one long leg up to rest his ankle over his knee, his free arm stretching along the back of the couch as if in invitation.

This thing *does not involve snuggling.*

"Yeah, like…what happens in the shower stays in the shower." She took another sip, this time longer. "Or in this apartment, at least."

"You're worried I'm going to tell someone?"

She snorted. "I guess not. You probably want people to know even less than I do."

He frowned. Joseph had a lot of different frowns— one for when he was angry, one for when he was sad, one for when he was confused. It was like his parents hadn't taught him any other facial expressions as a kid.

"Well, I can guarantee my mother knows now. No doubt the old man would have gone home in a rage because I didn't invite him in."

"Why didn't you?"

He settled his glass against his thigh. "I couldn't be bothered dealing with his shit, to be honest."

Annie blinked. In all the time she'd known him, Joseph had never said anything bad about Morris in front of her. It was a line he'd never previously crossed.

"Things have been a little...tense since I got back." He laughed in a way that told her he was making an understatement. "And he could tell the whole world for all I care. You came to me with a problem. I chose to help. It's none of anyone's goddamn business."

"Wow, Joseph Preston. Since when do you have a rebellious streak?"

He shot her a look. "People change, you know."

Had she changed since they'd broken up? She still cared about the same things: her family, her work, and now the people she could help with Bad Bachelors. Maybe she was more guarded.

Maybe?

Okay. She was definitely more guarded. But that wasn't change so much as evolution. Growth.

"Why did you do it?" he asked. "Bad Bachelors, I mean. Why did you create something like that?"

She sipped her drink. "Something like what?"

"Something so...controversial."

"It wasn't meant to be controversial," she replied.

"You had to know it would ruffle feathers."

"Sure. But sometimes feathers need ruffling." She watched him, waiting for a sign of judgment. Disappointment. But she got nothing. "I felt powerless when you left me. Then I watched Darcy get her heart broken. And Remi too. We all deserved so much better than to be discarded."

His jaw ticked. No doubt an argument or a rebuttal sat on the tip of his tongue, but for whatever reason, he chose to stay silent.

"I wanted to do something about it. I wanted to give women a tool to help them navigate the dating world. A safety net."

"It sounds like you have."

"You think so?"

He nodded. "I read through a lot of emails last night. It sounds like you've helped a lot of women."

"I've upset a lot of people too." She drained the rest of her whiskey and placed the glass on the coffee table. "Even my friends."

She had no idea why she was telling him this. She had even less idea why he would care. But it was like she'd popped the cork from a champagne bottle, and all the words fizzed out of her. She told him about Remi.

"The director of her show was reviewed a lot on Bad Bachelors. It caused him problems with his business, and he lost funding from one of their big investors. She came to me, wanting me to remove his reviews." Annie cringed at the memory. Remi had been so upset, and Annie had been forced to choose. From one day to the next, she vacillated on whether or not she'd made the right call. "I said no. The integrity of the site is based on the fact that I *don't* curate reviews. I don't want to influence people's opinions. I only want them to have the truth."

Well, after her slipup early on when she'd posted information about Darcy's fiancé, that was. What she'd done was utterly wrong; she knew that. And she'd made it a point not to repeat that mistake.

"And she wasn't happy with that?"

Annie shook her head. "No, she was furious with me because she said the reviews weren't only hurting her boss and the show. They were hurting her too. We haven't spoken since."

"Have you tried to make up with her?"

"I'm scared," Annie admitted. "I'm scared that she's going to hate me forever. If she did, I wouldn't blame her even a little bit."

Joseph didn't say anything. He simply sat there and bobbed his head.

"Aren't you going to tell me I've done something horrible?" Annie asked, shifting on the couch so she was facing him head-on. "Aren't you going to tell me that it's an evil idea to think we can rate humans? That it's simply my broken heart talking?"

It was easier to use her words as a defensive shield. Because he'd already gotten too close. Far too close. He'd waltzed back into her life, and *she'd* gone to him. It was just like the hacking attack she'd fallen for—effective because she'd made the connection. *She'd* been the one to suggest further contact.

And she couldn't blame him at all. It was her doing and hers alone.

"Why would I say that?" he asked.

"Because if you read the emails, you must have seen the bad ones too."

His blue eyes were so unnervingly still. Luminous. It was like stepping out onto a frozen lake and not knowing whether the surface would be strong enough to hold you. She waited with bated breath to see if a crack would form beneath her feet.

"I did." He studied her, and she clutched the throw pillow tighter to her chest. She hated the way he could see through her like that. Like he knew everything. "And if you think I'm going to side with people who are threatening your safety over the fact that you built a website, maybe you don't know me very well after all."

That was her Joseph, always so levelheaded. She'd been the firecracker in that relationship. Hot-blooded. Quick to spark. She was fire, and he was ice.

It's why they'd been so combustible, and ultimately incompatible.

"Have you told your family about it?" he asked.

She bit down on her lip. "No."

For a moment, she wondered if he might ask why, but he didn't. Her answer was ready—she didn't want anyone to know because the crazies would inevitably come after her, so the fewer people who knew, the better. It was a safety thing—for them and for her. But he wouldn't buy that. He'd know there was more to it.

They would be ashamed of you…

She shut down that nasty little voice in the back of her head. Her parents would understand. They'd seen firsthand what the breakup had done to her. How she'd crumbled and turned in on herself. They would support her… Wouldn't they?

"I should get to bed," she said, pushing up from the couch.

Joseph's eyes tracked her awkward movements. Her mind was at a disconnect with the rest of her—one part telling her to reach out and grab his hand, to lead him to bed with her. And the other part was ringing warning bells.

It was one thing to have hot and heavy sex in the shower, but it was quite another to crawl into his bed, knowing she'd fall asleep entwined with him the way she used to.

"Thanks for the drink," she said.

She headed to the guest room and closed the door softly behind her. When Joseph didn't follow, she knew he'd received her message.

Chapter 12

To: Query@Bad-Bachelors.com
From: Mr.Justice@fakemail.com
Subject: It's about time I introduced myself...

Dear Leanne (or do you prefer Annie? I found both names in your files.),

I guess by now you've figured out that I got a whole lot more out of your computer than just a happy snap from your webcam. I have your address, your phone number, your date of birth, your personal photos...

I could post that information online for the enjoyment of the thousands of men you've pissed off with your website and app. Did you know there are entire forums dedicated to what people would want to do with that information? I bet you hadn't even considered that. Why would you? You're stuck in your own little bubble, thinking about nothing and no one but yourself.

Now, I have to admit you've done a good job with protecting your site. Cloud hosting has made my attempts at a DDoS attack difficult. (Do you know what DDoS stands for? I doubt you've ever heard of it, so I'll tell you in case you'd like to google it. Distributed denial of service.) Not to mention your biometric encrypted passwords. Well done.

Oh…but you made one critical mistake. Do you know what else I have? The code for Bad Bachelors. That's right. Do you remember saving the source code to your hard drive for safekeeping? No?

I had a close look and found something *very* interesting. You left a little message in there. Do you even remember writing it? Maybe it was your way to remind yourself why you started Bad Bachelors. It's a dedication, of sorts. A love letter in a website that's clearly been created by someone who had their heart broken.

"To Joseph, this is for you."

It didn't take me long to work out you were referring to Joseph Preston. Lucky you kept those pictures of the two of you. You have a high-profile ex, it seems. He's a CIO now. What a big shot! I bet it would be awkward for him if it came out that his ex-girlfriend created Bad Bachelors. Maybe people would wonder if he had a hand in it. I could certainly make it look that way.

I don't have to release this information.

Shut the website down. Issue an apology to all the people you've hurt. I'll be kind and give you a few days because I'm a nice guy.

Mr. Justice

ANNIE WALKED INTO HER FAVORITE CAFÉ AND ORDERED A latte. The words came easily, because she was on autopilot. The truth, however, was that her brain had short-circuited. Overnight, Joseph had heard back from his contacts. It seemed no one had leaked her details online, at least not on any of the major forums where that stuff tended to appear.

Which meant they were likely dealing with one sicko instead of a mob.

Based on that, she'd convinced Joseph she would be fine to head out on her own and start doing some of the necessary things—like changing her phone number. He'd wanted her to go to the police, but that would have to be a last resort. After all, the police would want to know why someone might be targeting her, and she couldn't answer those questions without exposing that she was behind Bad Bachelors. As far as she was concerned, too many people knew already.

The plan was for her to go to work for the day and then meet Joseph back at her place in the evening. They'd check her apartment out together and figure out what to do next.

But that was before she'd received *the* email. The one that made her blood freeze in her veins and the breath catch in the back of her throat. The one that had given her the awful, sinking sensation in the pit of her stomach.

To Joseph, this is for you.

When she'd typed those words into the code—a little message for herself, a private reminder that nobody using the site would ever see—it had been with burning resentment. Bad Bachelors wasn't born right after he left. For almost twelve months after, she'd been a zombie, drained of emotion and purpose. Drifting through each day. Trying to be strong for her family.

It had taken that long for the numbness to burn away, leaving her with simmering anger. One day she'd done that stupid thing that all broken hearts do at some point: she'd searched his name. When an article announcing his engagement to Annika Van Beek popped up, it was no less painful than a sledgehammer to her heart.

Engaged. Barely a year after they'd split up. It was like the final twist of a knife already embedded deep in her chest. A cruel blow to her self-esteem. While she struggled to move on, tripping awkwardly through dates and going home alone every single time, he'd already found someone else. The worst part of it was that the article had quoted Joseph's father.

"Annika is a perfect match for my son. She's the kind of woman we always hoped he would find, and we look forward to joining the Preston and Van Beek families."

That day, Annie's vision had been a wash of red. It had descended like a fine mist, coating her completely. She'd saved the article, in case she had a moment of weakness and wanted him back. And then she'd started to code the website. It had taken her over a year to build it, since she was learning everything piece by piece. But when she decided to do something, she would throw herself into it. Some advice from a former coworker had helped her secure the site—cloud hosting with multiple redundancies, a super-secure encrypted password system.

And Bad Bachelors was born.

To Joseph, this is for you.

She *had* forgotten about that message. Maybe not forgotten…but ignored. Suppressed.

What had changed in the scheme of things? Nothing. He was still her ex, still the guy who'd shattered her understanding of love and loyalty.

Annie smiled at the server as her latte was passed over, but the expression felt brittle. She carried the cup to a small, empty table in the corner of the café and let the warmth of the drink infuse her with a semblance of normalcy.

Nothing had changed. So why did thinking about him feel a little less painful? A little less like punishment?

"Annie."

Her head turned at the sound of a familiar voice. "Remi, hi."

Remi stood, holding a paper coffee cup between her hands. Her ballerina's figure was encased in tight black jeans and a pink coat, a thick cream scarf wrapped around her neck. Being an Aussie, she always felt the New York chill more quickly than those who'd lived through the snowy winters from childhood.

"I wasn't sure you'd come." Annie's relief took the edge off her worries.

Remi bobbed her head. "Well, here I am."

"Do you want to sit?"

"Uh…sure." Remi set her cup down and shrugged out of her coat and scarf. Underneath, she had on a fitted sweater. "How are you?"

God, this was so awkward. It hadn't been like that

with Remi before. Not since the first time Annie had gone to visit Darcy after her new roommate had moved in and the three of them had ordered pizza and sipped wine out of plastic cups. She'd liked Remi right away. Liked her carefree attitude and snappy humor and genuine friendliness.

Then you had to go and flush all that friendship down the toilet.

"Good." Annie nodded. The silence stretched on until she was sure the tension was starting to infect the people around them. The couple next to them stood and left. "How's Wes?"

Remi sighed. For a moment, Annie thought she might unleash the fury. After all, that was how they'd ended things last time. Remi had asked her to choose between their friendship and Bad Bachelors. Annie had stubbornly refused to interfere with the reviews on the app and thus had picked technology over her friend.

It's not about technology. It's about purpose. Truth… Isn't it?

"What are we doing?" Remi shook her head. "I don't want to sit here and make bullshit small talk. I'm assuming you didn't invite me here for that."

That was Remi, always cutting to the chase.

"No." Annie shook her head. What reason was she supposed to give? That she was desperately trying to get things back to the way they used to be, even though she knew it was impossible? Could she even salvage things? She had no idea. "I wanted to apologize."

"Took you long enough." Remi folded her arms across her chest.

"I wanted to give you some space after…" Annie sipped her coffee, but it tasted like nothing. "You know."

"I don't know if space is going to help things."

"I know you're pissed off at me, and you have every right to be. But I *am* sorry and I don't want to lose you as a friend." A sick, twisting feeling took hold of Annie's stomach. "I've always been one of those people who shied away from being part of a big group. I'd rather have one or two great friends than an army of acquaintances. But I knew from that first night you moved into the old place with Darcy that you were one of us."

"Really?" A smile ghosted over Remi's shiny pink lips. "I never thought I'd fit in with cool New Yorkers."

"Maybe not, but you fit with Darcy and me. The *uncool* New Yorkers." That earned her a laugh. "I know I shouldn't have kept you out of the loop, especially after Darcy found out about…what I was doing." She hated talking in code, but the café was crowded. "We're supposed to be a team, the three of us. I betrayed your trust, and I didn't treat you the way a friend should."

"No, you didn't."

"And," she continued, needing to get it all off her chest. "I know you were angry that I wouldn't remove Wes's reviews. I really let you down."

Remi nodded. "I *was* angry. But I put you in a position where I forced you to choose, so I guess I can't really be upset that you picked a side simply because you didn't choose me."

Annie hadn't wanted to delete the reviews, not just because it would ruin the integrity of the site but also because it might create a link back to her. And since

protecting her identity had been her biggest concern—
and was still her biggest concern—she hadn't been able
to give her friend what she wanted. It was pure selfish-
ness on her part. Pure self-preservation.

"How's everything going with Wes and the show?"
She'd wanted to ask so many times in the last month,
but each time she'd gone to dial Remi's number, she'd
chickened out.

A dreamy look passed over her friend's face. "Wes is
great. And now that our relationship is out in the open
and the show is being well received, the pressure is off
a bit."

"You were amazing." Annie had gone to the opening
night of *Out of Bounds*—Wes's modern dance production
in which Remi was the star—and had bought tickets
for her team at work to show her support. She wanted
Remi to succeed, regardless of whether the possibility of
friendship was still on the table. "My coworkers couldn't
stop talking about it in the office the next day. I don't
think anyone had ever seen a show like it before. It was
incredibly unique."

"Thanks." Remi looked a little less wary now. "We
worked really hard to get it off the ground the second
time, but I'm glad we persisted. We've extended our
run since the shows were continuing to sell out, which
is great."

"Wes must be really proud."

"He is."

That awkward silence settled over them again. It was
unfamiliar. She and Remi had always been comfortable
talking about "real" things. Darcy had been the one in

their group who shied away from life chats and dissecting feelings. But Remi was an open book—honest and charming and unafraid of the sticky subjects.

Maybe that's what you need to do now. Just lay it all on the line and hope that Remi understands your position. Lots of people remain friends even if they don't agree on something.

"I had thought about killing it," Annie said. "The whole thing."

Remi's rich, brown eyes narrowed slightly, and she sipped her drink. "Really?"

"Yeah. I've thought about it a lot, actually. It's hard being a villain."

"You're not a villain."

"No? I've caused trouble for Reed and Darcy, and for you and Wes." She bit down on her lip so hard that the metallic taste of blood seeped onto her tongue. "I get people telling me every day what I'm doing is wrong and appalling and hateful. Am I just toying with people's lives?"

"You're not the one writing these reviews." Remi sipped her drink. "Do you think Amazon feels guilty if someone trashes a book? They provide the platform, not the reviews."

"We're not talking about books though. These are real people." The words caused something to shift in Annie's chest. She hadn't voiced these reservations aloud before—but that didn't mean they hadn't been circling in her brain. "Real relationships. And I give people a platform to say what they like. I draw attention to them."

"How much attention?"

She cradled her drink, looking down into the milky

depths. Her reflection was distorted. "I'm getting fifty thousand hits a day on the website, and it's growing. People are looking at it from all over the world. The app has over a hundred thousand downloads."

"Bloody hell."

"I know."

"And you didn't monetize it?" Remi shook her head. "You'd be filthy rich by now."

"The money isn't the point." In fact, the one thing she had to support her claim of really wanting Bad Bachelors to be a positive thing and to help women was her lack of monetization. It wasn't a get-rich-quick scheme. It wasn't a get-rich-slow scheme either.

Despite that, she got daily requests from brands wanting space for ads and investors wanting to buy in. But that wasn't what motivated her.

"My friend Mish has been using your app," Remi said. "The barista who works next to her Lexington barre studio asked her out a while ago, but she'd come out of a bad relationship. When she looked him up and found he had nice reviews saying what a sweet guy he was, she decided to go out with him. I haven't seen her this happy in a long time."

These were the stories that kept Annie going. Hearing how Bad Bachelors had brought people together, how it had helped them out of a dark place and into a better one, made all the threats and the shitty emails worth it.

"It made me realize I have to shoulder some of the blame for our fight," Remi said. "I *can* see how you're helping women."

"Am I helping more than I'm hurting?" That was the real question. "I honestly don't know."

"You can't be held responsible for what other people say. If the app didn't exist, they would still be saying these things. God knows the kind of shit I see on Twitter and Facebook on a daily basis. I doubt Mark Zuckerberg has a crisis of conscience over what people post on his platform."

The knot in Annie's stomach loosened. "I'm glad your friend found a good guy."

"She really has. We had them over for dinner the other night, and he's a lot of fun. He's good for her." Remi set her cup down and reached over the table to hold Annie's hand. "I don't want to lose you either."

The emotion and stress and confusion of the last few days settled on Annie like a boulder in the pit of her stomach. Tears threatened but she blinked them away, entwining her fingers with Remi's. "You and Darcy are like my family. It's been killing me to not pick up the phone and call you. I wanted to, but I knew you needed some time. And then after a week or two passed, I couldn't bring myself to do it. I was frightened you'd never want to see me again. It's been hurting like hell."

Remi nodded. "It's been hurting me too."

"Can you forgive me for being a shitty friend?"

"You're not a shitty friend, Annie. You know I struggled with the concept of the app. I still do, truth be told. I've seen the damage it can do, but I've also seen the good. It sucks to be hurt, and you tried to find a way to help people avoid that." She squeezed Annie's hand. "And I have to say, seeing what it's done for Mish, I think I understand the positive side a little more. I don't know if I agree with it on the whole, but I *do* see both sides."

Would she think the same thing if she knew that Annie had hidden a message in the code to take a shot at her ex? At one point in the not-too-distant past, Annie wouldn't have cared one iota if it brought his career down. But something had changed.

You're fooling yourself into thinking he has feelings for you because he agreed to help and because you had sex. That's not how it works.

Regardless, it was impossible to shake the guilt. For the past three years, she'd blamed him for everything, and that wasn't fair. Whether he had feelings for her now or not was beside the point.

"I shouldn't have shut you out," Annie said. "It was a dick move. I was so hung up on protecting myself that I didn't think enough about how you would feel. I don't want to be that person who puts her friends last."

"I'm glad you called," Remi said with a smile. "And I'm glad that we're stronger than one argument. I was furious at the time, but I've thought about it a lot. I don't necessarily agree with what you did, but I understand where you're coming from. What you've tried to create."

"So we *are* still friends?" She hardly felt as though she deserved it.

Remi leaned back in her chair and crossed one long leg over the other. "I can't only have one uncool New Yorker friend. I'm told you guys come in pairs."

Annie contemplated telling Remi about what was

going on with Joseph. But she wasn't sure talking about it would achieve anything. It wasn't like Annie and Joseph were going to become an item simply because they'd slept together. In fact, she was determined to make sure that was a one-time thing. Pleasurable as it had been, booty calls were not her style. Especially not booty calls with the potential for emotional damage.

She would *not* get sucked into believing that he cared about her.

"So what now?" Remi asked. "What are your plans for the app?"

"Honestly? I have no idea." Annie shook her head. "I never thought it would get to this point, and I don't know where it should go from here."

What she did know, however, was that priority number one was finding out who was messing with her *and* how she could keep Bad Bachelors going without ruining Joseph's career. If she'd learned anything from her fight with Remi, it was that keeping secrets made more trouble in the long run. And while she wasn't about to go public with her identity, shutting Joseph out when he was the only person who could help her wasn't the best approach.

And that meant she needed to come clean about the message in the code.

Joseph swallowed, his Adam's apple bobbing against the confines of his collar. It felt tight, like a fist squeezing around his windpipe. Which was stupid, since the damn thing was bespoke and made exactly to his measurements. Nevertheless, his fingers itched with the desire to slip underneath the collar to give himself some breathing room.

But that would be a mistake.

Showing weakness now, with bright lights and the shrewd eyes of the financial reporter in front of him, would undermine everything he'd been trying to achieve. He needed to be cool, calm, collected, and in control at all times. But *especially* with a camera trained on him.

"Our strategy is about putting the control back into the customers' hands," he said, reciting the words he'd run through with his communications specialist earlier that morning. "Banking is part of everyday life, and these days that means a mobile device is the preferred method of interaction. Ultimately, our goal is to allow customers to interact with us in a way that suits their lifestyle because our customers are young professionals, entrepreneurs, parents, business owners, *and* retirees. They all have different needs. But the one thing they have in common is that they want control over how they bank. So we're giving it to them."

"You've been very vocal about pushing forward with this aggressive digital strategy, but the fact is, you've got decades less experience than your competitors." The reporter adjusted her glasses. The action felt a little too practiced, almost like she was purposefully appearing accessible and nonthreatening, despite the statement she'd just made voicing the concerns he knew others were thinking. It was a technique: lull the target into a false sense of security. "What makes you think you're the best person to push forward with such an ambitious plan?"

"Who better to be at the helm than someone who's grown up in a digital world? I'm a perfect representation of our growing youth customer base because I've always had a computer close by. I know what our younger customers want and how they behave, because it's what *I* want and how *I* behave. Experience is important, of course, and I have that too. But the value that I bring to the table is that I'm comfortable breaking out of the old way of doing things. I'm here to shake up the status quo."

The reporter nodded, her expression showing some begrudging admiration. "Do you have anything to say to the people who are worried that you're not experienced enough for this job?"

"No, I don't." He looked directly at the camera. "I believe actions speak louder than words, so I'm ready to deliver this strategy and let my work speak for itself."

"Thank you for your time, Mr. Preston." The reporter nodded to the cameraman and he shut off the camera. "It was a pleasure. I'm always happy to see some fresh blood in this industry."

"Likewise. Banking is a small community at this level, so my appointment has certainly made a few waves." He rose up from the chair and secured the suit-jacket button at his waist. "Hopefully that fresh blood doesn't attract any sharks."

The reporter chuckled. "Like your father? Well, you've got him on your side, which is definitely an advantage."

You'd think that.

"Or does he think you should have done your time in the ranks like he did?" she asked. There was that sweet smile and the adjusting of her glasses again.

I'm not falling for it.

"I doubt any father would want to impede their child's career ambitions," he said, turning his wrist up to show the face of his Omega watch, hoping it would give her the hint that the interview was over. "Mine included."

"You could have a career in politics with an answer like that." This time her expression looked a little more cunning. She'd dropped the act now that the cameras were off.

"You never know, one day you might see my name at a polling booth. For now, I'm focused on this job."

"So no plans for a family. No girlfriend begging you for kids?" She leaned against the sleek boardroom-style table in the conference room they kept specially for media purposes.

The decor was a soft white, and the space was decorated with muted, unobtrusive pieces of art—a painting with mixed shades of gray and pale blue, a geometric vase holding a generic-looking plant. Everything was styled to look clean and fresh, modern yet conservative, which was the bank's attempt at a new image. The previous CIO had been an old-school eighties banker with a predilection for Rolls Royce town cars and gaudy diamond-studded Rolexes. A throwback from the gluttonous, pre-financial-crisis era.

Joseph was the pendulum swinging the other way. "I've got plenty to keep me busy at work. There'll be time for a family later."

"That doesn't answer my question about the girlfriend."

Was she coming on to him or simply looking for a story? Either way, he wasn't interested.

Why not? You're a single man.

Technically, yeah. He and Annie *hadn't* made any promises, and he wasn't sure he wanted to. Their relationship was over. But sleeping with Annie and then accepting a date from someone else was a hundred shades of wrong. Their situation was simply…

A problem that needed solving. He was giving her a hand because they'd once cared about each other. The sex was the two of them blowing off steam. It didn't mean anything…did it?

You know it means something. Stop lying to yourself.

The realization washed through him, bringing little relief to the knot in his stomach. Sex with Annie would never be casual; it would never be meaningless. No matter how hard he tried to separate physical desire and emotion, it wasn't possible with her. Because the reason he'd always been attracted to her was because of *who* she was, not simply how she looked.

There was no getting around it. Having sex with her *had* meant something to him, and it would continue to mean something to him.

"Can I say it's complicated?" he said.

"A Facebook answer. You *are* a man of the times." The reporter stuck her hand out, and he accepted it. "If things happen to get less complicated, you've got my number."

He shot Dave a look the second his back was to the reporter, who'd started talking to her team. Dave stifled a smirk, and they headed through the building's conference room and into the elevator that would take them back up to the executive floor.

"That went well," Dave said, scrolling through his tablet. "I haven't seen many interviews capped off with a come-on."

"Me either."

"You weren't in the least bit tempted?"

Joseph yanked at the tie at his neck, loosening the colored silk and popping the button on his collar. "I'm at work."

"Ah, so you're simply a man of principles." Dave nodded. "That's a good thing."

On some level, Joseph felt like he *should* have been interested. The reporter was attractive—with shiny, dark hair and sharp eyes—not to mention she knew her stuff. Capable women had always excited him. He'd worked with a lot of men who wanted trophy wives of the "look hot, stay quiet" variety. But that wasn't his style. He wanted a woman who had a spark to her, a fire. He liked people who could hold their own in a conversation, who enjoyed digging into a debate. He wanted an equal, someone who would challenge him and match him. Who wouldn't fade quietly into the background.

You realize you've just described Annie, right?

He shoved the annoying thought away. He'd likely also described the reporter, so it didn't mean anything. Besides, he had more pressing concerns than shifting through *that* mental minefield.

"That was the last meeting for the day, right?" Joseph's brain was so fried he could barely remember his own name.

Despite having had some of the best sex of his life, he'd barely slept. He kept reaching out in the twilight of almost-sleep, fingers groping for soft skin and silky hair, and finding nothing. It'd jolted him awake every single time. It was like his body had slipped into the past where Annie *was* by his side. They'd liked to sleep wrapped in each other, and he'd never felt right unless her head was tucked under his chin, the scent of her shampoo filling his nose.

"No, you've got one more." Dave tapped at his tablet. "Melinda Landry."

"You didn't tell me I had a meeting booked with my mother."

"Shit." Dave cringed. "It didn't register because the surname is different. I'm sorry, I would have brought it to your attention if I'd known. She didn't mention anything when she called..."

"Welcome to my fucked-up family," Joseph said drily as the elevators slid open and they headed to his office. "Where we book meetings via each other's assistants instead of calling one another directly."

"Melinda Landry as in Landry Cosmetics, right?" Dave asked.

"One and the same."

"It slipped my mind that you two were related. That's quite a pedigree."

Joseph let out a sardonic laugh. "Yes, it is."

The Prestons had been described as "having more money than God." Aside from his father's lucrative banking career, the Preston side of the family was no stranger to wealth. His great-grandfather had started a publishing company in New York that had been acquired for an eye-watering sum before Joseph's time.

His mother's side of the family owned one of the world's largest high-end cosmetics companies. Landry Cosmetics was a beast, aggressively acquiring smaller companies and using their clout to dominate a greedy global market. His mother had been CEO for two decades now and was grooming her niece to take over. They had a strict policy about keeping the company family-run, specifically by women. Since Joseph had three female cousins on that side of the family, he didn't have much to do with the business.

He and Dave rounded the corner to Joseph's office and found his mother waiting. Never one to blend into the background, she wore one of her signature pink suits—today it was a vibrant rose shade—with a black blouse and a necklace made of twisted strands of glimmering beads in pink and yellow.

"Mrs. Landry, it's a pleasure to meet you." Dave stuck out his hand, looking a little star-struck. "I'm a huge fan of your products. I wore Landry Homme on my wedding day."

Melinda smiled warmly and accepted his hand. "Well, you look to be a man of style, so I'm not at all surprised you wear Homme."

"Mother." Joseph nodded to his office. "Shall we?"

Melinda bid Dave goodbye and followed her son into the office. "I'll arrange to have a bottle delivered for him tomorrow," she said, shutting the door behind her. "We're about to launch the silver anniversary edition, and there are a ton floating around the office."

"I'm sure he would appreciate that." Joseph pulled off his tie and stuffed it into the pocket of his jacket. The second this "meeting" was over, he was getting the hell out of Dodge. "What's this meeting in aid of? Haven't you got important CEO business to attend to?"

Melinda took a seat on the other side of his desk, smoothing her hands demurely over her pencil skirt. At fifty-five, she'd mastered the art of being both formidable and approachable at the same time. She was highly respected for her business savvy and her head for numbers, and yet she didn't seem to suffer the fate many other powerful women did. That was, Melinda was not generally despised for her strength by men *or* women.

Over the years, Joseph had learned more about success in business from his mother than his father, though everyone assumed his father had been the one to groom him. Ingrained sexism was a bitch like that.

"I might be a CEO, Joe, but I'm a mother as well. Which means I tend to family business when it is required."

That was Melinda-speak for *Your dad told me everything*. He rolled his eyes. "What did he say?"

Her cool silvery gaze remained steadily on his. "That you had a guest when he came to visit."

"A guest." He shook his head. "Annie was staying with me. You don't have to skirt the issue like it's a taboo subject."

"Okay, let's cut to the chase then. Are you back together?"

"Not that it's any of your business, but no." He turned to face the view from his office. Winter was fast approaching, and not only were the days rapidly cooling, but they were shortening too. It was barely five, and the sun had started to sink against the horizon.

"She just happened to be staying at your apartment while you weren't there?"

"What's the point of this conversation?" Joseph turned and folded his arms across his chest. "If you think you need to reiterate everything you said three years ago, you don't. I know your views on her, and I don't want to hear them again."

His mother sighed. "I'm not here to upset you."

"Just a by-product, is it?" He looked up to the ceiling and prayed for strength. "I can only imagine what Dad said to her before I arrived."

"We're trying to protect you," she argued.

"No, you're trying to protect your money. Let's not kid ourselves about that." He all but spat out the words. "It's *always* about the money. I don't know how many times I've told you that she doesn't give a shit about it. She doesn't want to steal my inheritance."

His mother pursed her lips. "She certainly didn't hesitate to take the apartment from you. An apartment that you bought *with* your inheritance, I might add."

"One, I *offered* her the apartment. Two, it was our home. That's why she was happy to stay." His parents had been livid to find out about the arrangement he'd made without consulting them. In Joseph's mind, it was easier not to fight. Besides, Annie had needed it more than he did. The decision had been an easy one. "In any case, it was in *my* name. Therefore, I owned it and could do with it as I pleased."

"Despite what you think, it's not about the money."

His mother twisted a large ring with a winking yellow stone around her finger. "You're my son, and I care about you. So I don't want to see you getting hurt again. You deserve to be with someone who *wants* to be part of this family, someone who fits in with your lifestyle. Our life involves a lot of scrutiny and obligation, and that's not for everyone."

He wanted to rebut every point. Annie had never been given a *chance* to fit in with his family and the "lifestyle" that involved a lot of snooty charity events and snapping cameras. From day one, his father had ostracized her, labeling her a gold digger and doing his best to make sure she knew she didn't belong. His mother hadn't treated her so badly, but she'd never spoken out against her husband's behavior.

That's why he'd broken when he'd overheard Annie telling her family that she wouldn't move to Singapore with him. Because he'd *always* stood up for her. Always tried to show her that she was special. But years being stuck in the middle had worn him down, all the jabs—from both sides—chipping away at his patience and resolve.

And that's exactly why he wasn't going to engage in this discussion now.

"I'm not with her, Mom." He purposefully kept the ice out of his voice. "We had some stuff to sift through, and she stayed at my place. In the spare room."

It wasn't technically a lie, even though he was letting his mother believe nothing had happened between them. "Regardless, I wasn't about to let Dad throw his weight around and demand that I kick her out because he'd decided to show up unannounced."

She nodded. "I'll talk to him."

"Don't bother. It won't change anything."

Melinda rose and came around Joseph's desk, enveloping him in a hug. She smelled of violets and roses—her signature scent. Her grandmother had created the perfume Lindy in her name when she was only a little girl, and she'd never worn another perfume since. The scent always smacked him with memories, of her loving embrace as she kissed him good night hours after he'd gone to bed. His mother had never been home for dinners, always working hard on her business and missing the things that other mothers didn't. But he'd never once begrudged it because she'd told him over and over, "Never let anyone tell you that you can't do something. Never let someone else's limitations define you."

But the fact that she constantly backed his father, no matter how much it hurt her son, was still a barrier between them.

"We *do* want the best for you," she said as her slender arms squeezed him tight. "You're at such a pivotal point in your career, and I don't want to see her derail you."

He bit back his reply. There was no point. His mother would always think she was doing the right thing, and he would always disagree. At least where Annie was concerned. And none of it mattered. Because they weren't an item. They weren't getting back together.

For some reason, the finality of that thought hit him like a punch to the chest.

You'd better get over that feeling right now. Sex doesn't change anything.

Chapter 13

"In times like these, we need the truth more than ever. Thank you for giving us a platform."

—AlwaysTheBridesmaid

ANNIE WAS ABOUT TO LEAVE HER POSITION ON THE FAUX-leather couch in the reception area of her apartment building when Joseph finally strode through the front doors. He was still in his suit—black today—with a long, gray coat over the top and a red scarf around his neck. The sight took her breath away. There was nothing sexier than a man who knew the value of a good tailor.

With each long-legged stride, her body wound tighter and tighter. His slightly overlong hair looked as though it had been styled, but now it was mussed—either from the brisk wind or his fingers.

"About time," she said, aiming for a joking tone but missing.

"Sorry, I got ambushed." He pulled the scarf from his neck, and Annie's eyes tracked the smooth wool sliding against his skin.

"CEO?"

"*A* CEO, not *my* CEO." His mouth quirked.

"Ah, Mother Dearest dropped by the office, did she?" They headed to the elevator bay.

"Yeah. She made an appointment with my assistant and didn't bother to clarify our relationship." They squeezed into the crowded elevator, and the back of Annie's hand brushed against him. She quickly tucked her hands closer to her body. "Ten guesses what it was about."

"Only need one," Annie quipped. She could only imagine what Melinda Landry would have said about her. On behalf of her brutish husband, no doubt.

It was probably a good thing they'd never gotten married. Melinda and Morris were the stuff of in-law nightmares.

Yeah, keep telling yourself you're happy it all fell apart.

Against her better judgment, Annie asked, "What did she say?"

"Nothing of note." Joseph moved to the side to let another passenger out.

Within a few floors, they were alone again, and Annie positioned herself on the other side of the elevator. The scent of his cologne was doing funny things to her insides, and that one accidental brush of her knuckles against his leg had been enough to ignite memories of last night. Her body was hungry like she hadn't been screwed six ways from Sunday. She was a starving woman reintroduced to food, and now she wanted to gorge herself.

"Nothing of note, huh? Isn't that Preston code for *I'm too embarrassed to repeat it?*"

"Something like that. You're still fluent?"

A smile tugged at her mouth. They used to joke that his family had its own language, that speaking with his parents required an ability to read between the lines usually reserved for interrogators and FBI agents.

"My Preston is a little rusty," she said. "How do you say 'fuck off' again?"

"'There's nothing more to say.'" He shot her a crooked grin, and damn if it didn't nearly melt her. "Or you could also use 'This is a conversation for another day.'"

"Oh yes, I'd forgotten that one." The elevator dinged, and he held the door for her. "So are you going to tell me what she said?"

Gah! Why did she even want to know? Clearly it wasn't anything good. Why would it be? His parents had never said anything positive about her *or* her family.

"Dad told her you were at my apartment. She came to talk to me about it." Typical Joseph, shutting her out when she had questions. "That's it."

"And what did you say?"

"That it's none of their business."

They reached her front door. Annie fiddled around in her bag for her keys, her fingers shaking. Was it because she was frightened of what they might find in her apartment? Or was it resentment over the crap that his parents had likely been spinning?

"I never did anything to make them hate me," she said, regretting the words the second they left her lips. Too late. "Other than being the hired help."

"I know." He touched her shoulder.

She jammed her key into the lock and opened the door. The apartment was silent as they entered, their footsteps echoing on the floorboards. It only took a few minutes to establish that they were alone. And that her apartment appeared not to have been touched.

You have a high-profile ex, it seems. I don't have to release this information. Shut the website down. Issue an apology to all the people you've hurt.

Mr. Justice's words ran over and over in her head.

"I want to know what she said. What she *actually* said."

Why was she fixating on this? Maybe because it delayed the moment when she had to confess to Joseph that she'd put his career on the firing line. That as much as Bad Bachelors had its upside, she'd started it with hatred in her heart.

It doesn't matter how it started. It matters how it is now. The good you want to do now.

"Do you really want to get into this, Annie?"

This was the old Joseph she remembered—back straight, chin forward, eye contact unwavering. The beard gave him an extra level of toughness. He had the posture of someone who'd been in the military. Though, she supposed, living under Morris Preston's rule probably wasn't that different from living with a drill sergeant.

"I do." She swallowed and mentally prepared herself for the sting of his mother's words.

He made a gesture with his hand as if to say *It's your funeral*, and then he sucked in a breath. "She said I deserve to be with someone who wants to be part of my family and who fits in with my lifestyle."

No matter how hard Annie braced herself for the criticism, it still hurt like hell when the blow landed.

Of course, by fitting in with their lifestyle, Melinda was referring to the fact that Annie had never known which fork to use in their multiple-course dinners and that she'd laughed too loudly and worn the wrong things. Because people *actually* stuck to the "no white after Labor Day" rule. *Yeah, right.*

She shrugged out of her coat and hung it on the stand next to the front door. "They assumed we were back together? Interesting."

"Well, you *were* at my apartment," he said. Joseph was still in his coat, his red scarf bunched in one hand. "While I wasn't there."

"I suppose you putting Morris in his place didn't help."

"No, it did not."

"What else did she say?"

He eyed her warily. "Just that she wanted to protect me."

Wow. That was quite a comment. His parents had done nothing *but* hurt him—always putting their careers before their only child. Always pushing and pushing and pushing, piling on expectations until Joseph's shoulders sagged from the weight of them. Always teaching him to swallow his feelings.

The sad thing was, Annie had looked up to Melinda Landry. The woman was everything she'd wanted to become—successful, elegant, smart. As much as Annie loved her mother, she'd wanted the kind of success Melinda had. A thriving career, to break through glass ceilings. To be a businesswoman admired for her brains.

But Melinda had never returned Annie's admiration. No matter how many genuine questions she'd asked and no matter how many times she'd shown interest in Melinda's work. Annie had always suspected it was more about Melinda maintaining the peace with her husband than anything Annie had done.

"And what did *you* say?" she asked.

"That I thought she was more concerned with protecting her money than me." His face didn't show an ounce of hurt, but she knew it was there. Lurking beneath the surface like a sea monster, waiting for the right time to rear its ugly head. "And that we weren't together."

"I'm glad you clarified." Was she, really? Because it didn't feel like that. "The relationship is over, and I'm still causing you problems with your family."

"They're causing themselves problems by not minding their own goddamn business."

Annie held her hand out and gestured to Joseph's scarf and coat.

His blue eyes searched her face. It was like being scanned by a laser. "You want me to stay?"

"What, are you sick of playing bodyguard already?" She tucked her hair behind her ear, and he frowned. Dammit, she needed to stop being so obvious.

"Thought you might be sick of me hanging around."

They were circling each other. It was horrible being in limbo, not knowing whether to walk away or to stay and touch the flame like she so badly wanted. And her guilt hung heavy, like a thick chain around her neck.

"I should be." Her mouth was as dry as cotton wool. She stepped forward, reaching for his scarf again, but when her fingers clasped the soft cashmere, he didn't relinquish it.

So much for "What happens in the shower stays in the shower." Have you got an emotional death wish or something?

"Should?" He stilled like a hunter tracking a deer, his gaze holding her captive. Melting her defenses.

How did he *do* that? He made her feel like everything was right when it most certainly wasn't. He made her crave the security of his arms, the soothing balm of his kiss. Made her desperate for his touch because it blanked out all the messed-up, self-deprecating thoughts in her head.

She tightened her grip on the scarf. "I'm not sick of you playing bodyguard."

"Are you planning to screw me and then send me to bed alone?" His voice was rich and deep, like top-shelf whiskey and dark chocolate. His cologne mingled with the faded scent of rain on his skin, and she drew it deep into her lungs.

"What if I am?" she whispered.

"I don't want that."

"You seemed totally fine about it last night."

"Let's say I had an epiphany. I thought I could keep things casual, but I can't." He wrapped the scarf around his hand and yanked it toward him, bringing her closer. "This isn't just fucking to me. It can't ever be *just* fucking with you."

God. Why did he have to say things like that? It was so tempting to believe. So tempting to let herself be fooled. Her lip trembled. "That's all I'm offering."

"It's not enough." Another yank. She was almost toe-to-toe with him now. "Think what you want about me, Annie. But I didn't leave because I didn't care. I didn't leave because I stopped loving you."

No, please stop…

"I left because it was too hard to love you. Because loving you made me feel like I was splitting myself in half."

Dammit. Why did he suddenly have to be good at saying what he felt? Why couldn't he have done this three years ago? She squeezed her eyes shut. That was exactly how she'd felt—constantly trying to keep his family happy and failing. Trying to keep her family happy and hurting him in the process.

"No," she whispered. "I don't want to hear it."

"You *will* hear it," he growled. "Goddammit, Annie. I loved you so much I didn't know how to control it."

"You're not supposed to control it." She released the scarf, but his hand encircled her wrist before she could get away. "That's the problem, isn't it? We're both control freaks, and love is free-falling. It's crashing on your ass, and it's messy and painful—"

"And glorious."

It had been the most glorious thing in all her life. But love was also like being Icarus. And that's how every dream and hope she'd had for love and life had burned to the ground.

"Then why did you propose to someone else, huh? Was that glorious too?" She tried to tug out of his grip, but he held her fast. Tears burned in her eyes, but she'd be damned if she shed a single one in front of him.

"It was a mistake." He shook his head. "I should never have done it. I ended up making a fool of myself and hurting her in the process."

"Did you love her?" Annie didn't want to feel the sharp snap of jealousy whenever she thought of him with another woman, but there was no escaping it.

"For a second, I thought I did. But I realized I was making the same mistake as when I left here," he said. "I let my parents get into my head. But it wasn't love."

Her knees almost buckled. The day she'd seen the announcement of their engagement, Annie had wept on her sofa for hours. The shot of Joseph looking proud and handsome, with a stunning woman on his arm, was only made more painful by the close-up shot of the ring. The familiar hunk of stone. It was supposed to mean something. A future. A symbol of a bond.

"I regret proposing to her. I regret...hurting her." For once, Joseph's slick demeanor wasn't to be found. His eyes burned brightly like blue flames, his Adam's apple bobbing as he swallowed. "She didn't deserve to be treated like that."

"You broke up with her?"

"She called it off, actually." He released her hand, but she didn't step back.

"Why?"

"She said she could never compete with you."

The air evaporated in her lungs. "*She* couldn't compete with *me*?"

How were they even on the same plane of existence? Annika Van Beek was the type of person Joseph *should* have married. She had the social standing, the family pedigree, the looks. And as much as the photos could be trusted, it'd looked as though she was infatuated with him.

"She said I hadn't let you go, and she didn't want to

live in another woman's shadow." He let out a harsh laugh and rubbed a hand over his beard. "And she was right. I hadn't let you go. I wasn't ready to be with someone else."

The confession wrenched in Annie's chest, ripping her old stitches open and undoing all the work she'd put into moving on. But as much as she wanted to resist, the damage was done.

"What are you doing, Joseph? Are you toying with me?"

"No." He brushed her hair behind her ears. "You used to tell me all the time I was like a vault. I never gave anything away."

"I did say that." She let him tip her face up to his.

"So I'm setting the record straight. This isn't a booty call. It won't ever be like that between us." His lips brushed the corner of her mouth. "If you can't handle that, then tell me to stop."

Stop.

Her mind screamed it loud and clear, but her mouth was frozen as his lips burned a path along her jaw and down her neck. Deft fingers slid along the back of her head, sliding between strands of her hair and holding her captive.

Don't stop.

His lips parted hers, his tongue sliding into her mouth as he walked her past the couch toward the huge windows. Even with their eyes closed and hands occupied, they navigated the space with ease. He knew every inch of this place, despite the furnishings being different now. More importantly, he knew that Annie loved nothing more than the cold press of glass against her back.

When they'd walked into the apartment, they hadn't needed the lights. But the sun had sunk low, and the city was starting to shine as darkness settled over them.

Joseph was tightly coiled—the past and present fusing together until it was impossible to untangle them. Annie let out a soft gasp as she bumped against the glass. Planting one hand next to her head, he spread his fingers wide. Rain splattered, coating the outside of the window in glossy droplets.

"You haven't told me to stop," he said.

As much as it would kill him to walk away now, waking up tomorrow and having her regret it would be worse. But for once in his life, he needed to man the fuck up and be honest with her. For too long, he'd let his upbringing stifle his ability to communicate. And it had ruined them. Ruined any chance they might've had at happiness. And running hadn't fixed a goddamn thing.

"I don't want you to stop," she said, her hands coming to the hem of her cashmere sweater. The fabric lifted up to reveal her trim waist, then the pale-pink lace of her bra as she whipped the sweater over her head. "Whatever it means to you is your business."

The fabric hit the floor, and her hands automatically went to the fly of her pants.

"I've told you what it means," he replied. The sound of her zipper being undone cut through the air. "And

I'm not going to play this game if you think you can shut me out afterward."

Her hips wriggled as she pushed the fabric down her legs. Her dark gaze speared him like a lance to the heart. "You're seriously telling me you'll walk away unless I agree to cuddle afterward?"

"I wasn't thinking about cuddling as much as burying my face between your legs in the middle of the night." He watched as she continued to undress, peeling her pink panties down her legs and then reaching behind her back for the clasp of her bra. The action made her breasts thrust forward. "I want to fall asleep with those perfect breasts pressed against my chest and those legs tangled with mine. I want to wake you up with my lips on your skin, and I want to pull you on top of me while you're still half-asleep."

She stood naked before him, shadows playing off her porcelain skin. Her nipples were rosy and pointed, her skin dotted with goose bumps. Dark, soft curls highlighted the apex of her thighs. But her eyes were the giveaway—the blackness of her pupils eating away the rich brown irises he loved so much. They shimmered, alight with a potent mixture of defiance and excitement.

"I want to see your fists curling into the bedsheets when you come." His hand was still planted next to her head. His body growing hot beneath his suit and coat. The contrast of him being fully dressed next to her nakedness made it feel even more illicit. "I want to hear that sexy, raspy sound you make when my name is the first thing out of your mouth in the morning."

She tipped up her nose to him. "This is just sex. Nothing more."

"Will thinking that help you sleep better at night?"

"Going to bed alone will help me sleep better." Her voice didn't give him an inch.

Joseph leaned in and pressed a kiss to her lips. "Don't let the bed bugs bite then."

He turned and walked through the apartment, stopping to pick up his scarf from the floor. Annie hadn't made a move to get dressed and remained standing, staring him down. Her shapely figure was silhouetted against the Manhattan skyline, and it was possibly the sexiest thing he'd ever seen.

But trying to ignore what he really wanted was what had gotten him in trouble in the first place. She could huff and puff, but he wasn't going to sleep with her if she wanted him to act like it meant nothing. He'd rather go home and take a cold shower.

Or twenty.

At least being at home would prevent him from thinking with his dick in the middle of the night.

"Don't answer the door for anyone but me," he said. "I'll call when I'm on my way over first thing in the morning."

She didn't say a word as he pulled the apartment door open and let it swing shut behind him.

Chapter 14

"Dear Bad Bachelors, I won't be using your site anymore. Thanks to you, I'm getting engaged to the man of my dreams, all because you gave me the courage to ask him out!"

—BadBachelorsSupporter

ANNIE'S HEART POUNDED AS SHE PAID THE CAB DRIVER and then stepped out onto the sidewalk in front of her parents' place in Bensonhurst. After a night of tossing and turning, she needed to sift through the crap in her head and figure out what to do next.

So she'd fired off a text to Joseph, telling him she'd gone to stay with her parents and not to bother coming over. Her boss would probably flip that she was bailing on work for another day, but she hadn't taken a single day off this year so she had plenty of vacation days racked up.

Besides, she couldn't face being in the office, not with everything hanging over her. When was the last time she'd had so many competing emotions? So much uncertainty? Not in eons.

Maybe because you've tried your hardest not to feel anything at all for the last three years?

She glanced down at her phone. No response from Mr. Justice after she'd asked him for more time. She didn't want to close down Bad Bachelors, but she didn't want Joseph to suffer either. Why had all her biggest life decisions felt like that? Like choosing between her and him?

The one thing that always helped her sort out her feelings was talking with her mom.

Annie stuffed her phone into her bag and looked up at the house. It was similar to every other one on this street—semidetached, about ten years late for a new paint job, and still worth over a million. Not that her parents would ever move. They were the kind of people who committed. Forever.

The sound of her boots echoed in the quiet street as she jogged up the steps to the front door. It was early, seven in the morning. But her parents would have been up for an hour at least. She couldn't remember a time when they'd slept in past six, even on the weekends. Her stepfather usually tried to be at the café by seven thirty to open at eight. And her mother still prepared a proper breakfast every morning.

The doorbell made a shrill sound inside the house, and a second later, the door swung open. "Bella?"

"Hi, Dad."

Sal's deep frown was enough to bring the onslaught of tears she'd been doing her best to fight ever since she got out of bed that morning. They rolled fat and hot onto her cheeks, streaming down to her chin. His arms were around her in a second, her face pressed against his threadbare undershirt, her tears soaking through the fabric. The bristly scratch of his mustache was comforting and familiar against her head, and the smell of him—like coffee grounds and Drakkar Noir—helped what was left of her emotional guard come crashing down.

This house was the only place where she could truly be open. Her safe place. Family was the most precious thing in her life.

To the point that you let it make your relationship with Joseph come second?

There was no escaping the truth on that matter. She *had* put him second. But at the time, she'd thought it was the correct order. Family should *always* come first…right?

"It's him, isn't it?" Sal's question froze her to the spot.

She pulled away and swiped her tears with the backs of her hands. "What?"

He ushered her inside, closing the door behind her and flicking the lock. The house smelled like lemon and something buttery. Pastries.

"Joseph." It wasn't often that Sal's voice had a flint-like edge.

Despite what most stereotypes had told her about Italian men and their tempers, Sal was pretty much a Labrador retriever in human form. He was sweet, funny, fiercely loyal, and he adored the heck out of her mother and all the women in the family. He loved readily, wore his heart on his sleeve, and accepted people into his circle no matter where they came from.

But the way he said Joseph's name was like he'd discovered his capacity for hatred.

"That's why you're crying, isn't it? Connie told me he was back."

Shit. The universe seemed determined to test her.

"Yeah, he's back." She wrapped her arms around herself. Maybe she shouldn't have come here...

"Give me your coat." Sal held out his hand and waited while she complied. A neat line of hooks ran along the wall in the entryway, above a rack crowded with her mother's collection of colorful shoes. "Come. Let's have a coffee."

Annie's mother looked up as they walked into the kitchen. Her surprise morphed into a big smile, which quickly fell into a frown when she noted her daughter's expression. Sofia was also at the table, munching on a cornetto with lemon filling. A stray dot of it clung to her cheek, and she swiped at it with her finger.

"What's wrong?" her mother asked, her chunky gold earrings jangling as she jumped out of her seat. "What happened?"

To some people, the love of a family like Annie's could be smothering. They all knew each other's business, and the words *I don't want to talk about it* fell eternally on deaf ears. Since Annie's father had died when she was little, her mother had loved her hard enough for two people. Sometimes more. When Sal came along, Annie had been worried that he might steal some of that affection. That his presence would somehow diminish her relationship with her mother. How wrong she'd been.

It had been tough back in the day, with Connie's cleaning job and Sal's construction work only affording them the bare minimum. But they'd never been short on hugs or laughter in their house. Never short a shoulder to cry on or an ear to talk off. So Annie had gone into the world unprepared for the reality of relationships, unprepared that she might fall in love with someone whose family wouldn't accept her. Unprepared, ultimately, that one day she might have to choose between her family and something else.

"I just…" Annie stood in the doorway, watching Sal fiddle with the Bialetti coffee maker while her mother and sister stared at her with concern seeping out of every pore. "I needed to be here."

Sal shot Connie a look, but didn't say anything. Then her mother's expression developed an edge. How did they communicate like that? "What did he do? I knew he was going to be trouble the second I heard about him coming home."

Sofia raised a brow. "Who are you talking about?"

"Joseph." Her mother spat the name out in much the same way Sal had. Annie didn't know what to fear more—her mother's explosive anger or Sal's quiet wrath. "What did he say to you, huh? *Porco giuda!* You tell him to come here and explain—"

"Ma, stop." Annie shook her head.

"No, I will not stop." Connie was in full Mama Bear mode. Her curly brown hair moved as she shook her head, the tightly coiled spirals bouncing around her face. "*Che due coglioni!* He thinks he can come back here and upset *my* daughter like that. No. I will not—"

"Ma!" Annie came forward and gripped the back of an empty chair. Sofia's head swung back and forth between them like she was watching a ping-pong match. "Please. It's not like that."

God, how was she supposed to tell her parents what

was going on? Of course they were angry. While her mother was in surgery for her double mastectomy, Annie had sobbed like a baby. She'd refused to leave her mother's side once she was returned to her hospital bed, sleeping on the couch until Sal all but carried her out of the room, forcing her to go home and get some proper rest.

Annie had fallen to pieces during the time her mother needed her most, and her family had rallied around her. Telling them that she'd brought Joseph back into her life would be like spitting on all they'd done. On all the support they'd given her when they should have been focusing solely on Connie.

"What did he say to you? If he tried to say sorry, I hope you slapped his face." Her mother's cheeks were the same shade of pink as the flowers on her apron. "That man does not deserve to be forgiven."

"Connie," Sal growled. "That's enough."

The room fell silent as Annie's big bear of a stepdad came over to the table with a fresh cup of coffee. The steaming black liquid filled the air with a calming aroma, and he added a dash of milk—just the way Annie liked it—before handing it over.

"I'm just saying," her mother went on. "I will not tolerate people hurting my baby."

"He's not hurting me." Annie dropped down into a seat and brought the mug up to her lips.

If he was hurting her, it would probably be easier. She could cast him back to Voldemort status and move on. If he'd come home and decided to screw his way around Manhattan, then she could point the finger and say, "See, I told you he was a jerk." *That* would be easy. Comfortable, even.

But knowing that he regretted his engagement and that it had broken down because his ex thought he still had feelings for Annie was mind-boggling. She had no idea what to do about that. As for the sex he labeled as meaning something...

Yep. You're screwed.

Or *not* screwed as the case might be. Because how the hell was she supposed to admit it wasn't "just sex" to her either? That no matter how much she wanted to divorce the physical and emotional, she...couldn't.

"You're here, and you're in tears," her mother pointed out. "What other conclusions should I draw?"

Annie sighed. "I don't know."

"Come on, Sofia." Sal patted his youngest daughter on the shoulder. "Time to go to school."

It wasn't, of course. Sofia had at least another half hour before she needed to leave, but that was her stepdad's way of giving Annie some space. He grabbed a cornetto and his coffee mug and herded Sofia ahead of him, pausing only to plant a kiss on Annie's head before they left her and Connie alone.

"Eat." Her mother gestured to the pastries, but Annie's stomach was in knots. She'd be lucky to keep the coffee down, let alone anything else.

"I'm not hungry."

Connie looked like she was about to argue, but then she took a seat. "Tell me what's going on."

Where did she even start? Annie swallowed. "I don't know what I'm doing anymore."

"What do you mean?"

"With my life." She shook her head. How had she gotten so lost? Before the breakup, she'd been so focused. She'd known *exactly* what she wanted. Then Joseph had left and she'd started Bad Bachelors, and before she even knew what was happening, everything had spiraled out of control.

She'd almost lost her friends. Her safety was being threatened. Her performance at work had been slipping because she was so distracted and disengaged. Now she was fighting feelings for the man she'd loved so hard it had sent her down this dark path.

"I thought I was doing all the right things."

She hadn't gone the rebound route and jumped straight into bed with another guy. Or worse, jumped straight into another relationship. She'd found something to throw her energy into, found a purpose to keep her motivated. She'd coped with the stress of her mother's cancer by being even fitter and healthier, by working hard and keeping busy.

Wasn't that what all the articles said? Don't fall in a heap; drink your water and eat your veggies. Find something in life to be passionate about.

How did it all go so wrong?

"I'm trying to help people, but other people are getting hurt, and I don't know what to do. Am I supposed to quit because people are angry, or do I push on knowing that I *am* helping some people?" Annie was fully aware that she was babbling and likely making zero sense. "It's like everyone's screaming, and I can't figure out who to listen to."

"You never did well with gray areas." Her mother's dark eyes softened. "When you were a kid, you used to make me write out my rules so you could refer back to them if I got upset at you. We ended up with a list as long as *War and Peace*, because every time a new scenario came up, you'd make me write it down."

Annie's lip twitched, a smile close despite her worries. "I remember that."

"And then there was the time I had to go down to your school because you'd called Mrs. De Luca a 'bad teacher' because she gave you a C even though you said you'd satisfied all the assignment criteria."

"She *was* a bad teacher." Annie sipped her coffee, the tension slowly leaving her muscles. "You can't tell people to do XYZ and then grade them badly because they didn't include ABC."

Connie laughed. "True. But that's life, isn't it? You think you have everything covered, and then out of nowhere, you get hit."

"Yeah. It sucks donkey balls."

Outside, two car doors slammed and Annie watched Sal's truck pull out into the street. The large tree across the road was totally devoid of leaves now, and the spindly branches shuddered in the wind. Annie clutched her mug and turned her attention to the dark liquid.

"People are more resilient than they think," Connie said. "I never thought I'd survive after your father died."

Annie sucked in a breath. Her mother rarely broached this topic, and Annie had often wondered if she continued to think about her first husband, given she was so happy with Sal. All the fairy tales spoke of finding your "one true love," but Annie had never been able to reconcile with that. If love was a one-time-only deal, who was her mother's true love: Sal or Annie's father?

"The day he died, I remember sitting in the hospital while you played at my feet. I stared at the floor and I prayed, 'Dear God, please open a hole right now, and I will gladly jump in.'" She fiddled with the chunky gold hoop in her ear. "I wanted to die too. I wanted to go with him because I didn't think I was strong enough to face things on my own."

But her mother had turned out to be made of incredibly tough stuff. She'd worked multiple jobs most of Annie's childhood, sacrificing her own needs to see that Annie got an education, then she'd faced breast cancer head-on and with a *don't fuck with me* attitude.

"Do you still think about him a lot?" Annie asked.

Her mother nodded. "Yeah, I do. He was such a big part of my life. It's not like I can turn that part of my memory off just because I'm with Sal. And frankly, I don't want to forget him. But that doesn't mean I can't be happy now."

Maybe that's what was happening with Joseph. She was stuck in the limbo of wanting to move on but clinging to the good memories. Maybe all the desire she felt now was nothing but her brain trying to recapture the past. Her mother was proof that it was possible to move on. To find happiness and a second love.

Because the fact remained that Annie *had* loved Joseph. Him leaving couldn't erase that, as much as she'd wished for it at the time. Yet their breakup didn't have to mean she'd squandered her "one chance" at true love.

"What's going on, Annie?" her mother asked. "It's not like you to show up in tears."

"I had a moment of weakness." She shook her head. Her mother would never act like that—letting fear sweep her along until control slipped through her fingers. "I should have called first."

Connie rolled her eyes. "Leanne Carmela Maxwell, you are *always* welcome in this house. I don't give a shit if it's three in the morning. I am your mother, and I will always be here for you."

Annie got out of her chair and went to hug her mother. There wasn't a bad feeling in the world that couldn't be soothed by a warm, maternal embrace. Her mother smelled of coffee and orange rind mixed with the faded perfume lingering on her clothing. Her frizzy hair brushed Annie's cheek as they held each other.

"Whatever it is, you'll figure it out," Connie said, pressing a kiss to her daughter's cheek. "You're smart and strong, and you have a good heart. If you stop freaking out for a minute, you'll figure out what to do."

Annie wanted so badly to tell her mother about the whole mess—about Bad Bachelors and Joseph and how she had no idea what she was doing. No idea what she wanted. Lately, she'd lost interest in her day job, lost interest in everything outside Bad Bachelors. For someone who'd always had a strong sense of purpose in life, she'd become adrift.

"Why don't you come to my catch-up with the girls today?" Connie said. "We've got our monthly Fuck Cancer poker game."

Annie smiled. Growing up, she'd always been a little

embarrassed by how loud and brash her mother was. She cursed and wore outrageously colored outfits and never let people ignore her. As an adult, it made Annie love and respect her mother even more. She was who she was. And screw anyone who didn't like her.

"I don't want to intrude."

"Nonsense. We're going to Joan's house. She would love to see you again." Her mother winked. "Plus you're terrible at poker, so the ladies will take all your money."

Annie laughed and shook her head. Maybe getting away from her computer and her troubles for a few hours would be exactly what she needed to get some fresh perspective. "Okay," she said, nodding. "I'd love that."

A few hours later, Connie and Annie had driven to Red Hook to visit Joan and the rest of the Fuck Cancer gang. There were five ladies in total: Joan, their host, who'd survived breast cancer like Connie. Amity, a self-defense instructor and model who'd survived ovarian cancer. Martha, a foster mom to three boys, who'd survived endometrial cancer. And Bonita, an artist who'd survived colon cancer. They were a motley crew, a mismatched group of women who probably wouldn't have crossed paths if it wasn't for the cancer patient support group where they'd all met.

"The November meeting of Fuck Cancer is now in session." Joan banged a hot-pink, rhinestone-studded gavel on her kitchen table. Annie had no idea why they started the poker game with a gavel, but who was she to question it? "We're here for a good time, not a long time."

"Hear, hear!" Glasses were raised all around.

"It's nice to see you again, Annie." Martha smiled as

she shuffled the cards. Her voice barely rose above the sound of the other women catching up. She was the quietest of the group. "Are you on vacation at the moment?"

"I just took the day off work." She watched as Martha's hands deftly dealt the cards, her purple glittery nail polish catching the light. "I needed some peace and quiet to clear my head."

"And you came here?" Bonita laughed. "The only peace and quiet you'll get from me is when I'm dead."

"Amen to that," Amity chimed in. In contrast to Bonita's long, black dreadlocks, Amity had a shaved head. Something she'd decided to keep after losing her hair during chemo. That, coupled with the tattoos peeking out from the edge of her top, gave her a tough vibe. And she *was* tough, but she was also one of the sweetest, gentlest souls Annie had ever met. "In fact, I was teaching in my class the other day that being as loud as you can is just as important as putting up a physical fight."

"I may have to come and visit you at the studio," Annie said, picking up her cards. They were playing Texas Hold'em, and she had a two and a four. Unsuited. Not a good start, but she threw a few chips into the center anyway. "Pick up a few pointers."

"Why?" Connie's sharp voice made Annie cringe. For a moment, she'd forgotten her mother was sitting right next to her.

"It's good to know that stuff." Annie shrugged, aiming for nonchalance, but having no idea if she'd hit the mark.

"This isn't anything to do with Joseph, is it?" Her mother narrowed her eyes.

"The ex-boyfriend?" Amity raised a brow and tossed in a few chips herself. "Don't tell me that douchebag is back on the scene."

Of course, Joseph had been a hot topic of conversation among the ladies after the breakup, because Annie had been at the hospital with her mother a lot. Back then, Connie had only met Amity and Joan.

"He came back from Singapore with his tail between his legs," Connie clarified, and Annie shot her a look. "What? It's a fact."

Martha waited for everyone to finish betting. Then she dealt the flop. Two queens and a four. Annie watched for everyone's reactions.

"No, it's not. He came back for work," she said, still looking at her cards. As soon as that popped out of her mouth, she cursed herself. "Or so I heard."

Connie raised an eyebrow. "Did you hear it directly from him?"

Thanks to Darcy's quick thinking, Annie had managed to avoid telling the truth the first time her mother had asked. But now, face-to-face, she couldn't find it in herself to lie. "Maybe."

"Ease up, Mama." Amity placed a hand on Connie's arm.

"I'm sorry I didn't tell you." Annie tossed a few more chips into the center, having no idea if she should have folded or not. It was hard to concentrate under her mother's scrutiny. "I knew you'd be pissed that I'd seen him, and I didn't know well enough how I felt about the whole thing to answer all the questions you'd undoubtedly fire at me."

Her mother looked sheepish. "I *would* have asked questions. But only because I don't want you to get hurt again."

"Once a heartbreaker, always a heartbreaker," Amity added. "And I'm out."

"Not always." Martha shook her head and flipped the next card over. Another four. If the river turned out to be a two, Annie would have a full house. "My Daniel and I split up once, for a whole year. Sometimes you need time away to remember why you got together in the first place."

"Daniel did not leave you in the midst of a family crisis," Connie argued. "He didn't *abandon* your family."

Annie looked at her mother, the card game forgotten. For once, when the subject of Joseph arose, Connie sounded hurt rather than angry. Almost as though she'd taken his leaving more personally than Annie had realized.

"He was part of our family," Connie added. "I've known him since he was a little boy. He always used to play while I was cleaning his parents' house. Then, when you started dating, he came over a lot. We really got to know him like a son."

It had never occurred to Annie that the breakup might have affected her parents in that way. That *they'd* also lost someone the day he'd walked out.

"I liked having him around."

Annie swallowed, her throat swollen from all the emotion rising up. From all the things she didn't want to feel because it would be easier to be numb like she had been the last three years. But his return had been like taking a scalpel to her stitches. And now she saw her feelings for the bloody mess they were.

"I liked having him around too." Annie leaned her head on her mother's shoulder.

But there was no hope of them ever getting back together, was there? Not with Bad Bachelors potentially being a threat to his career, and all the baggage they had between them. Her family hated him; his family hated her. Literally, everything was stacked against them.

"He left because I chose to stay here while Ma was sick," Annie said.

"And that was a very noble choice." Martha nodded. "Your dedication to your family says a lot about who you are, Annie. You're a loyal woman. We need more people like that."

"Except I made that decision without him." At the time she'd been too blinded by hurt to really understand the nuance of their last fight. "He left because I made the decision and then told other people before I told him. I totally shut him out of the conversation."

Connie frowned. "You never told me that."

"I didn't think it mattered at the time. I needed him and he left, so he was in the wrong... Right?" But being with Joseph again and seeing him for the man he really was—imperfect but kind, smart, protective—had helped her understand even more where things had gone wrong. He'd never been the kind of person to be cruel or thoughtless. But it was easier to think of him that way so she could hang on to her anger.

I'm not going to play this game if you think you can shut me out afterward...

The man had walked away from her naked body because he didn't want to cross a line unless they were both on the same page. A line that said he still cared about her in some way. That she wasn't just sex to him. She wasn't just physical need.

"But that was *our* decision to make, and I didn't give him the chance to have a say." It was time for her to take responsibility for that. "I pushed him out just as much as he chose to leave."

Connie didn't say anything. It wasn't a normal reaction for her mother, a woman who had an opinion about *everything*. Now wasn't the time to dig further into the past, however.

"Sorry, I didn't mean to come here and derail the conversation," Annie said.

"Not at all." Joan, their vivacious host, waved a hand, causing a stack of bracelets to jingle. "This is a safe place where we can discuss anything, woman to woman."

"Or woman to *women*," Bonita said with a grin. "You need that group of people in your life. The ones who will let you say anything, who know when to listen and when to bring wine."

It made her think of Darcy and Remi. Of her sisters. Her parents.

And Joseph.

For better or worse, he fell into that category too.

"Now, are you in or out, girlie?" Martha asked with a grin.

Annie looked at her cards. She threw a few more chips into the middle. "In."

Martha turned the river card over. A king. Amity

crowed and showed a full house while the rest of the ladies groaned. "Come to Mama!"

Annie's phone buzzed with a notification, and she pulled it out of her pocket while the other ladies moved the conversation on and started dealing the next round. The text was from Joseph, wanting to know if everything was okay in his usual spare language. But the fact that he'd contacted her said more than the three-word text itself.

Just as she was about to tuck her phone away, she decided to scan the Bad Bachelors inbox to see if Mr. Justice had responded. He hadn't, but another email caught her attention. The subject line read: Acquisition offer for Bad Bachelors.

The first few times she'd received an email from a law firm representing someone who wanted to buy Bad Bachelors, she'd shrugged the whole thing off. But for some reason, now the idea of it being someone else's responsibility didn't seem quite so unappealing.

Chapter 15

To the owner of Bad Bachelors, it seems the letters from my lawyers have been ineffective in catching your attention. Maybe the personal touch will work better? Let's cut to the chase. I feel that Bad Bachelors has massive earning potential and global possibilities if managed by the right group. As such, I want to buy it from you. Of course, I will compensate you handsomely in recognition of the time and effort you've put into building and growing both the website and the app. My lawyers have said not to promise anything until we talk. But you're not talking, are you? I don't blame you. Bad Bachelors has certainly created some opposing views. But I love a little controversy. We should talk. How about we start negotiations at $5m?

JOSEPH HAD BEEN ON EDGE ALL DAY. AS IF GOING HOME last night with the biggest case of blue balls ever hadn't been enough to keep him on pins and needles, the fact that Annie had taken off to see her parents had pushed him into the stress zone. The thought of her leaving the safety of her apartment while some asshole was threatening her had him wanting to roar the roof off his office building. He knew it was illogical, but he needed to be certain she was safe. And that meant knowing exactly where she was at all times.

Never mind the fact that his stomach was in knots over what Connie and Sal would say if she decided to tell them he and Annie had seen each other again.

He leaned back in his chair, staring bleakly at the stack of board reports that required his review. They were tediously long. Inappropriately long. But that's how things were done at the bank—printed paper and plastic bindings. Highlighters. The old way.

In a burst of frustration, Joseph shoved the papers off the edge of the desk. The heavier reports fell straight to the floor with a *thunk*, and a few loose sheets fluttered in the air before landing. A second later, the office door swung open.

"Everything okay?" Dave raised a brow and looked at the mess.

"Yeah. Perfect." It was already dark outside, the weather as miserable as Joseph's mood. "What are you still doing here?"

"My boss was crankier than usual today, so I didn't want to bail early." Dave made a move to pick up the files, but Joseph waved him away.

"Don't. If I make the mess, I clean it up." He shoved his chair back and went around to the front of the desk, gathering the paper and reassembling his pile.

"You're not like most people in this job." Dave observed him. "I've been an assistant for fifteen years at the bank, and I've worked with eight different executives in that time. I can categorically say we need more people like you."

"People who throw tantrums?" Joseph tried to make a joke, but his tone was flat. Nothing would buoy his mood until he heard from Annie and knew that she was okay.

You're making life hard for yourself by caring about her. She's not your responsibility anymore. What part of that isn't clear?

"People who treat those around them with respect." Dave leaned against the doorframe. "You could have made me pick up your crap. You could have hit on that reporter the other day. You could have flipped out at the intern who spilled coffee on you this morning."

Joseph glanced down at the stain on his white shirt, which he'd deftly hidden all day by keeping his suit buttoned. He'd been in back-to-back meetings since seven, so there'd been no time to change. And he wasn't about to send Dave out to buy him a new shirt when there were more important business matters to take care of.

"A stained shirt is the least of my problems."

"That's exactly it though. There are a lot of egos around this office, and that's why we don't run this place efficiently."

"I used to put my ego first," Joseph said, almost to himself. "It never led to a good decision in my entire life."

Ego had driven him to ask Annika Van Beek out because she was the kind of woman he was "expected" to date, and for once he wanted that positive reinforcement. Ego had driven him to leave Manhattan—and

Annie—when he should have stayed. Ego had driven him to take this new job because it was prestigious and would cement his name in the industry. Worse than all those things was that ego had driven him to try to please Morris Preston, because he wanted some artificial badge of honor that said he was worthy of the family name.

But he hadn't cared enough for Annika, he hated this job, he resented his father, and he'd never stopped loving Annie.

The thought was like being flung off the Brooklyn Bridge.

You don't love her. You used *to love her. Big difference.*

"We need people to shake things up," Dave said. "People who are willing to get their hands dirty if it means achieving results."

Joseph studied his assistant for a minute, unsure exactly what he was referring to. "How so?"

"Not accepting *that.*" He pointed to the stack of papers in Joseph's hands. "Not accepting the 'that's how it's always been done' mentality. They think they can browbeat you because that's what they did to the last guy."

Joseph nodded. "So I heard."

"You're used to dealing with people like your dad, so you should have some practice in managing egos." Dave held up his hands as if in surrender. "And I don't mean to insult your family, but your father has a reputation. Much like the people on our board. They don't like change."

It was true. Joseph had come to the conclusion that anyone training for an executive position should be put through a "childhood learning" course along with their MBA, because it was like dealing with a bunch of misbehaving toddlers.

And for what? You get no personal satisfaction out of this job, just the kudos for managing to convince someone to hire you a good two decades before most people who take up this post.

He tried to ignore the sinking feeling in his gut. Personal satisfaction wasn't something he felt entitled to, because a career wasn't about that...or so Morris had told him. It was about a person applying their skills where they were best suited, working their way up to a position where they could make a name for themselves. Where they might build power.

And for what?

There was that question again.

"Maybe you need to play dirty," Dave said with a shrug. "Following the rules doesn't seem to be getting the results."

"That's not how I do things." Playing dirty was his father's approach—manipulation, coercion. Threats. "I won't stoop to their level by being a bully."

"Even if it's the only way to change things?"

"It's *never* the only way."

Dave nodded, but it was clear he didn't agree with Joseph's stance. "Is there anything else you need tonight?"

"No. Go home. Be with your family." Joseph dumped the papers on his desk in a messy heap. "We'll deal with this crap tomorrow."

Dave bid him good night, and Joseph paced his office for a few more moments, unable to relieve the tension coiling his muscles. When his phone rang, it almost made him jump out of his skin.

He snatched the device off his desk. "Hello?"

"Hey, it's me." Andrew's familiar voice sounded tight. Tense. "Remember how you asked me to give you a heads-up if I saw anything about Bad Bachelors?"

An icy hand clutched Joseph's heart. "Yeah?"

"I saw something."

Joseph did *not* like the vibe he was getting from Andrew, especially since he wasn't the kind of guy who usually enjoyed drama. If he was worried, there was a damn good reason for it.

"It was a cryptic message on one of the boards I've been monitoring for a private contract. I stumbled across it by accident." He paused. "The guy said he'd hacked the person behind Bad Bachelors. No real details. No doxing. But he said he got a name, address, and phone number. Apparently, he also got the source code for the website. But both the site and the app appear to still be up and running, so I'm not sure what that was all about. Maybe they tried a DDoS but couldn't take the site down?"

"Possibly. Anything else?"

"He made a comment about how he didn't just want to take 'this bitch'—his words, not mine—down. But that he wanted to make her understand the damage Bad Bachelors had done by hurting someone close to her." Andrew sighed. "I *know* you're not looking into this for work, so don't even try to feed me that crap. This is some serious shit, Joe."

He ignored Andrew's warning. Likely the guy had

already figured out what was going on, since Joseph's social circle in Manhattan was limited these days. But he wouldn't officially blow Annie's cover. "What about the guy who posted? Is there any information on him?"

"You know what these people are like. They're cocky, but they're not stupid. He's a forum regular. Gray hat, from what I can tell. Doesn't appear to be into anything illegal…well, other than the obvious." It sounded as though Andrew was looking at the guy's profile right now. "He's posted a few times in the general gaming area of the forums. He's also quite active in any threads where people are trying to catch cheating spouses."

"Was there much response to his post?"

"Yeah. Whoever is behind Bad Bachelors, if this guy decides to post their information…it'll be a shit show."

"I know." Joseph rubbed at the back of his neck.

"Is there something I should know?"

"No. Thanks for looking into it."

"Fine." Andrew's voice was tight, and Joseph could practically see his friend's frustrated expression. "I've emailed you screen grabs of what I found. It's not much, but it might help."

"Thanks, man. I really appreciate it."

"Call out if you need help, okay? Or if anybody you know is in trouble." His voice was heavy with meaning. "Even if you don't have a relationship with them anymore."

He resisted the urge to confirm what Andrew was hinting at. "I will. Thanks again."

When he ended the call, his phone beeped with an email notification. It contained the screen caps. He took a moment to look through them, studying the images and language. The user's profile was sparse, nothing but a name—Mr. Justice—and an avatar image of the Eiffel Tower at night. It was blurry, like someone's hand had moved when the photo was taken. Or maybe it had a filter applied. Either way, it wasn't much to go on. But something was better than nothing.

Joseph hit the home button on his phone and then dialed Annie's new number from his recent calls list. When she answered on the third ring, sounding surprisingly relaxed, he breathed a sigh of relief.

"Hey," she said.

"Are you still with your parents?" He wandered over to his big window and looked out over the East River.

"No. I just got back now…and don't worry, the apartment is fine. I checked every cupboard and behind all the curtains." She laughed, but it sounded hollow. Forced. "I, uh… I was thinking maybe we should grab dinner. I need to eat, and I'm guessing you're still in the office."

The invite shouldn't have warmed him at all, but it was like she'd found the heaviest thing resting on his heart and lifted it a fraction. "Yeah, I'm still here."

"Why don't we go to Vince's?"

It was their place. A small Italian restaurant that was a little run-down, but where the food was still melt-in-your-mouth good because Vince himself ran the kitchen. At least it had been that way three years ago. He and Annie had shared countless celebrations and plenty of "just because" meals there.

It's just dinner, nothing more.

But logic wasn't going to cut it right now. Why would she suggest that place, knowing what it meant? Was this her way of hinting that maybe he'd been right, that they *weren't* just sex? Or perhaps she was proving the point that she'd moved on. That old sentiments didn't affect her anymore.

"Meet you in half an hour," he said.

Why the hell had she suggested this place? Annie smiled politely at the waitress who pulled out a chair for her in the back corner of Vince's. The little round table was adorned with a candle almost burned down to its stump, a small bottle of balsamic vinegar and one of oil, and a set of wineglasses.

Memories assaulted her like a slap in the face.

So many birthdays and Valentine's Days and, of course, their first date. They'd been so young that they'd ordered sparkling water instead of wine because she wasn't legally allowed to drink yet. Annie had balked at the prices on the menu, but Joseph had insisted on paying because he was old-school like that. Of course, she'd taken him for coffee the next day in an attempt to make things feel more equal, because she wasn't used to anyone paying for her.

She thought back to how he'd looked then—tall and lanky like a beanpole. He'd worn his hair spiked up like all the guys did back in the post-NSYNC era. And she'd fallen hard. Before that, he'd been a figment of her teenage fantasies. The rich guy who lived in the house her mother cleaned. The house *she'd* cleaned a few times when money was tight and her mom was sick. It seemed kind of romantic then, like a Cinderella story. And he was her Prince Charming.

Of course, those fairy-tale notions were far more glamorous than reality. His parents were never able to see her as anything more than the help. Morris had said as much to her the Christmas before it all went to hell.

If he decides to marry you, I'll make the prenup so watertight you won't ever get a penny. You might become a Preston, but it'll be a formality only.

She'd wondered if maybe that was the reason she'd decided to stay when her mother got sick, despite his offers to fly her back as often as she wanted. Despite the fact that she wouldn't have needed to work in Singapore and could have split her time between the two locations.

Maybe she was over being viewed as a gold digger and a fake at that point. Never mind the fact that she'd loved Joseph in some capacity ever since that first time he'd asked her if she wanted to play Nintendo with him when she was six and he was nine. Their fast friendship as children had shocked Connie, who knew her daughter to be shy and almost standoffish. But not around him. Joseph had always boosted her confidence, even back then.

The front door to Vince's pushed open and Joseph strode in, his broad shoulders encased in a sleek black coat, his hair dampened with rain. He looked like an antihero—with Clark Kent eyes and the dark, brooding edge of Don Draper.

He stopped to talk to the waitstaff at the front of the restaurant, a reserved smile in place. Not his real smile. As he was led into the dining área, his gaze scanned the room until he found her. He was far from the lanky twenty-year-old who'd brought her here for a date. Far from the nervous and sweet boy who'd arrived with a bunch of flowers wrapped in canary-yellow paper like it was something any guy would have done. They'd split a tiramisu, their spoons clacking as they devoured the dessert, laughing over jokes that no one else would understand.

"Hey." She stood automatically to greet him, as if they *were* on a date.

Before she knew what was happening, he'd leaned in to kiss her cheek. The rough brush of his facial hair, the wafting scent of rain and cologne and the leather from his satchel hit her hard. He radiated warmth, his hand landing comfortingly on her arm.

But then he pulled back as if shocked out of the lingering habit. "Sorry, I—"

"It's fine." She waved his concern away and dropped back into her chair, burying her face in a menu. "I think we need wine."

"Yes."

The waitress was still hovering, looking awkward as if infected by their strange energy. Who could blame her? There was this weird push-pull going on. Annie ordered a bottle of Sangiovese and hoped the alcohol would loosen things up a bit. She *had* to tell him about the email from Mr. Justice. Murky as their past was, no amount of anger or hurt would justify her ruining his career. If only she could go back to the day that she'd put that stupid little note into the Bad Bachelors code!

She wanted to slap herself. It had been such an idiotic move. But back then the coding had been an outlet for her. It was almost a joke she told herself to help with the grieving process. She never in a million years thought it would go anywhere…

Never in five million, either.

"Everything okay?" Joseph studied her as he took a seat. His coat had been hung up, along with his scarf, and now he sat in front of her in a dark suit and open-collared shirt.

The man looked so good that it was borderline indecent.

"It's been a big day," she said, bobbing her head.

"How are your parents?" It seemed like he really cared, though she wasn't sure if that was simply the manners his parents had pounded into him.

But her mother's words from earlier that day rang in her head. *I liked having him around.* Perhaps it wasn't such a stretch to think that he'd missed them too.

"Good. Mom's crazy as usual. You know how she is." Annie toyed with her fork since she had no idea what the hell else to do with her hands. "Someone offered to pay me five million dollars for…well, you know."

Dammit, that's not *what you're supposed to be talking about tonight.*

But it was like her body physically resisted the idea of confessing. Every time she tried to put into words how to tell him she was sorry, she clammed up.

"Excuse me?" He blinked.

"Yeah, crazy, right?" She laughed. Nothing about the situation felt real. Maybe she'd fallen asleep, and this was some wacky dream.

"And they came out with that figure?"

"I've been getting emails from some law firm for a while now saying this person wants to make an offer, but this is the first time they've given a number. I never responded because I wasn't interested."

"Wasn't or aren't?"

Good question. A few weeks ago she wouldn't even have considered it. But things had gotten…messy. Complicated. Maybe selling Bad Bachelors would be a good thing? She could pay off her parents' house and set them up for retirement, get a new place of her own. Somewhere far away.

But the fantasy didn't sit right with her. Annie wasn't the kind of person who wanted piles of money, who was content to sit on her backside and have no purpose in life other than to count the zeroes in her bank account. Which was precisely what had made Morris's comment all the more ridiculous. Because she would have happily signed whatever prenup he put in front of her. She'd rather be penniless and in love than wealthy and alone.

And as much as she should have gotten over her notion of true love and finding the perfect relationship, deep down she'd never let go of that dream.

"I don't know." She rubbed at her temples. "It's a lot of money. I keep thinking about how much it would help my parents. I could set up a college fund for Sofia and pay off all of Allegra's student debt."

Then there was the idea that selling would remove power from people like Mr. Justice. If a big company bought Bad Bachelors, they probably wouldn't keep their identity secret since they'd have the kind of resources to protect themselves. Or if they did keep it quiet, they'd have hordes of people to deal with the problem of hackers and trolls.

"But?"

Of course he knew there was a *but* coming. "I never wanted the site to be a moneymaker. That's why I've never charged people to use it, and why I've never diluted the user experience with advertising. It's supposed to help people, and I think information should be free. If I sell it, those people would be looking to turn a profit. Wouldn't that be betraying the women who rely on me?"

They paused as the server arrived with their wine and poured them each a glass. Annie had barely glanced at the menu, but she always ordered the same thing: the arrabiata. Joseph ordered his usual carbonara.

"I guess that depends on whether you think the good outweighs the bad," he said as the server walked away.

"What do you mean?"

"Can you do more good with the money or with"—he looked around to make sure no one was in earshot—"Bad Bachelors?"

"I'm not sure. I hadn't really thought about what else I could do, given the opportunity." But now her brain was ticking, her body fueled with that fizzy sensation that accompanied new possibilities. That accompanied the best question of all... *What if?*

Maybe she could use the money to start a foundation aimed at helping women who'd experienced the darker side of dating. Who'd experienced internet stalking and aggression. Or who'd struggled to reenter the dating scene after a loss. She could have information online, but she could also run seminars too. She could teach women how to protect themselves, how to date safely and confidently.

"You've got that look," Joseph said, his cool-blue eyes crinkled around the edges.

"What look?"

"The look that you get whenever an idea sweeps you away. You sort of glaze over, but at the same time you look so…happy." The dim light of the restaurant made his hair look more golden than usual, highlighting the stubborn strands that curled over his ears no matter how hard he tried to tame them. "I always loved that look."

Her heart galloped in her chest. What the hell was she doing here? Playing happy couples? She reached for her wine and took a big gulp, fortifying herself. She was about to open her mouth when a familiar face loomed.

"Arrabiata and carbonara!" It was Vince, the owner of the restaurant, who was currently dressed in a sauce-splattered apron and had a huge grin on his face. Annie hadn't seen him in three years, but not much had changed other than a few extra gray hairs dotting his temples and the whiskers on his jaw. "I thought I might never see you two again."

Joseph stood and stuck his hand out, though Annie

could see the tension creating a subtle crease between his eyes. Talk about awkward as all hell. "Good to see you, Vince."

Vince chuckled and knocked Joseph's hand away, choosing instead to embrace the other man in a bear hug. In so many ways, the restaurateur reminded her of her stepfather. "And you, Bella. Beautiful as always."

The hug was warm and genuine. On many of the nights they'd popped into Vince's for a bite, he would come out to say hello. They'd been among his first regular customers after he'd opened the place, struggling to keep the kitchen running while also supporting the only server he could afford to pay. Annie had always tipped as much as her meager budget would allow, hoping that one day when she decided to quit the rat race to follow her dream, people would support her too.

"As soon as I saw your order, I came running out to see if it was you." Vince released her with a big grin. "Where have you been? I can't even remember the last time you were here."

Joseph looked at Annie, a silent question simmering in his light eyes. *Should we tell him?* Annie gave him a subtle no. What would be the point of trying to explain their situation? How *would* they even explain it?

We broke up, but now he's back and I invited him here, like an idiot. We're screwing, but I'm trying to pretend it doesn't mean anything. Oh, and I'm probably going to be responsible for the downfall of his career.

No big deal.

"I had to go overseas for work. Singapore," Joseph said. His voice was smoother than top-shelf whiskey, with not a hint of discomfort or uneasiness. That was him, always and forever in control.

That's how he'd been able to walk away the last night. Not even a woman stripped down to nothing could tempt him to bend his rules. Of course, part of her had always loved that he wasn't like the fuck boys and the players she'd seen her friends encounter. The first time they'd made love, he'd told her it would mean something. Forever. Whether they stayed together or not.

"Good for you," Vince said. "But you're back now?"

"New York will always be home."

"Ah, well, I look forward to seeing your faces around here more. I miss my regulars when they move away." He motioned for them to sit. "I'll send out some of the special garlic bread while you wait."

"Thanks." Annie mustered her friendliest smile. "That would be lovely."

As she lowered herself back into her seat, she tried to make sense of everything that today had brought. Now she'd have to wait until the dinner was over before she told Joseph about the code. The last thing she wanted was for him to flip and storm out of the restaurant while Vince could see. For some reason, her pride didn't want Vince knowing the truth. That she'd failed the man sitting across from her.

That she'd failed herself.

You'll make it right tonight. You'll tell him the truth, and then you can figure out what to do next.

Chapter 16

"If you really believe you're doing something good, then why don't you tell the world who you are? Why don't you publicly stand by your actions?"

—SuspiciousUser

JOSEPH HAD INSISTED ON WALKING HER BACK TO HER apartment, his coat draped around her shoulders because in her distracted state that morning she hadn't dressed herself appropriately for the late-fall chill. They had their heads bowed to the fine mist of rain, bodies close together, and footsteps mockingly in sync.

"I heard back from Andrew this evening," Joseph said as they walked along Fifth Avenue, past Saint Thomas Church.

The old building had always fascinated her, even if it *was* less famous than St. Patrick's. She loved the limestone exterior and imposing Gothic style and the neat rows of statues that always made her feel like someone was watching over her. In a good way.

She pulled Joseph's coat tighter around her shoulders as the wind whipped past them. "What did he say?"

"He found some reference to Bad Bachelors on a

forum he was tracking for a private security gig. There was a post from a guy boasting that he'd hacked your computer and found your details, although he didn't publish them."

Her stomach churned. "Well, that's good. I guess."

"The hacker also said he got the code for the website, although who the hell knows what he's planning to do with it. Maybe he wants to start up Bad Bachelorettes as a revenge thing?"

She snorted. "What's the point of that? He could just go onto 4chan or one of those ridiculous anonymous websites."

"Well, the guy's username *was* Mr. Justice, so I guess he sees himself as responsible for getting you back on behalf of douchebags everywhere."

The churning sensation intensified in her gut. "Mr. Justice."

"Stupid name, right? I've met a lot of hackers in my time, and many of them have a self-inflated sense of importance. Seems to go with the territory." Joseph shook his head. "Although I get it. The thrill of the chase is a big driver in that world. It's like a digital treasure hunt."

"You miss it, don't you?"

He looked down at her, his lips quirking at one corner. "A lot. I loved that job more than anything I've done since."

"Then why did you go into the corporate stuff? I thought you wanted to start your own infosec firm?"

He'd taken a role in banking two years before they broke up. After working his way up to chief information security officer of a smaller credit union, he'd gotten his big break when a friend of his father poached him into an IT operations manager role and put him on the fast track to his current executive position. At the time, he'd taken the job because it paid well and would give him the experience he needed to run his own company. But it was never meant to be a long-term career move. Just a head start.

"I did," he said. "But things happened. I changed."

But he hadn't changed. He still got that excited look of a kid with a new video game whenever he talked about his white-hat days. Undoubtedly it was the same look she got thinking about the company she could start with the money from selling Bad Bachelors.

"I have to tell you something," she said. Her building was approaching, and she didn't want to set foot inside without first coming clean. Because one more night with this weighing on her would mean another night sleeplessly fretting about what she'd done. And she needed a solution. "I got an email from that Mr. Justice guy."

Joseph frowned. "When?"

"Yesterday." She swallowed.

"Why didn't you tell me when I came over?" The apartment building loomed closer, flickers of last night distracting her. That searing kiss. Her standing in front of the window, naked.

"We got distracted." She bit down on her lip. "The thing is…he got my code. Like he said on the forum."

"Okay. And why is that a big deal?"

They stopped at the front door, the golden light from inside the building spilling into the street. People were coming and going, the doors letting out a blast of warm air each time they opened. Annie shivered.

"I…I did something stupid." Her breath was quick and shallow, guilt wrapping like a python around her rib cage.

"Whatever it is, we'll figure it out." He placed a hand on her shoulder, and the weight of his grasp was so comforting it made her want to scream.

"Why are you helping me?" She shook her head. "We're supposed to hate each other. I *did* hate you, and then you came back and…everything isn't clear anymore."

"I've never hated you, Annie." He pulled her close to him, wrapping his arms around her neck as they stood in the cold and the fine, glossy rain. "Not even for a second."

Dammit. Why couldn't he make this easier on her by being a total prick? Why did he have to be kind and sweet, and why did he have to smell *so* damn good?

"You should." She was so disgusted with herself that she wanted to throw up. "I'm going to ruin everything."

"Can we go upstairs and talk?" he said, pulling back and studying her. "We're getting soaked, and it's cold as fuck out here."

"I put something in the code," she said it quickly, like tearing off a Band-Aid.

He froze. "What?"

"I put a message in the code. A dedication." Her heart was like a wrecking ball now, slamming into her ribs. "To you."

"You put a dedication to me in the code of the website?"

The irony of it all was the only reason she even knew that people could do that was because he'd told her once. He had stories of hackers filing secret messages away in the code of a website they'd compromised. Like Hansel and Gretel–style bread crumbs for anyone who knew to look.

"Mr. Justice has it. I didn't put your full name, but he knows it's you." She squeezed her eyes shut. "I'm so sorry."

"I'm not having this discussion in the rain," he said. She couldn't discern anything from his tone or his expression. His face was blank, restraint fully in his grasp. "We're going upstairs. Now."

————————

Joseph didn't say a word the entire trip up to Annie's apartment. However, the lack of talking didn't mean his head was clear. The fallout was already flashing in his mind like a montage of his demise. It would be the spike upon which the executive members who wanted him out would mount his head.

Annie unlocked her front door with shaking hands. He was furious, but seeing her pain and remorse was as bad as knowing his career was about to come crashing down around him. He could only imagine what people would say. What his father would say.

It would justify every bad word Morris had ever said about Annie. It would validate the prediction that loving her would be Joseph's downfall.

She shrugged out of his coat and held it out, but instead of slipping into it, he hung it on the rack next to the door. No way was he leaving until this issue was resolved.

"Say something," she said, her eyes huge. It was the exact expression she'd worn when she'd found him packing his suitcase three years ago. "Yell, scream, do whatever you need to do."

"What would any of that achieve?" He ground the words out. She wanted him to throw his emotions around, to be an angry firework like his father. Not going to happen. "I want to know why you did it."

"I was angry. Hurt." She tucked her hair behind her ear. The rain had started to bring the curl out. "It was stupid."

"Of course it was fucking stupid." His voice was like ice. "This whole thing was stupid. I left when I didn't want to, and you stayed when you didn't need to. We could so easily have worked the situation out if we weren't both so…egotistical."

Maybe it wasn't even ego. Maybe it was a sense of entitlement born out of the fact that neither one of them had *ever* considered that they might not be together in the future. They'd been so convinced they could beat the odds, that they would stay together forever because they wanted to. But in the face of their first real challenge as a couple, they'd failed.

"You think?" Tears shimmered in her eyes. "Because I don't. We were doomed from the start. Your parents were *never* going to accept me. Your father cornered me the Christmas before we broke up and told me I was a gold digger and that he was going to have a watertight prenup drawn up if we ever got married."

"What?" He could feel the ice cracking now, composure sliding through his fingers. "Why didn't you tell me?"

"What would have been the point?" She threw her hands in the air. "You never wanted to take sides, and I respected that. I knew you loved me, and I didn't give a shit about your money. I would have happily signed the damn thing."

"You say that, but then on the other hand you say we would never have worked because of what my family thought. You didn't give me a chance to tell you what *I* thought." He was almost vibrating with anger now, his fists clenched as he tried with every bit of willpower to stay calm. To not be like his father. "There would have been a prenup over my dead body. I would have given you every last cent I had."

"I didn't want your money! I still don't. Prenup, no prenup, I didn't care." She rubbed her hands over her face, her cheeks flushed while the rest of her was pale with worry. "I only wanted you."

Were his parents really so worried about protecting their wealth that they would push away the one person who truly loved their son?

"You should have told me," he said. "I deserved a chance to speak for myself."

Her eyes were watery, and there was a slash of red dotting her lip where she'd bitten too hard. He should be furious. She'd risked his career. If it got out that he was connected to Bad Bachelors, his time as CIO would be done. He'd be disgraced. Damaged goods. Nobody would hire him.

"What did Mr. Justice want?" he asked, already knowing what the answer would be.

"For me to shut it down," she said. "He wants Bad Bachelors gone."

"And how are you planning to solve this problem?"

"I don't know," she whispered. "I don't have a solution. I asked him for more time. I made out like I was going to shut it down, but that I needed time to make it happen."

"So you stalled?"

She nodded. "Yeah."

If he knew anything about hackers, the damage would already be done. It was easy to shut a website down, even if it would take a little while to pull the app from all the major platforms. Mr. Justice would have to know that Annie was bluffing.

"Aren't you going to tell me I'm a horrible person?" she asked. "That I'm a vindictive villain who's going to ruin things for you."

"Going to?" he asked.

"That I already have."

He didn't know what to do. "What did you actually write in the code?"

"To Joseph, this is for you."

The words were like a sharp blade driving between his ribs, shaving the bone and hitting something soft on the other side. What must she have been feeling when she typed those words? "When did you do it?"

"The day I saw the picture of you and Annika." She faced him head-on, not shying away from her confession or trying to soften it. He'd always loved her inner strength, that iron will she used to face any tough situation without flinching. "I saw her wearing the ring, and it was like something snapped."

"You know if this gets out, I'll be fired," he said. "The bank took a risk in hiring me, and this kind of press won't be good."

"I didn't put your last name in the code." Her eyes darted back and forth like she was trying to come up with a solution. "Joseph could be anyone. I'll deny it was you."

"And how are you going to do that without giving yourself away?"

She wrung her hands. "I'll release a statement on the Bad Bachelors website. And I can push a notification to all users of the app."

"That'll add gasoline to the fire." He shook his head and wandered over to the window to look out at the view. The people of Manhattan were going about their business on the streets below. What he wouldn't give to be anonymous for once in his life. "It will only bring more attention to the rumors."

"Who's going to believe some faceless person on the internet?" she asked.

"Isn't that exactly what Bad Bachelors is predicated on? Users put stock in the opinions of people they don't even know."

Behind him, Annie was silent as she walked across the room. A few seconds later, her presence was strong behind him, almost like she was debating about reaching out to touch him. Their pull was something he felt down to the very marrow of his bones. Like an invisible thread connected them, he anticipated her. Craved her.

"Or do you think that an anonymous website user has more credit than a hacker?" he asked.

"I guess they're the same, aren't they? Why should we believe one and not the other?" She pressed herself gently to his back, her cheek resting against his spine with her hands sliding around his waist. "I'm sorry, Joe."

He shut his eyes, reveling in the feel of her embrace—the one she'd used every time they'd fought. For the first few years of their relationship, each little argument had resulted in her being convinced he would leave. That he would realize she was beneath him. Only he'd never come to that conclusion, because it was false. They were equals, then and now.

"I *was* going to ask you to marry me," he said. In front of him, the city glistened. He couldn't even remember how many times he'd stood in this spot, thinking about the future—*their* future—and making plan after plan for his fantasy life. The business he wanted to create, the places they would explore together. The family they would build. "I had it all planned out for when we landed in Singapore. I had a hotel room booked, champagne and flowers waiting."

"Did you think about me after you left?" Her voice was thick, and it cracked on the last word.

"Every fucking day."

But there was so much water under the bridge now. Damaged trust, resentment, a steaming pile of bad decisions that couldn't be erased. Two families who hated one another. If the odds had been against them before, where the hell did that leave them now?

"What should I do?" she asked, her arms squeezing him.

"Whatever you want, Annie. The damage is already done." His phone started ringing from the pocket inside his coat. When he slipped it out and saw that his messages had blown up, he knew the news was already out. So he turned his phone off and put it back into his pocket. "I don't want you endangering yourself by coming out with your identity."

"You think I should bend to him?" she asked.

"I think you should sell. Let Mr. Justice be someone else's problem. Someone who has the means to deal with him. Take the money and do something amazing with your life. You want to help people? Do that. Find a way to use the money for something that will fulfill you and benefit others."

Chapter 17

"The creator of Bad Bachelors continues to be a mystery. That was, until our attention was drawn to a blog post where a piece of the site's source code was published. Hidden between lines of code is a dedication..."

"DO YOU HATE ME?" SHE ASKED. JOSEPH'S JACKET WAS soft against her cheek, his body familiar and warm in her arms.

"Never." He extracted himself from her grasp and turned around. This was the old Joseph coming back, the one who shut down when emotions ran high. The one who walked away when things got tough. "What's done is done."

They had so much between them. So much history, so much pain. "I know I have no right to ask but...will you stay the night?"

His eyes flicked over her face. "You know my position on this."

"Will you stay with me, in my bed?" Asking this question was like ripping herself open. Exposing her vulnerabilities to him. "Will you fall asleep with me?"

There was a glimmer of something then, a tightening

of the muscles in his neck. A tensing in his jaw. He was fighting the feeling, fighting his reaction. "Will it mean something to you?"

"Yes." Her voice was shaky and raw. Roughed up, like her heart. "It will mean something."

He brought his head down to hers, lips meeting her open and hot. He tasted sweet, like the wine they'd had at dinner mixed with something salty. Tears. Hers. She fisted her hands in his shirt, and he slipped his palms down her back, over her ass until he lifted her up, coaxing her legs around his waist. She locked her feet behind him and wound her arms around his neck. Hanging on with everything she had.

"I'm sorry," she murmured against his lips. "I'm so sorry."

"I am too, baby." Their kisses were deep and rough, like they wanted to wrench every bit of passion out of this moment. Because this would be it.

Tomorrow he would return to work, and to protect his career, he'd have to keep his distance. She would sell Bad Bachelors and have the chance to do things right a second time. They would both lose one another again. But tonight, they could pretend it wasn't all falling apart.

Tonight, they could say the goodbye they'd never had the first time around.

Joseph walked them through the apartment, dodging every piece of furniture with ease and navigating to the bedroom without the use of his eyes or hands. Those never left her. His fingers tangled in her hair, cradling her scalp as he kissed her senseless. She returned fire by nipping at his lower lip and pressing her chest against his. Her nipples were hard, and each step caused her to rub against him, friction turning her wild with need.

But there was an undercurrent of fear beneath the inferno of lust. Because this *did* mean something to her. Hell, it meant everything. After what she'd done, Joseph could have walked right out of the apartment and vowed never to return. He could have done worse—exposed her before she exposed him.

But there were no words of retribution or threats. Once again—as he had done over and over in their relationship—he'd put her needs first. How had she never seen how selfless he was? That him leaving wasn't about putting his career before her family, but about him reacting to her placing him second?

She wanted to punch her old self. He was right. They *could* have made it work. If only she hadn't let his family get into her head…

"I should never have made you feel like you were second best," she said. "I let everything get to me. Mom's cancer, your dad's words…"

"I let them get to me too," he said. They were in the bedroom now, and he sank to his knees on the mattress, still holding her. Cradling her. "He pushed me so hard to take that job in Singapore. I thought it would…"

He thought it would make Morris love him, but now he saw the truth. Morris would never love anyone but himself. Her heart shattered all over again. All he'd ever wanted was the man's love and respect.

"I knew once I started the job that I'd made a mistake. Dad wasn't any different. He didn't suddenly think I was worthy of his time. And I'd lost you." He buried his face in her hair, his hands roaming her body—the blend of bittersweet and scorching hot making her mind swing like a pendulum. "I'd lost the one bright spot in my world."

"We've made a mess, haven't we?"

Joseph laughed, though the sound was anything but humorous. "We sure have."

"And now we're saying goodbye again." Why did it hurt so badly? It wasn't like she thought they'd ever get back together. "I wish I could fix this."

"The only way we can fix this is to go our separate ways." He stroked her face, gentle hands tracing the edge of her mouth and the angle of her jaw. She did the same, feeling the scratch of his beard and the firmness of his lips. "If I have any chance of salvaging my job, I have to get distance from Bad Bachelors."

The finality of his statement was like a punch to her gut. And she had no one to blame but herself. "I'll stay away."

An expression flickered over his face, but it was gone before she could interpret it. "You know why I have to do it, don't you? If anyone sees us together, they might figure it out. It's safer for us both to walk away."

"I know." She nodded, fighting back the emotion that reared up like a tidal wave. "I agree it's the right thing to do."

"Then let's not waste tonight. I don't want you thinking about the past or about tomorrow or about anything besides how good you're going to feel when I'm inside you."

"Yes, I want that too." She swallowed her doubt and regret. "I want you."

"If this is it…" For a second he was as vulnerable as her, his eyes finally revealing what was going on inside. "I don't want us to waste a second. Because I won't be coming back."

"I know."

"I will do everything in my power to make sure you're safe." He brushed the hair from her forehead, tucking it behind her ears. "But it won't be me guarding your door, okay?"

It hurt so goddamn much that she wanted to crumple into a ball and beg God to make her vanish. Was it possible that losing him was even more painful the second time around? Or was it simply that time had smoothed the edges of her memory, erasing the jagged bits and filling in the grooves?

"I understand." She pressed her lips to his so softly it was like kissing air. "Please, just make me feel good now. Tomorrow can wait."

He laid her down on the bed and rocked back to a standing position. There was nothing more blissful than watching Joseph strip down. His hands were unhurried, commanding. They turned the simple action of removing a suit jacket into an erotic act. As he popped the buttons on his shirt, revealing a widening V of skin and ridged muscle, Annie could only watch. He yanked the shirt from the waistband of his pants and then started on his fly.

He pulled the zipper all the way down, his erection pressed forward. Black boxer-briefs did little to hide his arousal, the fabric stretching taut over his straining cock. She swallowed as his thumbs hooked under the elastic and he shoved it all down—suit pants and underwear—so that he was almost naked. In seconds his shoes, shirt, and socks joined the pile of clothing and he stood before her, totally bare.

"Your turn," he growled, reaching down to wrap a fist around his cock. "Take it slow."

Her brain failed to get into gear, her body sluggish like someone else was controlling her limbs. Tugging on her strings. She fumbled with the fly on her jeans. All the while, Joseph stroked himself and she watched, mesmerized by the slow but strong up-and-down pumping action, by the way his head peeked out over the top of his fist with each downward stroke. Suddenly, her mouth was dry, and she realized she'd been frozen for a second.

"Keep going," he said. "Jeans off."

She shoved them down her thighs and wriggled her legs until the fabric fell over the edge of the bed. Then she pulled her top up and over her head, before sending it to the floor. Cool air brushed over her heated skin, making her nipples even harder. They pressed against the sheer fabric of her bra. Growing up, Annie had always been self-conscious about her less-than-buxom chest. But Joseph had treated her body like it was perfection, and over the years she'd come to believe his compliments.

She reached behind her back, unhooking the clasp and shrugging out of the straps. He came forward the second she peeled the fabric away, pressing his lips to her heated skin. "Yes."

He sucked on one nipple, gently at first and then roughly, using his teeth and tongue to test the edges of her restraint. Sensation overwhelmed her, short-circuiting her brain until she was running on nothing but arousal.

"Do I need a condom?" he asked, snaking his lips back up her neck as he gently pushed her back to the bed. His fingers toyed with the edge of her panties, breaching the elastic to tease her with barely there strokes.

"No," she said. "We didn't last time, and I'm on the pill."

Her eyes fluttered shut as he grew bolder, parting the lips of her sex and finding her clit. Each circular motion of his fingertips unwound her further and further, pushing deeper into sensation. How could she possibly let him go? How could she possibly wake up tomorrow and go on living, knowing this was it?

"If you want me to wear one, I will." He speared her with a serious look.

She shook her head. "No, it's fine. I trust you."

He rested his forehead against hers as he teased her, switching up the slow, sensual spirals to slip a finger into her. He let her find the rhythm, only to pull out and return to her clit. The maddening back-and-forth had her hovering on the edge of release, so close. Yet so far.

"There wasn't anyone else." The words slipped out before she could stop them. "Since you left."

"What do you mean?" His hand stilled.

"I haven't…" Her eyes flickered for a moment, because eye contact was too painful. "There's been no one else since you. Not a single person."

Joseph pulled back, and Annie was sure he was about to walk away. God, why the hell had she said that? What could she possibly hope to achieve by telling him that sorry piece of information? He probably thought she was pathetic.

But instead of moving away, he came down over her, slipping his hands under her body so he could hold her tightly to his chest. For a moment, they said nothing. She let herself sink into the safety of his embrace, let herself be held.

"Can we pretend I came with you?" She pressed her face into his neck. "Please. Let's pretend we didn't screw up."

"Okay." His voice was hoarse. It was a sound she'd never heard before. Because Joseph could sound cold as ice; he could sound gravelly and sexy and powerful in bed. But never this…ruined. "We're there now."

He reached between her legs and wrenched her panties to one side. The head of his cock nudged at her entrance, his hips rolling as he positioned himself.

"I've missed you," she whispered. Her voice was so soft, she had no idea if he heard her words.

But as he cupped her face and slid into her with one smooth, deep thrust, she let herself sink into the fantasy. She let herself pretend that they loved each other, that they'd never been apart, and that once the dawn broke, everything would be okay.

Mysterious creator of Bad Bachelors rumored to be linked to young CIO hotshot

By Peta McKinnis, *Spill the Tea* society and culture reporter

Ever since the date-rating app exploded online less than a year ago, the world has speculated about who created Bad Bachelors and why. Early on, it was thought to be a publicity stunt. A genius piece of PR for a matchmaking service or possibly a women's magazine. However, no company ever came forward to claim it.

Rumors also suggested that feminist blogger and women's rights advocate Marsha Hinley might have been responsible. But while Hinley praised the app for promoting safe dating practices, she refuted all claims of involvement.

Thus, the creator of Bad Bachelors continued to be a mystery. That was, until our attention was drawn to a hacking website where a portion of the Bad Bachelors site's source code was published. Hidden between lines of code is a message:

To Joseph, this is for you.

The post speculates that "Joseph" is none other than Joseph Preston—which appears to be based on a piece of information the source is not yet willing to publish. If you're outside tech circles and the elite of the Upper East Side, you may not recognize his name. But he's a high-profile bachelor, heir to a portion of the Landry Cosmetics fortune, and has recently been named the youngest CIO in JGL Bank's history. In fact, he sounds exactly like the kind of guy we'd expect to be reviewed on Bad Bachelors.

However, Joseph Preston has only recently returned to New York from Singapore, after a stint with HSBC, according to his LinkedIn profile. Which may account for his lack of reviews.

What remains uncertain, however, is who would have reason to dedicate Bad Bachelors to him.

Other than a brief engagement to Annika Van Beek, who you may know if you follow any top fashion blogs, Preston has kept his life relatively quiet. Recent hits on his name bring up interviews about JGL's digital strategy and footage from a presentation he gave at a FinTech conference in Sydney last year. But nothing about his personal life, other than a statement from Van Beek saying she was single again back in September.

Is Joseph Preston the Joseph referenced in the Bad Bachelors source code? No evidence seems to suggest it, but the blogger who posted the code certainly thinks so.

What's your take on Bad Bachelors? Have you used the site and found it helpful when navigating the dating jungle? We'd love to hear your stories.

Annie smoothed her hands down the front of her pencil skirt and practiced the breathing technique she always used before a big meeting. After saying goodbye to Joseph earlier that morning, and then spending all day in the office pretending like she wasn't coming apart at the seams, her nerves were shot. Of course, someone had circulated one of several articles published that morning that linked to a blog post naming Joseph Preston as the person Bad Bachelors was dedicated to.

Mr. Justice hadn't outed her yet, but the blog post was a show of force. A warning. He *would* pull the trigger.

Which meant she had to deal with the Bad Bachelors situation quickly. That morning, she'd fired off a response to the investor who'd written her about buying Bad Bachelors. Within minutes, she'd received a meeting request for that night. Not wanting to be ambushed in case this was another trick, Annie had set the meeting at a very public restaurant and given them a false description of what she would be wearing. She'd also given a false identity: Leanne Venturi. It was her birth name and a fake surname.

This was how she'd come to be sipping a glass of wine, alone, watching people coming and going from the bar. In other circumstances, she might have been excited at the prospect of playing the role of Bond girl. But her life was a pool of gasoline with a match hovering above it, so 007 fantasies would have to take a back seat.

The door pushed open, and a blustering breeze rolled through the front part of the bar. Annie was seated at the section closest to the door, wearing all black and blending into the background as much as one could without actually being invisible. A woman swept into the bar with an older man beside her. She wore a raspberry-colored coat with long, black pants that allowed only a peek of a pair of silver high heels.

Sasha Jenkins.

Several heads turned in her direction. At this end of town, the Financial District, Sasha was a celebrity. She'd grown up in Harlem, had cleaned offices in a few of the major Wall Street buildings while teaching herself computer programming. After mining Bitcoin in the days when it bore the bad stench of nefarious associations with sites like Silk Road and other shady corners of the dark web, she'd done what her parents had always taught her to do—save. When Bitcoin shot up in value, she'd become a multimillionaire overnight.

These days Sasha's tech company boasted several successful start-ups—a social games company that helped pioneer micropayments, a dining and entertainment app that was Tinder for restaurants, and a high-end matchmaking software company. Undoubtedly, *that* was the reason Sasha wanted Bad Bachelors. It was the perfect platform on which to advertise her matchmaking business, targeting the burned-out victims of Manhattan's dating jungle and offering them a low-stress alternative…for a fee, of course.

Sasha and her companion scanned the room and took a seat in the booth at the back that had a sleek, gold Reserved sign. A server immediately went over to take their orders. Annie counted to ten and then pushed off her barstool and made her way through to the back of the restaurant.

Sasha was reading something on her phone, her head bowed. Her tightly coiled black hair framed her face, where a pair of silver wire-rimmed glasses sat on her nose. The contrast of the light metal against her dark skin was dramatic and stylish, much like the woman herself.

"Ms. Jenkins?" Annie walked up to the table. "It's a pleasure to meet you. I'm Leanne."

"That's a strange-looking red dress." Sasha eyed Annie's black outfit. "I suppose Leanne Venturi isn't your real name either."

"No, it's not."

Sasha smiled and gestured for Annie to take a seat. The risk had obviously paid off, because she looked less pissed and more...appreciative. Begrudgingly appreciative, anyway.

"You can understand there are a lot of people who want to know who I am," Annie said, sliding into the opposite side of the booth. They had enough privacy to conduct business, as long as they didn't raise their voices. But it was also public enough that if things went south, Annie could disappear into the crowded room. "I can't take any risks by outing myself to the wrong person."

"I understand completely," Sasha replied. "This is my associate, Mr. Hawthorn. He's my legal counsel and personal adviser."

The older man had shrewd gray eyes and a firm handshake. "Pleasure to meet you, Ms. Venturi."

"Likewise."

"This is not how we normally do business," he said. It was clear Sasha had demanded the meeting against his advice, but like a good corporate soldier, he was biting his tongue. Somewhat. "But Ms. Jenkins is very interested in acquiring your website and app."

"I'm *extremely* interested," Sasha said. "I admire what you've been able to build in such a short time. Many tech start-ups fail to gain even a fraction of your prominence."

"Thank you." For some reason Annie couldn't have felt further from proud. What had it all been for if she was going to sell it off? If she was going to walk away with more money than she'd ever dreamed possible and nothing but personal destruction in her wake?

But what other choice did she have? The only way to get out of this unscathed was to either shut down the site or sell it off. And at least this way, Bad Bachelors would continue to help the women who relied on it.

But she wasn't even confident of that anymore.

"There's something you should know before we proceed," she said. "The only reason I'm entertaining your offer is because there have been some challenges behind the scenes and I'm at a point where I have to admit I can't handle it on my own anymore."

Sasha cocked her head. "Go on."

"My laptop was hacked recently." She explained the situation in detail, including the dedication to Joseph and the request to shut the site down.

"That explains the fake description and fake name." Sasha frowned. She thought for a moment, her hand toying with the rim of her glasses, her metallic polish a shade of pinky-red that matched her coat perfectly. "I'm under no illusion about the trouble Bad Bachelors has stirred up. It's precisely *why* I want to buy it."

"I know. But I also wanted to be transparent."

"I appreciate that. However, I have an entire security team at my disposal. I also know how to throw a punch, if it's required." Her full lips pulled up into a smirk. "I'm not concerned about some loser who's sniveling in his mother's basement."

There would be added advantages to the person running Bad Bachelors not having to keep their identity a secret. They could involve law enforcement. And there wasn't much to leverage against them.

"We've drafted an offer document for your review,

Ms. Venturi." The lawyer slid an envelope across the table. It bore Sasha's company logo on the front. "Take the weekend to read it over, and let us know if you have any questions. We'll expect a final response by the end of next week, which will give you time to have a lawyer look over it."

Annie nodded. "Thank you."

"I hope you consider this offer seriously," Sasha said. "You can do a lot with this kind of money. You can set yourself up for life."

Annie placed her hands over the envelope. It was true. Money like this would provide security for her family, for herself. She could pay Joseph back for the apartment. With wise investments, she may not ever need to work again.

But instead of comforting her, the thought brought a tightness to her chest. How would she fill her days alone, without a something or some*one* to care about? Would selling Bad Bachelors make her no better than a corporate raider who'd preyed on people's weaknesses to turn a profit?

"I'll consider it," she said, swallowing her worries.

The main thing you need to think about now is how to protect yourself. Your family. You're buying a second chance.

But no matter how she rationalized it, the whole thing seemed totally and utterly wrong.

Chapter 18

"I don't know how you can live with yourself."

—AngrySister

IT WASN'T UNTIL LATE IN THE EVENING THAT JOSEPH finally had the encounter he'd been anticipating all day. Despite feeling the constant prickle of people looking at him, no one had said a word about Bad Bachelors. If he was less experienced, he might have allowed himself the fleeting thought that perhaps it wasn't a big deal. But he was smarter than that.

His boss, a take-no-prisoners guy named Thomas Fairchild, walked into Joseph's office and shut the door behind him. He fit the stereotype of most executive officers at the bank—male, Ivy League–educated, edging into his sixties. But beyond that, he deviated in his thinking. Thomas was a disrupter, and it had been his plan to put someone fresh into the CIO role. Someone who would shake things up.

But the man was hard to read. Thomas crossed the room and popped the button of his suit jacket before sitting in one of the chairs across from Joseph's desk. "You know what this is about, I take it."

Joseph nodded. "Frankly, I was expecting to be summoned first thing this morning."

"Too many people in the office." Thomas nailed him with a sharp stare. The man was impeccably dressed—old-school banker shirt with powder-blue body and white collar and cuffs, subtle chalk-striped suit, silver tie bar. No doubt there'd be a Montblanc hidden somewhere on his person. "The last thing I want is to draw further negative attention to this problem."

Joseph could handle this one of two ways: fall on his sword and hope for mercy, or go on the defensive. Something told him that Thomas wasn't in a particularly forgiving mood.

"I had no hand in the creation of Bad Bachelors," Joseph said, leaning back in his chair. First rule of going on the defensive: stay calm.

"That's not what's being circulated. I understand your assistant has been inundated with calls from the media all day."

"He has. But that's not proof of anything other than media outlets wanting to sell advertising. This whole Bad Bachelors thing has gotten a lot of attention, so they're jumping on a piece of false information in order to further their own agenda." *Calm, blue ocean.* "And we all know journalistic integrity isn't what it used to be."

"I don't expect you to be glib, Joseph." Thomas narrowed his eyes at him. "When I brought you on, I wanted to draw attention to our digital strategy by employing someone young enough to sell it. I did *not* want some someone who would be associated with this…controversy."

"I'm not associated with it," Joseph repeated. "If you care to look up Bad Bachelors, you'll find that I am not reviewed on that site, nor is my name mentioned anywhere."

"Except in the source code."

"There are a ton of people named Joseph, for starters. And it could very well be doctored," he pointed out. "How hard do you think it would be for someone with Photoshop to make a fake screen capture? I could walk outside and find a kid to do it in under a minute on his phone."

Thomas considered this. "Why? What would be the point?"

"You said yourself during my interview that hiring me would ruffle a lot of feathers. Hell, that was the point of it. Do you trust everyone on the executive leadership team and the board *not* to stoop to this level?"

"You think someone is setting you up."

Joseph had wanted to get out of this conversation without explicitly lying. "It's a distinct possibility."

But that doesn't mean it's the truth…

"There are plenty of other ways to remove someone from their position in this bank. Doesn't that seem a little convoluted?"

"Not if you fire me," Joseph said. "You're the one who's trying to shake things up. If someone sets me up, you'll find a replacement to do what I'm supposed to do. However, if it's proven that a younger person in this role is too risky, then you'll be forced to go back on your plans and hire someone more in line with what the bank has always done."

"And what's that?"

"Hire someone like them who'll want the same thing. Less friction, no one challenging the money they're pouring into their pockets. No one trying to make them do things they don't want to—like change."

Thomas thought for a moment, his right hand going to the silver bar holding his tie in place and rocking it back and forth. He always did that when he was thinking. "Something needs to be done. We can't ignore it."

"How about an exclusive interview," Joseph suggested. "I know a reporter who would be thrilled at the chance to get me on camera talking about it."

"What's the angle?" Thomas steepled his fingers. "You can't publicly say the board has it in for you."

"Of course not. That would be inappropriate." Joseph almost had him. The next move would be a gamble, but something out of the box was required to escape this mess. "How about I tell them all the ways I've failed in my life."

"What?" Thomas blinked. "That's a terrible idea."

"Look at how we're moving to agile project management. Look at how companies like Tesla and SpaceX have a culture of embracing failure. The reason people hate banks is because they're never transparent when things go wrong. They're inherently risk averse and therefore stale. You wanted me in this role because I'm different. Why not capitalize on that? A personal interview, one-on-one. The youngest CIO in our history and how he got this position by learning from his mistakes. It'll be inspiring. We can also partner it with some internal PR, use me to show younger people in our ranks that they *do* have a future in this industry."

Thomas rubbed a hand along his jaw, clearly intrigued by Joseph's idea. "It's certainly a different approach."

"It'll work. We'll get agreement that the interviewer won't imply I had anything to do with Bad Bachelors, but they can ask about it in a general sense. I'll use this as an opportunity to show how we're not like other banks, how our strategy and approach can appeal to a younger customer. A customer who doesn't want the same old, same old."

Thomas bobbed his head. "Okay, set it up ASAP. But if this fails, you'll be looking for a new job."

He got up and walked out of the room, leaving the door open behind him. From his vantage point, Joseph could see that the office had mostly cleared out. He'd sent Dave home around six thirty, and his empty desk partially obscured the view of the executive floor. In the distance, he could hear the voice of the HR general manager talking to her assistant.

Letting out a long whooshing breath, Joseph tipped his chair back and tilted his face to the ceiling. Was it possible that he'd be able to dodge this bullet? The interview idea wasn't a guaranteed win. In fact, there was a very real possibility of it blowing up in his face. He had no idea if he could trust the journalist not to hang him out to dry. But perhaps if they offered an exclusive, she'd play ball.

Risky, but what other options do you have?

None. But even though he knew it was the right

thing to do, his mind cast him back to last night. Back to falling sleep with Annie's cheek against his chest and his arms around her shoulders. Back to her sleepy kisses in the predawn when he started to disentangle himself from her. Back to the tears sliding down her cheeks as they said goodbye.

The second he arrived at the office, he'd called an old friend who ran a private security firm. Joseph would pay someone to keep watch over Annie until this was all wrapped up.

Knowing she would be safe took the edge off his bad mood. But it was only a slight reprieve. They still didn't know who was behind the threats and whether her selling Bad Bachelors would stop the people targeting her. And Joseph didn't know whether his career would survive the speculation.

The only thing he could do now was get in touch with the journalist and set up an interview. He scrolled back through his calendar to the day of their original interview. But Dave had set the meeting up, and her phone number wasn't in the invite. It didn't appear to be in his contact list either. Perhaps Dave had a business card stashed at his desk.

Pushing up from his chair, Joseph wandered out to his assistant's desk.

He didn't want to go rummaging through drawers or invading the guy's privacy in any way, but he'd sleep better if he could set up the meeting now. At least knowing there was some progress would make him feel a bit more at ease. Joseph scanned the set of shelves next to the desk, looking for anything that might resemble a business-card folder. He was *sure* the journalist had handed one over when they'd first greeted her.

But nothing jumped out. Frustrated, he muttered a curse under his breath. He could call Dave, but he hated interrupting a staff member's time after they left the office unless it was absolutely necessary. And easing his own mind wasn't a good enough reason. Just as he was about to turn away, something caught his eye.

It was the picture of Dave and his wife. The simple silver frame caught the light and winked at him. When Joseph peered closer, one little detail made his blood run cold. The photo was taken in front of the Eiffel Tower and while the couple was in perfect focus, the background was soft and blurry. Swallowing against the rising tide of rage clawing up his throat, Joseph grabbed his phone out of his pocket and pulled up the email from Andrew with the details of Mr. Justice's forum profile. Sure enough, the profile picture he'd used looked exactly like this shot of the Eiffel Tower in the background of this photo. Almost as if the photo had been cropped to make his profile image. It must have personal significance to him.

How had he walked past Dave's desk every day without noticing it? The clue had been in front of him all this time, but Joseph had been in his own head too often to pay enough attention.

Maybe it's a coincidence? Lots of people go to the Eiffel Tower.

Possibly. Joseph would need to do some digging to confirm his suspicions, but his gut told him everything he needed to know: Dave was the person threatening Annie.

By the time Annie reached her building, her feet ached from the walk. In her jumbled-up state that morning, she'd forgotten to throw her flats into her bag. Sure, she could have hailed a cab. But that had seemed a bit ridiculous for what would be a ten-minute walk. If only she hadn't decided that her power stilettos were required to face the day. It became immediately apparent, however, that blisters were the least of her worries when she exited the elevator and found someone waiting by her door.

"Morris, to what to do I owe the complete lack of pleasure?" She really was *not* in the mood to deal with his shit tonight.

"Was it you?" he practically snarled.

"Was *what* me?" She folded her arms across her chest.

He might know where she lived, but she sure as hell wasn't inviting him in. They could have this argument in the hallway for all the neighbors to hear, as far as she was concerned.

"Did *you* post that bullshit about Joseph being connected to Bad Bachelors? Are you the person trying to ruin his reputation?"

Of course he thought she was the one posting rumors rather than the person who'd created Bad Bachelors. He'd always made it clear he didn't think her capable of anything. She bit back the desire to throw it all in his face.

"No, it wasn't me. Why would I do something like that?"

"Why not? I know you were livid when he left you,

and I can't imagine you were too impressed when he got engaged to someone else." Morris's eyes narrowed. For a second she thought steam might shoot out of his ears.

"Are you upset about the impact this will have on your son, or because you're worried about how it will affect you?" She raised a brow. "I sincerely hope that for once in your life, you're worried about Joseph. Lord knows it would be thirty years overdue."

"How dare you." His expression might have been fire and brimstone, but his voice was all ice.

Like Joseph, his father towered over her, and Annie wondered if maybe she should have already put in a call to the security firm that Joseph had emailed her about earlier that day. But she'd decided to invite Remi and Darcy over instead. It was time to come clean about what was going on. If this whole thing with Joseph and Bad Bachelors had taught her anything, it was that secrets were destructive. If she had any hope of regaining control over her life, she needed to start being honest— with herself and others.

Only she hadn't anticipated being accosted by Morris Preston. He was one person she didn't owe anything.

"How dare I what?" She looked up at him with full, unwavering eye contact and a calm, steady voice. It was like dealing with a snarling dog; you had to show it who was boss. "Voice my opinion? I'm not with Joseph now, which means I couldn't give two shits what you think of me. I only feel sorry for Joseph, that he's had someone like you bully him his whole life. It's a miracle that, despite your toxic influence, he's such an upstanding, caring guy. Because you have *not* done him any favors."

"Holy shit."

Annie whipped her head around and saw two very wide sets of eyes staring at her. Darcy and Remi were standing in the hallway, shell-shocked. No doubt they'd witnessed the verbal throwdown.

"You have no class, Leanne."

The fact that he continued to use her hated full name was a prickle under her skin. But she wouldn't let him see that, because it was precisely why he used it.

"Maybe. I come from nothing, and I don't know which fork you use for which dinner course. I have no idea what foie gras is, and I'll never have a closet full of ball gowns. But you know what, Morris? I'm okay with that. I'd rather be true about who I am than try to squish myself into some box to please anyone 'with class' such as yourself." It took every ounce of willpower not to let her voice shake. Because confident as she might seem, Morris always managed to reduce her to defensiveness. She would forever be a second-class citizen to him. "My family works incredibly hard. But they love harder. That's what you'll never understand."

Darcy and Remi came up beside her, like two guardian angels swooping in to show their support.

"You should probably leave now, Mr. Preston." Darcy looked the older man up and down, disdain dripping from her every word. "I'd hate to be forced to call the police about you harassing someone on private property."

"This apartment isn't hers," he spat out. "She thinks she's all about love, but she was perfectly happy to cut into Joseph's wealth without a second thought. You shouldn't even be here," he told Annie.

Remi slipped an arm around Annie's shoulders. "If you're worried about the bad press your family is getting right now, it would be unwise to add to it."

Morris looked as though he was about to say something else, but then he stormed off down the hallway. Without waiting to hear the ding of the elevator, Annie reached into her bag for her keys. By now, her hands were shaking from the effort of keeping her cool, and adrenaline rushed through her veins, making her jittery and light-headed.

"You should report it to the concierge desk," Remi said. "Someone obviously let him up here since he doesn't have a key card."

"Or he tailgated." Darcy shook her head. "Not cool."

Annie unlocked the front door, and the three women walked into her apartment. She hadn't even noticed until then that Darcy was holding a plastic tub containing a game console and controllers. They'd decided to stay in and play *Mario Kart* instead of going out, at Annie's request. She couldn't deal with the world tonight, and the thought of hanging out with her two best friends and dodging some shells sounded like bliss. But of course Morris had to come along and ruin any semblance of peace she might've had.

"I'm glad we came in time to catch that," Remi said. "You've got witnesses if he tries anything again. I'm happy to make a statement to the security team downstairs."

"It's fine." Annie shook her head. "His bark has always been worse than his bite. He's an asshole, but he'd never do anything physical."

"I'm assuming it's about all the articles that came out

today." Darcy dropped to her knees in front of the TV and started setting up the mini Super Nintendo, while Remi went straight to the cupboard and pulled out some wineglasses. The two of them moved around Annie's place like they lived here.

"Yeah. It was."

"I'm glad we were here for you," Remi said, giving her a quick squeeze.

Something settled in Annie's chest that made her realize how goddamn lonely she'd been the past few months. Since Darcy got engaged, she'd been around less. And then when Annie and Remi had their huge fight, their happy little threesome had ceased to exist. This was the first time all three of them had been in a room together since that happened—barring the *Out of Bounds* opening night. But Annie didn't count that, since Remi was performing and they didn't actually speak.

Keeping Bad Bachelors a secret had taken its toll on her. But worse than that, lying to her friends and to the world had made her shy away from all the things she loved in her life. She avoided conversations where Bad Bachelors might come up, and she'd spent less time with her family because it was getting harder to act like everything was okay when her parents asked what she was up to.

She had so many people who cared about her. And right now, she felt as though she didn't deserve a single one.

"Why did Morris think you had anything to do with it?" Darcy asked. She flipped a switch on the console, and the game fired up. Remi grabbed a bottle of wine from the fridge and brought it, along with the glasses, to the couch. "I mean, he can't know the truth. And just because Joseph is back in town doesn't mean that you have anything to do with him."

Oh boy. Well, if the "new Annie" was going to start somewhere, this would be it. She turned the game controller over in her hands, rubbing her thumb over the familiar buttons. "I was at Joseph's place when Morris came over, unannounced. He saw me there. So, that probably has something to do with it."

Darcy and Remi exchanged glances. "What were you doing at his place?" Darcy asked.

"It's kind of a long story," she said, noting Darcy's pointed expression. "But we have time."

Remi grabbed the other controller, and Darcy filled up their glasses. They sat on the couch and played a round of *Mario Kart* while Annie told them everything. She started with the hacking and the webcam photo, and finished with what'd happened between her and Joseph last night as well as the sale offer. For a few heartbeats after she'd finished, there was total and utter silence. Well, except for the enthusiastic signature *Wahoo!* from the game as the race ended.

"I don't know what to say." Darcy shook her head. Her blue eyes were wide. It wasn't often that their resident sarcasm chief was rendered speechless. "That's a lot to take in."

"You've been dealing with all this on your own?" Remi frowned as she took a sip of the pale-gold liquid.

"It's my problem, so I'll deal with it. Joe has really been a big help, but the only reason I went to him in the first place was because I needed his skills. I didn't really *want* his help…at least not initially."

"And now?" Darcy asked.

"I'm hoping I won't need it."

"Does that mean you're really considering selling Bad Bachelors?" Remi asked.

Annie's whole body rejected the idea. Every possible signal was there—the awful flipping in her gut, the resounding *no* in her head. It was like the idea repulsed her on some primal level. But what choice did she have?

"Yeah, I am." She reached for her wine and took a long gulp, but it tasted like sawdust. "It's the only way I can see to move forward. I told the buyer about the security issues, and they weren't concerned. Obviously, they have resources to deal with things like that. They'll announce the purchase, which should mean that the spotlight will come off Joe because he has no connection to the buyer. I'm also going to ask it be written into the contract that they'll make a statement saying that the message in the code was a hoax and he has nothing to do with it."

"So…five million dollars." Darcy let out a long whistle. "That's Monopoly money."

"I know. You'd think I would be more excited about it." Annie attempted a laugh, but it didn't sound authentic. Didn't feel it, either. "Stupid, right? How many sad millionaires are there?"

"There's got to be a reason for it," Remi chimed in. "You don't want to sell it, do you?"

"Not really. It's the only thing I've ever created. The only thing I've ever done that went right."

"Did it though?" Remi held up her hands. "I'm over what happened, truly. Forgive and forget and all that. But *has* Bad Bachelors gone right? Is this what you intended it to be?"

There was that rush of intuition again. The resounding *no* that repeated over and over like her heartbeat. Bad Bachelors had given her a glimpse of what she might do with her life, the good she might bring to the world. The positive stamp she might leave by helping women in vulnerable positions.

But Bad Bachelors wasn't it.

She'd been too stubborn to see it when Reed tracked her down. And she was clinging to the good parts when Remi came to her for help. But now, spending time with Joseph and being honest about the past had made her see that Bad Bachelors had grown into something tangled and unwieldy. Every day she was receiving emails about fake reviews, about people using the site to get revenge on their exes, to bring down an enemy at work. Selling now felt like failure, like she was leaving behind a legacy she wasn't proud of.

"I'm so torn," she said, because it was the only honest thing she *could* say.

Was five million worth it? What if Bad Bachelors continued down its dark path, only with advertisers shelling out money for the privilege of having their flashing banners sitting alongside hateful words? To a lot of people, the answer would be yes.

But Annie had said time and time again that she didn't live for money. As much as it would be nice to have that kind of security, all Joseph's family had ever taught her about being wealthy was that it gave people a mean edge.

Like you're a goddamn saint these days…

"Is it something to do with Joseph?" Darcy asked. Annie could tell she was trying not to sound judgmental, but her resentment of Joseph ran deep. "Did you… make up?"

"We didn't make up." Annie shook her head. "There was nothing to make up. Nothing to save. But I do feel like I got some closure, you know? Like I was finally able to forgive him and myself for what happened."

Her stomach churned. Early that morning, when he'd gotten out of her bed, she'd surprised herself by reaching for him. By trying to convince him that maybe they could have one more day.

One more day…

As if it would amount to anything. He'd been the stronger one, holding her tight and kissing her hair but ultimately walking away without a backward glance. That was them in a nutshell—he'd always been able to pull the trigger when she faltered.

"So what now?" Remi asked.

What now, indeed?

"I need to sleep on it. My head is too full of all this stuff, and I have no idea what to think about any of it."

"Do you still love him?" Remi asked.

The question sucked the life out of the room. Darcy shot Remi an *Are you crazy?* look, but their Aussie friend simply shrugged. "What? It's a fair question. You've been staying at his place, sleeping with him. I know you, Annie. You don't do booty calls or one-night stands.

You've barely dated. Has there been *anyone* since him? And I don't mean sex. Have you been attracted to a single other person since you broke up?"

Remi was asking her to answer the question that had been ping-ponging around in her head for days: Can anyone have more than one true love? She'd come to the conclusion that yes, it was possible.

But not for her.

"There's no point loving him. It's over, and we both know it." Annie sucked in a breath. "I need to make a decision, and then I need to do what I should have done the first time: move on."

Chapter 19

"There's something sad about the way the internet brings out the worst in people. Dating is supposed to be fun and exciting, but last night I had a guy ask me to sign an NDA before he agreed to take me out so I wouldn't review him on Bad Bachelors. Is that really what the dating world is coming to?"

—OldFashioned

IT WAS ANOTHER LATE NIGHT IN THE OFFICE. FOR THE three years Joseph worked in Singapore, that was the norm. He'd get in by seven thirty and leave somewhere between nine and ten most nights. Not to mention working every weekend. It was how he'd climbed the ladder so quickly—working hard and not being afraid to get his hands dirty.

But for the first time in his career, he resented how he'd whittled his personal life down to nothing more than a speck on his week. Down to nothing more than a quiet moment while he waited for his coffee to be served at the café near his office, or the brief patch of time where he zoned out in front of the TV before falling into a deep, exhausted sleep.

Is that because work demands it, or because you're using work as a distraction from the real problem?

It was probably a little of both, if he was being honest with himself.

But today he'd stayed late because he had a plan. Earlier that afternoon, he'd met with the journalist and she'd been only too happy to have an exclusive interview *if* she could ask a few questions about his thoughts on Bad Bachelors. They'd agreed she wouldn't spin the piece to make it sound like he was on the defensive. Only time would tell if his gamble paid off. But frankly, with the way he was feeling right now, if his boss walked into his office and fired him on the spot, Joseph would have struggled to give a shit.

Maybe this is a sign. You've stopped caring about anything.

Not true. He cared about Annie.

She popped into his head every few minutes, like an alarm that refused to turn off. Everything he'd done since seeking out this job and resigning from his position in Singapore had been about her. The day in the park was so serendipitous because he'd convinced himself that he wasn't going to reach out to her right away. That he needed to focus on his career and rebuilding his life.

Then fate had thrown her into his path—literally.

An email alert snagged Joseph's attention. It was from a contact in the IT Department.

To: Joseph Preston
From: IT Services—Security
Subject: Terminal 568 Browser Access Report

Hi Joseph,

    Further to our conversation earlier today, please find attached the browser access report for terminal 568, currently assigned to David Macintosh. There were two instances of him accessing forums on this computer, both times to the following URL for less than five minutes duration, collectively:

    www.hackmonster1337.com/member/forums

    Since the site is not on our blacklist, technically Mr. Macintosh hasn't broken any IT policies. But it's concerning that a staff member would be accessing this kind of website on a work computer, and we have since added this site to our blacklist. I have run a virus scan on the terminal, and it doesn't appear to have picked up any malicious software.

    However, I would recommend speaking with the Shared Services HR team in regard to how to handle the situation from a disciplinary standpoint.

Kind regards,

Michael Mitko | IT Manager, ISO & ITSec

Got him.

Joseph saved the report and replied, thanking Michael for the quick turnaround. Then he hit the intercom button on his desk phone.

"Hi, Joseph, what do you need?" Dave's voice sounded like it always did: relaxed and polite, as though he didn't have a worry in the world.

"I want to run something by you. Can you come in for a minute?"

"Sure thing."

A second later, Dave walked into the room and shut the door softly behind him. His easy smile dropped the second he saw his boss's expression. Joseph let the tension hang in the air for a moment. Perhaps it made him a bastard, but he wanted to see the other man squirm. He wanted to see the worry streak across Dave's face while he tried to figure out exactly how much Joseph knew.

"Take a seat," Joseph said, indicating the chairs on the other side of his desk.

Dave lowered himself into one of the black leather chairs, but he immediately started fidgeting. "Is everything okay?"

"You tell me." Joseph cocked his head.

"I'm not sure what you're talking about."

"No?" Joseph toyed with his pen, moving it back and forth between his fingers like a magic trick. He'd seen an old boss do this once, and it was a hell of an intimidation tactic. "I think you know exactly what's wrong."

Dave said nothing. But his face had turned a sickly white. This was the thing about hackers and internet bullies; when it came to face-to-face interaction, they had barely a fraction of the confidence they displayed online. If any at all.

"Do you want to tell me why you were accessing a hacking forum on a work computer?" Joseph asked smoothly.

Dave swallowed. His expression softened a little as though he believed this was just a disciplinary chat about inappropriate internet usage. "A friend sent me a link, and when I clicked on it and realized what it was, I shut it down. I should have raised it with IT and with you. I'm sorry."

"Your friend sent you a link that you accidentally clicked on twice for the same hacking forum?"

Dave shifted in his seat. "I've since asked him to stop sending me things. I know it was wrong to click on that link."

"Hmm." Joseph nodded as though considering the apology. "What about this website?"

He'd printed out a copy of the post that named him as the recipient of Bad Bachelors' not-so-secret dedication. When he slid it across his desk, Dave's eyes widened. "I had nothing to do with that."

"But you accessed it on your work computer."

Dave looked up at him, his eyes flicking back and forth as though trying to find a way out. Accessing the forum had been a dumb move, but that was hackers in a nutshell: cocky. Often they left crumbs around, thinking that no one would be smart enough to see the signs. They got a kind of twisted pleasure out of it. But ego was inevitably what brought them down. Because Joseph *was* smart enough to see the signs.

He'd contemplated telling Dave that it was the photo on his desk that had made Joseph suspect him. But he'd decided against it. Why give the guy information that might make him more careful next time?

Joseph had requested the internet browser report as soon as he'd seen the photo. Evidence that Dave had accessed the forum where Mr. Justice's messages were posted could mean nothing—it *might* be a coincidence. But Joseph knew how to extract information from people, and he'd find out soon enough if his assistant was behind the scare campaign targeting Annie.

"What are you insinuating?" Dave asked, his nostrils flaring.

"Are you denying you accessed this website?"

That's it, take the bait.

"I…" His breath was coming faster now. "I might have read it."

"You know that's not what I'm talking about. You *wrote* this. And before that, you posted on a hacking forum that you knew who was behind Bad Bachelors." He talked clearly and simply. "What I don't understand is why you're making up that there's some hidden message in the source code and that it's somehow connected to me."

"I didn't make it up. I *saw* it with my own eyes."

Gotcha.

"Really? And how would you have accessed it?" Joseph cocked his head. "I understand that code isn't open to anyone who looks."

"You're right. I found it." Dave smirked. Suddenly Joseph could see Mr. Justice, rather than the man Dave pretended to be in person. He could feel the venom pouring off him. "I hacked into the laptop of the bitch who runs the site."

Joseph willed himself not to look at his laptop screen. He'd set up a recording program to capture the confession. Part of him had been worried that Dave wouldn't confess, that he would be too smart to spill all the details. But perhaps the office environment and the fact that the conversation had started with a work focus had lulled him into a false sense of security. Did he know Joseph and Annie had been seeing each other recently? He'd have to gamble that Dave hadn't seen him coming or going from Annie's place.

Playing dumb was the only option. "So the message in the source code is real then?"

The other man looked far too smug for someone digging his own grave. "Yeah, it's real."

"But there's no last name. What on earth made you think it was me?"

"Because it was *your* ex-girlfriend. Leanne Maxwell." He leaned back in his chair, thinking he'd dropped some kind of truth bomb.

Joseph stared at him, letting his anger roll over his face and allowing Dave to think it had everything to do with his "revelation." He would be happy to wring this guy's neck for the pain and stress he'd put Annie through. A strong wave of protectiveness rushed through him.

You do this the right *way. The only way.*

That meant he had to get as much out of Dave as possible, to ensure he wouldn't hurt Annie ever again.

Joseph scrubbed a hand over his face. "You're sure?"

"I went through her computer. Trust me, it's her. I had no idea you two were even connected until I stumbled across a folder full of photos of the two of you." He laughed. "I'm guessing you dumped her, right? Makes sense. Good motivation to start a revenge site. Some women just can't let go. And I'm guessing since she had over a thousand happy snaps still sitting on her computer, you must have broken her heart pretty good."

Joseph's heart squeezed as he remembered finding

the folder on her computer that first night she'd asked him to come over. Wasn't that rule number one of a breakup? Burn the evidence? Or delete the evidence, in this case.

Why had she hung on to the photos when it seemed like everything else from their old life was gone?

"I'll take that silence as a yes," Dave said. "Oh, and you want to know something funny? The folder where all the photos were kept was called 'One True Love.' Pathetic, right?"

One. True. Love.

They'd talked about that once—the idea that there was one person for everyone. A soul mate. The way Joseph had grown up, he wasn't sure he believed in such notions. He didn't really understand the love his parents shared. They weren't affectionate; he'd never seen them hold hands or kiss. Most days it was like they were two colleagues rather than people in love.

Annie's family was the opposite. Sal and Connie had both found a second chance at love, and they seemed to have no shortage of affection. Of hugs and welcoming smiles and laughter. All the things that had been sorely lacking in his own childhood.

"Trust me, I'm doing you a favor." Dave nodded as though convinced of his own bullshit.

"But why out me publicly and not her?"

"Because I'm trying to get her to shut Bad Bachelors down quietly. She'll be a martyr if I out her. I want her to shut it down and slink off into the night anonymously. She doesn't deserve to have the world know her name." He shook his head. "Sure, there will be a lot of angry people after her. But I'm not stupid. There will be plenty of people who will praise her too. If I have to out her, I absolutely will. But I'd prefer that she doesn't get any credit for Bad Bachelors."

Which meant his threat of posting her personal information online would only be acted upon as a last resort. Mr. Justice had simply been bragging, as hackers often did. "So you're pressuring her by threatening *me*? What happened to all that bullshit about this industry needing more people like me?"

"Publishing the message from the source code won't hurt you that much. You've got that interview now, and you came off like a beacon of light for the banking industry. The main goal is to get Bad Bachelors wiped off the map," he said. "For good."

Dave's speech about sometimes needing to get one's hands dirty for the greater good now made a whole lot more sense. It was how he viewed his actions—flinging a little dirt Joseph's way was acceptable if it meant taking down Bad Bachelors.

"And where are you going to stop, huh?" Joseph asked. "Are you threatening her?"

"Do you really care? You've moved on."

No, I haven't.

It hit him like a bolt of lightning. He hadn't moved on, and getting out of her bed and leaving their old place this morning was just him going through the motions. An attempt to feel how he wanted to feel rather than letting the truth sink in.

Would he have gotten so involved in this situation if he didn't want her in his life? He could have protected her while maintaining his distance by hiring someone to watch over her. But he'd wanted to be the one looking after her; he'd wanted to be around her. And all the times when he wasn't, he thought about her. Constantly.

"I care, because what you're doing is illegal." Joseph ground the words out through gritted teeth. "I care because I'm your boss, and you've been accessing inappropriate websites on a work laptop during work hours. That alone is a terminable offense."

Dave stared him down. "You don't want to fire me."

"I think I do."

"If you fire me, I'll dox her on the black-hat forums so that other people can hunt her down. *They* won't be praising her, believe me. I'll go on every dark-web forum I can and encourage people to take action." Dave's eyes narrowed to slits, his fingers digging white-knuckled into the arms of his chair. "There are a lot of psychos online, you know."

"One is sitting right in front of me," Joseph drawled. "Your behavior is abhorrent."

"I thought you'd appreciate it, someone taking action instead of simply complaining. I thought that's how *you* were. But maybe you're more like the dinosaurs here than I thought."

Joseph was done with this conversation. He reached over and clicked the end-recording button on his laptop and made sure the file was saved to the company's shared drive so it would be automatically backed up.

"What was that?" Dave's eyes grew wide. "Were you recording me?"

Fucking hackers, always so cocky. The guy hadn't even

thought for a second Joseph might be recording the conversation.

"Yes, I was. I needed to make sure you didn't try to claim that I fabricated this story." He nailed his employee with a hard stare. "Now, if you do *anything* to Annie, I will take this recording to the police and make sure she presses charges. Hacking and internet stalking are tough to prosecute, but between this conversation and your browser history on your work computer, you've left quite the bread-crumb trail. You know what this means, right?"

Dave's expression turned brittle, and he clenched his jaw.

"I'll take that silence as a yes," Joseph said, tossing the man's words back at him.

"If you out me, you'll also be outing yourself. And her," Dave snarled.

"Fine by me. But I won't be outing her. Bad Bachelors will have a new owner by then, so Annie won't be connected to it anymore."

"I can't believe you're taking the side of a woman who created such a *disgusting* thing."

"She created a website to help women. The people using it made the decision to write the questionable reviews." Of course, Joseph saw both sides of the coin. Annie was absolutely operating in a gray area—but he wasn't going to get into it with Dave. He didn't owe the other man his opinion. Joseph stood, indicating the conversation was over.

"Do you have *any* idea what damage those reviews are doing?" Dave shot out of his seat. "My friend might lose his kid because his bitch ex-wife convinced all her friends to post crap about him online that made him look like a bad dad."

"I'm sorry for your friend, but that doesn't justify you stalking and threatening people." Joseph would have a word with Annie about the reviews though. Because *nobody* should lose custody of their child over something like this. That was wrong, plain and simple. "I've arranged security for Annie, so don't even think about doing anything stupid."

Dave stormed out of the office, slamming the door behind him. Prior to calling him into the room, Joseph had given Andrew the heads-up about his plans so he could keep an eye out for anything that might pop up. But something told Joseph that Dave would slink away into the night like the slug he was.

Joseph slumped into his seat, the weight of the day crashing down like an avalanche. There was so much to process. Until now, he hadn't thought much about the photos of him that Annie had kept in a folder called *One True Love*. That information had taken a back seat to other things, but he'd be lying to himself if he didn't admit that knowing she'd kept the photos warmed something inside him.

Despite the circumstances that had brought them together, being with Annie again had made him feel like the old Joseph. The guy who'd had more in his life than a job he didn't love. The guy who'd cared about something other than board packs and spread-sheets and strategies.

He looked around the office. The sleek white walls

and gray carpet and silver shelving might as well have been a prison. He didn't want to be here. He didn't want to be this guy.

More importantly, he didn't want to be the person who let love—real love—slip through his fingers. But he and Annie had so much water under the bridge. Such a tangled past to deal with. And it wasn't only about them. Family was involved, and he needed to take that into consideration because her family was everything to her, and he'd never known that kind of love. That kind of bond.

If he had any chance of reconciling with Annie, there were other people he needed to talk to. Because the qualities he loved about Annie—her determination, her loyalty, her fierceness—were ones she owed to her family.

He hadn't only let her down. By abandoning them in a time of need, he'd let her family down too. And that meant he owed Connie and Sal an apology.

———

As the days crept on, Annie's sense of unease swelled around her. She'd heard nothing more from Mr. Justice, nothing more from Joseph, and all the while the weight of her decision sat heavily on her shoulders. The deadline was fast approaching, and tomorrow Sasha Jenkins would demand an answer.

Five million dollars…

Her whole future could be taken care of. She would have to be crazy to turn it down.

What's the point of a future with a permanent reminder of your failings?

Because that's what Bad Bachelors had become. The idea was a good one—wanting to help women protect their hearts and themselves—but the execution was fundamentally flawed. Only she'd been too blind to see it, too bitter to listen to her friends when they questioned the good it did, too stubborn to change her thinking.

She'd been wrong to create Bad Bachelors.

This was the point at which she could rectify those problems. Because once she sold it to Sasha Jenkins, Bad Bachelors would continue to do more damage. And she would have no way to make up for her mistakes.

Which meant there was only one real path to take: she had to shut Bad Bachelors down.

Not sell it or try to rebrand or turn it into something else. It needed to be gone. Only then could she live without a noose around her neck. It was a conclusion she should have come to much sooner because all the signs were there. If she couldn't tell her family about it—people who would *never* have ratted her out or compromised her safety—then how did she really feel about it?

Ashamed. Embarrassed. Regretful.

It was like standing in the bottom of a well, staring way up to the glimmering light above. She didn't want to stay living in the darkness and solitude. She didn't want to spend every hour of her days worried someone would find her out. She didn't want to have to choose her own security over important relationships.

In trying to find something to care about in life, she'd only secured the lock on her own prison.

For the first time in three years, Annie felt lighter. She'd been coming to this conclusion ever since she'd run into Joseph at Central Park. Her life had been missing something: a path to the future. Hope. Honesty.

Because hiding and secrecy and lies weren't who she was. Dwelling in the shadows and being in a constant state of fear and defensiveness wasn't the existence she wanted for herself. The old Annie would *never* have allowed this to happen. She'd had dreams, once. Real dreams of doing something meaningful with her life, of leaving her mark on the world in some positive way.

Wasn't that what Nonno had always said to her? *Leave your patch of the world in a better state than how you found it.*

Could she honestly say that creating Bad Bachelors was the way to improve her patch? No, she could not. Which meant the only way out was to make a change.

Bad Bachelors had to go.

The five million dollars had to go.

The cracks on her heart had to go.

Releasing a shaky breath, she reached for her laptop and opened the Bad Bachelors email account. With every word of her response to Sasha Jenkins, Annie grew more confident in her decision.

Of course, she had no idea what she would do next. If Mr. Justice would come after her. Or if Joseph would accept her apology for…well, everything.

But she had to try. Because that idealistic girl who'd graduated from college with her head full of ideas, the woman who'd promised her mother she would make something of herself one day, was worth saving.

As soon as she sent the email, Annie would hit the kill switch on Bad Bachelors.

Chapter 20

"Dear Sasha, it is with regret that I must decline your generous offer. After much thought, I know the only path forward is to shut Bad Bachelors down totally and completely."

JOSEPH PULLED ONTO THE STREET IN BENSONHURST where Annie had grown up. Despite knowing her since they were kids, he'd been in his early twenties by the time he'd seen where she lived. The first time he'd come to her house had been like opening his eyes to another world. Like seeing the families he'd watched on TV—the small kitchen where everyone sat around the table to eat, the loud, enthusiastic chatter and warmth. People who hugged one another.

He hadn't understood why his home was so different. His father had never told Joseph that he loved him, or that he was proud. It was always criticism under the guise of making him a better person, all the while hinting at Morris's disappointment or disapproval. But the second Joseph had walked into Sal and Connie's place, they'd opened their arms to him—physically and emotionally.

In fact, he remembered Sal embracing him in a

big bear hug not more than a month into his relationship with Annie, and the family had joked that Joseph looked like a deer caught in headlights. The truth was, he hadn't known how to behave like that—to be affectionate. And he'd been so fearful of making the wrong move that he'd stood there like a statue until Sal had released him.

But it had felt *so* good to be part of their family unit. As much as he'd resented the way Annie had put him second and the way she'd shut him out of her decision-making, he'd missed them all. A lot.

He pulled his car up behind Sal's work truck. They would be finishing dinner by now. He could practically see it in his head: Sal still at the table, hacking into an orange and using the knife to bring the juicy pieces of fruit to his mouth. Connie yelling at Sal for teaching the girls bad habits. Sofia and Allegra giggling and rolling their eyes.

He sat in the car for a moment and watched the house. Like most residences on this block, it looked a little run down. There was peeling paint and a few dying shrubs in decade-old pots. But the warm glow emanating from the front rooms filled his heart with hope.

Would they hear him out? Accept his apology? He wasn't sure he deserved it.

Sucking in a deep breath, he got out of the car. His feet were heavy as he walked up the steps to the front door, fear tugging at him. He needed to do this. Even if it led nowhere, and they slammed the door in his face, he needed to try. He needed to apologize.

Not for Annie. But for Connie and Sal. For the girls.

For the family who'd embraced him right up until the moment he'd betrayed them.

Happy family sounds emanated from the kitchen, which was right near the front door. When he knocked, rattling the screen against the wooden frame behind it, there was a cheerful "Coming!" from inside. A second later, the door flew open.

Sofia stood behind the screen, a polite smile hovering on her lips for a second until recognition set in. She was far from the fourteen-year-old he remembered—the one who was all limbs and elbows, a gangly baby llama of a girl with braces and waist-length hair.

"Joe?" She squinted, her voice low. "I almost didn't recognize you with the beard. What are you doing here?"

"Are your parents home?" he asked. "I'd like to speak to them if possible."

Sofia bit down on her lower lip, clearly unsure how to proceed.

"I can wait," he said.

She nodded and went back into the house, leaving the door open. The scent of basil and tomato wafted out, and music played in the background—something sixties and groovy. Connie's favorite. He stuffed his hands into his coat pockets, regretting not bringing his scarf as the wind whooshed past.

"What in the hell?" Sal appeared in the doorway. In contrast to his daughter, he looked exactly the same as Joseph remembered. A man with a big barrel of a chest, and an even bigger mustache. Warm eyes and salt-and-pepper hair. Sauce stain on his shirt, as always. "What are you doing here?"

Joseph swallowed. He had to remind himself that, as with his own father, the bark was worse than the bite. And it wasn't Sal he should be worried about. It was Connie.

"I wondered if we might talk," he said, rocking back on his dress shoes. He felt ridiculously overdressed in his cashmere coat and bespoke suit with the monogrammed silk pocket square his mother had given him and the Ferragamo double monks that cost the earth.

"What could we possibly have to talk about?"

It started to rain. With a crack of thunder, the heavens opened, and rain poured down in sheets.

Sal rolled his eyes. "Christ. Come inside before you get sick."

Even in his angriest moment, Annie's stepfather couldn't refuse a person on his doorstep. "Thank you."

"Connie," Sal called, his head angled to the back of the house. "We've got a guest."

Sofia poked her head out of the kitchen to watch, her eyes darting up the hallway to where her mother would materialize any second. Always the quietest of the kids, she didn't say a word. But concern showed in the knitting of her brows.

"Who is…" The words died on Connie's lips. Then, "What the fuck are you doing here?"

"Mom!" Sofia came out into the hallway at the same time Sal threw his hands up.

"Connie." He frowned. "Please. Not in front of Sofia."

"I'm sure she hears worse at school, Sal." Connie walked right up to Joseph. She was all of five foot two, with a wild halo of frizzy hair and earrings that made music when she moved her head. "What do you want?"

Joseph found himself tongue-tied. Throughout his career, he'd never had a problem speaking in front of an audience. He'd stared down seas of journalists at press conferences, looked into the blinding spotlights of a five-hundred-person auditorium. He'd faced down powerful CEOs and board members. But the sight of this woman vibrating with anger made him want to turn tail and run for the hills.

No running. You need to do this. You need to own up to your mistakes.

There was no point beating around the bush. Best to get it out in the open and pray for mercy. "I'm long overdue for an apology," he said. "I'm here to say sorry."

"About three years too late, isn't it?" Connie arched an eyebrow.

"Absolutely." He nodded.

"Sof, why don't you get some coffee going," Sal said to his youngest daughter. "Don't worry about the dishes. We'll do them after."

Sofia reluctantly went back into the kitchen, and the sound of cupboards opening and closing came a minute later. The three adults stood in the entrance, awkwardly silent as though waiting for someone else to make a move.

"Since I came back to New York, I've been doing a lot of self-assessment. The way I ended things with Annie and with you has been weighing on me." Joseph kept his hands in his pockets to stop himself from fidgeting, but the discomfort burrowed into his bones. In his family, his father was always right. There was no discussion, no talking through bad decisions or failures. Just stony silence. "Leaving the way I did, after your diagnosis, is something I will always regret."

Connie's fiery anger had diminished a little, but her arms were still folded tightly over her chest.

"Even if Annie and I weren't able to make our situation work, I should have come to say goodbye. To be an adult and not run away from the situation because I didn't know how to handle it."

Connie didn't say anything. She stood there, regarding him as one might a scientific experiment with warning signs all over it. Like she couldn't tear her eyes away, but at the same time she didn't want to get too close.

"Why don't we sit instead of standing in the doorway," Sal said gently.

"I didn't want to interrupt your evening," Joseph replied.

"Well, you have." Connie sighed and walked into the living room. "So we may as well sit."

The space was small, with two couches in a faded floral covering crowding the space. Photos of the family filled one wall—Annie in plain clothes with the girls in ballet costumes on either side of her. They had those cheesy family portraits, the ones where pets were encouraged to attend. So Lupo was there too, looking proud and strong while almost being strangled by a young Sofia, her spindly arms wrapped around his neck as she pressed her cheek into his fur. Then there was one of Annie on her graduation day—her smile so bright and wide it made something shift in his chest.

He'd been there, clapping and cheering alongside her parents and sisters. One of them. Part of the family.

Connie and Sal took their spots on one couch, and Joseph sat on the other. God, what else was he supposed to say? He wasn't sure how much Annie had told them about Bad Bachelors and her recent troubles, if anything at all. His gut told him she'd likely kept it all a secret.

"I guess the main thing I wanted to say was that I'm sorry. For hurting Annie and for vanishing."

"You hurt us too," Connie said, her hands folded in her lap. "When we accept someone into this family, we love them like one of our own."

His throat tightened. It was true. He'd felt more acceptance from this family than he ever had from his own parents.

"I've known you since you were a little boy," she said. "You used to run around while I cleaned your parents' house, always smiling and cheeky. You were good for Annie. You helped build her confidence, and you grounded her. After you left, she…turned into a different person."

"I turned into a different person too." He swallowed.

He'd turned into the kind of guy who could get engaged to a person he didn't love, a guy who put career prestige before the things that really mattered in life. A guy who shoved his own aspirations into a box in order to please his father, a man who didn't even know him.

"I was glad to hear you pulled through the treatment so well," he said.

Connie tilted her head, surprise streaking across her

face. "And how did you find that out? If you weren't talking to Annie, that is."

"I asked a mutual acquaintance to check in and report back. I knew it wouldn't be right to add any extra stress by reaching out myself, but…I wanted to know you were okay."

Her expression softened a little, but she made a derisive huffing noise to cover it. Sal reached over and enveloped her hand in his big bear paw. "Connie's a fighter," he said.

"You are tested in those moments," she said, and he got a glimpse into how vulnerable it had made her. "Your beliefs of what is right are tested, your desires are tested, and you find yourself understanding what is really important. That all the things society has led you to believe you want—riches and fancy things and to be envied—aren't worth shit."

Joseph let out a raw chuckle. The past few weeks had taught him that exact lesson. What he'd left behind in Manhattan were the very things he should have been chasing—love, family, belonging. Not some mythical acceptance his father would never give him. Morris would find the next thing, dangle another carrot in front of his son just to see if he'd be obedient and chase it.

He curled his hand over the arm of the couch. At that moment, Lupo trotted into the room and then, recognizing Joseph, bounded over to the couch. The big dog leaped up and settled next to him, draping his huge paws over Joseph's suit pants and resting his head there.

"Lupo! *Basta, vai!*" Sal got up to shoo the dog, but Joseph waved him away.

"It's fine." He gave the dog a scratch behind the ears,

struck with memories the second he touched the wiry gray fur. The dog made a satisfied little whine when Joseph found his favorite spot, right behind his ear. "Good boy."

"Apparently dogs don't hold grudges," Connie said, shaking her head. "That damn beast always had a crush on you."

"Do you remember the first time he came over?" Sofia appeared in the doorway with three cups precariously cradled in her hands. She set one down in front of Joseph and then handed one each to Connie and Sal. "Lupo was barking so loud that Joe didn't want to come inside."

"Not my bravest moment," Joseph admitted with a self-deprecating smirk. "I'd never seen a dog that big before."

"Not many people have." Sal puffed his chest out. He'd rescued Lupo from a scrap yard when the dog was just a puppy and already too big for most families.

The dog, an Irish wolfhound, only understood commands in Italian since Sal's father had looked after him for the first three years. The limited Italian that Joseph learned had mostly revolved around issuing doggy commands in Lupo's native language.

Sofia squeezed herself into the corner of the couch, earning a slight grumble from Lupo who shifted further into Joseph's lap.

"I see he's still under the impression he's a lapdog," Joseph said.

Sofia smiled, her expression tentative and unsure. "I don't think that will ever change."

Joseph wasn't sure what else to say. But simply sitting here, with them, made him see how much of an idiot he'd been. It hit him like a ton of bricks. In light of Connie's breast cancer diagnosis, *of course* Annie had needed to stay. Her mother was everything to her. Her family was everything. And he should have been part of that, instead of being her opposition. While he wasn't going to waver that it should have been a joint decision, he understood her actions now. Family was more important to her than her own needs.

She hadn't put him second, she'd put *herself* second.

"Does Annie know you're here?" Connie asked.

He shook his head. "No. This wasn't about trying to score points. The apology was for you, and I have a separate one for her."

"Why did you go?" Sofia asked. Her eyes were bright, perceptive. She never missed a beat when it came to people.

"My father pushed me to take the job, and I thought it was the right thing to do. I thought he wanted what was best for me. Plus, Annie and I had dreamed of seeing the world together, and she'd always wanted to go to Asia. It was the chance of a lifetime…"

His voice trailed off as it hit him. Morris must have hoped it would break them up, knowing how close Annie was with her family. After learning of Connie's diagnosis, Joseph had gone to his parents for advice. His father had told him not to be stupid, that of course he should still go, that her family would understand if they wanted a good life for him. That Annie herself should understand his career was their future. That this move would set them up for life. And if she didn't understand that, then did she really care about him?

Why didn't you see what a manipulative bastard he was at the time?

"I should have listened to my gut," he murmured. "Not my head."

"We all make mistakes," Sal said. Although he wasn't as fiery as his wife, Sal's approval went a long way in this family. "Not all families have their priorities straight."

Connie nodded and sipped her coffee. "Do you plan to stay in Manhattan this time around?"

Joseph nodded. "This is my home. It's good to be back."

"It took balls coming here," Connie said. "I appreciate that."

"Does this mean you're getting back together with Annie?" Sofia asked.

Joseph laid a hand on Lupo's head, and the dog nuzzled against him. "I want to. But it's entirely up to her. All I know is that I haven't been able to move on…and I don't want to. She's it for me. She always has been."

"Are you asking for our blessing?" Connie watched him closely.

"No, because I couldn't help loving her even without it." He met the woman's stare, hoping that she could see right into him. That she could see his truth. "I've tried so hard to forget about her, but I can't. Walking away didn't change how I felt. About any of you."

"Then it's a good thing you came home," Sal said. "Family always hurts when one of their own is on the wrong path."

"I'm sorry I wasn't here for you, Connie," Joseph

said. "I won't ever make that mistake for someone I care about again."

She rose out of her chair and came over to him, wrapping her arms around his shoulders in a crushing hug. Lupo whined and tried to get between them, wanting the affection for himself. "Don't hurt her again."

"You have my word." He hugged Connie back, feeling like for the first time since he'd returned to New York, he was with family again.

What has become of the Dating Information Warrior?

By Kiera Cox, *Spill the Tea* society and culture reporter

Outside of politics and baseball, it's been a long time since something divided New Yorkers quite like Bad Bachelors. The website and app, which allowed the women of Manhattan to rate and review their dates, had equally vocal supporters and detractors. Even among the *Spill the Tea* staff, Bad Bachelors generated a lot of debate.

Adding fuel to the fire was the relentless anonymity of its creator. Countless people have speculated on who's behind it and what their motives might be.

However, last night New York's most talked-about website went dark. Avid Bad Bachelors supporter and power user Hailey Redman noted that when she attempted to log on to the website last night around seven, she received an error.

Rumors of a security breach exploded on social media. After all, anyone who knows anything about the internet could see why a website like this would be the target of groups content to use illegal means to silence female voices. To bolster this argument, people have pointed to the anonymous hacking website that recently posted a portion of Bad Bachelors' source code with a supposed hidden message dedicating the site to someone called Joseph.

However, this morning something new appeared. Where once the Bad Bachelors' home page had stood proud, with its pink banner and blog posts signed by someone calling themselves only by the moniker "Your Dating Information Warrior," there was only a single line of text. The once-thriving site has been reduced to the following message:

> I never meant for this to get out of hand. I want to help people, and I realize now this isn't the way to do it. I'm sorry.

A legitimate note from the person who created Bad Bachelors? Or a false message from someone who has a lot to gain by shutting it down? The app also appears to have disappeared from most major app stores.

Does this signal the end of Bad Bachelors?

For now, we will have to wait and see what becomes of the Dating Information Warrior and the Bad Bachelors franchise. Does this mean we need to go back to bitching about our dates over margaritas in the Village? Likely.

Annie burrowed her chin into the depths of her coat and scarf, bowing her head to the chill. Most of the leaves in Central Park were now on the ground, the trees swaying in the wind like ghosts. Today was gray and miserable, and it felt like someone had turned New York's thermostat way down. Though winter didn't technically start for another week or so, it was threatening. Soon they would have the first flurries of snow, and the city would begin its annual transformation into a Christmas wonderland.

"Perfect time to turn into a recluse," Annie said to herself as she walked along the path, her eyes fixed ahead of her.

Christmas wasn't her favorite time of year, though most people didn't really know why. They assumed it was because she eschewed all things traditionally romantic, especially after her breakup with Joseph. But the fact was, Christmas was when her dad had died, and she'd always found it hard to feel festive because of that. She made an effort for Sal and the girls, but usually she spent a good portion of the week between Christmas and New Year's in hiding, wallowing in her grief and creating a strong Annie-shaped dent in her couch.

As much as she loved Sal like a father, she also missed her dad. According to Connie, Annie was more like him than she was like her mother. Her dad had been an engineer, and he'd liked numbers and order and rules. Just like she did. Secretly, Annie had always assessed herself on how proud she thought her dad would be of her if he were still alive.

But lately the answer to that question had raised some uncomfortable feelings. That was, until she'd shut Bad Bachelors down.

Annie strolled toward the pond. Today the water's surface rippled with the wind. Though it was a Saturday morning, the park wasn't as busy as usual. The gloomy weather must have driven people into the surrounding coffee shops and stores. Which meant Annie was able to find a bench to sit on. She tucked her knees up to her chest and wrapped her arms around them, resting her heels on the edge of the bench.

The future stretched out in front of her like a long, unending tunnel. Everything was murky, hard to see. For most people, the chance to start fresh would be an exciting prospect, if a bit daunting. But Annie felt the weight of responsibility on her shoulders. This time, she was going to get it right. This time, she was going to start something from a place of goodness, and then she would keep it that way.

Her phone buzzed.

REMI: Where are you? Bad Bachelors is down, and Darcy said she couldn't get hold of you. Please tell us that you're safe!

ANNIE: I'm fine. Just taking some time out to think. Bad Bachelors is done. For good.

REMI: Are you okay?

ANNIE: I will be.

Of course she would be. Annie was a fighter, a survivor. Like her mother. She would take the lessons she'd learned and pour her heart into something better. She would *be* better. A better friend, a better person.

A better lover?

That she had no idea about.

Something made her look up, a flash of movement

out of the corner of her eye. Joseph was walking toward her, like he'd stepped straight out of her head and onto the path. Was he here to see her? Or was he here to think? This spot had had a gravitational pull for both of them, even from the beginning.

"I thought I might find you here." He wore a pair of jeans and a puffy black coat over a gray hoodie.

As much as she loved the way he looked in a suit, this was almost worse. Because the suit was his armor, his uniform. This Joseph—with the worn jeans and crooked smile—was *her* man. The man who'd been a childhood friend, a teenage crush, the man who'd made her fall head over heels in college, the man who'd been her first and only…everything.

"I needed to get out."

"Got space on that bench for a friend?" He jammed his hands into his pockets.

Friend. She swallowed. They would never be friends. Because what she felt for him couldn't be contained by such a gentle term. That was part of her problem—with him, she would need to be all in or all out.

And that was terrifying.

"Sure." She shuffled over, and he sat next to her.

"So, anything you want to tell me?"

She let out a short, humorless laugh. "Ah, so you know."

"I know everything," he said with a wink. "Okay, well, maybe not everything. But I do know that Bad Bachelors is down."

"How?"

"I tried to look at it this morning."

"Did you want to see if anyone had written about you?" She turned to him.

"I don't care what anyone has to say about me," he said. "Except you."

"Now you'll never know. Bad Bachelors is nothing but pixel dust."

His easy expression morphed into something more serious. "Until the new owner rebrands it, you mean?"

She shook her head. "Nope, I mean forever. I didn't sell it."

Joseph's silence was deafening—it rang in her ears like a foghorn. His blue eyes flicked back and forth like he was trying to figure something out. "You didn't sell it," he said. "Then why did you take it down?"

That was the five-million-dollar question.

How could she say she loved him if the consequence of their breakup still existed?

Because she *did* love him. She'd never stopped. It was precisely why she'd hung on to her anger. Because it allowed her to keep thinking about him, to keep him present in her soul. It was the reason she didn't have any success in dating. There was no one else for her.

"It was time," she said. "And I'm not trying to be cryptic. I was done. I'd learned my lesson, and in order for me to move on, Bad Bachelors needed to be gone."

"So it had nothing to do with me?" he asked.

"It had *everything* to do with you," she replied. A lump formed in the back of her throat, strangling her words. "From start to finish."

"You gave up five million dollars." He shook his head. "Are you crazy?"

"I needed to do something for me, something that's good. Positive. I, um… I can't pay you back for the apartment yet, but I will. I—"

Joseph held up his hand. "I don't care about the apartment. I don't care about anything you owe me, because we were never that couple who tallied points and counted pennies."

She didn't need to point out that Manhattan property could hardly be classified as "pennies" by anyone. "And the thought that I'd hurt your career made me sick to my stomach. Your job is so important to you, and if I did anything to make people doubt you, I'm sorry."

"I hate my job."

She blinked. "What?"

"I hate it. It's not what I wanted to do with my life at all. You were right. I wanted to have my own security consulting company. I wanted to tackle puzzles and build things and teach people how to protect themselves. And then I got caught up in the ladder-climbing and the prestige. I should never have taken that job in Singapore."

Annie watched a brown leaf skip along the path in front of them, until a gust of wind picked it up and blew it over the water where it landed softly and floated away. "You were so excited."

"I thought I was." He slipped his arm along the back of the bench, and she scooted in closer to him. "But in hindsight, I was chasing my father's approval. I thought if I kept doing what he wanted, eventually he'd… I don't know, accept me? Love me? Not treat me like I'm a constant disappointment?"

"How could anyone think you're a disappointment?" She frowned. "You work so hard, and you're good at everything you do."

He shook his head. "Not everything. I let him manipulate me into forgoing the life I wanted. I lost you. I lost hold of my dreams."

"What are you going to do about it? The job thing, I mean."

"What I should have done three years ago. I'm quitting the corporate world."

"Really?" She shook her head. "What about your dad? What will—"

"It's none of his business what I do. I should never have let it be his business in the first place." He sighed. "Like you said, it's time to walk away."

"Good for you."

"What about you? What comes after Bad Bachelors?"

"I want to do something that helps people. My mom has a friend who teaches self-defense. I want to take that and apply it more broadly to women…and men. I want to teach people to protect themselves physically as well as online." The idea was brewing, gathering steam. "I'm thinking of a website that's like a one-stop shop for fixing your life. I want it to be empowering, but also about lifting people up instead of bringing them down. It's a place where people can learn to be confident, where they can heal after something bad has happened. I want to help people come to terms with loss and heart-break, and I want to help them rebuild."

"What are you going to call it?" he asked.

"I don't know." She leaned her head on his shoulder and

brought her bare hands up to her mouth, blowing warm air on them. It was starting to rain. A fine mist descended on them, and Joseph reached behind her head to pull her hood up over her. "What's the opposite of Bad Bachelors?"

"Good People?" he suggested.

"I like that." The name made her smile. "I promise I won't dedicate this one to you."

He chuckled. "Thanks."

They sat in silence for a moment. She had so much to say, and yet no words came to her lips.

Tell him you love him.

The need to confess rushed through her like a river.

Tell him. Tell him. Tell him.

But what would be the point? Even if he said he loved her back, it wasn't like they could be together and magically everything would work out. Morris would hate her more than ever now, especially if he thought she had anything to do with Joseph quitting his job. She'd never be accepted by his parents, and it would create a wedge whether she wanted it to or not.

And God only knew what her family would say about it. Her mother had been calling all morning, but Annie couldn't find the strength to pick up the phone. She knew it was time to come clean with them about Bad Bachelors and Joseph and everything…but it would have to wait until tomorrow. She needed today to figure out what her next steps were.

"What are you not telling me?" he asked. "I can hear your brain working from here."

She laughed. The rain pelted down harder now, but neither one of them moved. A second later, an umbrella popped open and he held it over them. They were going to get soaked if they stayed here too much longer, even with a bit of coverage. The wind roared and shook the trees and sent the fabric of the umbrella flapping in protest.

"I'm not telling you that I love you," she said, looking straight ahead. Tears spilled onto her cheeks, mixing with the spray of the rain. "Because I'm sad it's over and I need time to figure out what to do with my life."

"It doesn't have to be over." Underneath the black nylon, his face was close to hers. She could easily lose herself in the reflective blue pools of his eyes and let herself forget everything. All their troubles and their differences and their mistakes. "I don't want it to be over."

His lips lowered to hers, one arm snaking around her neck as he held her and tried to keep them sheltered at the same time. He tasted of comfort and tears, of fantasy and the dark, gray reality. All things that didn't belong together.

She kissed him back with everything she had—with her lips and tongue and teeth and nails. With her hands and her arms. She kissed him like she was trying to get a lifetime's worth of kisses out in one go.

Could she believe him when he said it wasn't over? Could their sacrifices possibly make up for all the mistakes and the hurt and the anger? Were they strong enough this time?

Chapter 21

"Dear Leanne. There are not many people in this world who would turn down $5m for the sake of personal principles. I'm not sure whether to think you're crazy or stronger than the rest of us."

—Sasha Jenkins

JOSEPH'S HEART HAMMERED AS HE SAT ROOTED TO THE bench as though someone had taken a staple gun and pinned him in place. The nylon of his umbrella flapped as another breeze whooshed past, spraying them with more rain. Overhead, the clouds were thick and black.

If you can't man the fuck up now and tell her exactly how you feel, then you will lose her forever.

It didn't matter how uncomfortable it made him. It didn't matter how little experience he had. Right now, he had two choices: let her walk away and earn his misery, or fight for the chance to get her back.

"You're not saying anything." He'd told her he didn't want it to be over and her silence was killing him.

"I don't know what to say." Her eyes were wide, black pools, and her cheeks glistened from where the rain had sprayed her skin. "I'm scared."

He was scared too. Terrified. More than he'd been in all his life.

Coming across her sitting at "their spot" wasn't entirely a coincidence—he'd come looking for her after getting no answer at her apartment. There was a small box in his pocket, rose petals on his bed, champagne chilling in his fridge. Everything he'd planned for the night he was supposed to propose.

"Why don't we go back to my place? We're going to get soaked out here." He brushed away the moisture on her cheeks. "I may even be able to lend you a small towel."

Annie laughed, and it was like the sky had split open to allow the sun to shine through. "Are you going to send me home in it?"

"Who would do something so cruel?"

He stood and held the umbrella over her, reaching out with one hand. She hesitated a moment, emotion warring in her eyes. Her pale face was framed by the hood of her parka. Wide eyes drank him in as she wrapped her arms around herself, almost shrinking into nothing. She was vulnerable now. Because she'd loved him hard before, and it had hurt them both so much.

But this time would be different. This time he would get everything out of his head and into the world, so she knew *exactly* what he felt. The time for running away from hard conversations and feelings and emotions—all things he'd been taught to avoid—was over.

"Can you trust me?" he asked.

"I *do* trust you."

They walked along a path curving around the pond and out onto the street, hailing a cab on West

Fifty-Ninth. Neither one of them spoke a word as they slid into the back seat. Rain pelted the cab, creating a drumming sound that blocked everything out. Joseph ran through his speech over and over in his head, until the words jumbled into a big mess. By the time they made it to his place, he had no idea what to say anymore.

Just tell her how you feel.

Could it be that easy? That after all this time, could he just lay down the simple fact that he still loved her?

When they walked through his front door, Annie didn't slip out of her coat. Was that a bad sign? Was she prepared to leave at any second?

"What am I doing here, Joe?"

Joe. Not Joseph. "I came to find you at the park because I've left too many things unsaid."

"Like what?"

"Every day I spent in Singapore without you was like giving up a piece of myself." He stepped toward her, drawn to her the way he always was. The way he knew he would never *ever* be drawn to another person. "By the end, I had given so much of myself away that I had no idea if there was anything left worth caring about.

"I kept a picture of you inside my passport wallet, and I looked at it all the time. I can't even tell you how many times I thought about tearing it into little pieces just to be free of the hold it had over me. But I couldn't bring myself to do it. I couldn't let go, and for so long I didn't know why. Then I realized…I didn't *want* to let go. I didn't want us to be over because I never stopped loving you, not even for a second."

"Once you say these things, you can't take them back."

She was afraid they'd go down the same path again. That something else would rock their security and that one of them would walk away.

"I don't want to take them back. I should have married you, Annie. Like I had planned to all along. You're the only person who makes me feel like I can be myself."

"That's how you make me feel," she said. "But it's not that simple. There's so much more that goes into loving someone."

"Like what? Our families? Because I want to be part of yours again. I tried to make you choose, and it didn't work because I missed one fundamental thing: we were already family. The ring wasn't going to make a lick of difference, because it was a symbol of something that already existed. You were right to want to stay with your mom. I shouldn't have seen that as you choosing sides, because there was only one side."

She looked up at him, her eyes bright and shining. "They loved you, you know. They wanted you to stay as much as I did."

"I know." He bobbed his head. "I went to see them last night."

"What?" She blinked. "Why?"

"Because I owed them an apology too. God. I made a mess of things, but I will happily spend my whole life trying to right those wrongs for you." He brushed a strand of damp hair from her forehead. "I will spend every day I have left working out new ways to tell you how much I want you, how you make me feel life is full of possibility. I know I've never been good at saying these things before, but I'll learn."

She pressed her hands to his chest. "I can't believe you went to see them. Did my mother try to kill you?"

He chuckled. "Thankfully, Lupo seemed to be the only one who hadn't held a grudge, so she gave me a chance after that."

"Maybe we should all be a little more like Lupo." A soft smile lifted her lips. "You have no idea how much that means to me, Joe. The fact that you went there not knowing what they would say…"

"I know *exactly* how much it means to you. And it's a poor repayment for what I should have done the first time around."

"I don't know if there's anything I can say that will make your parents forgive me." She bit down on her lip. "I'm afraid I can't return that favor."

"I don't need that from you." He lowered his forehead to hers. "Maybe I'm selfish, but all I care about is having you with me. Forever. I just want you."

Her eyes fluttered shut. "Even after everything I've done?"

"You gave up more money than any person could ever need because you wanted to stand by your principles. In my eyes, that makes you far stronger than anyone I've ever met. Sure, you lost your way after we broke up. But I know you, Annie. I know you have a good heart, you have a kind soul, and you want to do positive things in the world. And I believe that you will. I believe it with every part of me."

When her eyes opened, she looked up at him with the full force of her love, this time without walls and without reservation and without the past standing between them. "Can you forgive me for not talking to you first that day? For not letting you be part of that decision? I know it was wrong and I regret treating you like that with all my heart."

"I forgive you."

"I should never have shut you out like that. After all the times you'd supported me and loved me, it was a huge slap in the face. I see that now. I don't blame you for walking out, because I probably would have walked out on me too." Her eyes glimmered. "Of all the dumb things I've done in my life, I regret that moment most of all. I regret losing you most of all."

He took her hand and pulled her through the apartment toward his bedroom. He'd left the house a few hours earlier, having everything in its place—hoping this moment would be perfect. The second she stepped into his room, her eyes popped open.

"Joe." She clamped a hand over her mouth. "What are you doing?"

He got down on one knee, just like he'd planned to three years ago. "Annie Maxwell, I have waited far too long to do this. I don't ever want to walk away again. You're the best thing in my life, and I'm never going to make the mistake of not fighting for us."

He reached into his pocket and pulled out a small box. It had a diamond inside but no ring, which was *not* how he'd originally planned for things to go down.

"Don't the diamond and the ring usually come together?" she asked with a cheeky smile, but the shake in her voice told him how much she was fighting back tears. "Is this a 'some assembly required' proposal?"

"I didn't want to give you the ring as it was, because I'd hate for you to look at it and think of that day." That day, which had started them both down the wrong paths. "And I want us to create something that's uniquely perfect for you. Something that makes you smile when you look at it, that makes you remember *this* moment. And all the other good moments."

Her hands knotted together and she had an expectant smile on her lips. "Are you going to ask me, Joe? Because I want to say it so bad."

"Will you marry me?"

"Yes!" She didn't give him a chance to get up. Instead, she snapped the box closed to protect the diamond, and then flung her arms around his neck. They were on the floor, a tangle of limbs and the scent of rain and fresh roses dancing in the air. "Yes, I will marry you."

Her lips met his, greedy and hot. He placed the box gently up on the bedside table before pulling her close. Then they were undressing, the sound of zippers flying and clothes landing with wet slaps on the floorboards around them. She straddled him, her near-naked body pinning him to the floor.

Dark, wet hair curled around her cheek as she reached behind herself to unhook her bra. She peeled the soft pink lace from her skin and tossed it to one side.

"You're so beautiful," he said, his voice ragged. This was everything he could have hoped for, his Annie—his *fiancée*—in his arms and a second chance at forever. "We have so much lost time to make up for."

"Don't look at it like that." She trailed her hands down his naked chest, raking lightly with her nails. There was the bite he loved most about her—the sting behind her sweetness. "We *saved* all the years ahead. We rescued those years. I want us to do great things together."

He grabbed her hand and brought her fingertips to his mouth, kissing each one in turn. "Like what?"

"I want us to do the work that fulfills us. I want us to fall into bed exhausted and excited about our lives. I want us to be honest and to communicate and to fight clean and fuck dirty."

He threw his head back and laughed. "Fight clean and fuck dirty. Like right now, on this very floor."

"On this very floor."

"Baby, you have no idea how happy that makes me."

"You have no idea how happy *you* make me." She leaned forward, and he wrapped both arms around her, holding her tightly against him. So tight, it felt like they'd never be split apart again. "I love you. I always have."

"I love you too. You're good people, Annie Maxwell."

She grinned. "That has quite a ring to it, doesn't it?"

"Yeah. Must have been a smart guy that came up with that name."

"And a smart girl who's going to run with it."

Epilogue

Six months later…

ANNIE STOOD AT THE EDGE OF THE CROWD, WATCHING her engagement ring wink in the light. The center stone that Joseph had given her was now flanked by two small pearls, to match the studs she always wore in her ears. On their wedding day, he had surprised her with a band of diamonds that perfectly hugged her engagement ring. But the most important detail was the engraving on the inside: *See you at the pond.*

Their spot. The spot that had drawn them back together after a long absence, the spot where he'd found her the night he proposed. The spot where he'd told her he loved her for the very first time all those years ago. The place was magic; she was sure of it.

Clutching a glass of sparkling water, Annie forced herself to count the bubbles as they raced to the top. *One, two, three…*

"Breathe." A deep, commanding voice sounded next to her. She hadn't even heard anyone approach.

"It's the dress," she said, craning her head up to where Joseph stood beside her. "I think I ate too much while we were on vacation."

"You mean while we were on our honeymoon." He slipped an arm around her waist and pulled her closer, his chuckle sending lightning bolts of anticipation through her. "I would have thought all that sex burned off the calories."

"You'd think that." Her lip twitched.

It was certainly a plausible explanation. Maybe she'd eaten her way through the guilt of running off and eloping without her friends or her family to bear witness, despite them all being perfectly understanding after the fact. She'd promised them a celebration on home turf soon. Nothing fancy, a BBQ at her parents' place to celebrate love and the important things in life.

But eloping had been the only way they'd been able to start married life without making the same mistakes they'd made last time. To make it about them first. Of course, they would still care for their families. And they would still throw their hearts and souls into their businesses. But their relationship had to be number one.

Only now there'd been a slight wrench thrown in the works.

"I don't think calories are the problem here," she quipped, pressing a hand to her stomach. She'd hit twelve weeks, and although there wasn't much of a bump to speak of, she did feel changes happening in her body. She'd put on a little weight, and her boobs were tender as hell. "I should have picked a different dress."

"You look incredible." Joseph tucked her hair behind her ear. "You're going to sound incredible when you get up on that stage."

Her chest squeezed, and her stomach rocked

violently. "Oh God, you know I hate public speaking. Can't you do it?"

Just the thought of standing up there, looking down at the sea of faces, had her feeling like she was going to hurl. Add to that, the fear over launching her new business, and she was a bundle of nerves.

"This is your baby, Annie. Your creation. You need to take the credit for it." Joseph cupped her cheeks with both his hands. "You're going to do amazing things with your life, and this is the first step."

"No, not the first step. The first step was getting you back in my life." Her eyes shone with unshed tears. Dammit, the hormones were making her even more emotional than normal. "I couldn't have done this without you."

He lowered his head to hers, coaxing her lips open for a searching kiss. It filled her whole body with shimmering energy, with confidence and love and determination. All the things he brought out in her. All the things they brought out in each other.

And all the things they would pass on to their little boy or girl.

"I love you so much," she whispered.

"I love you too." He pressed a kiss to the tip of her nose. "You're going to kill it. Good People is going to blow everyone's minds."

Good People. It was the antithesis of Bad Bachelors. It focused on creating a positive impact on people's lives through counseling, workshops, and online resources to help people navigate life's ups and downs. They had recruited a small but powerful team to help build out

Good People's offerings—a psychologist, a financial adviser, a doctor, and Connie's friend Amity as the self-defense and safety expert. Plus, they had Joseph and his information security company, providing help to those who'd suffered from online bullying and cyberstalking. And then there was Annie, CEO. Out in the open.

And it felt amazing.

"You think so?"

"If there's one thing I know about you, it's that when you set your mind to something, you make good on it. I have no doubts at all."

They looked up to find Joseph's mother walking toward them. She wore a simple sheath in cotton-candy pink. A heavy strand of pearls hung around her neck. As usual, she looked every bit the put-together CEO. A power woman. Someone Annie *should* look up to.

To her surprise, Melinda approached with a soft smile. "Joseph. Annie."

"Mom." Joseph waited for a moment, but leaned in when his mother reached for him. All he'd ever wanted was for his family to accept Annie…and now, their baby. Would things change with the news of their child? When they'd told her parents earlier that day, Connie's scream could have been heard on the moon.

"Hi, Melinda," Annie replied, determined to be polite no matter what. She and Joseph had decided together that both of them were done letting him be stuck in the middle.

"It's nice to see you. I'm very much looking forward to hearing all about Good People." She sounded genuine, which was a surprise. "I think it's a fabulous idea."

Annie blinked. "I'm glad you think so."

"In fact," Melinda continued, "I would love it if we were able to strike a partnership between Good People and Landry Cosmetics."

Whoa. Annie was so stunned that no words immediately came to her lips.

"I know we've had a very rocky relationship so far, but I also know my son loves you very much. Now that you're married—"

"And expecting, actually." Joseph's voice was firm, but not unkind. "We were planning to tell you soon."

Annie waited for the response, to see if it would be the news that caused the happy facade to crack.

"Oh my gosh!" Melinda shook her head, her hand rising to her décolletage. "That's wonderful."

"You're not going to freak out about being a grandmother?" Joseph asked.

"Of course not." Her eyes were watery. It was the most emotion Melinda had ever shown, at least in front of Annie. "I'm so happy for you both."

"Good." Joseph's quiet response might have sounded like a simple word to anyone else, but Annie could hear the layers underneath. The cautious hope, the worry, the protectiveness.

"We want the baby to have a good relationship with his or her grandparents," Annie said. "Family is really important to us."

Melinda nodded. "I know. I respect you for that, Annie."

Annie blinked. It was the first time she'd ever heard anything like that from Joseph's parents. But Melinda had been thawing over the last few months, especially after Joseph made it clear that he wouldn't be put in the middle anymore. He *would* choose a side, if they forced him. And they might lose their son in the process.

"And I meant what I said about partnering Landry Cosmetics and Good People. I know that I could have done so much more to include you in our family from the start, and I deeply regret that. I'm willing to put my money where my mouth is if we can start again on the right foot."

"I would really love that," Annie said, meaning every word of it.

"Where's Dad?" Joseph asked.

Melinda's expression said it all. He hadn't come. "You know how busy your father is. He wanted to be here."

"I doubt that," Joseph replied with a scowl.

Annie placed her hand on his arm and squeezed. After Melinda disappeared back into the crowd, Annie turned to him. "Baby steps. He'll come around eventually."

"You think?" Joseph asked. A groove had formed between his brows.

"I hope so. And we're a team, remember? You and me and the little bean." She pressed her hand to her stomach. They'd made a pact to try to rebuild things with Morris, for the sake of the baby. But Joseph had also learned to stand his ground where his father was concerned. They wanted a relationship with Morris, but on their terms this time. "That's always going to come first."

Joseph pulled her into a warm embrace, and she

knew—without a doubt—that she'd made all the right moves this time. *This* was where she belonged: in his arms and on the verge of something new and exciting.

The squawk of a microphone brought everyone's attention to the front of the room. Their emcee duo—Reed McMahon and Wes Evans—looked handsome in their tuxedos as they addressed the room together. In making amends with them and dismantling Bad Bachelors, Annie had finally been able to get her life back on track. To start atoning for her sins. And the fact that they were here tonight, along with their amazing partners, Darcy and Remi, meant the world to Annie.

"We'd like to call forward the host of this evening's events," Reed said. "Please join us in welcoming Annie Preston to the stage."

She still got a buzz from hearing her new name after the wedding.

Sucking in a shaky breath, she planted a kiss on Joseph's cheek. As she ascended the steps to the stage, she held the length of her shimmering gown in one hand. Reed kissed both her cheeks, as did Wes.

"You've got this," Wes whispered in her ear.

Smiling, she took her place at the microphone. "Thank you all for being here tonight. I know some of you are expecting me to launch into the benefits of my new business, Good People, and to ask you to pull out your wallets and your checkbooks for a good cause. Don't worry, that will come soon."

The audience tittered.

"But instead, I'm going to open with a confession. I've made a lot of mistakes in my life. Perhaps one of the biggest was starting an app and a website that you might all be familiar with. Bad Bachelors." She held her breath as whispers and gasps skittered through the audience. "But tonight, I am here to ask New York's forgiveness. I'm here to apologize for the pain and anguish I caused so many people."

She paused to let that sink in. With six months between her and the closure of Bad Bachelors, she'd had a lot of time to think about what she'd done. About the mistakes she'd made. The people she'd hurt. And those she'd helped. Those she wanted to help.

"I'm also here to announce that I will be taking the good parts of Bad Bachelors—the help it gave to women, the confidence boost and the feeling of safety— and growing those good parts into something even better and brighter."

She looked over to where Joseph stood at the edge of the crowd, love and admiration shining in his eyes.

"And I want to tell you about two women who inspired me to be a better person, my best friends Darcy and Remi." She gestured to where they both stood in the audience, looking amazing in stylish cocktail dresses. Darcy in her trademark all-black, and Remi in a pretty ballerina pink. "Let's start with Darcy."

Darcy made a motion of groaning and buried her face in her hands. Beside her, Reed stood strong and tall, his arm around her waist and a proud expression on his face.

"Darcy is a librarian who works tirelessly to improve her community. She campaigns for funding to run programs for the children who visit her library. She started a series of book clubs to get more people through the doors, and raise awareness of the important role liter-ature and reading play in our community. She will talk your ear off about her favorite book and then make you promise you'll come and borrow it. Lord help you if you break that promise."

The audience laughed, and Darcy shook her head, burying her face in Reed's shirt.

"She's going to kill me after this. Because Darcy hates the spotlight. She does all this work quietly, not for praise or recognition, only for the passion of what she does. For the love she has for her community. I can say with absolute certainty that she's a true role model."

Annie swung her gaze to Remi, whose face was wide and open. A huge smile split her lips as she held hands with Wes, who looked down at her dotingly.

"My other best friend is someone you may have heard of. Remi Drysdale. She's one of the most talented and fearless people I know. For anyone who thinks ballerinas are dainty and cute, let me correct you. Ballerinas are *warriors*. They work harder than you would even think is possible. They push their bodies to extremes. They spend their lives perfecting an art form that repays them with pain. They have the mental fortitude to face constant rejection and criticism in their careers, while making their performances look as easy as possible. Remi is the bravest and most hardworking person I know."

Remi pressed a hand to her chest, looking like she was about to cry.

"This woman barrels through life, always trying to do her best. She speaks her mind, wears her emotions on her sleeve, and tells it like it is. I have learned so much about honesty and openness from her. She's truly changed my life for the better."

Annie swallowed. Emotion clogged the back of her throat. It felt like she was standing at the edge of a cliff, baring herself to the world.

"Why am I telling you about these women and not my amazing husband who's stood by my side for most of my life? Well, he'd have no issue in telling you himself just how good he is." The audience laughed, and Joseph shot her a mock stern look, that he could barely hold for a second before his smile broke through. "But these two women wouldn't ever list their achievements. It seems to be ingrained in us, as women, *not* to tell the world how awesome we are. Not to feel comfortable sharing our achievements.

"But Good People is going to change that. I want to give women the resources to stand up for themselves, to speak their truths, and to follow their dreams. The truth is, I couldn't have done this without Joseph. Because I wouldn't *be* the person I am now without him. He's lifted me up, challenged who I thought I was. He backed this idea from day one. So, on that note, let me talk you through my vision."

Annie glanced to the tech guy sitting in his booth off the side of the stage. A curtain was drawn back, and the logo for Good People filled an enormous screen. This was it. Good People was really happening.

This next step would be scary, but with Joseph, Darcy, and Remi by her side, she felt as though she could conquer it all—family dramas, business, motherhood. Love.

Because together, they could face anything.

Acknowledgments

The reason I continue to write about families is, without a doubt, because I'm so blessed in my own family life. Thank you to my mother, who doesn't swear quite as much as Connie but who is a survivor and always puts her family in priority position. Thank you to my father for being the kind of man who isn't afraid to show his emotions and who never fails to make me feel loved. Thank you to my sister for her constant encouragement and thoughtfulness. If I could have even half the goodness she carries in her heart, then I'll live a very full life.

Thank you to my husband, who's been by my side since our first year of university. Who's pushed me to grow and to challenge my beliefs of what I can achieve. Without your love (both tough and kind), I would not have made it this far. Thank you for respecting my crazy deadlines and for continuing to buy me adorable tiny plants even though I keep killing them.

Thank you to the friends who enrich my life. To Shiloh, for being my (kiwi) twin, to Myrna for being the most authentic person I know; to Madura, for always telling the best stories; to Jill and Luke, who are my Canadian family and always make me laugh (remember! Vision sockets!) Thank you to Taryn, for being one of the most caring people I know. To Denise, who makes every conference more fun and who gives the BEST dramatic readings. To all the other people in my life, I wish I had enough pages to list out all the ways you make my days brighter. Thank you.

I must thank my agent, Jill Marsal, who has guided me through so many ups and downs. This past year would have been impossible if I didn't have you on my side. Thank you.

Thank you to Sourcebooks for giving Bad Bachelors a home and helping my stories reach new readers. And thank you for the *incredible* covers I've had for this series, they absolutely rock!

Most of all, I must thank my readers. Without you, I wouldn't have the incredible opportunity to do what I love every day. Your emails, messages, comments, and tweets truly mean the world to me. I put my heart and soul into my books for you. So, thank you.

Don't miss the first book in Stefanie London's
Bad Bachelors series, available from Sourcebooks Casablanca

Bad Bachelor

Chapter 1

"Reed McMahon is a master manipulator. He knows
exactly what to say and how to say it. Don't believe
a word he says."

—MisguidedinManhattan

SWEAT BEADED ALONG DARCY GREER'S BROW AS SHE
smoothed her shaking hands over the full skirt of her
wedding gown, her fingertips catching on the subtle
pattern embroidered into the silk. Long sleeves masked
her tattoos, turning her into a picture-perfect bride. Her
mother had been so pleased when she'd chosen this

dress because the priest wasn't too thrilled with her ink. Truthfully, Darcy hadn't been thrilled with looking like a cake topper. But she also hadn't wanted any drama to mar her big day. Besides, it was only a dress.

I can't believe I'm doing this…

She sucked in a breath and surveyed the picturesque blue sky with clouds so white and fluffy they looked like globs of marshmallow. A flawless day, the photographer had assured her, all the better to capture this important moment.

Empty space stretched out from all sides, making her feel small, like a blip on the surface of the earth. A smile tugged at her lips and she tilted her face up, letting her eyes flutter shut as a cool breeze drifted past.

Just breathe…

Her best friends stood before her, looking immaculate in their bridesmaid gowns. They each wore a color that matched their personality—Remi, the ballerina, in soft pink and the ever-practical Annie in a classic royal blue. These women had gotten her through the toughest times in her life. They'd made sure she was here today in one piece, finally ready to release her old life.

"All right, ladies." The photographer raised his camera, the big lens pointing in Darcy's direction, unblinking like a Cyclops's eye. "Everyone get into position. I want this first shot to be perfect."

Darcy's heart skipped a beat. This was it, her last opportunity to put a stop to this madness.

You okay? Annie mouthed.

Darcy nodded. She would be okay, she would be okay, she *would* be okay.

Pop!

The first shot hit her straight in the ribs and stung like hell. She gasped, her hands clutching at the spot where crimson bled across the white silk. The camera clicked. A moment captured.

The pain was more than she'd expected, but there was something deeply satisfying about seeing the splash of color against the ugly, white silk.

Pop! Pop! Pop!

"Wow, guys, give me a minute." Darcy backed up, dodging a green balloon sailing through the air. "And don't look so happy about being able to throw stuff at me."

She reached for a water balloon of her own and took aim, Remi's soft-pink dress in her sights. Her throw was off and the balloon burst against the ground, splashing orange paint over Remi's feet and legs.

"Now you look like a beautiful sunset," Annie said, hiking up her long skirt in one hand and reaching for a ketchup bottle filled with red paint. She ran over to Darcy and squeezed a stream of it all over the sweetheart neckline of her wedding dress. "Ah, much better!"

"I look like I'm starring in a remake of *Psycho*." Darcy glanced down at herself. Red paint dripped along her body, running in rivulets across the silk. "I need more color."

"Coming right up." Remi grabbed a small paint can and a tiny brush. "Watch me unleash my artistic side."

She splashed purple paint in a flamboyant arc, turning Darcy from a horror movie extra into something out of a modern art exhibition.

"This is wonderful, ladies." The photographer clicked and clicked, capturing Darcy's shock as Annie paint bombed her out of nowhere. "These photos will be amazing."

A high-pitched shriek pierced the air as Annie turned on Remi and the two girls battled it out with their respective weapons. Soon, the elegant dresses looked like a finger-painting lesson gone horribly wrong. Splotches of orange and green peppered Remi's blond hair.

They'd decided against using the proper paintball guns on advisement of the venue owner—safety first and all that jazz. Getting shot at close range apparently stung like a bitch. So they'd spent a painstaking hour filling up water balloons and other containers before the shoot.

Darcy picked up another ketchup bottle filled with paint and used it to make a sad face on the bottom of her gown. "I hate this goddamn dress."

Annie covered her mouth in a failed attempt to stifle her laughter but instead smeared paint across her cheek. "Sorry, Darcy. I know you only picked it to keep your mom happy."

"You're right." She frowned. "The whole damn wedding was more about her than it was about me."

Annie slung an arm around Darcy's shoulder. "Come on, this is your anti-anniversary party. Your 'thank God I got out while I could' bash. It's time to celebrate, not mope about your family issues. That dress is ugly as hell anyway."

The beginnings of a smile tugged at Darcy's lips. "It *is* ugly, isn't it?"

"Fugly even. Seriously, I didn't have the heart to say

anything because you know I love your mom"—Annie wrinkled her nose—"but I wouldn't even bury my cat in that thing."

Out of nowhere, a balloon burst between them. "Hey!"

"Two for the price of one," Remi crowed, her Australian accent amplified as she raised her voice and pumped her fist in the air. "You beauty!"

"We were having a moment," Darcy said in mock protest.

"Yeah, and now it's a rainbow moment." Remi toyed with two fresh water balloons, a cheeky grin on her face.

"Do it," Annie said. "I dare you."

"Do you double dare me?" Remi walked toward them, her arms swinging in that dainty, fluid way of hers.

Annie tried to make a break for it, but Darcy wrapped her arms around her waist and held on tight. "Get her, Remi."

The balloons exploded and both girls screamed.

By the time they'd run out of things to throw at one another, Darcy was famished. The owner of the venue—which was normally an outdoor paintball arena—had kindly allowed them space to conduct the photo shoot and let them make use of the open-air cafeteria as well.

She glanced at the picnic table full of cupcakes and let her eyes settle on the top tier of what would have been her wedding cake. Apparently, you were supposed to save it for the first anniversary.

But what if the wedding never happened? Surely that was an excuse not to keep it. Except her mother had; she'd saved it when the rest of the cake had been thrown into the trash. Now, a year after Darcy *should* have been married, her mother had foisted it on her like some kind of cruel joke.

It said a lot about their relationship.

The offending lump of cake—covered in thick, Italian-style marzipan icing—sat in the middle of the table. Poking at it with her forefinger as if it were an alien species, Darcy considered her options. Eat it or toss it?

"Let me show you how to deal with this." Remi picked up the cake and signaled for the photographer to follow her. She hurled it into the air and it landed with a satisfying splat on the ground a few feet away.

"See?" she said. "No more devil cake."

Annie clapped her hands together. "Now we can get this party started."

This "party" was something that had taken a lot of convincing. Darcy had wanted to let the day come and go without ceremony or recognition. She would have been perfectly happy to sit in her sweats and eat ice cream straight out of the tub like a Bridget Jones cliché. But she was the kind of woman who could admit when she was wrong—the trash-the-dress party had proved far more entertaining than she'd first anticipated. Plus, it made for an interesting catch-up rather than their usual wine-and-vent sessions.

Every week, the three friends got together to unload their latest funny stories and problems on one another. It'd been a tradition since high school, when Darcy and Annie would meet to do their homework together. Translation: talk about boys and update their Myspace profiles or whatever else sixteen-year-old girls did before smartphones.

Remi had completed their trio when she'd moved to New York from Australia a few years ago and ended up being Darcy's roommate. These women had glued her back together—and *kept* her that way—since her wedding had been canceled the previous year.

"These look delicious," Annie announced as she pored over the tiered cake stand filled with cupcakes supplied by Remi. "I wish I could bake like you."

"I wish I could bake something without setting the oven on fire," Darcy quipped as she washed her hands at the small outdoor sink, scrubbing at the green paint under her fingernails. "But we can't all be Martha Stewart, can we?"

"Just don't tell my family that I'm using sugar and wheat flour—they'll think I'm poisoning you." She cringed. "Everything in their house is hemp-infused, plant-based bullshit."

"Well, I can't cook *or* bake," Annie said. "According to my mother, that means I'll make a terrible wife."

"Ugh." Darcy forced down a wave of nausea. Nothing could recall her lunch faster than the thought of motherly expectations. "Please don't use the *W* word around me. Mom's been trying to set me up with her friends' sons. Literally any and all of them. I don't think she cares who it is so long as I get a ring on my finger."

"Did you remind her what happened the last time she set you up with someone?" Annie snorted. "Or won't she take any responsibility for that?"

"She dropped off the top layer of the wedding cake as a reminder that I should be trying to find 'the one.' *And* she had the audacity to tell me she hadn't given up on me, like I'm some hundred-year-old spinster who's about to be eaten by a houseful of cats."

Annie blinked. "Right."

"If only she could see you now." Remi grinned.

The photographer hovered around them, snapping pictures of what must have been a hilarious scene: three women in full hair and makeup, wearing paint-splattered dresses and eating cupcakes. What a sight.

"Maybe she meant it as an encouragement," Remi said.

"The message couldn't have been clearer. It's been one year and she wants to know why I'm not out there trying to find a man so I can fulfill my purpose as a woman and start making babies."

"Screw that." Remi wrinkled her nose.

Annie opened the champagne with a *pop* and poured the fizzing liquid into each of the three champagne flutes. She measured precisely, ensuring each glass was equal.

"Here's to you, Darcy. Happy anti-anniversary." She handed the glasses out and held up her own. "Congratulations on dodging a bullet."

"Still feels like I got shot." She shook her head as their flutes all met in a cacophony of clinks.

"Better to have loved and lost than to have gone down the aisle with the wrong guy," Remi said, sipping her drink. "Here's to moving on."

There was a chorus of "hear, hear" from the girls as they clinked their glasses again.

"Nothing like a new fling to take your mind off the old one," Remi added, gesturing with her champagne. "Forget about relationships and have a little fun. You've earned it."

It sounded so simple when she said it like that, but

Darcy was out of practice. Besides, there was this little, tiny problem that had developed since the almost-wedding. The very few times she'd gotten close to getting physical with a guy, her nerves had kicked in and she'd lost all sense of excitement. Was *sex anxiety* a thing? Because that was probably what she had.

"I don't know…" Darcy sunk her teeth into the pile of frosting on her cupcake.

"Think about it. If you quit a bad job, you would start looking for another one, right?" Annie said. "You don't stop working because you had *one* bad job."

Remi snorted. "Only you would compare a relationship to a job."

"I'm serious. Getting a job and dating aren't all that different. You have to assess each other to see if you're a good fit and then you have a trial period to see if it's going to work out."

"Do you make your dates sign a contract too?" Darcy teased.

"I'll tell you when I have enough time to go on a date." Annie sighed. "Like in the year 2045."

Remi peeled back the brightly colored paper on another cupcake. "As ridiculous as that comparison is, she has a point. One bad experience doesn't mean a lifetime without sex. It's perfectly acceptable for men to enjoy casual sex, so why not us too?"

The group murmured their agreement. Even the photographer nodded emphatically.

"Have you been with *anyone* since Ben?" Annie asked.

The girls looked at her curiously. Darcy hadn't spoken much about the demise of her engagement or her failed attempts to put herself back into the dating scene. She'd always been the most private one of the group. Growing up with a mother who was emotional to the extreme had made her develop a natural resistance to showing her feelings.

Maybe that's why you never saw it coming. You didn't ask enough questions or pay attention to the right things.

"The only kind of sex I've had in the last year has been with me, myself, and I." Darcy sighed.

"Oh, a threesome." Remi winked. "Kinky."

"And even that hasn't been too spectacular," Darcy said. "Not for a lack of trying, mind you. I've had a few dates, but anytime the guy even tries to kiss me, I freeze up."

Annie reached out and patted her knee. "You're stressed. That's totally understandable."

"What do I have to be stressed about? I love my job, I'm healthy, I have a great family…"

Annie raised a brow.

"Okay, not *great* but they're decent human beings… most of the time." Well, barring the cake incident. "Finding your fiancé making out with someone the day before your wedding doesn't have to ruin everything. Single is the new black, right?"

"I love you, Darcy, but this #foreveralone thing is stopping right *now*." She set her drink and half-eaten dessert down on the table. "You need to break the dry spell."

After the split, getting back into the dating scene had gradually moved from the "too hard" basket to the "never, ever again" basket. Except there had been this little voice in the back of her mind lately, whispering dangerous thoughts to her, asking questions she wasn't sure how to answer, like whether she was happy being alone. Or if she'd be able to watch her beautiful friends walk down the aisle and be okay missing out on that experience herself.

Despite hating her mother's über-conservative ways, deep down, she still wanted the white-picket-fence dream—a wedding, a loving husband…even the babies.

But all that required her to date. And that meant facing up to the fact that she had no idea *how* to date. She'd given up her chance of learning those lessons when she'd fallen head over Dr. Martens at nineteen. Now, eight years later, she was starting from scratch with no skills and no real experience to draw on.

Casual sex might sound like a piece of cake to some people, but the idea of dating was terrifying enough. As for casual sex? Darcy had never had a one-night stand. Ever.

"I wouldn't even know where to go to meet someone," she muttered. "And I deleted Tinder the second I started getting dick pics. Not to mention that I'm so out of practice even if I *could* make it past a first date. I can't flirt. I can't do witty banter. I can't play the temptress. So how am I supposed to have casual sex?"

And that wasn't even the hard part. Being able to trust someone again and not be paranoid that they were secretly living a double life, now *that* was the real challenge.

"Being celibate is so much easier."

"Hey, if that's what you want, I support you one hundred percent." Annie reached out and squeezed her shoulder.

"Say the word and we won't mention the dating thing ever again," Remi chimed in.

Darcy scratched at a fleck of dried paint on her dress. "I *do* want to get back out there," she admitted. "But I'm scared I'll pick the wrong guy again."

"Then you need to find a guy who's trustworthy," Annie said, pausing to sip her drink. "Someone who wants the same things you do."

"And how would I find a guy like that? It's not like I can trust what they write in their dating profiles."

"You could try the Bad Bachelors app," the photographer piped up. All eyes turned to the young man in the vest and bow tie. A heavy-looking camera hung from a thick strap around his neck. "I read about it the other day."

Darcy shook her head. "What on earth is the Bad Bachelors app?"

"Oh!" Remi bounced up and down in her seat. "I heard about this. Apparently, someone started this app that has all the single guys in New York listed and you can rate and review them."

"You're kidding." Darcy blinked. "So it's Yelp… for guys?"

"Or Uber? You know, go for a ride and then rate your driver," Remi said and Annie choked on a mouthful of cupcake.

Darcy shook her head and downed the rest of her champagne, immediately reaching for the bottle to refill her glass. "You're making this up."

"I swear, I'm not. Does anyone have the app?" Remi asked, but the girls shook their heads. "Give me your phone."

Within minutes, they'd downloaded the app and

were browsing through profile after profile of gorgeous, single New York men. Each profile had at least one photo, a brief description, and a star rating. It looked as though the app was fairly new, but there were already a ton of reviews posted.

"These are hilarious," Remi said, swiping across the screen. "Look at this one. 'Trenton Conner, thirty-eight. Doctor. The only thing that's large about this guy is his ego and his credit limit.'"

"Let me read." Annie grabbed the phone and swiped a few times. "'Jacob Morales, thirty-nine. Technology executive. Things were going well until he rolled over and fell asleep right after sex. Then his maid came into the bedroom to shoo me out of his apartment.'"

Darcy laughed. "Oh my God."

"This one's nice." Annie held the phone in one hand and her drink in the other. "'Darren Montgomery, thirty-one. IT manager and entrepreneur. Darren is a lovely guy, very sweet and kind. Romantic. But we didn't have much in common—I hope he finds the right woman for him.' I'm going to mark this one as a favorite for you."

"Gimme." Remi grabbed the phone back. "What about this guy? 'Alexei Petrov, thirty. Investor. This guy will take you on the ride of your life…' Oh no. Looks like he might've been dating a few women at once. Next!"

Darcy pressed her fingertips to her temples. "No cheaters, please."

"Oh dear." Remi turned the phone around to show a photo of the most beautiful man Darcy had ever seen. And yes, *beautiful* was the right way to describe him.

He was so perfect looking, and yet there was a hardness to him, like a marble statue—beautiful and cold and unyielding. "'Reed McMahon, thirty-two. Marketing and PR executive. Reed McMahon is a master manipulator. He knows exactly what to say and how to say it. Don't believe a word he says. He goes through women like candy.'"

Darcy wrinkled her nose. "He sounds like one to stay away from."

"Look, you can sort by highest and lowest rated." She laughed. "This guy is the lowest rated—number one on the Bad Bachelors list. Fifty women have rated him already. Serial dater, not interested in commitment, colder than an iceberg…looks like he always has a different woman on his arm."

"What about the good guys? *Are* there any decent men on that thing?" Darcy sighed. "I feel like I'm searching for a unicorn."

"We'll find the right guy." Remi's eyes sparkled at the thought of playing virtual matchmaker. "Why don't we swipe through and put a list together?"

"A list will make it easier. I like that idea," Annie said.

Remi rolled her eyes. "Of course you do."

"Say I *hypothetically* agree this is a good idea," Darcy said, drumming her fingers on the edge of the table. "What am I supposed to do? Walk up to these guys and say, 'Hey, you've got a five-star rating. Let's date'?"

"It's called recon." Annie grinned and Darcy could already see the cogs turning in her mind. "We'll go through the top-rated list and help you narrow down some options. You never know, with six degrees of separation and all that, you might have a friend in common who can introduce you. But at least you know up front that the guy is a decent person…unlike if you met someone randomly at a bar."

Darcy rolled the idea around in her head.

Maybe this wasn't such a terrible idea: a lower-risk, research-led type of dating. As a librarian, that appealed to her. She could get all the information she needed up front and avoid the dangers associated with spontaneous dating.

Besides, what harm could a little research do?

Chapter 2

"When something seems too good to be true, it usually is. Reed McMahon is not the guy you want him to be."

—LittleMissMidTown

EVERY MUSCLE IN REED MCMAHON'S BODY TENSED, anticipating, assessing. He shifted his weight, moving his hips as he prepared to unleash all his frustration into a single powerful swing. He'd had the kind of week that made him want to pound something into oblivion.

With a white-knuckled grip, he pulled back and focused on his target until the rest of the world fell away. The baseball whizzed past him and his bat connected with air.

Reed swore under his breath and reset his position. His team, Smokin' Bases, was one run down in the final inning with two outs. Losing to a group of Columbia graduates who loved to fist-bump one another was *not* an option. The week from hell would not be made worse by a crushing ball game defeat.

Reed *had* to make this swing count.

The pitcher went through his routine of rubbing the ball in his gloveless hand and stretching his neck from side to side. He drew his arm back and sent the next ball sailing in Reed's direction. It was perfect—fast, but perfect. He swung and the bat made a satisfying crack as it sent the ball flying through the air, eventually bouncing in the empty pocket between right and center field.

He took off, pumping his legs as fast as he could toward first base. An outfielder scooped the ball up and threw it hard, but he overthrew it and it grazed the top of the first baseman's glove, giving Smokin' Bases enough time to get a runner across home plate.

That tied them. "Keep going!" the third base coach shouted as their captain, Gabriel, legged it down the home stretch.

Reed ran for second, but the other team recovered and their second baseman landed the tag perfectly across Reed's midsection.

"Out!" the pitcher called. But Gabriel had already made it home and the run counted.

Reed's hit had given them a one-run victory. The rest of his team whooped and jogged onto the field to shake hands with the opposition.

"I knew you'd save us." His teammate and friend, Emil Resnik, slapped a hand on his back as they walked off the field.

Reed grabbed his workout bag and fished around for a bottle of water. "Just waiting for the right moment to attack."

"Like a snake." Emil flattened his fingers against his thumb and made a striking motion. "I think we've earned a beer or three."

"God yes."

Reed brought the water bottle to his lips and tossed his head back, relishing the slide of the cool liquid down his throat. After a game, his body felt looser. The tension he carried with him Monday through Friday eased out of his muscles. This was the thing he looked forward to each week.

He pulled his phone out of the small pocket on the side of the sports bag and turned it on. Multiple alerts made the device buzz in some kind of digital battle cry.

One hundred notifications. That *couldn't* be good.

He scrolled through the list and sure enough, the majority had "Bad Bachelors" in the title. "God fucking damn it," he muttered. "Not this shit again."

"That was a killer hit you had there, man." Gabriel came over to where Reed stood, ready to congratulate him on locking in the win. "What's going on?"

A new message appeared in his inbox from a colleague titled *I knew you got around but daaamn*.

"There's some bullshit new app that rates New York 'bachelors.'" He made air quotes with his fingers. "And apparently I'm top of the bad guys list. I've been getting emails about it since Friday."

"Have you checked it out?" Gabriel asked as he whipped off his T-shirt and changed into a fresh one.

Reed glanced at a woman leaning against the black railing that sectioned off the North Meadow diamond from the rest of Central Park. She was dressed in a suit, which was an odd choice given it was the weekend. "Hell no. I couldn't care less what these women are saying about me. Probably that I'm some heartless brute who only cares about sex."

"Accurate," Emil said with a grin. "And it's nothing you haven't heard before."

"Except now it's out there for the whole world to see and the guys in the office are having a field day." He shook his head. "They think it's hilarious."

He'd come back to his desk after a meeting on Friday afternoon to find some cheap plastic trophy with Reed's picture affixed to it, along with the words *#1 Lady Killer* in bright-red letters. This person had also taken the liberty of "enhancing" the little gold man's appendage with putty.

Classy.

But Reed wasn't worried. Gossip like that tended to fizzle quickly, in his experience. There was *always* something more scandalous to worry about than a man having sex.

"What's wrong with loving women so much you can't have just one?" Gabriel chuckled when his pregnant wife, Sofia, whacked him in the arm with the scoring clipboard. "What? I'm talking about Reed."

Reed stuffed his phone into the pocket of his sweatpants. "They know what they're getting into, but then they cry foul when I don't want to see them again."

"Because they all think they could be the one to change you." Emil dug his elbow into Reed's rib cage. "They think they can tame the beast."

"There's nothing to tame." He picked up his gym bag and slung it over one shoulder.

The sun hung low in the sky. Central Park was busy as always, full of tourists and locals out soaking up the rays now that the cold weather had finally started to disappear. Everything was green again, and that usually put a smile on his face. But Reed's frustration settled like a weight on his chest.

"I'm sure it'll blow over." Emil slung an arm around Reed's neck and pulled him away from the field. "I'll buy you a beer. That should cheer you up."

They made their way to the edge of the field, heading in the direction of the path that would lead them out to West Ninety-Sixth Street. It was Reed's Sunday ritual: baseball in Central Park, beers at his favorite sports bar in Brooklyn Heights so they could watch a game—preferably the Mets—and then he'd head over to Red Hook to check on his dad before going home. Nothing messed with his Sunday routine, not even a shitty mood.

"Doesn't matter anyway," Sofia said with a cheeky wink. "He's got enough money for a therapist. Isn't that how rich people handle their problems?"

Gabriel and Emil, along with a few other guys and girls on the team, were mechanics, and they loved to rib Reed about his white-collar job. Sofia joined in the fun, even though she had a degree and worked in an office just like Reed.

"None of you seem to have an issue with my money when I'm paying for drinks," he responded dryly.

"Yeah, that's right. Maybe we won't buy you a beer after all," Gabriel quipped. "Although we did get a new client at the shop. Some trust-fund baby with a hard-on for Audis. God knows why he'd spend so much money on them when he could have something better."

Gabriel and Emil dissolved into their long-running argument about the best luxury car manufacturers and

Sofia pretended to stick her fingers in her ears. Reed tuned out the familiar banter. Despite having a salary with enough zeros to make most people's eyes bulge, he didn't live in Manhattan or drive a sports car. A huge chunk of his money went to paying for health care and a near full-time caregiver for his father. The leftover cash was funneled into conservative investments.

Beyond keeping up appearances at work—which required a wardrobe fit for dealing with upper-crust Manhattanites—his home life was fuss free. He'd paid off his DUMBO apartment a year ago when he'd made partner and received a generous signing bonus, and had turned that place into his personal sanctuary.

"Reed?" The woman who'd been watching their game waved to catch his attention. She wore a light-gray suit and her eyes squinted behind a pair of black glasses. "Are you Reed McMahon?"

"Who's asking?" Emil piped up.

"I'm Diana Lay with *Scion* magazine. I was hoping to grab a few moments of your time, Mr. McMahon." She looked directly at him but he could see the hesitation in her face.

In his sweats and a red baseball cap, he looked totally different from the photos floating around online, which were mostly corporate headshots and a few professional photos from galas he'd attended for work. But they all showed the same image—a polished, curated, and tailored level of perfection he prided himself on. A fake version of him that didn't exist at a weekend ball game. Or any other time when he wasn't at work.

Ugh, he should have guessed she worked for *Scion*.

They'd been trying since the previous Wednesday to get ahold of him. The "society journal," which could only be referred to as such in the loosest of terms, was now mostly online. But it continued to boast a half-million readership of gossip-hungry people with no lives of their own. *Scion* wrote about the upper echelons of the "socially prominent" in New York, Greenwich, and the Hamptons. Surrounding the articles was extensive advertising for boat shoes and diving watches.

"You missed him," Reed said without breaking his stride.

"I don't think I did." The woman hurried after him, her sensible, low-heeled shoes no match for his well-loved sneakers. "How do you feel about being rated New York's Most Notorious Bachelor?"

"You'll have to ask the man himself."

"So you're denying you're Reed McMahon who works at Bath and Weston?" she asked, out of breath as she tried to keep up with his long strides. "And that you're the son of Adam McMahon?"

At the sound of his father's name, Reed stopped dead in his tracks and the woman almost slammed into him. "Leave him out of this."

She smiled like a cat who'd gotten the cream. "Were you aware of the Bad Bachelors app before today?"

He was tempted to keep walking, but the last thing he needed was for her to think there was a story here. "No comment."

"Come on, you must have something to say about it." She used a cajoling tone that made his blood boil.

He knew her type—parasitic gossip columnists who

called themselves journalists but were more likely to talk about a sex tape than anything of substance. However, he wasn't about to let his anger show. That would only make her dig deeper.

He gave her a cool, well-practiced smile and shrugged. "I'm afraid I don't have anything for you."

"Does it bother you that all these women are airing your dirty laundry to the world? Or does part of you believe you're getting what you deserve?"

He kept his gaze steady. "No comment."

"What does your father think about all this?" She looked at him with a bland expression, although he had no doubt bringing up his father was intended to incite an ugly emotional reaction in him. "Do you think you've disappointed him?"

Hell would freeze over before he gave this woman— or anyone—an ounce of satisfaction in seeing him break over this nonstory. "You mentioned you worked for *Scion*, correct?"

"That's right." She held her phone out, the recording app on, ready for a juicy quote he'd never give her.

He'd had dealings with *Scion* in the past, namely when he'd needed to help a wealthy businessman get his family-friendly image back on track after photos leaked of him and his wife engaging in some more unique BDSM activities. As much as he wasn't a fan of *Scion*'s work, he'd never done anything to piss them off.

"So you work for Craig Peterson?" He kept his tone even.

Her tongue darted out to moisten her lips. "I do."

"Craig's a close personal friend of mine." It was a

total lie, but he'd met the guy on a few occasions at work functions. He allowed the awkward silence to stretch long enough to make the woman shift on her heels. "In fact, Bath and Weston does good business with *Scion*. I'm not sure he'd appreciate you harassing the source of some important advertising money. Money that, if I'm not mistaken, is quite critical to keeping the company afloat, given how your CFO has been suspected of embezzling company funds."

Thank God he had *that* little tidbit up his sleeve. Rule number one of working in PR: always keep your ear to the ground.

Her face paled. "I'm just doing my job."

"I understand. I'm also doing mine." He paused. "If I find out that you or anyone from your establishment has gone near my father, I will make sure more people know why *Scion* is in such bad shape."

"You'd do that to your close personal friend?" Her lip curled.

"To protect my family? Sure." He leaned in closer to her. "And if I'd do that to Craig, imagine what I'd do to someone I don't care about." Reed didn't wait for a response. Instead, he turned and stalked to where Emil, Gabriel, and Sofia waited for him. "Come on, let's get out of here."